D0341977

Nantucket Grand

Books by Steven Axelrod

The Henry Kennis Mysteries
Nantucket Sawbuck
Nantucket Five-spot
Nantucket Grand

Nantucket Grand

A Henry Kennis Mystery

Steven Axelrod

Poisoned Pen Press

Copyright © 2016 by Steven Axelrod

First Edition 2016

10 9 8 7 6 5 4 3 2 1

Library of Congress Catalog Card Number: 2015949418

ISBN: 9781464205538   Hardcover
      9781464205552   Trade Paperback

All rights reserved. No part of this publication may be reproduced, stored in, or introduced into a retrieval system, or transmitted in any form, or by any means (electronic, mechanical, photocopying, recording, or otherwise) without the prior written permission of both the copyright owner and the publisher of this book.

Poisoned Pen Press
6962 E. First Ave., Ste. 103
Scottsdale, AZ 85251
www.poisonedpenpress.com
info@poisonedpenpress.com

Printed in the United States of America

For Annie, who knows all the reasons why.

Acknowledgments

The usual thanks to Nantucket Police Chief William Pittman— as before, the mistakes and the poetry are my own. I also need to thank Ginger Andrews for her no-nonsense fact-checking, and a certain M/Y ship's engineer, who asks to remain anonymous. He taught me everything I know about sinking a luxury yacht, for the austere pleasure of living vicariously.

Contents

Part One: Off Season

Chapter One

Samaritans

Before the harbormaster pulled the body from the saltmarsh creeks, before the drug overdose and the arson, before the murder that triggered the biggest scandal in the island's history, there was a teenage boy, all alone on an autumn night, trying to rescue the girl he loved.

It all began with a book: a biology textbook that belonged to Alana Trikilis. She had left it behind after class.

Jared Bromley had known her since first grade. They both worked on the student newspaper, *Veritas,* they had even acted in several school plays together, but she had never shown even a flicker of romantic interest in him. It made sense—he was skinny and clumsy, generally unwashed with a bad complexion and a big nose. She was impossibly clean and graceful. A character very much like her was the catalyst for the action in every one of Jared's screenplays. She was the girl who dares the boys to steal the whale bone from the museum in *Swiping Moby.* She was the hostage turned peacemaker for 'Sconset and town in the *The War Between Nantucket.* And she was the haughty girl who spurns a serial killer when he's alive and then drives his zombie back into the grave in *Hoyt's Homecoming.*

Jared also wrote about her on his blog, referring to her only as "The Girl," but even after *sharkpool.com* became notorious, even after people found out that it was his website, Alana never glanced at it. She was one of the few girls in school who didn't spend time online. She never posted pictures on Instagram, she didn't Snapchat or instant message her friends. She had no Facebook account, no Twitter handle, no Google+ circle. Mean girls had tried to cyberbully her in ninth grade; she never noticed.

Jared was one of two *Veritas* editors this year. He ran Alana's cartoons every week, and she accepted his compliments with the same weary smile she managed at the dump, when her mother offered a wrinkled shirt from the take-it-or-leave it pile. She'd accept it to avoid a fight, but she'd never wear it.

Her dad hauled trash for a living and she'd been to the top of garbage mountain with him more times than she cared to count. Jared had heard her describing the view in the dining hall a few days ago. He had been tempted to break into the conversation—he had written a story for the paper about the man who got run over and killed in the C&D building the year before. But trash-related death hardly seemed the ideal subject matter, and she was surrounded by her friends. The sound of their talk and laughter, the smell of their skin, and the flash of their hair formed an estrogen bubble he couldn't penetrate. She was never alone. Girls traveled in packs, like feral dogs. He resigned himself to that. Anyway, she had a boyfriend, because girls like Alana always had a boyfriend.

But now Jared was staring at her biology textbook and formulating a plan.

It was an obvious plan, but that was the best thing about it. What could be more natural than one student returning another student's misplaced textbook? From there they could start chatting about biology class and how Mr. Felder trimmed his beard from his ears to his chin to create the illusion of a jawline, and why anyone could think that dissecting mice was a useful life skill.

He might get her laughing, and then he'd be on his way.

So that was how he came to be parked outside the Trikilises' house this evening, watching Alana climb into the cab of Mason Taylor's pickup truck.

Jared had been stalling, trying out different opening lines, bracing himself for the cognitive shutdown he always experienced looking into those pale blue eyes. He needed to know exactly what he was going to say beforehand, because there was no chance he'd be able to think of anything when he was actually standing in front of her.

He almost decided to leave the damn book on her doorstep, but now he slid down in his seat and watched Mason amble to the front door. What was the allure? Well, Mason was tall and his family had money. That stuff seemed to matter. Jared was short and poor. Apart from wearing lifts and winning the lottery (and he could use the lottery money to buy some really excellent lifts), there wasn't much he could do about either problem.

Mason walked back to the truck with Alana, and Jared sank lower, peering over the dashboard. He looked like a pathetic stalker. Was he actually turning into one? If they drove off and he followed them, it would be case closed.

Alana's parents weren't home. Did they know about this school night date? Probably not. He didn't like the possessive way Mason put his arm around Alana as they walked to the truck. She looked nervous. It was almost as if he was forcing her to come with him. Jared wasn't sure he could help her if she needed it, but he couldn't quite bring himself to drive off and abandon her, either. So he followed them.

If that made him a stalker, fine.

He kept a safe distance as they went around the rotary and started up Milestone Road. They passed the Monomoy and Polpis turnoffs. Jared kept a couple of cars between them, watching the truck's red taillights. They drove on, beyond the roads to Madequecham and the airport, where Jared lost one of his cover cars, then Tom Nevers Road, where the second one veered away.

Alone with Mason's truck as they headed downhill for the straight shot in into 'Sconset, Jared fell back and let the distance between them build up. There weren't many people living out at the east end of the island this time of year. Any car would look conspicuous.

Past the cranberry bogs, still-shallow ponds now rimmed with ice from the last hard freeze, past the new golf course—Jared's father had bid low and then "sharpened his pencil" even more to get the electrical contract for the rebuilt clubhouse—and finally up the gentle rise to 'Sconset's Main Street.

The huge leafless elm trees lined up like an honor guard on the wide sweep of lawn that flanked the avenue. Big houses loomed behind their hedges, dark and uninhabited. The owners rented the places out in June and July, then showed up for a couple of weeks in August—that was it. The rest of the year 'Sconset was virtually a ghost town, with maybe twenty families scattered between Sankaty and the old dump. Jared's family had lived out here for a couple of years. He'd been glad to move back to town. The windy, wide open spaces gave him the creeps.

He slowed down as Mason's truck skirted the rotary and took the sharp left toward Sankaty. Where could they possibly be going? The population thinned out even more as you approached Polpis. But Mason hooked the right turn onto Baxter Road. This was high-end real estate, tinged with a crazy King Canute sense of entitlement—lavish homes teetering over the Atlantic on the crumbling cliffside, as if the ocean would never dare to approach their houses. Empty lots marked off with yellow police tape told a different story. The bluff was sliding into the sea, a slo-mo avalanche that had been grinding away since the Laurentine ice sheet headed north twenty-one thousand years ago. It wasn't going to stop anytime soon, no matter how much money people threw at it.

And they were throwing plenty. But they generally did it from a distance, in November anyway. Maybe Mason's dad had some caretaking gigs out here, and maybe Mason had borrowed the keys. That was possible. Jared shrugged. Mason better have the alarm codes, too, or it was going to be a bad night for everyone.

The truck disappeared around a curve and Jared pulled into someone's driveway. He'd do the rest of this on foot. There was no chance of losing them now: Baxter Road dead-ended at the lighthouse. He killed the engine. Should he take the book?

Absurd question—that plan was part of a different night, lost the moment Mason Taylor drove off with Alana.

He climbed out into the damp chill wind and shivered, zipping up his jacket. It wasn't that cold—only forty degrees or so—but the damp air penetrated him. He recalled a ski trip to Vermont a few years before. It had gone down to zero one night, and the dry still air was more comfortable than this.

He jogged around the bend and saw the taillights angling into the driveway of the one lit house ahead.

He approached cautiously. He peered around the hedge, but the yard was empty. He could hear the ocean beating at the base of the cliff, and a halyard slapping a flagpole down the road somewhere. He caught his breath—he was in terrible shape—and then eased around the privet, through the arbor and along the side of the house. He could see people through the big living room window. He moved closer. They wouldn't be able to see him, the glass would be a mirror against the night outside, but he couldn't hear them through the storm windows and the thermapane sash.

He recognized some of the people inside—Chick Crosby, who ran the local TV station, and Brad Thurman. Jared's dad worked for Thurman sometimes, on big jobs. Wiring one of these big new construction jobs could get the family through a whole winter and maybe even pay for a week in the sun during a February vacation.

Who else?

There were a couple of faces Jared recognized, but he couldn't pin names to them—the tall thin white-haired guy who was pouring drinks, the chubby red-faced Mr. Man type jabbing a finger at him. Jared had seen both of them around town, maybe on one of those summer nights when he worked as a waiter at the big fundraisers. He drew a blank on the other one-percenters. And there was some thug in Nantucket Reds and a Great Harbor Yacht club polo shirt. Who the hell was he?

It reminded Jared of the year before, when a girl he'd met at summer camp came to visit. People would come up to them at the Stop & Shop or the Fast Forward parking lot and Jared would chat with them, ignoring his guest. She thought it was rude. She thought he was ashamed of her. Why didn't he introduce her to anyone? The simple fact was he didn't know their names. What was he going to say? This is Mike something from Nantucket Sailing, and this is the older brother of that kid Tommy I did Strong Wings with five years ago, this is my guidance counselor from tenth grade, we just called him "boogers"?

It was hard to explain stuff like that.

There were faces he'd known all his life he'd never attached a name to, and famous names he couldn't pick out of a lineup. Like these people tonight. He wished he'd brought a camera, but how was he supposed to know he'd need one? He'd just have to remember.

A beautiful blond woman in a short black dress came in from the kitchen, carrying a pot of coffee and some mugs on a tray. They had logos on them. Jared squinted through the glass. He was steaming up the window. The design on the mugs looked like a C and an L linked together. It meant nothing to him.

Jared knew the woman, though. Everyone knew Ms. DeHart. She was the new school psychologist. The district had created the position for her after a rash of student suicides a couple of years ago. Smart hire: the crisis wound down, and the school settled into the old routines again after she arrived. The girls all loved her and the boys were all in love with her. She was way too good-looking to be working at a public school, that was for sure.

She was passing out the coffee while Alana stood in the corner talking to—what was her name? Jill something. A pale blonde, Alana said she looked like a mouse, but Alana thought everyone looked like some kind of animal. Jill Phelan, that was it. She was one of Ms. DeHart's girls, always in and out of the guidance office. Was she crying now? Jared couldn't quite tell. They were standing too far away.

Jill's new boyfriend, Sam Wallace, a hefty lug, who would turn obese when his metabolism could no longer keep up with the burgers and fries, hovered nearby in a Whalers hoodie sweatshirt.

He had nothing to say but obviously wanted to look like he did. Alana touched Jill's shoulder. Jill twisted away.

Mason was talking to the Yacht Club shirt dude. Despite the Nantucket costume the guy looked like he should be working as a bouncer in some New Jersey nightclub.

Then the night tipped over.

Yacht Club grabbed Alana's arm and pushed Mason away. He staggered a few steps, recovered and pushed back. They were both shouting. Sam jumped Mason and wrestled him into a bear hug. The scene had a bizarre silent movie quality, framed by the window. Jared shivered in the chill wind, watching. This was really happening—whatever it was. He wanted to help, but there was nothing he could do. Call the cops on his cell phone? That would get everyone in trouble and, besides, he doubted he had any bars out here. Physically intervene? Even if he could get inside the house, everyone would see him so there'd be no element of surprise. He'd wind up getting his ass kicked for nothing. Well, not nothing exactly. Alana would know he tried to help.

No, that was stupid. He was no karate guy, no hero. He might even wind up making things worse. All he could do now was wait, watch, and study the faces.

Yacht Club, still with a vise grip on Alana's upper arm, ran two fingers down her cheek, caressed her neck and let his hand slip lower, inside her unbuttoned coat. She reared backward away from him, but she couldn't get loose.

This was crazy. Jared was about to break the window with a big decorative stone in the mulch at his feet, but he didn't have time. Mason stamped down hard on Sam's instep. The impact of the heavy-soled work boot made Sam leap backward, releasing his grip, and Mason launched at Yacht Club. The big man had to let Alana go to deal with the kid. Alana picked up an end table and swung it into Yacht Club's back, knocking him down. A lamp crashed to the floor. Jared stood gaping, amazed and awestruck. He would never have had the courage or the presence of mind to do something like that. Alana wound up and threw the table at Yacht Club's prone form. He managed to deflect it with his arms, but it did something to his wrist and his mouth gaped open in what must have been a howl of pain.

Alana sprinted for the door with Mason right behind her.

Jared took off around the side of the house, toward the front door. He stumbled around the corner in time to see Mason and Alana dashing to his truck. Alana helped Mason into the passenger side, slammed the door, ran around the cab and jumped in. But for some reason she couldn't start it.

Jared felt a crazy vertigo. He felt himself moving while he was standing still. Sam Wallace, star running back for the Nantucket Whalers, sole bright spot of yet another losing season, burst out of the door, sprinting for the truck. Jared threw himself wildly at the monstrous running form. He managed to catch an ankle—a perfect "shoestring" tackle. Sam pitched forward face-first into the dirt as Jared heard Mason yelling at Alana, "Put in the clutch, put in the clutch!"

She flooded the engine. Sam was thrashing to his feet. Jared jumped up first and hurdled at him, face-planting him again. Jared banged his shin on the front bumper and reeled around to the driver's side of the truck.

"My car's on Baxter Road!" he panted.

Alana stared at him "Jared?"

"Come on! You've gotta get out of here. Come on!"

He opened the door and pulled her out. But he couldn't make her step away from the truck. It was like her feet were stuck in the mud.

"Mason!" She called out.

Mason was bailing from the passenger side. In a second he was face-to-face with Sam Wallace. Another figure was bounding out of the front door, pounding toward them: Yacht Club.

"Go," he shouted to Alana.

"But Jill—"

"You heard her! She's not going anywhere. Get the fuck away from me!" This last was directed at Sam. They tussled beside the car as Yacht Club reached them.

But he grabbed Sam, not Mason. "Fuck are you doing? I told you to get the kid!"

"Somebody tackled me! How was I supposed to…?"

Mason used the momentary distraction to scramble back into the truck and over the seat to the driver's side. He locked the doors.

"He's okay," Jared said. "Let's go."

"But what if he can't—?"

"This is for you! He's stalling them for you! Now come on."

That cut the cable holding her to the scene behind them. They were almost out of time and she finally realized it. Jared took her hand and they dashed up the shell driveway, along the road to where he had parked his crummy white Ford Focus station wagon, possibly the most uncool car ever produced in the continental United States.

They heard the engine note of Mason's truck—he had gotten it started!

As they climbed into the Focus, the truck skidded out of the driveway in a fan of shells and accelerated toward Polpis. He was going to have to cut back to Sankaty Road on one of the little side streets. There was only one left before the street dead-ended at the lighthouse. Bayberry Lane, it was called. Mason knew the streets. The turnoff wouldn't slow him down too much, and he had a good head start.

Jared started the Ford and headed in the opposite direction, back toward 'Sconset.

"This way they won't know who to follow," he said.

Alana just nodded. They said nothing until they turned onto Milestone Road. Jared realized he was speeding, pushing the little car up to seventy miles an hour. He lightened his foot on the gas, let his breathing and his heart rate slow to normal.

"What was going on in there?" he said finally.

"I don't get it. What are you—how did you find us? Why were you even—?"

"Your book. On the floor. By your feet."

It had fallen off the seat at some point. Alana leaned over to pick it up. She stared at it. "This is—wait a second. How did you…?"

"You left it in class. I was returning it. That's all. But I saw you get into the truck with Mason."

"And you followed us."

"I was worried."

She sighed. "You were worried? Why would you—?"

"I don't know. It was a school night, your parents weren't home. I mean—their car wasn't in the driveway. And it kind of—it looked like he was dragging you."

"He wasn't."

"Okay."

"It was my idea."

"Okay."

"I was worried about Jill. She broke up with Oscar Graham for no reason and started dating that creep and acting weird, like nodding off in class. And she snapped at me when I asked her about it and…I don't know. There were lots of things. She hasn't taken a shower in a week. She's dressing like a slut and, seriously—Sam Wallace? He's a total druggie. And I don't mean weed or whatever. He sells oxy. And God knows what else. Mason said they were both going to be there tonight, so—"

"There? Where? What was going on?"

"The house belongs to this McAllister guy. I don't know his first name. My dad picks up his trash."

"So what was he doing with a bunch of high school kids? And what was Ms. DeHart doing there? What the hell is happening? This makes no sense." They drove in silence for a minute or so. "Alana?"

"This so totally sucks."

"Tell me."

"There's nothing I can do about it. I don't even know what I was trying to accomplish out there. I can't save anybody. What am I supposed to do—draw a stupid cartoon? That would get me kicked out of school for good. I should have stayed out of it. But Jill's been so fucked up lately and Oscar was freaking out and…I just—Mason invited me out there and I thought…I don't know. I have no idea what I was thinking. You can't talk people out of doing drugs. Obviously."

"So—they're doing drugs?"

Alana laughed a hard nasty laugh and turned in her seat to face him. "No. They're making dirty movies and paying girls to be in them, with drugs."

"What?"

"Don't make me say it twice, Jared."

"Are you fucking kidding me?"

She turned away again to look out the window, pitch pines blurring past in the dark. A line of cars behind a slow-moving van swept past them and disappeared in a smear of red taillights. They were alone on the road again, no houses in sight. They could have been driving down any deserted country road, anywhere. Jared liked that idea. Anywhere but here.

"That old guy? And Chick Crosby? Brad Thurman?"

Alana sighed.

"Okay, whatever, they're all assholes. Fine. But what was Ms. DeHart doing there?"

Alana picked up a crumpled scrap of tinfoil and started pulling it open with her fingernails.

Jared pushed on. "I really need to know what she was doing with those people."

"Why? Are you in love with her?"

He almost blurted "No, I'm in love with you," but some part of him, some heroic World Cup goalie, managed to block that ball before Team Crazy could score.

Instead he said, "Are you kidding? She's like thirty years old. She's my guidance counselor. Jesus."

"She's giving great guidance out there. She should be fired."

"She seems okay to me."

"Well, she's not! What do you think she was doing out there? Want to guess?" Alana stared at him, letting silence build up under the word, letting the pressure push it out of her. "Recruiting."

"What?"

"You heard me."

They drove along, listening to the wind against the car and the rasp of the engine. Finally Jared let out the breath he'd been holding. "I don't believe this."

"Well, believe it. She tried to recruit me, okay? Like I was some kind of drug addict. I don't even take aspirin."

They started around the rotary.

"I'll take you home," Jared said. Then, as they passed the Stop & Shop construction site, he asked, "What are we going to do?"

"We can't do anything. If we go to the police, they'll just deny it. Jill's the only person who'll get in trouble. And maybe Sam Wallace."

"Yeah. He deserves it, but…"

"She doesn't. It would be our word against theirs. A guy like McAllister could really hurt us, too. I mean—my family. If he got all his friends to cancel my dad's contracts…Miles Reis has been trying to get that route for years. We'd be fucked. I'm not supposed to know how close to the line my dad lives. It's always paycheck to paycheck, and he doesn't even charge some people! His dad didn't, so…" She shook her head, as if there were gnats in the car. "Like this was the old Nantucket! If there ever was an old Nantucket."

Jared was thinking. "Thurman could blacklist my dad. All those contractors stick together. The big ones."

"Yeah."

"But we have to do something."

"Yeah."

"We could report it anonymously."

"They know I was there. And Sam saw you. They could hurt Mason's family, too. His dad's a Selectman, and with Mason involved…"

Jared nodded. "It's a small town."

"That's why I'm moving to the city. As soon as I get my diploma."

He glanced over at her. "Which city?"

"Any city. Kabul. Detroit. I don't care. Except, not Manhattan. No more islands. Ever. Not for me. I want dry land around me and lots of escape routes."

Jared had to laugh. "I know what you mean."

They drove past the high school and the softball field. He turned up Bartlett Road.

"So what can we do?" Alana said.

Jared squinted into a set of oncoming headlights—some asshole in a truck who refused to lower his brights. There were assholes everywhere and so many ways to be one.

"Chick Crosby must be shooting the movies. We could steal them from him."

Alana closed her eyes. It seemed to take her a few seconds to summon the energy even to answer such an idiotic point. "You think he has cans of film sitting around? People don't even use film anymore. They're probably encrypted files on his computer. Anyway, I'll bet you anything he locks his house, with all the equipment lying around. I mean, he's a criminal, and criminals always lock their houses because they think everyone else is a criminal, too. He probably has alarms. In case you were thinking of stealing his computer and having some super-geek get past his firewalls and passcodes and whatever, which by the way we don't even know anyone like that."

"Okay."

"That's just stupid."

"Okay!"

Jared pulled into her driveway. "So here's what we have to do," he said. "First we have to figure out who every one of those people were—the ones we didn't recognize. They probably have their pictures in the *Foggy Sheet*. Gene Mahon probably knows their names. He might help. Or the newspaper. They take pictures at those fundraisers. Then we have to figure how they're all connected to each other. And we have to talk to Jill. And Ms. DeHart."

"Ms. DeHart would just close me down, and I already tried talking to Jill."

"But now you've seen what's going on. Everything's different after tonight. If she goes to the police she could trash the whole operation, single-handedly."

"And lose her drug connection."

"That has to happen anyway. She's seventeen years old. I mean, fuck. You can't be a drug addict at seventeen years old! Or, that is—you can, obviously, but..."

"I know. She wants to get clean. But it's not that easy, okay? My dad wants to quit smoking. He's been trying for twenty years and he's finally down to one pack a day. If you were ever addicted to anything you'd know what I mean."

But he was addicted. He was hooked on the rush of feeling he got talking to this girl. It was a legitimate drug addiction, even if the drugs were manufactured inside his own body: adrenaline, testosterone, endorphins—a potent mix. He certainly didn't want to give it up. That was why he had followed her tonight, that was how he had gotten into this mess in the first place.

Then a thought slid into his mind like a cold wind under a doorsill.

He turned off the motor, twisted around to face her. "Tell Jill you'll go to the police if she won't. Her best shot is to talk to them before you do."

"That's harsh."

"But it's a plan. And it just might work. She'd be fucked if you turned her in."

"I'm supposed to be her friend."

"You are her friend. This is what friends do. Like an intervention."

"I guess." They sat in silence for a while, then Alana nodded. "I'll do it."

Good decision—but it was already too late.

Chapter Two

Bedside

The day after Thanksgiving, I started the morning at Nantucket Cottage Hospital and finished it at a friend's memorial service—not much to be thankful for.

At the hospital I was visiting a girl named Jill Phelan in the second floor ICU. At least that's what they call it; in fact our Intensive Care Unit is one room they can seal off while they stabilize patients. Anyone in critical condition, they transfer by helicopter to Mass General. This girl had dropped into a coma after a drug overdose, but with the winds gusting up to fifty miles an hour the medevac crew was stuck waiting for a break in the weather. For the moment they were grounded.

My most experienced detective, Charlie Boyce, took the initial call. He'd already talked to her family and friends, her teachers at the school, and the doctors at the hospital, but no one knew anything and so far he'd gotten nowhere. He was determined to track down her source, but drugs were all over the island these days. She could have gotten it from anyone; she could have even been selling the stuff herself.

I was interested in the girl, though. She didn't fit the profile of a juvenile opiate addict. She had come in second at the previous year's Junior Miss Pageant where she played something by Mozart on her flute for the talent section. She was shockingly good, and you didn't get that far by the mere accident of talent. You had to work, you had to practice long hours to burn those arpeggios into the muscle memory of your fingers, and that kind of discipline didn't square with a drug habit. Something was drastically askew. I needed to check out the situation for myself.

I had plenty of time. My ex-wife, Miranda, and the kids were back in Los Angeles with her parents for the holiday. They'd made the right choice. Los Angeles was at its best in the late fall, when the occasional storm off the Pacific scrubbed out the smog and the crystalline desert air flooded the basin. Not much chance of that in a drought year, but you could always hope.

Nantucket was having its own storm, a dark gusty nor'easter. The island presented itself to the odd straggle of visiting home-owners and tourists at its most bleak and dreary: cold rain, raw wind, gray skies, the Sound torn with turbulent chop, the streets slick with rotting leaves. Christmas trees lined Main Street, set up but not yet decorated. The stores were full of Christmas merchandise, but nothing could draw people out into the pen-etrating damp and the Atlantic gale.

I had gotten a twelve-pound turkey from the health food store—Annye sourced them from a farm in Vermont—and defiantly cooked it for myself. I could warm it up in the gravy for a few more dinners, have a week's worth of turkey sandwiches for lunch, and there'd be soup when the kids got back from L.A. But it made for a lonely night. I had slept badly, and my mood fit the weather when I got to the hospital.

It was quiet inside the old building as I walked the long corridor to the elevators, my shoes squeaking on the linoleum. Upstairs at the nurses' station, Marilee told me the patient already had visitors.

I could hear their voices before I got to the room: a deep Scottish brogue and the higher lilt of a Jamaican accent—Liam Phelan, the father, and Oscar Graham. I'd only met Phelan a couple of times—he had helped me break up a drunken fight on the docks during Race Week the year before. He was chief engineer on one of the big yachts, a burly Santa with a mean left hook. No sign of his wife, Margaret. They were estranged, separated but not divorced. He had refused her ultimatum to stop working the big yachts and settle down on the island. No doubt there were other problems. They made it a point to never be in the same room together, even their daughter's hospital room. That took careful planning in a small town, but I guess they thought it was worth the effort.

Oscar, I'd known since I first arrived on the island. He was my first near-arrest, in fact, brought in for throwing a snowball at Lonnie Fraker's cruiser. I often felt like pelting those dark-blue-and-green cars myself, but this had been my first exposure to the State Police, as well as the local juvenile delinquent population. I have to admit I preferred the juvenile delinquents. I let Oscar off with a warning—Lonnie had just launched his "scared straight" crusade, and wanted to ship the boy off to Walpole for a week. Oscar and I had been good friends ever since.

I paused outside the door now to eavesdrop.

"How did this happen?" Oscar was saying. "How could she even—?"

Liam's intimidating baritone: "You tell me!"

"Wait a second. I—"

"You're the boyfriend! You're the one she refuses to talk about and now I see why!"

"That's—I am not…what are you talking about?"

"You're black! And she thinks I'm some kind of racist, as if I cared a row of pins for that shite. All I want to know is where did you get the drugs?"

"I didn't—I'm trying to tell you, I'm not—wait a second—"

"Did you steal someone's prescription?"

"Hold on. I'm telling you—"

"Or do you know a doctor? Some of these bastards will do anything for a few extra bucks under the table."

Tim Lepore appeared behind me. He was doing his morning rounds, about to walk in on them. I grabbed his arm, crossed my lips with a warning finger. He shook his head, raised his eyebrows in an expression of amused contempt. He had no business acting surprised at my snooping, though. It's part of my job description.

"I'm not Jill's boyfriend," Oscar was saying. "I'm just her friend. All right?"

"Her friend, are you? Her school chum? Then what the hell are you doing here? How did you find out she was in hospital in the first place?"

"Everyone knows. It's a small town, Mr. Phelan. Other people have come to visit. School friends. Teachers. I wanted to see her, I wanted to talk to her for a few minutes. Maybe find out what's going on."

"Well she's not talking just at the moment."

"No."

"So you're not the boyfriend."

"No."

"And you didn't sell her the drugs."

"No."

"Jesus Christ. What a cock-up. How could a thing like this happen?"

"Well, if you were ever around you might—"

"I've got a job, you little prick. I work for a living. I was halfway between here and Bermuda when I got the news. What was I supposed to do?"

"You were supposed to get back here, and you did."

"Fucking right, I did. Thank you for that at least. Have you seen Margaret? Mrs. Phelan?"

"You just missed her."

"Thank God for small favors."

"She couldn't stay. She had to go to work."

"But you stayed."

"I got the day off, Mr. Phelan. I just want to be here, you know—when Jill wakes up."

"If she wakes up."

"She'll wake up."

"You're sure of that are you?"

"A hundred percent."

"Good lad."

I nodded at Lepore and we entered the room together.

"Mr. Phelan—Oscar," the doctor said, nodding at them in turn. "I'm going to have to ask you to leave now. You can wait downstairs. I'll let you know if there's any change in her condition. The same goes for you, Chief. They'll be taking her out in a few minutes, and you'd only be in the way."

We left the doctor to organize the airlift, and walked back to the elevators together.

"You have to do something about this, Chief," Oscar said. "You have to—I don't know, find the drug dealers and arrest them and…"

"And?"

"I don't know. Hurt them somehow."

Phelan laughed. "That's my boy. But I wouldn't count on the police, begging your pardon, Officer, sir. Could be it's a policeman who sold her the drugs in the first place. They confiscate a lot of contraband and who's to know if a bit goes missing here and there?"

Oscar slumped. "So what can I do?"

"I'll tell you what I'm going to do, lad. I'm going to find these bastards for myself and fucking shake them until their brains scramble."

I touched his arm as the elevator doors opened. "Not a good idea, Liam."

"And you have a better one, then?"

"Leave it to me. It's my job. And I'm good at it."

"That remains to be seen, Officer. That remains to be seen."

Outside in the parking lot, the storm had cleared off to the north, and we watched the medevac team wheel Phelan's daughter to the helicopter. It lifted off slowly, the blades chopping the air into a private hurricane, then it arched away over the hospital toward the harbor.

"They'll take good care of her at Mass General," I said.

Phelan's storm was still raging. "They better. I'll take care of the rest."

"I don't want you getting yourself in trouble, Liam. That won't help anyone."

He was staring away at the diminishing speck of the helicopter. "That's my daughter in there, Chief Kennis. You've got a daughter. And an imagination, I've heard. So don't talk like a fool."

I left him standing there studying the clearing sky. There was nothing more I could do for him, and I had a memorial service to attend, half the length of the island away. I didn't want to be late.

Chapter Three

A Folded Flag

Todd Macy's memorial was being held in Madaket, at the old Admiralty Club, a big, rambling old building that mostly consisted of one giant room dominated by a massive fireplace. Long tables were set up in rows under the high wooden beams, with seating for seventy-five or eighty. The fire was roaring and the place was jammed—a least a hundred friends and family crowded the place, taking up every chair and lined up against the walls, standing room only.

Todd had served with the Marine Corps in Iraq and he got the full military send-off, with the cannon on the lawn banging a hole in the day, and the geese flapping by overhead harmonizing with the bugler on "Taps." A grizzled old vet presented Todd's widow, Sandra, with a folded flag before everyone retired inside to hear their neighbors remember their friend. Todd had been a prankster in his youth, painting out the "l" in the Madaket Public Landing sign, drag racing on Milestone Road, and organizing a famous party at Fortieth Pole, where three jeeps and a Range Rover got caught in the rising tide. A puttering techie and strident environmentalist, he had more than ten thousand followers on his Twitter account, where he posted occasional musings like "Daylight savings time—jet lag without travel" and "'Why would I lie?' should never be taken as a rhetorical question." Just last month he had begun to tweet on the subject of the coming global climate apocalypse. "They say it takes 20 years to wreck a town. 200 to wreck a planet." And "Give us 2,000 more years, we'll take out the whole galaxy."

Todd had found a home at the Land Bank, where in the week before he died he managed to forestall chairman Chuck Forrest's efforts to scuttle a major land-trade. A couple wanted to barter thirty undeveloped acres around Long Pond for a bank-owned old house in Tom Nevers. At the last minute, Chuck tried to back out—someone offered the Land Bank a couple of million for the place, and he wanted the cash.

"The Long Pond property is worth ten times that much," Todd pointed out.

"But we can't sell it! That's the whole point!"

"We're not supposed to sell it. But we're not supposed to sell the Tom Nevers parcel, either. And you're about to do that."

That was how he had described the argument to me, at least. He'd won that battle. He'd convinced the buyers to pull out of the deal with a secret tour of the old mansion that included the full inventory of Nantucket entropy: crumbling chimneys, carpenter bee drill holes in the trim, wasps' nests under the eaves, dry rot, termites, and a powderpost beetle infestation—not quite the "turnkey" home that Chuck Forrest had promised. But that was only a skirmish. Todd had confided to me that he feared much bigger struggles ahead.

I had to wonder—who was going to fight them now?

Even his death struck me as symbolic—shot by a stray bullet as he walked the moors in deer hunting season. He and his dog had both been wearing their bright orange vests, but it hadn't made any difference to the trigger-happy drunk who took him out.

I turned my attention back to the side of the big room that had been cleared out to accommodate a podium. A woman was telling the story of how Todd had delivered her baby in her car, pulled over to the side of Polpis Road in a whiteout blizzard, twenty-two years ago. The child was a boy named Connor, recently graduated from MIT and living in Boston.

He stood beside his mom and described Todd tutoring him on eighth-grade math homework. I smiled. Todd had done the same for Tim this year, dropping by for a beer to chat about Land Bank issues, and staying to work some algebra problems with my son. When I thanked him he'd just shrugged and said, "This stuff is easy. Teachers try to complicate it to make themselves look important."

Connor announced to enthusiastic applause that he was adopting Todd's black lab, with his landlord's blessing. Other people took their turns at the lectern, describing a home-brewer whose beer could "knock a lumberjack on his ass," and a gourmet cook who had prepared Christmas dinner at the Our Island Home nursing home every year for the last decade.

Billy Delavane stood up to talk about their surfing days in the eighties, before a damaged rotator cuff made Todd hang up his wetsuit for good. On one memorable autumn swell in Madaket, Todd managed to break three surfboards, take a ten-stitch gash in his forehead, and get his car towed. His response? Drive Billy's truck to the emergency room, return an hour later, borrow one of Billy's boards and paddle back out.

"He broke that board, too," Billy said with a rueful smile. "I think that's some kind of record."

I thought of saying a few words, but this meeting was for old-timers only. I hadn't hung out at Jim Powers' shack or gotten drunk at Preston's. I only had one anecdote, and Connor's story made it feel redundant. Apparently Todd helped lots of kids with their math homework over the years. I was probably one of the last people to hear from Todd, but it was—and remains—a ghostly Boston accent speaking on my office voicemail. The day before he'd been shot, Todd called the police station and insisted on talking to me. I was out, so he left a message. A short one, just three terse sentences: "Something bad is happening. I need to talk to you, and not over the phone. Call me."

I did, but by the time I got around to it the next day, he was lying among the brambles of North Pasture in the Middle Moors with a two-inch hole in his chest.

After the service, everyone milled around on the lawn, small groups talking, people taking turns for a moment with Todd's family. A small gap of blue sky opened up in the clouds to the north, casting a shaft of light onto the Sound. I paid my respects and stood by the big anchor at the edge of the property with Billy Delavane.

"Great guy," he said.

"Yeah."

"Who else could get all the Thayers together in one room?"

I looked around. All three brothers were there, Andrew, Mike, and Larry, along with Billy's old flame, Joyce. They had a daughter together, Debbie, now a restless and gangly thirteen-year-old, standing apart from her mother, obviously feeling oppressed and unfairly tyrannized by these meaningless family rituals, staring at the crabgrass, waiting for the moment when she could start texting her friends. She lived most of the time with Billy and he kept her on a loose rein; but Joyce shared custody and she had rules. One of them was clearly being broken. She said something and Debbie looked up to speak with Sandra, who pulled her into a hug. Debbie controlled a flinch and reluctantly hugged the widow back.

"Good girl," Billy said. "Debbie likes hugs about as much as Dervish." His pug definitely abjured displays of physical affection; I could testify to that.

Joyce and her daughter said their final condolences and started strolling toward us. I wished my son, Tim, could be here. This was first moment I could recall seeing Debbie without her clique of friends. On second thought, it wouldn't have mattered much—if Tim had attended the service, my daughter, Caroline, would have been there also, and she was part of that clique. I would say the leader, but the balance of power shifted on a daily basis. She would have effectively insulated Debbie from Tim's advances, all by herself. She'd been doing that for weeks.

Billy pulled a silver flask out of his coat pocket, twisted the cap off, took a quick pull and passed it to me. "It's Notch."

"You've got to be kidding."

Notch was a local single malt priced at eight hundred eighty-eight dollars by Triple Eight Distillery. Even $88.08 would have priced it above sixteen-year-old Lagavulin I preferred, so I could buy a case of the stuff for that price. The whole enterprise was hilariously delusional, but typical of Nantucket. We're always looking for new ways of making rich people feel richer, skinning them smartly in the process.

Billy laughed. "Dean Long gets it for me free, dude. I found the leak in his living room a couple of years ago. I had to pull off half the shingles on the east side. Turned out it was coming in from one of the dormers on the third floor. It was like this insane puzzle. I kept after it long after Dean gave up. I wound up not charging him for the last few weeks. Why should he pay to finance my hobby? So instead he slips me a bottle of Notch every year. That works for me. It's nice stuff, if you don't have to pay for it."

I took a swig. I had to admit it was good. But I wasn't paying for it either. I could see Billy studying my squint. He knew I was trying to do the math. But that was his specialty. "About twenty-five bucks a sip," he said.

"Jesus Christ. What a racket." I took another pull. "I feel richer already."

I handed him back the flask and scanned the crowd again. Charles Forrest had taken Andy Thayer aside, and they were standing near the cannon across the wide lawn from us, talking intently. Chuck jabbed at Andy's solar plexus with a stubby finger. The second time he did it, Andy reached across his chest and grabbed the finger, twisting it up and back. Chuck's yelp carried sharply across the lawn, a pale echo of the cannon shot earlier. People turned, and then turned away.

I started toward them but Billy grabbed my arm. "Let it play out, Chief. It's finished already."

He was right. Chuck stepped back, cradling his injured hand, and bumped into Jane Stiles. He glared at her briefly and then stalked away. She studied his retreat for a few seconds, then started across the rabbit-bitten lawn toward us.

She was wearing a short black dress and black stockings under an unbuttoned gray overcoat with wide lapels that looked like something out of a forties movie. The damp weather had teased her curly hair out into a wild frizzy mane, tamed under a charcoal head scarf.

Billy nodded at her appreciatively. "She cleans up good."

I nodded. It was a pleasant shock—I had never seen Jane in a dress before. Mostly she wore her landscaping clothes—jeans and a tee-shirt, or a moth-eaten Fair Isle sweater. She was a writer, too—she wrote what they call "cozy" mysteries, but of course you couldn't make a living from that. So she kept her all-girl landscaping crew and scribbled on the side. That was typical of the trades on Nantucket. Everyone had something going on the side—the carpenter with a darkroom in the basement, the plumber with a recording studio in the garage, the housepainter who kept a falcon. And the police chief wrote poetry.

I'd been published in a few small magazines, but Jane Stiles was the real thing. She had three books in print, all part of a detective series set on the island, featuring a local librarian/sleuth named Madeline Clark. Jane's small-scale success hadn't changed her attitude and lifestyle at all. She still worked sixty hours a week, belittled her success, and deflected compliments with acid wit and a cringe of genuine discomfort. Her fashion sense hadn't shifted, either. She still managed the same trick, turning a complete indifference to her appearance into a kind of high style that you'd have to work hard to copy effectively.

It was an "old money" look—I often thought of Katherine Hepburn in baggy sweats tooling around New York on her bicycle. Later I found out that Jane's family had burned through their money a long time before. But a certain residual elegance remained. It was the way she held her head, her hand gestures—there were generations of gracious hostesses lurking in her DNA.

She could have been hosting this affair, the way she moved from group to group with a light touch on the arm and a word or two. She seemed to know everyone, and everyone knew her. She whispered something to Sandra, paused a moment for our premier real estate shark, Elaine Bailey, and kept angling toward us.

"Hi, Chief. Billy," she said when she reached the anchor. Billy tilted his head in greeting.

"Hey, Jane," I said.

"Sad day."

"Awful. Senseless and stupid. What a waste. I wish we could ban hunting sometimes."

Billy snorted. "Then the deer would take over this island, Chief. Them and the rats. Chase all the rich people away. Can't have that. I'll tell you something. It's a good thing people jack a few out of season or we'd never keep a lid on it. Not that I'd ever do that."

I lifted my arms, palms out. "Of course not."

"So, you're sure it was an accident?" Jane said.

"Oh, boy," Billy laughed. "The whodunit lady strikes again! 'I suspect foul play, sir!' Your Maddy Clark always finds clues the police don't catch. Hence the term 'clueless,' am I right? 'This isn't plaster dust, Officer Dimbulb. It's dandruff…just like I noticed on Least Likely Suspect Guy's blazer!'"

Jane punched him on the arm. "Very funny. Can I use that dandruff idea, though? I like it."

"My pleasure. But you better mention me in the acknowledgments. And sign me a copy."

"I always sign you a copy."

"But make this one more personal. 'To Billy, who felt me up at our senior prom.'"

"I had totally forgotten about that."

"Liar."

She turned to me. "Seriously, though, Chief. I heard something a little weird back there."

"What was it?"

"Well…Chuck Forrest was talking to Andy Thayer—I didn't hear the whole conversation but I sneaked over to eavesdrop because that's what I do for a living when I'm not weeding flower beds and mowing lawns. It is! Anyway, they didn't notice me. I'm quite unobtrusive."

"Chuck walked right into you!" Billy said.

"My point exactly. So this is what he said." She closed her eyes for a moment of concentration, then opened them wide. "'Tough break. But it could happen to anyone, Andy. Life's a minefield. You better watch your step.' Wait, I just re-wrote that! I was trying to make it sound more threatening. Hold on. No, no—he actually said 'you have to' not 'you better.' Like, the general 'you.' People in general. 'You have to watch your step.' But then he said, 'Word to the wise.'"

I nodded. "That sounds pretty specific to me. And pretty threatening."

"I know. That's what I'm saying. What a creep."

"So you're saying—what? You think Todd was murdered?"

"I don't know."

"And Chuck Forrest pulled the trigger?"

She started to laugh but it collapsed into a sigh. "That's how it would be if it happened in one of my books, Chief. Maddy would be out in the moors, looking for spent rounds and shell casings while Chief Blote worked on his memoirs and told her to keep her nose out of police business."

"He always tells her that," Billy said.

Jane shrugged. "He never learns—supposedly. But he's not above asking Maddy a question or two, from time to time—on the sly. Of course he never gives her the credit when he finally solves the case. And that's fine with Maddy. She works behind the scenes."

"Sounds familiar," I said. I was thinking of my old flame Franny Tate and the late, unlamented Jack Tornovitch. Franny had taken over Jack's old job at Homeland Security. I read about her in the newspapers from time to time. She was finally getting the credit for her work.

As for the fictional Police Chief Blote, he couldn't be quite the pompous buffoon everyone thought, if he was smart enough to take Madeline's Clark's advice. I could do a lot worse myself.

Jane's words stuck with me, as did Chuck's ominous "word to the wise" remark. I hadn't visited the spot where Todd had fallen. At this point the patch of moorland where the kids discovered his body hadn't even been listed as an official crime scene.

That was probably the right call. Jane spun out fantastic theories for a living, She was more interested in drama and intrigue than the boring facts of any actual case. I looked across the lawn as the mourners started to disperse. Chuck Forrest was on his iPhone, talking intently to someone, shaking his head, performing a spot-on pantomime of an agitated suspect. All the more reason to give him a pass. No real killer would put on that show fifty feet away from the local police chief.

But it couldn't hurt to check.

Chapter Four

Hunting Grounds

It was a typical weekend outing with my kids—breakfast at Fog Island, followed by hot chocolate at Jim's on the Broad Street Strip, and a drive out into the moors, where we bundled up and hiked the deer paths. The kids found a cache of arrowheads that had tipped the quiver of a Wampanoag hunter half a millennium ago.

I found the bullet that killed Todd Macy.

I kept my purpose secret. Tim had been shaken by Todd's death, unusually quiet, but waking me up in the middle of the night to talk about God and death and the meaning of life… or the lack of it. I didn't want to exacerbate the situation (or prompt another of Miranda's "your-job-is-poisoning-their-lives" diatribe), but I was stealthy and they were easily distracted, so it was worth a try.

We parked at the cranberry bogs and walked southwest toward Altar Rock. I had chosen the route carefully—I had the GPS coordinates for the spot where Todd's body was found and I wanted to inspect the scene for myself. The hole in Todd's chest was big. The bullet passed through him and disappeared, according to the ME's report. But the medical examiner had a plane to catch, and no real interest in one of a dozen hunting accidents in a busy season.

We had examined the body together briefly. Shotguns are the only legal weapon for hunting at that time of year on Nantucket, and the damage to Todd's body was not consistent with the twelve-gauge buckshot standard for island hunters. This was one bullet, not a spray of pellets. It made a small hole going in, and a much bigger one going out. The ME acknowledged that the round was illegal but found my suspicions amusing. "Right. Someone's rifle hunting during shotgun season. Wow. I'm shocked. I have literally never heard of that before. Next thing you'll be telling me people are still hunting after the season closes. What'll they go for next? piping plovers? I hear they taste like chicken."

We chuckled at that reference to a locally famous bumper sticker, but I had continued to examine the body. The bullet had entered around the third thoracic vertebra and exited just above the solar plexus. The angle indicated a shot from above, so as I tramped through the bracken now with my kids, I was looking for a nice concealed perch in the low hills above the moors that the hunter might have been using for a blind.

The kids had other concerns. Caroline had no interest in digging for arrowheads. She wanted to drive out to Great Point.

"We always do what Tim wants," she muttered, kicking through a stand of beach plum. "I hate these stupid bushes! It's like they're attacking you all the time. Ow! They prick you right through your pants! This sucks."

"We never do what I want," Tim said. "That is such—" He caught my look and cut the rest of that sentence off. "This is the first time I ever got to—"

"Are you kidding me? All summer we had to go to Dionis because you're scared of the waves! Dad got me a boogie board and I never got to use it once!"

"I am not scared of the waves!"

"Oh, really? So what bothered you so much then?"

"Jellyfish. There were tons of jellyfish at Surfside last summer."

"Oooo, that's scary,"

"They sting!"

"All right," I said. "Enough." I turned to Caroline. "You're supposed to find some arrowheads for school, right?"

"Tim could just give me some of his."

"That's not the point. Come on, Caro. It's fieldwork. You're supposed keep a journal and write down where you find them and try to figure out where the nearest Wampanoag settlement was located, and—"

"I can fake that. Hello—Wikipedia."

"Just because you can doesn't mean—"

"Besides, you told us that learning to bullshit teachers was—"

"Caroline!"

"You said it! You said it was the most important thing you ever learned in school."

"That was college!"

"I'm starting early!"

Tim laughed and I started laughing, too. "Okay, but we're going to do some real work right now, No bullshit, pardon my language. And it's actually fun. That's what you're going to learn today."

"Fine." In other words—anything but. Still, I chose to take it as a victory and move on. We pushed into an open field. A few minutes later Caroline said, "Can I go to Debbie's sleep-over tonight?"

"She's grounded!" Tim said. "That's why we couldn't go out last night."

Caroline spun to face him. "First of all, she isn't grounded. She just told you that to get rid of you, and second of all—going to movies with a bunch of other kids and getting picked up by somebody's mom isn't exactly a *date*."

This one-two punch rocked Tim into a stunned silence.

I said to Caroline, "Will Billy be there?"

"Dad!"

"Well, sorry. I don't like the idea of a bunch of eighth-grade girls running around that house unchaperoned."

"Of course he'll be there. God."

"Your mom said it was all right?

"She said it's up to you. She also said you don't want to lose a night of being with me."

"That's true, but it's okay. Tim and I can have boy time. Too bad you can't go to her mom's house, though. It's so much bigger."

"It's horrible there. They fight all the time. Debbie's mom and her uncles."

"You're lucky. You only have one uncle and he's never around."

"Do you fight about money?" Caroline asked.

I laughed. "Neither of us has any so there's nothing to fight about."

"But he's a big FBI agent."

"Right. With a government paycheck."

"How about Grandpa? Didn't he leave you anything?"

"He did. It's called your college fund."

Caroline mulled this for a few steps. "Well, Debbie's grandmother left them a lot. I mean, like a real lot. So all they do is fight. Everyone wants to do different things and so they're all mad now all the time. The last time I stayed over, Billy came and got me and Debbie and took us back to Madaket."

"Yeah, I remember that. I asked what happened and he said, 'The kids just wanted to hear the ocean.'"

Caroline shrugged "It's better than crazy grownups screaming at each other."

"Good point."

"I found one!" Tim shouted. He had lagged behind us, poking through the rosa rugosa, ignoring the prickles. He actually dug up a nice cache of arrowheads and I left the kids to sort them out because we had come to within ten yards of the spot where Todd Macy was killed. I vectored the exact location on the GPS and started digging with the trowel I'd brought along. The ground was hard with the cold, and tangled with stiff spiky bushes. The bullet must have buried itself in the turf at high velocity, cutting through the brambles and lodging itself deep in ground. I figured I had an area of roughly two or three square feet in front of the impact zone to search. It doesn't sound like much but it took me almost an hour to find it. By the end, my wrists were bleeding from the prickly bushes, and of course the kids had figured me out. Carrie was annoyed. I'd tricked them, dragging them out to the moors on police business, bribing them with hot chocolate and distracting them with arrowheads.

But Tim surprised me. When Caroline pronounced the project a pointless waste of time, he turned on her. "Dad's trying to solve a murder!"

"Not exactly. I'm trying to figure out if there even was a murder."

"Probably there wasn't," Carrie said. "People don't get murdered on Nantucket."

"Yes, they do," Tim snapped. "People get killed all the time here! The people who died in the bombings last summer and Preston Lomax and—tons of people."

"Tons of people," Caroline mimicked him. "That's what you say when you run out of examples."

"There are," Tim insisted. "Like—that lady who was killed by her boyfriend. And those guys at the Chicken Box."

Caroline shrugged. "Whatever. It's not like some big city, I'm just saying."

"*Whatever.* That's what you say instead of admitting I'm right!"

"You are such a useless little—"

She lunged at him. I stuck my arm out, separating them. "Enough! Look, I found it."

It was a big bullet, deformed by impact into a rough oval shape. The kids crowded in and then stepped back.

"Ugh, that's creepy," Caroline said.

"It actually looks like an arrowhead—the ones we saw at the museum last summer."

Tim just stared down at it quietly. I took a picture with my phone and sent it to my assistant chief, Haden Krakauer. He had served in the military, so I thought he might recognize the round.

He did. The phone chimed when we were halfway back to the car. Haden sent a picture of a tall gleaming brass cartridge pointed at the tip like a miniature rocket, lying across two dollar-bills—maybe five, five and half, inches long. The kids clamored to look at it.

"What is that?" Tim asked.

"I'm not sure, but I think it's what our bullet looked like before it was fired."

I read Haden's e-mail quickly to myself. The bullet was an M82 series 0.50 caliber sniper's round, probably fired from a Barrett M107 rifle. That's a military grade weapon the Coast Guard uses to disable smugglers' boats, shooting from a helicopter. It can take most vehicles out with one shot to the engine block. According to Haden, a typical sports rifle has a muzzle energy of two to three thousand foot pounds. This rifle's muzzle energy measures between ten thousand and fifteen thousand—five times more powerful than the sport requires. So this was not a hunter's gun—not a deer hunter's, anyway,

And Todd Macy's death was not an accident.

◇◇◇

That night I got the call from State Attorney General David Carmichael. I had just put the kids to bed, reading them the long passage in *Catcher in the Rye* where Holden goes to see his sister Phoebe. Tim had calmed down—I think he was glad to see me working the case. That was the part Miranda never understood.

It was a little after nine and I didn't expect a call. Haden? Some problem at the station? Miranda? But it was a Boston number. I took the call out of curiosity.

"Kennis? It's Dave Carmichael."

"Dave? It's kind of late to be calling."

"We work late here. We have seventeen ongoing cases and six more pending. I'm preparing nine jury trials right now, I'm hip-deep in discovery and jury selection and opening arguments. I'm shorthanded and I need help."

"I know the feeling."

"No, I don't think you do. This is the real world and these cases matter. I have four RICO investigations ongoing, a couple of huge drug busts, and a corruption scandal on Beacon Hill.

Big stuff. You've got some rich punk with an open-container violation."

I thought of the deformed sniper's bullet I had just dig out of the ground. "I may have a murder on my hands."

"Really? Well, I have fifteen murder cases going right now, and I'm dead-ending on most of them. Leads are going cold because I don't have the manpower to chase them down. But that's not even the problem. Clues are falling through the cracks because my guys don't have the brains to see what they're looking at. I don't even know what evidence I'm missing because I can't add up *what I can't see*. I know we're falling behind, though, Henry. I can feel it."

"So what can I do for you, Dave?"

"Work for me. Quit that dead-end bullshit job and come to Boston. I have an opening for chief investigator and I want you to fill it. I know the way your brain works. You're a chess master and you're down there playing checkers with the day-trippers. It's a waste."

Knee-jerk arguments twitched along my nerves as he spoke. We had big cases on the island—obviously. I'd first met Dave during the Preston Lomax murder investigation, and I knew he'd followed the bombings that had threatened the island last summer. But it was pointless to argue because I knew he was right.

This was an extraordinary opportunity, the break I'd been looking for since I left Los Angeles. It was the difference between a job and a career. The only limit to working for Dave Carmichael would be the line between what I wanted and what I was able to achieve. I'd been pacing in circles in a tiny closed room and Dave knocked the walls down. Turns out the room had been sitting in some vast alpine meadow that stretched away to the high peaks in every direction. All I had to do was step out into the coarse grass and start walking.

But it was impossible.

I couldn't leave the kids, and Miranda would never let me take them. The silence on the line said everything, but I still had to fit the words to it. Speak the syllables, make the truth manifest, make it real. The wonder and the glory of language. "Sorry," I said. "Maybe when the kids are grown."

"I'll be governor when your kids are grown and you'll be too old to keep up."

"You're probably right, at least about me."

"Thanks for the vote of confidence, buddy."

"Just kidding. But seriously—"

"You could commute."

"Not really."

"Give them that quality time!"

"Kids don't care about quality. Just quantity."

He was quiet for a second or two. Then: "At least think about it, will you?"

"I will."

"I mean, seriously consider this."

"I will."

"All right, family man. Go and get some sleep."

I couldn't sleep that night. I went into the kids' room and watched them for a while, Carrie wrapped like a little burrito, Tim with the covers thrashed off after the exertions of some dream. I pulled the comforter up over him, eased his right leg back onto the bed, thinking; "If a body catch a body coming through the rye," just like Holden Caulfield.

You and me, Holden. You and me.

Chapter Five

The Burning House

As it turned out, I had more homegrown crime to investigate, anyway.

I was out in the moors the next Monday afternoon, poking around for some additional scrap of evidence in the Todd Macy shooting, when I saw the column of smoke. This wasn't the lazy curl from a chimney with someone inside, sipping tea next to a cozy hearth. This was thick and toxic, a pulsing black column like a million ants swarming a tree trunk, a spreading noiseless stain on the clear blue sky.

I took off, crashing through the bracken, hearing the distant sirens as I ran. By the time I had cleared the last tangle of wild grapevines, I knew I'd been out there before. This was Andrew Thayer's house—Debbie Garrison's uncle. My kids had attended a birthday party at the cottage last summer. The big fireplace in the living room had made me nervous—all that resinous raw pine timber, all those canvas slipcovers on the old wood furniture. One errant spark…the place had struck me as a fire hazard all the way back in August, but of course that was fire season where I came from, and the big stone hearth was cold with disuse. No one was going be roasting any marshmallows in there until… well, until now. The thought of my kids in there struck a nerve. This was all edging a little too close to home.

The place was empty that day, fortunately. And there were five witnesses to the fire. That fact alone was slightly odd—the cottage sat out in the middle of nowhere, near the pout ponds, and the chances of anyone seeing the blaze were nil, especially so late in the year, during that gray, dismal patch between Thanksgiving and Christmas. But pyromaniacs linger at the scene of the crime—that's the rule. The fire lights them up and they love to watch it.

That made everyone on the scene a suspect.

If they had plausible alternative reasons to be out in the moors that day—as I did—we needed to find out quickly. *Eliminate the innocent*, that was what Chuck Obremski, my mentor in the LAPD, always used to say. That's the quickest way to find the guilty.

As the fire trucks parked and watered the surrounding bushes—it was too late to save the house—I spoke to the witnesses one at a time, pulling them away from the subsiding blaze and the sagging skeleton of support timbers.

They made an odd cross section of island life. David Lattimer, an old money septuagenarian crank who lived on the edge of the moors nearby. Alana Trikilis, the seventeen-year-old daughter of local garbage man and homespun philosopher Sam Trikilis. ("Show me a man's trash and I'll tell you his life story.") House-painter Mike Henderson. Local newspaper owner and editor David Trezize. And an off-island visitor. The trades, the media, the high school, the island aristocracy, and a tourist. You could make five seasons of *The Wire* out of that catalog, if Nantucket were a city like Baltimore. I glanced around the wind-bent scrub pines and brush-tangled holly trees. It could happen. Manhattan had looked like this once. But Nantucket would probably drown from rising sea levels long before anyone tried to get the first skyscraper past the voters at Town Meeting.

The witnesses agreed to meet me at the station, and I left the site to Sam Culbertson, the fire chief, and Detective Charlie Boyce. Charlie had taken some classes in arson investigation at John Jay College, and picked up some experience with this particular crime working in Boston before he came back to the island. Lonnie Fraker, our bulky and squeaky-voiced, grandstanding but good-hearted State Police captain, would show up any minute. His first move would no doubt be to fly in an off-island expert, but it never hurt to get a jump on the Staties. Charlie's "Go Whalers!" pride would spike if he found something before the big shots did.

Stumping back to my car, I heard the house collapse into a bed of charred planking and coals behind me. The fire was shocking, but at that moment I felt more irked and stymied than anything else. The Todd Macy investigation was going to have to wait now, at least for the next few days. I could send someone else out to work the case but I didn't feel confident that my other detective, Kyle Donnelly, would do anything but contaminate the crime scene. I felt overworked and outnumbered. Things were piling up fast.

And this was supposed to be the quiet season.

Chapter Six

Daughters

As it turned out I had a fair-sized crowd waiting for me at the cop shop. Liam Phelan was standing on the big compass cut into the brickwork in front of the station talking to a Laurel and Hardy team—Laurel was a tall, thin gent in what looked like a thousand-dollar suit under a cashmere overcoat. His dark steel-gray hair rose off his long bony face like a hat and he sported a thin, perfectly trimmed moustache—a policeman's dream, when it came to eyewitness descriptions. He cut a distinctive figure; even a bunch of scared people remembering a brief incident a few days before would agree on the basics, and it would be easy to pick the lanky gray-maned aristocrat out of a lineup.

I had to smile as I approached them—this guy was much more likely to be the victim of a crime than the perpetrator. Still I found it obscurely comforting to cast a jaundiced eye on the island's ruling class. Cops see everyone as potential criminals, anyway—at least the cops who taught me did.

"Just give 'em a chance," Chuck Obremski used to say, whether he was talking about a banker, a politician, or a movie star. During my first year with the LAPD, Winona Ryder got busted for shoplifting from Saks Fifth Avenue in Beverly Hills. That day, Chuck dropped the *Times* on my desk with a dramatic shrug. The story was on the front page, below the fold.

"That's what I'm talking about," he said. "It's a bug. Anyone can catch it." He caught it himself later on, but that's another story.

The Oliver Hardy standing next to the old man struck me instantly as a private detective. One more balding overweight schlub in a pea-coat—but he had the wary, attentive posture of a man who expected the worst and paid close attention to everything all the time, so he wouldn't miss it when it finally arrived. He scanned the parking lot as I walked toward him, eyes flicking past me to the cars pulling in behind me and the two officers crossing toward the side entrance, then back to Liam and the tall man, who patted Liam's shoulder and let Liam pull him into a hug.

Liam broke away from the conversation and jogged over. He stopped in front of me, blocking my way. He was panting, his face looked wind-burned and I could smell whiskey on his breath. "I know what happened."

"Are you all right, Liam? You look—"

"I know what happened to my daughter. You're a copper. You've got to do something about it."

"Your daughter suffered an overdose of some opiate drug. The lab reports aren't in, but it was probably heroin. People often shift from oxy to heroin because it's cheaper. But it's also much more dangerous. You can never tell the true quality of the load or what they cut it with."

He grabbed my shoulders. Liam was a big man, maybe six-three, a couple of inches taller than me, and at least fifty pounds heavier, most of it muscle. "Listen to me! I'm telling you how she got the heroin in the first place! Do you understand me?"

I shrugged out of his grip. "Calm down, Liam. Take it easy. We can talk about this after I—"

"You don't get it, lad. Talking's finished with. Talking's done." He lowered his voice. "There are men on this island, bad men. Terrible men, Chief Kennis. I served in the British Navy during the Falklands War. I saw my own paratroopers executing Argentine prisoners after the battle of Mount Longdon. Just putting a gun to a man's head while he sobbed and begged for mercy and pulling the trigger while the others watched and knew they were next. I never thought I'd see anything so dreadful again. That was enough for one lifetime. That was my quota, you understand? Or so I thought. But this is worse."

"Liam, you need to—"

"I need to tell you this and you need to listen. These men are getting girls hooked and making them pay for the drugs by doing things…by performing…on film. Turning themselves into—"

I grabbed him this time. "Who told you this? How did you find out about this?"

"A girl told me. One of my daughter's friends. They tried to… recruit her, as well. But she was having none of it, thank God."

"Okay, hold on. Wait a second. Who is this girl? Why didn't she come to me directly?"

"I canna tell you that. I gave my word. She thought if you heard about it from another man, you'd take action. Especially a man like me, someone who'd lost…"

"Jill's not lost, Liam. She's a fighter. The doctors in Boston say the prognosis looks good."

"I hope that's true. I'm praying that's true. But in the meantime, you find these people and bring them to justice. Or someone else will do it for you."

"Is that a threat?

"It's an oath. It's a sacred vow."

"Don't turn yourself into criminal over this, Liam."

He gave me a chilly smile. "I'll do what I have to do, Chief Kennis. You do the same."

I watched him stalk off across the parking lot, glad that I had Alana Trikilis coming into the station. I had a lot more questions to ask her now.

"You've met my engineer," the old man said as I approached them. Clearly I had to talk to him. The wind kicked up, pushing an icy gust across the plaza. It was cold and getting colder. I wondered for second if I was ever going to get inside.

The tall old man stuck out his hand. "Sorry. Jonathan Pell. And this is Louis Berman."

I shook the smaller man's hand. "Private investigator?" I asked.

"At one time. Currently, head of security for LoGran Corporation."

"I assume you have a license for that gun."

"I—uh, yes. Yes I do."

"How did you know he had a gun?" Pell demanded.

I looked Pell over. He had the chiseled Roman coin features of a movie star from some earlier era, when press agents enforced privacy, and glamour—that exotic creature driven to extinction by the Internet—still flourished in the high-canopy habitats of Bel Air and the Holmby Hills. Pell had a radio voice to match his face, a mellow baritone that made you want to buy whatever he was selling. I wondered what he was selling today.

I tilted my head toward Berman, answering the old man's question. "He has the look. And he should cut his suits better if he wants to conceal a weapon." I turned to the detective. I was on a roll. "Beretta?"

He nodded "PX4 Storm compact."

"Nice gun. Don't use it on my island."

"I was saying…" Pell cut in, "my engineer and I—"

"Your engineer?"

"On my yacht. The *Nantucket Grand*. Phelan is chief engineer. He keeps the ship afloat, keeps it running and on course. Sort of genius in his own way. Idiot savant. But absolutely essential to the life. He'll be bringing the *Grand* up from Bermuda for race week. If he can get those fuel manifold valves repaired in time."

I glanced longingly at the front doors of the station. Had I really been complaining that it was overheated inside? "Right now he has more serious problems to deal with."

"I know. I fully sympathize with his daughter's tragic circumstances. We share a concern regarding the…efficacy of the local police."

"Meaning me."

"To the extent that you stand for your department, yes."

"What's the problem, Mr. Pell?"

"The cottage on the LoGran property has been broken into three times in the last several weeks. On all three occasions the alarms went off—and they are keyed into the police station, at great expense. The official response was woefully inadequate. Officers arrived, but too late to catch anyone. And each time the response was slower. Do you have the figures, Mr. Berman?"

The little detective pulled a folded sheet piece of paper from his jacket pocket, straightened it out and squinted at the numbers. "Six minutes...fourteen minutes...twenty-two minutes. No land speed records there, Chief."

I ignored him. "Did you file a report? What was missing?"

"We filed three reports. Nothing was missing, but the place had obviously been searched. And we haven't seen hide nor hair of the police since that last call-out."

"Well, if nothing was missing...have you called the alarm company? There may be a problem on their end. Some of the alarms use motion detectors. If you have a mouse inside, or a rat... they could be setting off the alarms. It happens a lot out here."

He stared at me. "There are no...vermin in the LoGran compound. We have a human intruder and I demand that these incidents be investigated. Is that really so unreasonable?"

"Not at all. In fact, I'll take care of it myself."

That seemed to derail his next angry salvo. "Well...thank you. Thank you very much. I appreciate that."

"I'll check it out today. Have someone in the house to let me in."

"Keep in touch with Mr. Berman, here. He'll inform me of your progress."

"Fine."

"Then I suppose we're done." He reached out to touch my shoulder. "Let me know if you hear anything. Sorry I was short with you before. But these break-ins have put us all on edge. Louis is a stranger here. You know this island, you have your ear to the ground. That's like gold, as far as I'm concerned. Twenty-four carat gold."

I clasped his shoulder, our arms and bodies briefly forming a square before we stepped back and shook hands. The sudden thaw in his attitude, dropping the gruff pose of the impatient captain of industry, combined with his nervous smile, made me want to help him; and something more. I wanted to confirm his good impression of me, win him over to the side of small-town police in general.

He turned and strode away, the squat detective hurrying after him.

Chapter Seven

Witness Interviews: Alana Trikilis, David Lattimer, and Mark Toland

A few seconds later I was pushing into the blissfully warm air of the police station. Jane Stiles was waiting for me. I was happy to see her, but momentarily confused. She hadn't made an appointment, and as far as I knew she had no connection to any ongoing investigation. Could she be here inquiring about resident visitor status for someone on her crew? Protesting a parking ticket?

It turned out she was making a social call.

She lifted her hand in a half wave. "Hi, Chief. I wanted to remind you about Emily Grimshaw's salon tonight. You're not listed in the phone book and there's no way to get anyone's cell number, so I thought I'd just stop by. Someone should put out a listing of people's cell phone numbers. They could make millions."

She was dressed in the usual jeans and Fair Isle sweater, under an old tan barn jacket, the whole outfitted topped off with a battered Patriots cap. Her curly blond hair was wind-scattered and it looked like the cold had slapped her face recently, so she hadn't been waiting long.

"You could have called the station," I suggested.

"I suppose so. But I had this theory that it might be more fun to see you in person."

I smiled. "How's that working out?"

"Pretty good, so far. But you look like a man on a mission, so maybe my timing was bad."

"A little," I admitted. "I have to keep moving now. I'll see you tonight, definitely. What time does it start, again?"

"Oh—seven o'clock or so. The stragglers show up by seven-thirty. Eight Orange Street, first floor. See you then."

She dodged past me and out the door. I watched for a second and then turned away. The view was distracting, and I needed to concentrate.

We have three fully outfitted interrogation rooms at the station, with state-of-the-art camera and recording equipment and ergonomically designed uncomfortable chairs (the seats tilt down just slightly) for the suspects. But the people I was meeting were not officially under suspicion and the last thing I wanted to do was make them feel that way. I made sure Barnaby Toll gave them coffee and a fresh box of Downeyflake donuts, and took them one at a time into my office upstairs.

I suppose I should have taken the tourist first. But I felt bad for Alana Trikilis. She had better things to do than cool her heels in a police station waiting room. Plus she was probably scared, since police stations are designed to be scary, and she had no reason to be. She was no arsonist. She drew cartoons to make her points, though she had certainly burned some people with those drawings during her tenure at *Veritas*, the NHS student newspaper: the Peeping Tom coach she sketched from behind with his plumber's crack showing, the school board emerging in full makeup from a circus clown car. She almost got suspended for that one. She had done a drawing of me a couple of years before, a far more flattering one, which I still kept.

She edged into my office now, unbuttoning her cable-knit cardigan.

When we were both settled, I said "Would you like coffee? My assistant chief is obsessive about his Chemex, and I have to admit, it tastes pretty good."

"No thanks. I'm fine. I mean—actually…my stomach is kind of upset. Coffee would probably be bad right now."

"So…can you tell me what you were doing out at the Thayer place today?"

"That's a long story."

I smiled. "My favorite kind."

She shifted in her chair, pulled off her sweater. I took that as a good sign. "I guess I just wanted to feel like I was in control of something. Like I could do something that made a difference."

"Life was getting out of control?"

"I applied for early admission to some art schools. RISDE? Parsons and Pratt? I didn't think I'd hear from any of them until January, but I got the last rejection letter today. So I'm done. And it's still only December."

"I'm sorry. That sucks."

"I felt…it was like I'd been launched into outer space. There was no air to breathe, no air pressure…nothing was holding my insides in. I had nothing—no present, no future. I blew it all, I've got the magic touch. I couldn't move. There was nowhere to go. I just stood there, looking down at this Formica counter top with the crumbs and I thought maybe I'd just stay there for the rest of my life. I wanted to go upstairs, close my door, put on dry socks, climb into bed, pull the covers up and hide under the sheets. But I couldn't move. Finally, I took the letters to the wood stove and burned them. That felt good."

"Direct action," I said. "Beats legislation."

She perked up. "You know, Ford Madox Ford got furious when Hemingway stole that line. He said he was sick of reading his private conversations in other people's books."

"I didn't know it was stolen," I admitted. "Some detective."

"Well, Bill Gorton is, like, the only character in any Hemingway book who had a sense of humor, so…"

"Good point. I should have been suspicious."

"What a pair."

"Excuse me?

"You don't see the clues in the book and I don't—I can't even…I just—I'm not good enough. That's the point. That's what they're saying."

"What do they know?"

"They know who's good enough and who isn't. That's their job. They know who deserves to go to their school and who doesn't."

"So you're going to let some admissions guy at Parsons decide if you have talent?"

"No, but—"

"You were good enough for Superintendent Bissell."

"What?"

"You were too good for him. You think he tried to suspend you because you did a bad drawing? That drawing was great. I always think of that clown car when I have to attend a School Board meeting. And I still have the sketch you did of me—at Osona's auction."

She smiled. "I forgot about that. I'd seen you at the school the week before, talking to Bob Coffin. Ugh. I couldn't believe it when he passed the police exam. But I knew it was true when pulled me over on Bartlett Road last Halloween. I thought he was wearing a costume, like he was out trick-or-treating or something, But he was really a cop. Do you mind if I say 'cop'? I mean cops say it, but is it like the "c" word and only cops can say it?"

"It's more the *way* people say it. You're fine."

"Anyway…all I had was a learner's permit, and he wouldn't let me go with a warning. You probably think that's great. But getting a traffic ticket from some ex-babysitter who ate your dad's Captain Crunch cereal straight out of the box? While he made you watch Japanese anime DVDs? That's one of the best reasons I can think of for getting the hell away from here pronto. That's my dad's word—pronto. 'I want you to get that bed made, pronto!'"

"So, you saw me at school, talking to Officer Coffin. I remember that day—it was like…a year ago, last November. Someone tried to frame your friend Jared Bromley for drugs."

"He never used drugs."

"I know."

"Jared's probably the nicest boy in school. He's definitely the smartest. No one else ever says anything interesting. He'd be a good policeman, Chief Kennis. No, seriously—better than Bob Coffin. Jared notices things, like when Ms. Hamer stopped wearing her wedding ring last month, or when I got this haircut. They took off less than an inch, no one else paid any attention. My own dad didn't notice, and neither did Mason. Mason Taylor, he's—"

"I know who he is."

I had helped Mason at a bad moment a couple of years ago, and secretly played Cyrano for him with Alana. But she didn't need to know that. More recently, I'd been reading his increasingly political editorials in *Veritas*—attacking Israel's Gaza blockade, defending Edward Snowden, talking about drone strikes, suggesting that Yemeni shepherds who'd had their flocks dry-roasted by American missiles might hate us for more than our freedom. The school principal loathed Mason, but hadn't censored him yet, most likely because he didn't relish the prospect of a visit from the boy's bloviating dad, Selectman Dan Taylor, storming his office in high dudgeon, declaiming the First Amendment and threatening a lawsuit.

I tipped my head, gesturing her to continue.

"Well, he's kind of why I'm here," she said. "He's why I was out at the house, I mean—him and Jared."

She stopped at that point, the way you stop when you're driving in the moors and the dirt road narrows into an overgrown footpath. She couldn't go forward and I wasn't letting her go back. "Alana?"

"I'm not supposed to tell you this."

"What aren't you supposed to tell me?"

"Any of it. Why I was there, what's going on, who's involved. Any of it."

I sat forward. "Did someone threaten you?"

"I should go."

"Because we can protect you."

"The Nantucket Police Department?"

"It's possible."

"Twenty-four hours a day?"

We sat staring at each other. I tried to regroup. She had to be the girl Liam Phelan mentioned. But she'd assume he'd broken his word if I used his name. I'd have to work around it. "No one needs to know you told me anything. There's no way they can know—unless the NPD goes after these people, whoever they are. And I can promise you we won't do that until we have enough evidence to put them away."

"Well, that won't happen. That's the whole point."

"I think you should let me decide that."

"But no one threatened *you*."

I stood and walked to the window. I found the dreary view of the parking lot and the traffic on Fairgrounds Road obscurely comforting at that moment. Everything looked dull and ordinary—just the way I liked it. The wind rasped against the big window and the gray sky promised snow. But the office was warm. The big furnace in the basement made the building hum softly. I touched the pane of glass—the fragile integument of civilization.

I turned to face Alana. "Here's what I can offer you. Nothing you say leaves the room, until I know I can take action, and if I do choose to arrest these people, I'll make sure you're protected. If we gather enough evidence, we'll never mention you at all."

"But you won't gather any evidence. It all got burned in the fire."

"Then you have nothing to worry about."

"You won't believe me anyway."

"Try me." I walked back and sat down. She was looking down, picking some dirt or a speck of dried food off the knee of her jeans. I said nothing and waited. Silence exerts its own pressure, and I let the pressure build. When she began, it was as if I'd caught her in the middle of a conversation. Maybe she had just turned the volume up on the monologue running inside her head.

"This group of men is getting girls hooked on a new drug like oxy, I don't what it's called, and then using them in these... movies they make. Mason asked me to help him. We're just sort of friends now and he was totally sprung over Jill Phelan."

"Sprung?"

"Sorry. He was falling in love with her. He knew she was with Oscar, but I think he likes being—unrequited? When you feel as much as Mason does, another person just gets in the way. At least that's how it seemed with us. We're much better just being friends. Anyway, he was freaking out and he had this crazy scheme where he'd pretend to recruit me and we'd both hear their pitch and then we'd know what was going on."

"And you did that?" She nodded. "That was incredibly brave." She studied her knees with a rueful smile. "Now he tells me."

"Go on."

"We went out to this man's house in 'Sconset. His name is Howard McAllister...I went back the next day and looked at the letters in his mailbox. My dad picks up his trash, but I didn't want to ask my dad about him. There were other people there, too—Chick Crosby and Ms. DeHart from school, Charles Forrest from the Land Bank, and this contractor Jared knows, Brad Thurman. I made a list—"

"Jared was there too?"

"He followed us that night. He had come to the house to bring me a textbook I left at school, and he wound up following us. We never would have gotten out of there if not for him. We've been trying to identify the rest of them, but...I saw a couple of them on *Mahon About Town*, but he never includes any names and I thought if I started poking around and someone found out..."

"That was smart. So what did you do?"

"First I tried to get Jill to come forward—Jill Phelan? She's in my class, and she was out there that night. She was obviously involved, but she denied everything. Then she admitted everything, but she wouldn't talk to anyone about it, and got mad at me and made me swear I'd never tell anyone, but she must have told someone about me because this guy, Doug Blount? He's a caretaker? He came up to me in the Stop & Shop and walked me back into the stockrooms where they have a bathroom and pushed me inside and told me if I said anything to anyone I'd be next, and I didn't know what he was talking about, so he said they'd get me hooked on heroin, or that other horrible stuff they use. It only takes, like, one hit sometimes, and then when I needed drugs bad enough I'd be their next little movie star. That's what he said, their next little movie star. I started crying and he slapped me and told me to shut up and left me there in the bathroom. I didn't come out for like an hour."

"His name was Doug Blount?"

"You can't talk to him! That's what I was telling you! You promised!"

"Okay, okay. Don't worry. I just want to get all the names straight. The ones you know."

"He was serious."

"I'm sure he was."

"He was trying to scare me and it worked, and I could tell he really, really liked that."

We sat in silence for a few moments while Alana caught her breath and I fought down the urge to go out and arrest these people, praying they'd resist arrest, and sweat them until I got the rest of the names and then book them all and scrub them off the island, like you'd tent a house for termites.

"Jill must have been planning to go to the police. They found out and gave her an overdose."

I stared at her. "That's attempted murder."

She didn't look away. "That's why I'm scared."

"You can't know that."

"No."

"It could be a coincidence."

"Maybe, but—"

"You don't trust coincidences." I nodded. "Well, cops hate them."

"So…?"

"Jesus, Alana." I ran both hands through my hair and squeezed my temples hard with my forearms. This was exactly the kind of horrific bullshit I had come to Nantucket to escape. This was big city stuff, L.A. stuff. But it was following me, like one of those dogs in the movies that sniff their way across the country chasing after their owner, having adventures and getting reunited at the end. Except this dog had rabies and needed to be put down—pronto, as Sam Trikilis would say.

I decided to get the conversation back on track. "You were out at the Thayer place today. How does that fit in?"

"I—this sounds crazy."

I offered a reassuring smile. "You and Jared are the only sane parts of this story, so far."

"Okay, well…I started following Chick Crosby. Alana Trikilis, girl detective. But I didn't know what else to do and I had to do something."

"Why Chick?"

"I guess…he seemed the most harmless, and he had to be the one actually making the movies, he has all the equipment. Plus, he's so clueless and into his own head I knew he'd never notice. I mean, you wave to him in the street and he doesn't notice. So anyway…I started watching his house whenever I could, nights when I told my dad I was at friends' houses studying, and weekends, and whenever he went anywhere I trailed him."

"Go on."

"One night I followed him to that house and I peeked in the windows and saw him setting up cameras and lights in the bedroom, and I got really scared and I was going to run but the others showed up. They had this girl, Emily Trott, with them. I sort of knew her, we were on the basketball team last year but we both dropped out. Guys were stamping around the house and I lay flat in the bushes, my heart was beating so loud I was sure they could hear it and I was trying not to breathe, but it was a really windy night, so…finally they were all inside and I realized this was my chance so I filmed everything they did with my iPhone."

"You're crazy."

"Yeah. They caught me. They must have seen light reflecting on the screen or something. Blount and the rich guy came out and grabbed me and I was screaming but there was no one around to hear it and Blount said they should give me a shot of heroin right there and then, like he had threatened before, but McAllister called him a 'stupid thug' and said, 'I have a better idea.' He took my phone and smashed it and said 'Now she has nothing.' And I just ran."

I let her catch her breath. "But you went back. You were out at the house looking for evidence."

She nodded. "They burned the place just in time."

I took a pad out of my desk drawer and made a few notes, more to let a little air into our conversation than anything else. I wasn't likely to forget a word she said.

I looked up from my pad. "How much of this did you tell Mr. Phelan?"

"Nothing. None of it. I mean, I told him what was going on, but he freaked out on me so bad and I just got out of there. I thought he might kill somebody himself. I mean—what if it was the wrong person? Or, even if it was the right person, that's totally whacked. That's crazy."

I nodded. "Good. I'm glad. You did the right thing. No contact with him since?"

She shook her head. "I don't know what to do now."

"Leave it to the police. It's a police matter."

"But if—I don't see what you can…the evidence is gone, the people are mostly bigshots who'd laugh at you if you accused them of anything."

"Not all of them."

"No, but—come on. Someone like Doug Blount? He's ten times more scared of McAllister than he is of the police. All he has to do is stonewall. He could accuse you of slander and he'd probably win."

"Unless the victims come forward."

"But they won't. Jill's in a coma and Emily's parents are shipping her off to some boarding school in Maine. I don't know who the other girls are. But I know one thing for sure—they're too embarrassed to go to the police. No one wants to admit this stuff—being addicted to drugs and—all the rest of it. So it's hushed up and the house where they did it is gone, and who knows where the films are. On some flash drive somewhere, which you'd need a warrant to even look at and you could never get a warrant on hearsay from some girl."

The diatribe wound down. I blew out a breath while she took one. "You've obviously thought about this a lot."

"It's all I've been thinking about. For weeks."

"Could you get Mason to come forward? If he corroborated your story…"

"No way."

"Maybe I could talk to him."

"He's too scared. He'll just deny everything. He told me so."

"How about Jared?"

She shook her head. "Those people could ruin his father. He does most of his work for Brad Thurman. And it's the same for my dad. One word and his whole 'Sconset route goes to Myles Reis. McAllister is Dad's customer and they're all pals on Baxter Road, and my dad doesn't have a ten-customers-more-or-less, easy-come, easy-go lifestyle. Sorry. I'm not going to wreck his business to make some useless point and turn myself into a bigger loser than I already am, for nothing. I'm just not."

"I could talk to Jared anonymously."

She stared at me. "They saw him that night. Not just me. Maybe I didn't make that clear. They know who he is. 'Anonymous' doesn't work around here, anyway, Chief Kennis. Everyone knows everything about everybody. That's why I didn't say anything before. That's why I was trying to…to do things on my own."

"But you're going to stop that now. Because you understand how dangerous it is."

"I guess."

"I need you to be certain about this, Alana."

"Okay, okay. I'll leave it alone. I will."

"Thank you." Time to move on. I had an arson fire to investigate. "Tell me about the house. Was it deserted when you got there?"

"It was burning when I got there. I looked inside and I could see the curtains flaming in the living room. And the couch. It was really smoky. I tried to get in but the doors were locked."

"Really?"

"I know. Nobody locks their doors around here. I don't even have a key to my own house. My dad must have one somewhere but he never uses it."

"You said doors...so you tried the back door, too?"

"Yeah and the bulkhead. The whole place was locked up tight."

"So when you ran around to the back...did you see anything—or anyone suspicious?"

"Just Mr. Toland—and Mike Henderson. They were shouting at each other. When we were leaving I saw the newspaper guy, Mr. Trezize? And some crazy old man—could he have set the fire?"

I thought about David Lattimer. The only way he could set a fire would be smoking his pipe in bed. It was a class issue for him. Felonies were for the *hoi polloi*. I remembered him quoting with evident relish Winston Churchill's response to his first view of real poverty, after touring the East End of London during an early campaign: "How strange it must be! Never to see anything beautiful, never to eat anything delicious...never to say anything clever." Snobs like Lattimer didn't burn down a house, they filed suit with the Boston Land Court to have it taken by eminent domain.

I shook my head. "Not likely."

"I know Mike Henderson didn't do it. That's a painter's worst nightmare—setting a house on fire."

"Yeah, Mike's no arsonist. How about the other guy?"

"I talked to him. He's a movie director. He was scouting locations, taking pictures. That's what he said. He had a really expensive-looking camera. If he wanted to burn down a house he'd wait until he was shooting his movie. I mean, if there was a fire in his movie. Why waste it? Like in *Gone With the Wind* when they burned down all those sets at the MGM studio."

I nodded, thinking: I want to take a look at those photographs.

"Let's go back a little further. How did you get to the house? Were you driving? Walking?"

"I was riding my bicycle. It's a Specialized mountain bike. I can go anywhere with it."

"That's good. People in cars don't really look around that much—they're just staring at the road in front of them. Bikers pay attention. They're actually in the environment. That's the whole point."

She smiled. "Yeah."

"So what did you see?"

"I don't know…the usual—hawks and cardinals and turkey buzzards, lots of bushes. Some beer cans and paper cups. Someone had dumped an old refrigerator out there."

"The actual dump is taking them for free right now."

"I know but…this one looked like it had been there for a long time. The door was off and I think something was nesting in it."

"Anything else?"

"Not really."

"No traffic?"

She sat up a little. "I almost got driven off the road by some jerk."

"Which way was he coming?"

"Right at me."

"So he could have been coming from the house."

She took a quick breath, contemplating that idea. "Wow. You really think so?"

"What kind of vehicle? SUV? Truck?"

"It was a black Ford F-150. A new one. I didn't get the license plate." She must have caught my skeptical look—everyone watches the cop shows. She'd be dusting for fingerprints next. "No, really, I tried! I wanted to get the number. I wanted to report the guy. He was going like forty miles an hour on those dirt roads. I hope he bottomed out or hit a deer or something. Asshole."

I pushed my chair back. "Okay. Thanks, Alana. You've been a huge help."

"But nothing's going to happen to those people."

"Something's already happened. Their secret is out. And like you said—there's nothing anonymous on Nantucket. They tried to scare you, but they can't be sure you won't go to the police, anyway. You were a witness to the fire and there were other witnesses. That's an open arson investigation. Jill Phelan could wake up tomorrow, and her father's on the rampage. Apart from everything else, their little soundstage just burned down with all their equipment in it. They may be safe, but for the moment they're out of business. They're not going to be making any more movies for a while."

"I guess."

"And by the time they do poke their heads up out of whatever hole they've climbed into, I might have enough evidence to put them away. Thanks to you."

"The Ford?"

"The new black F-150. How many of those can there be on the island?"

"Lots?"

"We'll track it down, don't worry. And I'll have my boys keep an eye on you for the next few weeks. Cruise by the house from time to time. Make sure you're safe."

"Can you really do that?

"I have a lot of officers and a lot of cars. We may actually outnumber the criminals right now."

I stood up and she did, too. The interview was over. "Okay, great," she said. "That would be really nice. Thank you." She extended her arm across the desk awkwardly and I shook her hand. "I really want you to catch these guys."

"Me, too."

◇◇◇

Lattimer was next, but he had little to add: he'd seen the fire from his house and called 911. No one at the station took it that seriously—he had called the emergency number twice before in the last couple of weeks, both false alarms. A possibly senile old man freaking out about non-existent "prowlers" didn't strike anyone as a major law-enforcement priority. But other calls, several to the fire department, got everyone moving. Lattimer had an excellent vantage point—the Thayers were his neighbors. They owned a huge parcel, mostly undeveloped, and he hadn't seen any of them since the summer. After he called in the alarm, he stumped across the property line to have a look at the blaze, as anyone might have done.

"It's December on Nantucket, Chief Kennis. There's not much else to do, and very little in the way of entertainment." He saw no one and nothing suspicious, but he wasn't looking for anything, either.

Mark Toland, the film director, was equally unhelpful, though he promised to e-mail me the photographs he'd taken at the scene.

Chapter Eight

Witness Interviews:
Mike Henderson and David Trezize

Mike Henderson clarified the situation for me.

"Am I a suspect again?" He walked into the office. A nasty combination of motive, opportunity, and the apparent lack of an alibi had put him in my sights a couple of years ago, but only briefly.

"No, no—not at all. But I have to ask…what brought you out to the middle of the moors on a cold winter day?"

"It was personal."

"Bad answer, Mike. Most serious crimes turn out to be personal, one way or the other."

"So, I am a suspect."

"Not unless you turn yourself into one."

We studied each other across the desk.

Finally he said, "I really don't want to talk about this."

"Think of me as your Father Confessor."

"So everything I tell you is secret? Nothing leaves this room?"

"Unless you do actually incriminate yourself."

"Embarrass myself, maybe. But that's it."

"Then you're fine."

I let a silence trundle by, like a line of traffic inching past some road construction. Finally I lifted my hands, palms up, eyebrows raised along with a half-smile, as if to say "So?"

"I'm not sure where to start."

"How about the middle?"

He laughed, more out of surprise than amusement. "Okay. I was following Mark Toland."

"You know him?"

"Not exactly."

Then I remembered. I'd been flailing around, trying to hit the dangling light-switch string in a dark bathroom. Now I grabbed it and yanked it, and the light came on. "Cindy was staying with him at the Sherry Netherland hotel the night Preston Lomax was killed. You were supposed to be in New York with her, but you were staying at your customer's brownstone."

He stared at me. "How can you possibly remember that?"

"Are you kidding? It was the best non-alibi ever. You couldn't account for one second of your time off-island. That was a record."

He started to speak. "I mean—you couldn't prove anything. No paper trail at all. It was amazing."

"That's one word for it. I was scared shitless."

"So let me fill this in for you. Cindy came back, and you thought it was over, and then he shows up on-island two years later and Cindy's been a little distant lately, with the toddler wearing her out every day, and you see this guy, or read an e-mail you shouldn't have, or hear the end of a phone call—"

"The name was on her phone. He's on her contact list."

"So you were stalking him."

He shrugged. "Basically. There was a text about his flight time. Cindy didn't meet the plane. Maybe she was having second thoughts. I haven't really talked to her about this yet. Anyway, I was there and I was just…keeping track of him."

"Well, he's gone now."

"Hopefully for good."

"Hopefully."

We sat in silence for a few seconds. "Do you know what happened at the house?" Mike asked. "Was it arson? Were there painters working there? A pile of thinner rags or a bag of floor sanding dust with all that urethane in it…?"

"That's what we're trying to find out. State investigators are flying in to look the place over. I'm asking questions like—did you see anything today, notice anything unusual, or…?"

"No, sorry. I was just watching Toland. I'd make a shitty detective."

◇◇◇

David Trezize had an equally embarrassing reason for his trip to the moors that day. But, unlike Mike Henderson, he actually enjoyed talking about it. As a newspaper editor, he knew a good story, and he appreciated a funny one, especially when he was the butt of the joke.

David sat down in the chair facing my desk, rumpled and unshaven, looking as though he'd been up all night in the basement office of his little newspaper, which he probably had, with deadline one day away, despite all the writers he had recently poached from *The Inquirer and Mirror*. "No matter how many writers I steal, I still have to do all the work," he said. "Anyway, I was spending some of my extremely limited free time out at the Thayer property because of my ex-wife's diary, so I really should start by telling you why I was reading it in the first place."

"Are you sure you feel comfortable doing that?"

"Who else can I talk to? Kathleen wouldn't want to hear it, that's for sure."

I could understand why David would want to conceal his stubborn obsession with Patty from Kathleen Lomax. The daughter of the island's most prominent murder victim, she had fallen in love with David and saved his newspaper from the old man's efforts to destroy it, bailing the business out financially after Preston Lomax died. David owed her a lot. She didn't deserve to suffer through his irrational adolescent crush on the ex-wife. It wasn't even love in any ordinary sense. Like so many stalker types—and he was turning himself into one—David needed to remain part of Patty's life, to be fully included in his own exclusion, in complete control of his own helplessness. I'd felt a twinge of that when I first got divorced, but it passed like a twenty-four-hour virus. David had a full-blown case, complete with the fever and the body aches.

"I was okay until I heard that Grady was moving in with her," he said.

In the last year, over half a dozen five-dollar burger nights at Kitty Murtagh's, I'd gotten a fairly complete picture of David's Grady Malone problem.

Grady Malone was an architect, the glamour architect of the island. He'd built notoriously stark corporate headquarters and prize-winningly lavish private homes. He'd designed every house in a gated community on Prince Edward Island. He had moved to Nantucket to relax, but had built a huge practice in less than five years. He designed the Preston Lomax mansion on Eel Point Road, and he was supposed to be the favored architect for several huge residential developments on the island, none of which had materialized yet.

Grady had taught at Stanford and RISDE, worked on Habitat for Humanity with Jimmy Carter. He had consulted with Frank Gehry on the Guggenheim Museum in Barcelona and had a design in the finals for the New York 9/11 memorial. He had the casual air of having seen and done it all, and the irritating fact (you had to admit it) was that he actually had seen and done quite a lot. More than most people; much more than pudgy, plodding David Trezize, for example—as Patty took every opportunity to point out.

"Why can't you be more like Grady?," Patty would ask, after Grady had calmly but forcefully ejected a drunken heckler from a lecture at the Unitarian Church, hooked up their Blu-ray player to the television, or cooked them his famous Osso Buco.

He had no good answer, so Patty divorced him and started dating Grady. It wasn't quite that simple, but it seemed that way sometimes.

This new rumor of cohabitation had pushed David over the edge, which was why he broke into her house and read her diary.

"Are you sure you want to be telling this part to a police officer?" I asked him gently.

"It wasn't breaking and entering! I used to live there! I have a key."

"I thought you told me she changed the locks."

"Yeah, and she hides the new key under the same old shingle. That's high security! Like putting your money in your shoe when you go for a swim at the beach. Come on."

"Sorry. So you found the new key and let yourself in."

"I don't even know what I was looking for exactly—some sign of Grady—an extra toothbrush in the bathroom, or his brand of beer in the fridge. He drinks Stella Artois. Maybe a bottle of some weird aftershave in the bathroom, or a Yanni CD. Anyway, what I found was Patty's diary. It was in her underwear drawer. I was checking for new racy lingerie. Hey, that would be a sign! But she was still wearing the same old plain cotton panties, for what it's worth."

"David—"

"No, no you might as well hear it all. If you're going to make an ass out of yourself, do it right! That's my philosophy. So, the diary was at the bottom of the drawer, kind of a pink-and-gray flowered cover held shut with an elastic ribbon. So there I was, alone in the house, with everything I needed to know about Patty's state of mind lying there. What would you have done?"

"I wouldn't have been there at all."

"So you wouldn't have copied her passwords and hacked into her e-mail?"

"No."

"I kind of figured that. I didn't know what I was going to do, myself. Really. I stood there, just kind of staring at the diary, turning it over in my hand. I knew I could never violate Patty's privacy by reading it…and at the same time, I'm studying the elastic ribbon to be sure I can replace it exactly. Who was I kidding? Anyway, I don't know how long I was stuck there, when I heard someone at the door. I totally freaked out. I had no excuse to be there, and no way out. I mean—my car was in the driveway. But it was just the mailman."

"So you took the hint and got the hell out of there."

"Not exactly. I knew I was never going to get another chance to do this thing. I'd never get the up the nerve again."

"So you read it."

"Yeah."

"My grandmother always used to say, 'Don't eavesdrop—you won't hear anything that makes you happy.'"

"Well, your granny had a point on that score. But there was plenty of good stuff. And I'll tell you something. Even the worst of it helped me. She described sex with Grady like a lapsed Catholic walking into a church after being born again. Can you believe that? She said something like 'those cheesy stained-glass windows are suddenly illustrating miracles.' So she never had an orgasm with me—yeah, that's in there, too. But sex with Grady is religious experience! Thanks so much. There was a lot more, and it cured my stalking problem for good. Apparently I'm like an old smelly dog that won't leave you alone, and you feel guilty about wanting to kick it, so you pat it and then you have to wash your hands afterward. That's exactly what she said. Nice, huh? But fuck all that. What matters is the land deal."

I sat forward, palms braced against the edge of the desk. "The land deal?"

"You don't know about that? Your ex-wife is all over it. She and Elaine Bailey. It's making Patty nuts—she wants a piece and she can't touch it. The only upside for her is that Grady Malone's the architect."

"The architect for what? Can't touch what?"

"You know the Thayers own a huge chunk of land out in the moors. Hundreds of acres. The family's been fighting about it since the old lady died. Some want to sell, some want to sit on it. Some of them are hurting for money and some of them are doing okay. Some of them care about the island and some don't. It's the same old story. Remember Pimney's Point?"

"Sorry."

"It was before your time, I guess. The Crosby family owned all this land on the harbor and when the grandma died she left it to the church. Kids were furious but they couldn't break the will. Then the priest she had left in charge—can't recall the guy's name—he subdivided it and made a fortune. It reminded me of something Billy Delavane used to say, quoting old Mrs. Thayer, talking about the new people. She hated the new people. I guess that meant anyone who came here after 1926. She said, 'Divide and conquer? Not these people. Subdivide and conquer, that's their strategy.'

"It seems to be working pretty well. You ever walk around Sanford Farm? Ann Sanford's kids went to court to break the will, and all Ann's friends testified that she was in her right mind when she gave the land to the town. So the kids lost, obviously. Fuck them, they were all millionaires anyway. Nothing's ever enough for them. It's like a disease. They have to have more."

"So the Thayers sound like a classic Nantucket story."

"They finally decided to sell to the Land Bank. They're getting a pretty good price and all the kids are already planning their new trophy houses. That's where Grady Malone comes in. They could have made a hell of a lot more selling out to a developer but they would have been pariahs in this town after that. And some of them do actually live here. It's like it was 'Sconset. If you own a house in Codfish Park and you decide to sell it? Better make plans to leave the island. You'll never play tennis at the Casino again. These people are vicious."

"But it sounds like everything worked out fine."

"Except there was one holdout. Andrew. And his house burns down a month before the sale deadline."

"I don't think that fire had anything to do with real estate, David. There was a lot of bad stuff going on out there."

"Which you can't talk about."

I shrugged.

"I wanted to check it out myself. But by the time I got there the fire engines were pulling up. So…"

"And you didn't see anything suspicious?"

"Just the fire."

I stood. "Thanks, David. Thanks for coming in."

"And the stuff about the diary…"

"That stays between us. Since it's never going to happen again."

"Don't worry. I'm done."

"Good."

"I can wait for her to ask for another bullshit favor, dangling the chance that we might get back together again in front of me. That's one of her favorite tricks." He stood with a sheepish smile. "This is actually very liberating."

"I'm glad. And if you think of anything else, remember any details, anything odd about today…give me a call."

Chapter Nine

The Holdout: Andrew Thayer

My last interview was with Andrew Thayer himself. He was distraught, barely able to talk until I gave him two fingers of whiskey from my Lagavulin stash. It was against regulations, but that's one of the perks of being the chief.

"I can't believe this," he said, for the tenth time in five minutes. "I just can't believe this. It makes no sense."

"Maybe, maybe not, That's what we're here to find out. Was the property insured?"

"Of course it was insured! But I'd have nothing to gain from that! It's all done through the Thayer Trust. Any insurance settlements or litigation awards get donated to the Maria Mitchell Association. Edna was on the board for years. She helped with fundraising for the Loines Observatory and helped them buy the new telescope. No one could coax a thousand-dollar check from a hedge fund manager like Edna. She used to say—'that's like getting steak bone from a Boston terrier.'"

"I see, so do you—?"

"I loved that house! That was my mother's house! Her grandfather built it with his own hands. That was our whole family history, right there. Not just the house but the photographs and diaries, the letters and clippings and…yacht club party invitations. My grandfather was a member when it was still only a rinky-dink offshoot of the New York Yacht Club. We go back…that house—it was the…It was us, it was who we were."

"So you don't think anyone in the family might have set the fire?"

"God, no!"

"Someone who knew you were against selling the property?"

"Absolutely not!"

"You're sure?"

He took a big swallow and set the glass down, reaching over to place it on the blotter, not my desk. His life might be falling apart but he wasn't going to leave a wet circle on a piece of fine cherry wood.

"Chief Kennis, my siblings may be awful but they're not horrible."

"I'm not sure I see the distinction."

"A horrible person burns down houses! That's the distinction."

I nodded. "And an awful one?"

"Larry went in there with his own key and took every light-ship basket before Mom's body was cold. He was late for the funeral—that was why! He claimed she wanted him to have them and there's nothing in the will, so…but it wasn't right. Ransacking the place like that. Do you know what my sister, Joyce, said? She swore, I won't quote her, I don't use language like that. She was furious she let him get there first! That was all. He beat her to the punch! The idea of actually sharing…of sitting down together and talking things out…not in my family. It's every man for himself with the Thayer clan. Or woman. Especially woman. My sister is a devious, meanspirited harpy. But she's no arsonist. She's afraid of fire. Always fretting that the chimneys are going catch and burn the house down."

"Could that have happened?"

He shook his head. "Not out there. No one has built a fire in that cottage for a decade. The flue was closed up in '07. Largely due to Joyce's badgering."

I spun around once in my chair, and caught the edge of the desk to set myself facing him again. "Have you heard any rumors about the house?"

"Rumors?"

"For instance, that it was being used as a sort of studio for making films."

"What sort of films?"

"You tell me."

"I have no idea."

"Pornographic films?"

"That's ludicrous."

"How many people had keys?"

"Just the family. And the caretaker—Billy Delavane. He's family now."

"You never noticed anything odd out there? Film equipment? Lights?"

He cocked his head in thought. "Well, Chick Crosby has been storing some equipment at the place. He's making a documentary about bird migrations or something. Saves him hauling everything out to the moors and he's a good friend of Larry's. I don't see anything sinister there."

"No."

"Are you sure it was even arson at all?"

"They suspect a propellant was used. We don't have the lab work back yet."

"This is awful. Just awful. I simply can't believe it."

That was number eleven. I decided to get him out of my office before he tried for a record-breaking twelve. But he hit it at the door: "This is just so…unbelievable. I can't believe it. I just can't."

I gave him the benefit of the doubt on the variation in usage and silently awarded him a very small trophy for his thirteen repetitions. I'm not overly superstitious, but in retrospect that seemed like bad luck.

Once Andrew was gone, I called a meeting with Haden Krakauer, Kyle Donnelly, and Charlie Boyce. I hated to delegate but there was too much for one person to do, and according to the Selectmen, I wasn't supposed to do anything but push papers, attend administrative meetings, and talk to the newspaper when we had a blizzard. That would have been a nice, easy sinecure, but I get bored too easily, and my staff was still learning on the job.

You learn police work by doing it, so I gave them their marching orders.

I wanted every house within a mile of the Thayer cottage canvassed. I wanted statements from anyone who might have heard or seen anything. It was still shotgun deer-hunting season, so I wanted every license pulled and every hunter who'd bagged a deer that day interviewed, whether they lived on-island or not, and most of them didn't. That would mean getting the cooperation of various other local jurisdictions and I left that to Haden. If any of those hunters were anywhere near the Pout Ponds, they might have heard or seen something. I wanted them debriefed before their memories faded.

Next on the list: copies of the State Police arson report and the ballistics report on the bullet I dug out of the moors. Those documents needed to be analyzed, point by point.

Then there were the family members—both Macy's family and Thayer's. Unfortunately, statistically, despite Andrew's protestations, they were the most likely perpetrators. The random act of destruction and the wraith-like hit man were staples of crime fiction, but as rare in real life as Bigfoot.

I also set my detectives poking into the victims' business dealings, social activities, friends, romantic involvements, social media—everything they could dig up without a court order or a search warrant.

My first mission: I wanted another visit with Andrew Thayer, to see him in his own space. Our interview felt incomplete. Lonnie Fraker called me as I was on my way out the door, with news on the propellant—it was jet fuel. That made no sense to me, but Thayer might know something. He might own a jet, or know someone who did.

I drove over to Andrew's house on Union Street. As a day trader who had left his big firm to work alone, he spent most days in his attic office working three computers, the NASDAC, and NYSE, and the NIKKEI simultaneously. He was also short-selling commodities futures this afternoon, and apologized for being distracted.

"Multi-tasking is my specialty."

I glanced at the three Apple desktop monitors as he sat down in front of the middle one, and sipped from his mug of coffee.

"Good thing," I said.

"Crap. I have to do this. Hold on." He typed furiously for a few seconds, then spun his ergonomic desk chair around to face me. "I quit because I was working too hard. Now I'm working harder than ever."

"But you get to keep all the money."

He nodded. "And no office politics. Unless you count Buster. And he's very demanding." Andrew was referring to his black Lab, who had followed us up the stairs and was pawing Andrew's knee at every break in the petting. "Great dog. If there was a Nantucket flag, the black Lab would be on it. Maybe not this black Lab—" The dog cocked his head, sensing the change in tone. "Just kidding, buddy." The dog's tail thumped on the floor. I gave him a pat myself, while Andrew attacked the computer keyboard. "So how can I help you, Chief?"

I didn't know what I was looking for, or exactly why I had needed an immediate follow-up to his interrogation at the cop shop. I had no specific questions—just a general one: who was this guy?

I glanced around the cramped office: floor-to-ceiling book-shelves, a canvas-covered wing chair with a floor lamp, and one of Jane Stiles' Madeline Clark mysteries on the end table next to it. An oval hooked rug on the wide-board floor held a scatter of newspapers and magazines and a plate that had obviously been licked clean by Buster. It struck me as odd: the downstairs was scrupulously neat, with the exception of the kitchen table, which had the look of a very temporary glitch in the clean machine. I would have guessed the office was Thayer's sanctuary from the housekeeping tyranny of a more exigent wife or girlfriend. Having done my homework, I knew Thayer was divorced.

Suddenly the trip seemed worthwhile. "I'd like to talk to your girlfriend when she gets home."

He flinched. "Girlfriend?"

"When does she get off work?"

"I don't have a girlfriend. Currently."

"Fine—roommate, then. I just need to double check some things with her—or him."

"What are you talking about? I live alone."

I sighed. "No you don't."

"How can you say that?"

"Well, there were two coffee mugs on the kitchen table when I came in."

"I leave dishes for the maid."

"One of them had coffee in it."

"I'm absent-minded."

"Coffee with milk." I nodded toward the mug on his desk. "You drink it black."

He stared at me. "You noticed that?"

"It's my job description. Noticing stuff."

"We walked past the kitchen door. The table was visible for two seconds! We didn't even go in."

"I'm a snoop."

"This is ridiculous."

I pushed on. "As we were walking upstairs I could have sworn I heard the back door open and close. And a minute or so later, I heard a car start. It's probably just a coincidence, but your house backs onto the town parking lot. So the timing is good."

"That's crazy."

"Who is she?"

"She's no one."

I smiled. "So, it is a she."

"What does this have to do with my house burning down?"

"You tell me."

He took a breath and let it out slowly, jammed his eyes shut and opened them as the carbon dioxide vented. "Okay. There is someone staying with me. Temporarily. But she's not an—an arsonist. There's no—it's not possible. I don't want her caught up with any more—with any trouble. She needs a break."

"Who is she?"

"Just a friend."

"A high school friend? A new friend?"

"She used to come here in the summer. She's had a shitty life, and it's—oh, I know what you're thinking—poor little rich girl. Nantucket summer chick couldn't find the right lipstick at Murray's. Well, sorry, but rich people have problems too. Just not money problems. There's lots of problems besides money problems. You'd know that if you ever had any money."

"Father issues?"

He coughed out a humorless laugh. "Stepfather."

"What happened?"

"Just about everything. I'd rather not talk about it and it's not my place anyway. I'm on the sidelines here. Trying to help. And she has nothing to do with—" He cut himself off.

"With what?"

"With anything. With anything bad. She's a victim, not a—what do you call it? What's the word? A perpetrator. She couldn't steal a penny candy from a dime store."

"Maybe I could help her."

"The police? Are you kidding? The police don't help people. They make trouble. They think everyone's a criminal because that's all they see. Sorry, but it's true. I dated a girl when I was in college, her father was on the Highway Patrol. He acted like I-95 was a fucking Mad Max movie. No, no, no. The last thing she wants is to get tangled up with the police. I mention the police and she's gone."

"Don't mention the police. Just let me talk to her."

"Is there some law? Do I have to do this?"

"No. Not right now. But eventually, under oath, you'd be required to—"

"Under oath? Wait—what? There's going to be a trial?"

"I certainly hope so. That's usually what happens, after we arrest someone."

"Right, sure. Yeah, of course. A trial. But I mean—how do you know it wasn't just an accident? It wouldn't have to be from the fireplace—a chimney fire, like we said before. It could have been anything—a cigarette, kids smoking a joint. That place was a tinderbox."

"The State Police investigators recovered traces of a propellant. Someone started the fire with jet fuel. Do you know anyone with access to a jet?"

He stared at me. "A jet?"

"That's what the report says. The fire was started with jet fuel."

"The jet set. Right. I don't have that kind of money and neither does anyone I know. I hate those assholes anyway. I heard one of them say he has a separate plane for his dog."

"It wouldn't have to be an owner, Mr. Thayer. A pilot, someone on the ground crew, maintenance people, fuel delivery guys, airport security…"

He sniffed. "I don't exactly hang out with those people, either. I guess that makes me middle-class. At least in this world. Where ten thousand dollars is a 'Nantucket grand.'"

"Do you think you might have pissed any of them off?"

"Jet maintenance mechanics?"

I blew out a breath. "Working people. Tradesmen. House cleaners, gardeners. The support system that keeps this island running."

"And required this island to build a police station roughly the size of Buckingham Palace."

"Excuse me?"

"We let the riffraff in and we have to protect ourselves from them—that's the attitude. That's the dirty little secret. Think about it. When I was growing up, we had five police officers on this island, which worked for everyone because we also had *no crime*. But we also weren't the premier gateway destination for illegal immigrants. Don't get me wrong, Chief. I like change.

I like a more diverse population. I like hearing Portugese and Lithuanian and Spanish and whatever else in the grocery store. Jamaican patois, Belarusian. This place was turning into an inbred nightmare. I voted against the police station at Town Meeting, but facts are facts. Even well-off people feel poor living here, cheek by jowl with billionaires. Get a crowd of actual poor people angry enough, rouse them up—you've got a rabble. People lose their heads when that shit goes down. Their actual heads. Ask Marie Antoinette. You thought 'Let them eat cake' was bad? Try 'Let them eat Cumberland Farms donuts.' That's really adding insult to injury."

"So the fire was an act of revolution?"

"A misplaced one. If it was."

"So, no enemies, no grudges, no stalkers? No bad debts, no ongoing litigation? No squatters? No firebugs in the family?"

"Nothing. No one."

"You have no idea why someone might have done this?"

"People do crazy things all the time, Chief Kennis. Maybe my house was built on an Indian graveyard. Maybe someone thought aliens were going to be using it for a landing pad. Why speculate? I'd rather look forward and rebuild. I may install some surveillance cameras this time around."

I stood up. "Well, thanks. If you think of anything else, give me a call."

"I certainly will."

I doubted it. He had lied about almost everything else—at least that was my instinct, and I trusted it. But why? That was the question. Who was he protecting, beside the houseguest who ducked out when I arrived? Or maybe protecting her was enough.

I needed to find out who she was, without actually arresting Andrew Thayer. I could set one of the junior officers, maybe Barnaby Toll, to watch the house, and get another one to take down all the license plate numbers in the town parking lot. We might find something out if we ran them all, and it would give the young cops something to do besides writing out parking tickets and answering prank calls.

This mystery woman was my only lead. Without her, my interviews with Thayer were useless: one more set of evasions and half-truths delivered by one more venture capitalist with things to hide—most them, probably all of them, irrelevant.

For the moment, I let it go. My day's work was done. I went home to take a shower and find some civilian clothes. Miranda had the kids that night and I actually had a social engagement, the first one in weeks.

Chapter Ten

At Emily Grimshaw's Salon

I didn't expect to find a clue in that cluttered, hothouse living room, crowded with would-be poets and authors, but until that night I never thought a poem could be a death threat.

Still, if anyone was going to compose such a document, the late Todd Macy's son, Chris, was the guy. A spoiled brat with father issues, though the term probably applied just as well to Lord Byron or Ezra Pound, both of whom (it turned out) Chris used in the poetry workshop he ran at the Community School. Mason Taylor took Chris' workshop and thought he was a genius. There was nothing I could do about that. Maybe he was a good influence when he was sober.

The poem was an odd piece of work, but so were most of the stories and poems people performed at Emily Grimshaw's house. And almost all of them concerned some sort of tortured family relationship. One began: "Daddy, Daddy, Daddy, why are your eyes so silent, why does your mouth refuse me, why are your broken hands fisted with grief?"

There was a limit to how much of that stuff you could listen to, but I still enjoyed attending these soirees. I liked the Bohemian atmosphere, the books and trinkets piled on every surface, the smell of incense. Emily made excellent hors d'oeuvres, and served good wine. She was proud of her little salon and always had a few young writers around that she was mentoring; most of them strapping twenty-year-old boys. They adored Emily and did most of the heavy work, moving furniture and setting up the little apartment for the art installations and readings. It looked like Chris Macy was one of them these days. He had the tormented look she preferred.

He was hauling the big lectern to the arched opening between the bedroom and the living room when I pushed inside out of the cold. Emily, bulky and intense, was talking to Jane Stiles, while Jane's six-year-old son tugged at her pant leg.

"I expect a *real* poem to *change my life*," Emily was saying. She stepped back from the door. "Oh, hello, Chief—you're late. We're about to start. Shut the door and introduce yourself to anyone you don't know. We have some newbies tonight, and you need to assure them they won't be arrested. I'm going to open more wine."

She disappeared through the crowd, back toward the kitchen at the far side of the little apartment.

"Something had better change her life," I said, "as soon as possible."

Jane smiled. "You came."

"I wouldn't miss one of Emily's evenings."

"This is my first. I think she's interesting. Until Emily, I'd never met anyone who wore black as a lifestyle before."

"There must be more to her lifestyle than that."

"You're right. I'm being unfair. I shouldn't leave out the self-help seminars, the nuisance lawsuits, and the continuous low-grade nervous breakdown. She feels the pain of the world—which makes her better than you. Just ask her. She calls it *Weltshmertz*, basically because things sound more important when you say them in German. She's in court with her ex over custody of their Siamese cat. That's been going on for six months. Last year she announced that she was the bride of Jesus. But apparently that marriage didn't work out either."

I smiled, unbuttoning my coat. Emily kept the heat cranked, regardless of the expense. It was one of her few luxuries, and she prided herself on having "thin blood."

"Jesus, huh?" I said, "Well, it makes sense. The guy's never at home, he's got *issues* with his father, like everyone else here tonight."

"I can just hear her nagging him—'Follow *me*, believe in *me*, heed *my* words—it's all about *you*, isn't it?"

I laughed, as much at the perfect shrewish squint on her face as for what she said.

She lifted up her little boy. "This is Sam." Sam looked away. "He's a little shy."

I shrugged. "Me, too."

"It runs in our family. I'm going to have to drink a lot of wine before I try to read anything tonight."

"Are you embarrassed?"

"No, but I hate reading my stuff aloud. I get so self-conscious. If there's one person yawning or looking bored or something I just feel, you know—what's the point, they all hate it. Which is pretty distracting. I guess I get distracted too easily. A drink or two helps. When I'm drunk I don't care what anyone thinks. I get sort of hostile, in fact. I think stuff like—oh, boy, they thought they were bored before! Wait until they hear *this next part*!"

"I bet no one is actually bored, though. You're the only published writer here."

"What about you?"

"I don't think three poems in *Mulch* Magazine really count. That was their final issue, anyway. I think I may have killed it."

"I'll put my detective Maddy Clark on the case."

"Uh, oh. I'm sure I left some telltale clues lying around."

She laughed. "Gotta have those telltale clues."

"Anyway—people yawn because they're tired, not bored. Especially around here. Most of these people worked a ten-hour day today."

"I shouldn't let it bother me."

"I'm thirsty, Mommy," Sam said.

"We'll get you some juice, honey." She turned back to me. "I'm sorry—"

I held up my hands. "It's okay. I'll see you later."

Sam led Jane off toward the kitchen, and I moved deeper into the house. I saw a few people I knew: Mike Henderson and his wife, Cindy, clutching a folded piece of paper tonight, but I could tell she wouldn't have the nerve to read. I had seen her here before, with that same look of quiet panic on her face.

Alana Trikilis was sketching, sitting in a corner beside Jared Bromley. No sign of Mason Taylor.

Who else? David Trezize, of course, with another chapter from his divorce novel. He took the podium first, after Emily thanked everyone for coming and announced a "found art" show she would be presenting next month.

David's story was grim. But fortunately, he couldn't take it any more seriously in his writing than he did in my office. Staggering out of a catastrophically bad marriage and flirting ineptly with girls half his age, the narrator was "as horny as a fourteen-year-old boy, and about as likely to get laid."

Chris Macy laughed at that one. Kathleen Lomax sat near the window at the back of the room, saving David's place. I'm sure she was hoping that the next book would be a more cheerful one, detailing their new relationship. She laughed and applauded with everyone else, so David must have buried the incident with his ex-wife's journal—at least until he turned it into Chapter Twelve.

I didn't see Jane Stiles again until she was picking her way through the people sitting on Emily's floor toward the antique lectern. Sam followed a step behind, clutching Jane's thumb.

Jane's pants, a torn old pair of blue jeans, were a little too big on her, so was the loose white long-sleeved tee-shirt. It was as if she'd recently lost a lot of weight and hadn't bothered with a new wardrobe, though she told me at some point later that she'd worn the same sizes since high school. The clothes contrived to look as if they might just fall off her body at any moment. She slouched a little, as if she wanted to disappear into them. It was only when she stretched her back and squared her shoulders as she prepared to read that I noticed she wasn't wearing a bra. The four buttons that descended from the crew neck were unbuttoned but once again, it seemed negligent rather than intentionally provocative; she was too busy and distracted to bother with them.

She knew how to wait for people's attention. There was complete silence in the room when she finally began.

"This story is part of my new book, *Poverty Point*," she said. "Spoilers: Don't feel too happy for this girl. She gets murdered in the next chapter."

> Eleanor could see immediately that it was impossible. The box spring was not going to fit up the stairs. It was a queen size and it was just too big. She had an excellent sense of spatial relations, which generally annoyed people. She could fill grocery bags or moving vans with the same gratuitous perfection, fitting an end table or a box of pancake mix into the last little jigsaw gap that no one cared about but her. It was the same with parking. She had a trivial genius for it that made David crazy. Whenever she tried to help him, he would turn icy and polite. Finally he'd say, "You do it, then" and get out of the car. So she did it, but he never paid attention and he never improved. To learn something from her would be a defeat. Blaming her was better. Anything unpleasant made more sense to David if it was someone's fault. She thought about those primitive tribes she had read about in Sociology class at college, where the king was celebrated if the crops were good, and killed when the crops were bad. That was David's kind of world.
>
> "I'm sure we can do this," he was saying now, squinting up the stairs in the dim hallway light. It was a brilliant, sparkling early November afternoon outside. But not in here. The stuffy, overheated passageway felt like midnight in August. Eleanor yawned. The two moving men shifted from foot to foot awaiting orders.
>
> "It's not going to fit, David," she said again.

The chapter ended with Eleanor ducking out for a breath of fresh air, overhearing another crazy argument in the street between hopelessly at-odds family members—this one between a father and daughter. Eleanor sees her own life revealed with a shocking clarity, and makes a snap decision:

> She turned and started walking, away from the cramped stairwell and the jammed box spring and her waiting fiancée, into the sharp autumn morning and the bright conspiratorial streets of Boston, never once looking back.

When Jane was done she lifted her son into a hug while she endured the applause. I was standing in the doorway to the front hall. She eased past me.

"I have to get Sam home," she said. "It's past his bedtime."

"That was great."

"It was awful. Everyone hated it. I knew they would."

"I liked it, Mommy," Sam said. "I thought it was funny."

Jane replaced a stray hair behind her ear. "My fan club," she said. Then she was into the hall and helping Sam with his coat.

"I'd like to hear more."

"And I didn't get to hear any of your poems."

I was inspired. "Let's have our own private salon. I could come out to your house, bring wine and dinner, and we could read our stuff."

She touched my arm. "Sounds great. How about next Friday? Phil has Sam on Fridays."

"Perfect. Any food I should avoid?"

She stood on tiptoes to kiss my cheek. "I eat everything." She left me to ponder that comment while she took her son and slipped out the door.

I didn't get much time to mull it over, though. Chris Macy stepped up to the lectern and started to read.

Chris looked like his father, the blue eyes set far apart, the wide nose, the thin-lipped mouth. He was even starting to lose his hair in the front the same way his father had, with the same high forehead that made him look like a college revolutionary taking over the science building, especially when he put on his wire-rimmed glasses.

The poem was short, and he chanted it in a soft, singsong monotone that made you feel he was infatuated with every word.

"Patricide"

Yeah, that was the title. It stuck in my mind.

> *I am all the brothers:*
> *I live their lives,*
> *They remain the same:*
> *I am Alyosha who forgives*
> *I am Dmitiri who takes the blame*
> *It's no use, I still bleed:*
> *I am Ivan, who makes excuses*
> *I am Smerdyakov who does the deed.*
> *I am on fire,*
> *I live the Oresteia*
> *But it's no accident:*
> *I lure Jocasta with purpose*
> *I slaughter Laius*
> *With intent.*

After the reading, I got a beer from Emily's fridge and moved between the patches of conversation in the little apartment. Chris stood alone, leaning against a teetering bookshelf, drinking from a bottle of Bud light.

"Interesting poem," I ventured. Plucking a bacon-wrapped scallop off a tray on the nearest table.

"It was the last thing I wrote before my father died."

I bit, chewed, and swallowed. "Anything since?"

"Nope."

"Writer's block?"

"I was always writing for him, I guess. Now I don't know who to write for."

"So tell me—how did he feel about your patricide poems?"

"He understood metaphor and symbolism."

"And that was metaphorical and symbolic, what you read tonight."

"God, yes. I mean, I just lost my father, Chief Kennis. What are you trying to say?"

I took his arm and led him around the corner to the cramped alcove beside the bathroom door. Someone had pulled out a guitar and people were singing in the living room.

"It's possible your father was murdered, Chris."

"It was a hunting accident!"

"I found a sniper's bullet at the scene. This is shotgun season. And Todd told me you argued about guns all the time. He didn't think the second amendment applied to automatic weapons and stinger missiles. He was more of an organized militia-with-muskets type of guy. But you were hardcore NRA all the way down the line. He told me you had quite a gun collection. Any sniper rifles in there?"

He stared at me. The crowd in the next room applauded the first song. "Do I need a lawyer with me for the rest of this conversation?"

"I don't know. Do you?"

"Jesus Christ. I'm like a guy with a model train set, and you're accusing me of hijacking the Acela! Not to mention the implication that I—that I could have…"

"Sorry. But that was not a friendly poem."

"I loved my dad, whatever you may think. And I couldn't have—it takes years to learn how to shoot one of those rifles. You need military training. I collect them! I'm no sniper. They wouldn't even let me in the army because of my fucking asthma, all right? Why don't you look for someone who hated my dad and knew how to shoot? That would be a good start. Like the Vietnam sniper *with seventy-five verified kills* who's hated my dad's guts and lived right here on the island and never wears short-sleeved shirts because of all his fucked-up military tattoos! Start with that guy. Not me. I write poems. That's not a crime in this country, at least not yet."

"Who are you talking about?"

"You figure it out. You're the detective. Now unless you're actually planning to arrest me tonight, I'd like to grab another beer and go have a nice sing-along with my friends."

He pushed past me and rejoined the group in the living room. It was time for me to go.

I caught Emily's eye as I pulled on my coat, and lifted an arm. She blew me a kiss. I stepped out of the heat and smoke into the frigid night air and took a deep, grateful breath. Apart from the faint rattle of conversation from inside Emily's house, the town was silent. Orange Street was deserted. I stamped down the front stairs and headed uphill toward my car. The cold air clamped around my head. My ears were already stinging. But I stood still in the empty street anyway. I heard a distant car engine and the steady rush of the wind, studied the lighted windows in the old clapboard houses. It was the perfect metaphor. After six years, I still felt like an outsider so much of the time, sniffing at the margins, unable to penetrate the affable Yankee cordiality of the people around me.

Important things were always happening just out of my sight, at another table in a restaurant, behind a closing door in the town building, in the swiftly silenced chat in Emily Grimshaw's front hall. People stopped talking when they saw a cop. It was probably a smart move.

I had no way to unmask the military sniper Chris Macy described, but that didn't matter, because I had Haden Krakauer. Haden had lived here his whole life. He had to know the guy. And yet...holding the lethal bullet in his hand, admiring the precision of the shooting, he had chosen to keep the shooter's secret.

Why? What possible reason could he have for doing that?

I was going to find out, and I wasn't going to wait for morning.

Chapter Eleven

The Sniper

"You shouldn't have braced that kid at the party," Haden said.

"It was a reading."

Haden snorted a laugh. "Did you read him his rights?"

We were sitting in his messy living room in two old armchairs angled in front of the woodstove. The old yacht club race pictures, Audubon prints, burgees, and theater workshop posters from the 1980s (his father had been a prominent local actor) hadn't been moved in decades. The small house in 'Sconset was a time capsule. The last time I was in here, it was a little more than a year ago—I'd been tossing the place for evidence that Haden was plotting a bomb attack on the Boston Pops concert. Haden didn't hold a grudge, but I hadn't been back since.

"I didn't arrest the kid," I said.

"You accused him."

"I know."

"And that was way out of line."

"I know."

"He could file a formal complaint."

"I know."

"But he won't."

"I know."

"Which doesn't change the facts."

"I know."

"Right. You know and I know you know I know. So what'ya know?"

"I know you know me, and you know why I did it."

He took a sip. "You found something."

I stood and pulled off my coat. It was warm in there, the dense, starchy heat that radiates from hot metal. "I found a sniper shell in the moors. We have an ex-Army sniper living on island who was apparently feuding with the victim, and you never mentioned it to me. Why?"

Haden let a silence pass. A log popped with a gunshot exclamation and a fan of sparks.

"It's a dead end, Henry."

"Why don't you let me decide that?"

"Was that a real question? Because there's a real answer. David Lattimer would never kill anyone. Even if he still could—and he hasn't picked up a rifle in more than thirty years."

"David Lattimer?"

He nodded.

"David Lattimer was an army sniper in Vietnam?"

Haden said nothing, just finished his drink and set the glass on the carpet next to his chair.

"Sorry, but that sounds like one of those crazy Nantucket rumors," I ventured.

"Look it up. Google the guy. He has a pile of medals stashed away in that house. A Bronze Star, a couple of Silver Stars that I know about. An Army Commendation medal, maybe more."

"But he wouldn't shoot anyone?"

"He walked away from all that shit. He's a pacifist. I mean, really a pacifist, an official one. He belongs to all these organizations—Peace Action, the War Resister's League, Food not Bombs, the International Physicians for the Prevention of Nuclear War."

"He's a doctor?"

"Thoracic surgeon, retired. Worked his whole career at Brigham and Women's. He does a volunteer shift now and then at Cottage Hospital, when they're jammed up in the summer. But that's it. His wife was a nurse. That's how they met."

I finished my drink. I could feel the day catching up to me. "I still have to talk to him."

"Okay, but play nice. Lattimer is beloved around here."

"Why did I never hear all this before?"

"It's New England, Chief. We don't talk to strangers and we don't brag."

"Jesus Christ. So when do I stop being a stranger?"

He smiled. "Give it thirty years or so, you'll be fine. Most of the old geezers at the Wharf Rats club will be dead by then."

"Well, that's comforting."

"Just don't ask Lattimer to bump them off for you. He patches people up now."

"Very funny." I yawned. It seemed like a week since I'd stood in the moors watching Andrew Thayer's house burning. In fact it had been just twelve hours. And I had a feeling that the next twelve were going to feel even longer. The dog years of police work. At this rate I'd be dead before the old codgers at the Wharf Rats club.

◇◇◇

Searching the moors the next morning, Kyle Donnelly found an iPod nano in the brambles near the sniper's perch. He had also noticed some tire tracks in the mud nearby, photographed them with his iPhone and e-mailed the pictures to the State Police forensics lab.

"Because you never know," he said.

"Nice work," I told him. "Keep it up."

He shrugged, embarrassed by the praise. "I figured it wouldn't hurt to take one more look."

"Exactly. We should cut that into a quarterboard, and make it our new motto."

An hour later Haden Krakauer was standing in my office with the playlist printout from the little iPod. He had traced the iTunes account to David Lattimer's computer.

I studied the playlist. "Talking Heads, Caetano Veloso, Kassav, Johnny Clegg and Savuka, Vampire Weekend, Pink Floyd, Mahotella Queens. The guy's got interesting taste, anyway."

"For a killer. Say it."

I shrugged. "For a killer."

The faxed ballistics report topped the pile of papers on my desk. I'd been reading it when Haden walked in. I twirled my chair away from him to face the big windows and the wide early winter morning outside: freezing rain and winds gusting to thirty miles an hour.

"You know someone planted that iPod, Chief."

"Broke into his house, pulled the songs off his computer?"

"Why not?"

"Because it's crazy, that's why."

"His house isn't locked. There's no security on his laptop. They're out tramping in the woods every afternoon. It'd be a cinch."

I rotated back around. "But why?"

"Misdirection. Lattimer's the obvious choice if you want to set someone up for a sniper kill."

I nodded. "Or maybe whoever wanted Todd Macy dead wanted to get rid of Lattimer at the same time."

"Two birds with one stone."

"It's surprisingly difficult to hit even a single bird with one stone, you know. Much less two."

"And yet."

"Yeah."

We sat in silence, rearranging the pieces of the puzzle, until Charlie Boyce stuck in head in the door.

"I think we have a lead on the F-150."

Chapter Twelve

Truck Rally

Charlie and his team had done their homework—the tedious, detail-crunching slog that made up about ninety percent of effective police work. The figures broke down this way: Don Allen had records for twenty-two black Ford F-150s purchased over the previous five years, new and used. Three of them had been resold, two of the sales for cash, and Charlie was trying to track down the new owners, who could be visitors, or off-island contractors, or illegal aliens who re-sold the vehicles themselves. It got a little murky down at that level. Up in the sunlight of legal transactions with valid paperwork, fifteen of the vehicles—and their owners—had solid alibis for the afternoon in question: off-island, or parked at various jobsites. Four could be placed at Marine Home Center, Valero's, or Island Lumber in the time frame we were looking at.

That left four trucks unaccounted for. One was being cannibalized for parts by a local mechanic, one was a Christmas gift to a high school senior named Ken Podell, who was serving a detention at the high school that Saturday afternoon. One was registered to David Lattimer, who couldn't have been driving it, since he was on the ground as the vehicle left the scene.

The fourth one belonged to Brad Thurman. "Jane Stiles' soon-to-be-ex boyfriend," Haden pointed out. "According to the infallible Nantucket rumor mill."

"He doesn't go to her readings."

I thanked Charlie, dismissed Haden and started pacing my office. On the upside, it was nice having an office big enough for pacing. On the downside, Brad Thurman. The contractor's relationship with Jane made him a confusing person for me to investigate—if I was, in fact, interested in Jane as more than a writing colleague and one-woman critique group.

Because, if Alana Trikilis and Jared Bromley were right, Thurman was involved with the drug-fueled movie-making that had been using the Thayer place for an ad hoc soundstage. That gave him motive and opportunity for the arson. I should send one of my detectives to see Thurman, but neither of them knew the link to the pornography ring, and I had promised to keep Alana's name out of the investigation until I had enough evidence to arrest these people and was able to justify the expense of protecting her to the Selectmen.

Haden Krakauer would have given a simpler explanation—I was incapable of delegating responsibility. He would have been right. This was one case I wanted to handle myself.

I called Thurman's home number. No answer, but the voicemail offered his cell number; no answer there either. I left messages and then went down to the Town Hall to check the building permits.

Gail behind the counter saved me the trouble of a long search. "He just filed for a big job in Shawkemo," she told me. "Is he in trouble?"

I had to think fast. The last thing I wanted to do was fire up that infamous Nantucket rumor mill. "No, no," I improvised. "It's personal. His mom is in the Island Home and I was thinking of moving my mom in there, too. I just want to get the inside dope on the place, but he never returns a phone call."

"Well, the Island Home is wonderful, I can tell you that much. My grandmother is in there and she loves it. The MassHealth part is bad, it's like the state hates paying for her, and it's always trying to find some excuse to kick her out. But the people are terrific. They're really on your side. And they all love Grams."

I smiled. "I think you just saved me a trip."

I had told her half the truth. I didn't know about Brad Thurman's mother, but I was missing my own, and all her friends in Northern California had died off. She was ready for assisted living, with me living three thousand miles away. My itinerant FBI agent brother wasn't much help. He visited her maybe twice a year. It wasn't an urgent issue; Mom was fine for the moment. The important thing was derailing Gail's interest in Brad Thurman's possible criminal activities, and discussing our local skilled nursing facility had served the purpose *to a T*, as my mom herself would have said.

I drove out to the jobsite, a big house framed and half-shingled, surrounded by trucks parked in the mud. I saw a Bromley Electric van, with its lightning bolt logo, and Ted Bromley himself, bald and hawk-nosed, rummaging through the shelves inside. The van was right next to the front door of the house, a prime space as befitted an electrician, the acknowledged royalty among island tradesmen. Anyone could equip themselves with a hammer or a paintbrush, but taking apart your own fuse box was illegal, not to mention a terrific way to get yourself killed.

Ted carried his elite status lightly. He sensed me beside him now, pushed off to stand up straight, and turned to face me. "Chief Kennis," he said, "thanks for looking after my boy."

"Jared's a good kid. It's not often you find someone who's a good friend and a good writer. Jared is both."

He grinned. "*Charlotte's Web* fan, I see."

I nodded. "Some pig!"

"So what brings you out to this hellhole today?"

"I'm actually looking for your boss."

He cocked his head in surprise. "I'm my boss."

"I meant…your GC."

"Brad Thurman doesn't sign my paychecks, Chief. That would be Polly Culbertson. Her husband owns this dump, but she's in charge. He only bought the place to keep her out of his hair for a year or two—that's my theory."

I smiled. "So you see a lot of her."

"Oh, yeah. We're changing the wall sconces again. And I haven't even got the place wired yet."

"So…Brad?"

"He eats lunch every day at the drugstore in town. Don't ask me why. I think he uses the soda fountain for an office. Beats paying rent."

◇◇◇

I thanked him and drove back into town. I found a slant parking spot in front of the Hub, and walked the half block to the Nantucket Pharmacy. The Christmas trees lining the sidewalk had been decorated, now mostly by businesses and school children. Laminated crayon drawings of Santa vied with miniature jewelry boxes and tiny anchors. It all looked messy to me, and the jewelry boxes reminded me that the island had a few more jewelers than it really needed.

When I first arrived on the island there were two drugstores side by side on Main Street, but Congdon's had closed. The space had been renovated into yet another high-end jewelry store, but the words *Congdon's Pharmacy* could still be seen, cut into the panels below the front display window. David Trezize had photographed that storefront to illustrate a screed about the new Nantucket. But the picture nailed it.

"A thousand words, exactly," he had said, after performing a word-count on the editorial. "I'm not sure why I bothered."

Thurman wasn't at the lunch counter but I found him sitting in a silver Toyota Tundra in front of the store. Not a good start—he was driving the wrong pickup truck.

"Hey, Chief," he called out. I walked over, leaned into the window. "I got a bone to pick with you. Listen to this. I was driving my kid's Range Rover, it's a used '97 model. He rebuilt it himself, so don't tell me I'm spoiling my kids. Anyway, I'm out for a spin on Milestone Road, doing the speed limit, driving like an old man which I'm getting to be, let's face it. And one of your goons pulls me over—flashers, sirens, the whole nine yards. I'm like—what the fuck? So the big dumb cop strolls up, looks inside and says, "Sorry, Mr. Thurman, I thought it was your son." Can you believe that shit? Don't tell me you're not targeting Tommy, Chief. That idiot admitted it. I were you, I'd fire his ass just for that. He couldn't think of any excuse? So he just blurts out the truth? What a loser. And Tom's been clean for eight months, FYI."

"Did you get the officer's name?"

"No, but he's a big fattie and he needs a haircut. Acne scars. Bad breath. He needs to go to a dentist, get those teeth cleaned. Unless he's got stomach cancer or something. Which wouldn't surprise me given the crap he probably stuffs in his pie hole every day. Anyway, he's a disgrace to the department."

Thurman was talking about Byron Lovell. Not my proudest hire. But Byron was Haden Krakauer's nephew. I'd let him handle the situation.

"Got a minute?" I said.

"Climb in where it's warm."

I opened the door and folded myself into the front seat of the big truck.

"Didn't you used to own an F-150?"

"Yeah, until the coil packs crapped out, the injectors starting leaking, and two timing chains failed. All just as I hit the magic sixty-thousand-mile mark. Then the shift cable broke, while I was driving it into Don Allen! They were gonna charge me three grand to get it fixed. I sold it to some Brazilian instead. Jorge something, he paid cash. Said he likes working on cars after work. The guy's a mason, works eighty hours a week, then fixes cars for fun at night. How are we supposed to compete with that?"

"Work harder?"

"Or hire some Brazilians. That's my solution."

"So when did you sell the truck?"

"Back in October. I didn't want to go through another winter with that shitbox."

I looked around the cabin of the Toyota. "Nice ride."

"It's loaded—heated seats, back up camera, bluetooth, you name it."

"Plus that new car smell."

"Can't beat it."

We sat quietly for a moment, then the bluetooth function lit up, alerting him that it was syncing to a phone he had programmed into the system.

Thurman hit the horn two short blasts and someone on the sidewalk sprinted away. I twisted around in my seat to watch as the figure pivoted around the corner onto Centre Street and out of sight.

"Who was that?"

Thurman shrugged but I could tell he was spooked. "Could have been anyone. Most of my subs are synched to my bluetooth."

"So they can use their own phones hands-free when they drive your truck?"

"Why not? They use my vehicle for a supply run, they can't charge me for the mileage."

I stared at him. "Most contractors I know are more possessive about their wheels."

"I just want to get the job done. These guys are driving my trucks, I can keep track of them."

"Trucks?"

"I have three now. I'm a self-serve taxi service. But on the other hand I don't have some kid getting his used Chevy Malibu stuck in the mud all the time. Or whatever."

"Do me a favor, Brad. Get me a list of everyone with a phone synched to your bluetooth."

"Why? What's the problem?"

"I just want to know why that guy took off so fast."

"Are you kidding? He saw you. These punks want nothing to do with the cops, okay? Probably thought you were going to sic the INS on him."

"Should I?"

"Yeah, sure. Have 'em do a sweep. Half the workers on this island'll be on the next boat home."

"And you were just trying to help him when you honked."

"I'm a nice guy. I don't want to make trouble."

"Really? Then get me those names."

I climbed out of the truck and slammed the door behind me. I didn't trust him to give me a complete list and I thought briefly of deposing his carrier—probably AT&T, since they were the only company that had a coverage at the far ends of the island. But I'd need a court order for that, and I had a better idea anyway.

The Hub had installed a webcam last summer, aimed directly at the corner of Main and Federal streets. It took a picture every twenty seconds and when they scrolled it back for me, I got one usable picture of my quarry: six-foot-two, broad Slavic face, tangled brown hair clamped by a watch cap. Whoever it was, it wasn't one of Thurman's Brazilian subcontractors.

I printed out the screen-grab, intending to show it around and see if anyone recognized it. But the first person who looked at it saved me the trouble.

"Pumpkin latte with a double shot," said the Jamaican girl behind The Hub's coffee counter.

"Excuse me?"

"That's what he orders. Doug. I don't know his last name. But he comes in all the time."

"And orders the pumpkin latte?"

She looked hurt. "They're good! Want to try one?"

"Not right now. Does he ever park in front of the place?"

"Sure, I guess. Sometimes."

"You ever notice the kind of car he drives?"

She nodded. "It's a big black pickup truck."

She saw my expression, and hers changed too, the smiles echoing back and forth like a shout in a canyon.

After a few seconds I said, "I think I will try that pumpkin latte, after all."

It was actually pretty good—not as sweet as I expected. Haden Krakauer filled in the rest of the information: "Douglas Blount. He's the caretaker handyman guy out at the Pell place."

And the porn group's enforcer, according to Alana. With her as my only link to him, I had promised to leave the guy alone. But now I had an independent lead. I was standing in the door to Haden's office. I turned to go.

"Heading out?" he asked.

"Yeah."

"Want backup?"

"You just want an excuse to get one of these pumpkin lattes."

"The thought had occurred to me."

"I'll bring you one. With a double shot, just the way Doug likes them."

Chapter Thirteen

The Major Domo

The LoGran corporate mansion gave me a jolt of déjà vu—the company had purchased the house out on Eel Point Road where Preston Lomax was killed. I hadn't been back in the two years since, but the place looked pretty much the same—big high-dormered gambrel roof rising three stories above the crushed-shell driveway and elaborate stonework that terraced the steep front yard. The white widow's walk would have a spectacular view of the harbor.

The house had a shuttered, closed-down look. Haden had told me that, apart from Doug Blount, who lived in the guest cottage during the off-season, the only resident was a woman named Sue Ann Pelzer, who was the "major domo" of the place, making sure everything was clean and sparkly when the visitors showed up, or some big function had to be organized, deploying armies of tradesmen to work on the plumbing or the furnace if necessary, fixing the cracks in the walls and the mold on the grout, filling the fridge and the potholes in the driveway, changing the old shingles and the sheets, restocking the bar and the wood shed and the pantry, making sure the blu-ray players in every bedroom could stream Amazon Prime, Hulu, and Netflix. She made sure the bills were never overdue and the propane tanks were never empty, the pillows arranged and the gardens weeded just so, the window boxes blooming with pansies in the summer, cleaned out and stored for the winter, and the new toilet paper in every bathroom sporting a folded triangle of tissue at the top of every roll.

"Cleaning isn't an easy job," Sue Ann said to me. We were standing in the giant high-ceilinged living room with its massive fireplace featuring alabaster mermaids holding up the mantel. Sue Ann stood about five-foot-one, with a starved and steely marathon athlete's body and a blocky, wide-eyed face. The piercing blue eyes looked out from below a curtain of bangs, her hair knotted into a tight braid at the back. She wore a gray wool cable-knit cardigan over a white-collared shirt buttoned to the neck, khakis, and running shoes.

Standing feet apart with her fists on her hips, she seemed to be guarding the place. The trumpet of her big Southern voice filled the room.

I studied her while she continued her lecture. "You have to know where to look and you have to be able to see what you're looking at. It sounds simple, but it's not. In fact, it's a talent, Chief Kennis. Just like your poetry. Oh yeah, I read your poetry. I read everything. I'm a reader. I even learned one of your poems by heart, I liked it so much. Don't believe me? Then listen up.

> *I watch the lawnmower*
> *Make another pass*
> *Across the field of wildflowers*
> *Cut to look like grass;*
> *Hacked to their stems.*
> *The sweet green turf*
> *Keeps its secret,*
> *Trimmed and discreet—*
> *Like a circus clown*
> *In blue jeans*
> *Like an acrobat*
> *Merely walking*
> *Down the street.*

"That one's called 'Incognito.' Am I right?"

I had to smile. "Absolutely."

She laughed. "You should see the look on your face! Writers love to be quoted. I know that for a fact. The magazine said you were a detective and I loved that. It's a detective's poem. You see what isn't there, and what was there before. It looks like grass now but you know the truth. You see the wildflowers when everyone else just sees grass."

She had me off-balance; I had actually never thought of the poem that way. "Well…I hope so," I managed.

But she was already moving on. "Anyway, like I was saying, a good house cleaner has to be able to see dirt. That's their talent. You got to see it to clean it. Most people spend their whole lives trying not to see it! But a good cleaner's got to search it out. I write my girls an instruction sheet for every task. You know item number one on my bathroom clean-up list? Can you guess? No? Okay, I'll tell you: 'Turn on the light'! Don't laugh. You can't believe how many times I've caught those crazy kids trying to scrub toilets in the dark."

She ran out of steam for a second.

"So, Sue Ann—"

"You need help solving a crime? Because we've had several break-ins down at the cottage."

"Mr. Pell told me. I'll take a look while I'm out here, but for right now I need some information. It's about Doug Blount and his truck."

"That's not his truck, Chief Kennis. That truck belongs to the LoGran Corporation. It's one of three corporate vehicles currently in use on the island. There's also a little Prius for me, and a Range Rover for ferrying the guests to and fro when they hold conferences here or whatever. Douglas Blount can't afford to pay for a brand new F-150. He can't afford to pay *attention*." She chuckled at her little joke, then dropped a frown over her features. "Is the truck part of your investigation?"

"That depends where it was last Saturday."

"That's easy. It was in the shop, getting its brake lines replaced."

"Do you have some proof of that?"

"I have the bill, dated and paid this morning, and Toby Keller was working on it all weekend at his garage. Keller Automotive? It's out by the airport, on Nobadeer Farm Road. I'm sure he'd testify to that. He'd remember. That truck's been in and out of the shop for months. It's a lemon. Toby says we should just give up and run it in the Demolition Derby this year. But Doug loves that truck."

"Where's the truck right now?"

"Oh, Doug has it. I think he's picking up a new filter for the dryer. I like to keep him busy. Idle hands are the devil's playground. Anything else?"

"Could I take a look at the invoice?"

She got it for me; she had it filed away with all the other invoices for automotive repair, in a special file for the truck. I followed her to the little office off the living room and I noticed that the house was immaculate—not a speck of dust or an unfluffed pillow anywhere. Whatever Pell paid her, it wasn't enough.

She gave me the bill, and it proved I had hit another dead end. Every truck on the island was accounted for, but one of those accounts had to be a lie. Unless someone had come over on the steamship. The Authority records the make, model, and length of every car that crosses with them. But no Ford F-150s had come over from Hyannis in the last month—at least, none with an originating ticket off-island. Some trucks had come and gone, but always departing from Nantucket and returning in a day or two.

So someone was lying, or Alana Trikilis was hallucinating, but I had no way to verify either of those theories and nothing to do but fret about it. I had a suspect I didn't believe in for Todd Macy's death, which meant some kind of frame I couldn't verify, a lot of hysteria and suspicion about a drugs-for-sex ring that I couldn't prove, and an arson fire with no meaningful leads. The only new piece of information from the State Police was the aviation fuel, but no one involved owned a jet or had any dealings with the airport. It was just one more jagged little jigsaw piece that didn't fit anywhere in the puzzle. Nothing fit, nothing came together. We couldn't even track down Jill Phelan's drug dealer.

But then, the next morning, not ten minutes apart, Kyle Donnelly handed me the State Police forensics report on the tire tracks at the Macy crime scene, and Alana Trikilis' father showed up at my office with a letter he'd fished out of a garbage bag that turned those tread-marks into a death sentence.

Or so it seemed.

Chapter Fourteen

Crimes of Passion

November 10th, 2015

My dear darling Daisy –

    I don't know what to do or say any more. I feel like an old fool and there is no fool more pathetic than an old one. How could I have imagined you might be truly interested in someone like myself? One unguarded glimpse into a mirror should have disabused me of that illusion. Yet your kiss felt so real to me. Words lie, but the touch is true. You must have known that when you touched me. Everything brings me back to you. The harbor is an iron gray this morning, exactly the color of your eyes. The wind is relentless from the Northeast and I can hear you say, "I feel like it's brushing my teeth." I don't know what to do with these memories. There is no one I can share them with. My friends are all dead, and these revelations would surely kill Phillipa. My thoughts

turn to suicide, and even in the dark hours
before sunrise, to murder. It would be so easy to
kill one of my rivals, with his habitual walks
through the moors, and to vacate the island of
the other would only require a lit match in the
wrong place. He has remarked in my hearing
on more than one occasion that the only filament connecting him to this place is his little
cottage, which lies a stone's throw from my own
house. Or I should say, a stone's throw in the old
days, when my arm was stronger. I think about
these things and Phillipa says, "Darling you
are brooding again," and I have to invent some
plausible excuse for my despondent mood. It gets
harder and harder and I know that just seeing
you once would

The letter ended there, unfinished and unsigned, dated almost two weeks before Todd Macy's killing. I dropped it on my desk as if it were radioactive, pushed my chair away from the desk feeling contaminated by it, the Geiger counter-crackle sizzling up from my fingertips.

I glared at Sam Trikilis, hunched over my desk, memorizing the wood grain. "Where did you get this?"

"It was…I got it—from the trash."

"It was sitting on top of an open trash can?"

"No, I had to open the bag…and—you know…rummage through it a little."

"Jesus Christ, Sam."

"I'm sorry."

"Why would you do this?"

"It's—Alana's got me worried. All the crazy stuff going on. Andy's house burning down. Lattimer was right there when it happened, and everybody knows firebugs like to watch things burn. And, I mean…the rumor is that Todd Macy got shot—like, by a sniper, a real military kill. Everybody knows about Lattimer, Vietnam and the tattoos and all. It adds up. Except for the motive. So that's why I started digging around myself. And I found that."

He pointed down at the letter as if was a dead animal.

I said, "Lattimer kept the letter for a long time."

"Maybe he was trying to figure out how to finish it."

"Or get up the nerve to send it."

"Or both."

"Yeah." We sat in silence for a minute or two. I had more questions. "So, who is this Daisy?"

"That's Ms. DeHart—she's one of the guidance counselors at the school."

I wasn't sure how much Alana had told her father about that night in 'Sconset at McAllister's house. I decided on a gentle prod. "Have you met her?"

"We had some meetings after Jill Phelan's overdose. Everyone was worried about the kids and they brought in some kind of grief counselor from off-island. But Ms. DeHart was right there, too, coordinating with the administration and the parents."

"So you like her."

"I did. I mean—at first. Until I found out she was…procuring, is that the right word? Getting girls involved with this…this…"

So Alana had told him everything. "I know what she was doing."

"So why not arrest her?"

"I have to be able to prove it, Sam. And I have to be sure myself. That's not the kind of mistake you want to make in a small town. Unless you're planning to move. With no forwarding address."

He nodded. "Good point."

Another thought occurred to me. "Where did you hear that Todd Macy was shot by a sniper?"

"I don't know. Someone was talking about it at Bartlett's when I went to get my Christmas tree. Two guys were arguing about it at the Stop&Shop. It's all over the island, Chief. Sorry, but it's like—what are you gonna do? People talk. It's how we get through the winter. But the letter...Is it—can you use it? I mean, in a trial?"

I nodded. "It's admissible. And you didn't even break any laws. Trespassing would be the usual charge but you had business on the property."

"So, I'm not in trouble?"

"Nope."

"And Lattimer's going down."

"We'll see about that. Meanwhile, I have to ask you to be quiet about this. For Alana's sake, as well as for the good of the investigation."

He nodded vigorously—maybe too vigorously. "Not a word, Chief. Not a word."

"Not even to Alana."

"But I—okay."

"I mean it, Sam. If this gets out I'll know they heard it from you."

"Okay, okay. I understand."

"Good. I appreciate that. Thanks for coming in."

He left and I picked up the report Kyle Donnelly had brought me. The tracks at the scene were Goodyear Wrangler AT/S tires— the most common you could find on an F-150...and various other light pickups, also. So it wasn't conclusive, but Kyle had also attached a separate report, detailing his alibi investigation for the date of the shooting. He managed to locate and clear every truck on the island—except Lattimer's.

Out of curiosity, I double-checked the LoGran vehicle—it was in the shop getting a coolant leak fixed, along with an oil change and new brake pads. The sinking feeling in my stomach was buoyed slightly by the thoughtful, meticulous work Kyle Donnelly had done to give it to me. The kid was turning into an effective police officer. That was good news for the NPD.

And bad news for David Lattimer.

I drove out to his house after a quick lunch at the airport. I took my second coffee in a takeout cup, and before I got to the house—driving the long way around, skirting the whole east end of the island—I had my thoughts in order.

◇◇◇

I parked on Polpis Road and walked up his driveway. The old Jeep Wagoneer was gone and the F-150 was parked in the grass beside the house. The day was still and cold and silent. I could see the harbor through the screen of trees—the livid water that had reminded Lattimer of Daisy DeHart's eyes. Interesting word, livid—from the latin *lividus*—an exact translation that filtered into English mostly as a descriptive term for bruising: black and blue.

Lattimer would probably appreciate that fragment of etymology this afternoon.

I walked up the driveway and circled the truck. The hood was cool to the touch, the cab scrupulously neat, the bed empty except for a fitted rubber liner. But I immediately saw something wrong. Somewhere in an interview transcript, Lattimer mentioned that he rarely drove the big Ford. They used it mostly for antiquing trips off-island, or the occasional dump run.

That was where I had to start.

Worst case scenario: Lattimer took the Jeep, leaving Phillipa at home. I didn't feel like manufacturing some bogus reason for my visit, and I certainly didn't want to tell her the truth, at least not yet. But Lattimer came to the door. After a moment of surprise he invited me in and offered me a cup of coffee.

"Thanks, David. I'm wired enough as it is."

"Well, what can I do for you, Chief?"

"I just have a few questions. The first one would be—when was the last time you drove your truck?"

He rubbed his chin, the perfect pantomime of the thoughtful patriarch. "Hmmm, excellent question. I would have to say… Oh, my goodness, quite a while ago. I think it was the final toxic waste collection day last summer. Late August sometime. I could check the date. We cleaned out the basement, found paint cans from the nineteen sixties all the way up to a couple of years ago! The labels made a fascinating study in the changing styles of graphic design over the decades. I prefer the older, simpler labels. But I suspect people who mourn for past eras. They're really just missing their own youth."

I let him chatter. It was classic suspect behavior. Finally he wound down. "Tracks matching your vehicle were found at the blind where the sniper took his shot."

"You mean the perch."

"I defer to your greater knowledge, sir."

"My military record is no secret. I'm proud of it."

"Of course. Thank you for your service."

He barked out a laugh. "I didn't serve you! I served the politicians and military contractors who reaped the profits. And I never even got a tip."

We were drifting. "Every other truck on the island that day has been cleared, David. We know exactly where they were. Most of them are work trucks, parked at jobsites. A few were in the shop or off-island. The only one we can't account for is yours."

"You're saying I killed Todd Macy?"

"You were certainly thinking about it."

I handed him a copy of the letter. The original was safe in the NPD evidence locker.

His face darkened—a blush of anger, not embarrassment. "Where did you get this?"

"I can't tell you that."

"You were picking through my trash!"

"Someone was."

"I knew I should have burned that letter."

"But you didn't."

He stalked into the living room and collapsed onto the couch. "This is a nightmare. Phillipa must never know about this."

"David—"

He crumpled the letter in his fist, as he must have done before. "This isn't real! Nothing happened! This had no...I—it was an old man's dream. I was deluded. I was pathetic. I know that now. Daisy had no interest in me! Of course she didn't."

"But you were obsessed with her."

He stared down at his knees. "Yes. Obviously."

"To the point where you were wanted to kill your rival."

"That was a fantasy! You can't put someone in jail for a fantasy. You've never dreamed of killing someone…someone who stood in your way?"

"No."

"In any case, you'd never admit it me."

I smiled. "No."

He stood and dropped the ball of paper into the trash near the writing table by the big picture window. "Do I need a lawyer?"

"That's up to you. I'm not arresting you. I just want to talk."

"Nothing I say will be used against me in a court of law?"

"No. Not today."

"So what's next?"

"Come outside with me. I want to show you something."

We walked out into the chilly afternoon. The humid air hung still, poised and tense, as if eavesdropping. That was just my imagination. There was no one around to overhear our conversation and the great dome of blue sky above us was defined by its indifference.

We stopped at the truck. "You shouldn't park on the grass," I said.

"I know, but there's no room for Phillipa to turn around in the driveway, and we had couple of absurd fender-benders before…what are you saying?"

"Look at the tires."

"What am I looking for? Tell-tale blood spatter? Some personal item caught in the treads?"

"Just look." I waited but he didn't see it. "The grass beside the tires," I said. "Those little rectangles of sod. They're crushed and brown, because you were parked there for a long time. But you didn't put the truck back in exactly the same spot after you finally drove it."

He stared down. "Yes. But why should I care? I have nothing to hide."

"You went out driving. Where did you go?"

"Nowhere. I don't remember. It was just a drive. I took the old truck out for a spin! Nothing illegal about that."

"When was this?"

"I have no idea. Weeks ago."

"Would Phillipa recall?"

He answered much too quickly. "She was off-island. Our daughter is getting married and she—oh, I see. I do know when. Exactly when."

"Can you verify that you were at home any time that weekend? Did you make any calls from your landline? Rent a movie from Comcast? Download anything?"

"I don't download. I make clippings. From actual newspapers and magazines. And as you can see, I don't e-mail, I write letters. With a fountain pen."

"So you stayed home all weekend but you can't prove it."

"That sums it up, I'm afraid."

I put my hand to the driver's door handle. "Do you mind if I take a look inside?"

"There's nothing to see."

"So?"

"Go ahead, Chief Kennis. Be my guest."

But it was obvious as soon as I pulled the door open. "Who drove this car last, David? It wasn't you."

"Phillpa may have—"

"It wasn't her, either. She's almost as tall as you are."

"Yes, but I don't see what that has to do with—"

"This seat is set for the shortest possible driver. As high and far up as it can go. You wouldn't even fit inside. Care to try?" He shook his head. "Who was driving?"

He released a shuddering sigh. "Fine. It was Daisy. We were together that day. But I'll destroy the letter, move the truck, and adjust this seat—you'll never be able to prove anything."

"That will wreck the only alibi you have. Do you want that?"

"It doesn't matter. I'll go to jail. I'm old. I won't be around much longer anyway. And frankly I'd rather die in prison than have Phillipa discover any of this."

"Let's say we do arrest you. What will your story be? What was your motive?"

"I went crazy. How about that? I have PTSD. Macy was a liberal pro-immigration gay-rights tree-hugger. I read one interview too many and took things into my own hands. Like the classic George Price cartoon. You know George Price?" I nodded. I had grown up on his *New Yorker* cartoons. "The old man sitting in his rocking chair with a smoking shotgun? The radio blown to pieces? That was before your time. His wife is saying, 'Harold has his own way of dealing with Walter Winchell.' Something like that."

"Then why not just shoot the TV during the Rachel Maddow show?"

"I kill people, not appliances. I'm a trained killer, remember? I just snapped."

"This is crazy."

"Good! I'll take the insanity defense."

A dark speculation obscured my thoughts for a moment. I half-expected a cloud to drift across the sun and drape us in a wintry shadow. But the world remained neutral, and the hard frosty sunlight continued to sting the eyes, glittering on the chrome of Lattimer's truck.

"I wonder if someone else knew that," I said.

"Knew what?"

"That'd you'd go to jail before revealing where you really were that day. It makes you the perfect patsy."

He flinched as if I'd raised a fist. "You're saying Daisy was part of some—some conspiracy? That she was using me, using my feelings…"

"It's possible."

"I refuse to believe that."

"Okay."

"She's a good person."

"Good people do bad things sometimes."

"Not her."

He was adamant. There was no point in arguing. I had other things on my mind anyway. "You still keep your sniper rifle, don't you?"

"I—what? Yes, of course. Of course I keep it. I haven't used it in years. That alone would put paid to this preposterous frame-up idea of yours."

"Could I take a look at it?"

"Why?"

"If what I'm thinking is true, it gets you off the hook and no one will ever have to know anything about you and Daisy."

"Fine. Follow me."

He had stored the weapon in the back of his bedroom closet, behind a rack of seldom-worn evening clothes draped in dry cleaners' plastic. When he pulled out the rifle, I saw a look of baffled chagrin twist his face. He held out the gun as if it had turned into a large snake. He almost dropped it and let it slither away, but he was too good a soldier for that.

"What the hell? How is this…What is going on here?"

"It's not your rifle, is it David?"

"It certainly is not! How could you know that?"

"I didn't know. I guessed."

"You guessed that someone stole my rifle."

"Borrowed it. They've been trying to return it for weeks."

He stood very still. "The prowlers."

"They're not trying to take anything. They're trying to put something back."

"But—oh, of course. The ballistics! The round and the casing won't match the barrel of my rifle. That would prove I had nothing to do with the killing and wreck the plan. So… this thing was slipped into my closet as some kind of decoy, on the off-chance I went looking for my tuxedo, and all they had to do was replace it with the real thing when they were done."

"That's turned out to be kind of a problem for them."

"If I hadn't noticed…if you hadn't come…if they had managed to—"

I patted his shoulder. "That's a lot of ifs."

His mood shifted again, now that he knew he was in the clear. He was a mercurial old geezer. "I want my rifle back."

"We'll get it. I promise."

"And I want to know who did this."

"So do I."

"You have to find out! Be tireless! Leave no stone unturned!"

"That's my job. Turning over the stones. And I'm actually pretty good at it."

"Yes, you are. Of course you are. You're a tribute to your profession. I'm sorry. This has been quite a shock." He extended the rifle to me. "I suppose you'll be wanting this. As evidence. It's of no use to me."

I took the big gun, which was surprisingly heavy. "Thanks, David. Maybe we can trace it."

"You're sure you don't want some coffee? It's George Howell Mamuto AA—freshly ground."

"No, thanks. But I would like to check your iTunes account."

He stare was almost comically blank. "I don't have an iTunes account."

"Yes, you do."

We went into his office. I handed him back the rifle, and booted his computer. I noticed all his passwords on a notepad next to the keyboard. Hacking into his system wouldn't exactly have been a challenge—more like walking into unlocked house.

He looked over my shoulder as I scrolled down through his library. "There! You can tell it's not mine! No Beatles, no Dave Clark Five. I was a big fan of the Dave Clark Five. No Brubeck. No Miles Davis. And no Schubert! This was sloppy work. I would never own a music collection that excluded the B flat and the E flat trios."

"So, I take it you mostly listen to vinyl?"

"It's very hip now. According to Daisy. Everything old is new again. Except me."

"Can I take a look at your collection?"

"Of course."

All the African music from the iPod was there. He seemed authentically shocked. "I have never seen any of those records before. Besides, why would I have both?"

"People like to take their music with them. They listen while they're walking or driving, or working in the garden."

He sniffed. "Multi-tasking. A feat which human beings are incapable of. For your information. When I listen to music I sit in a comfortable chair properly placed in front of two speakers and I give that music my undivided attention. I am a longtime advocate of undivided attention, Chief Kennis. As—I suspect—are you."

"It helps in police work." I admitted.

"Well, there you have it. Clearly these…items…were placed here when the perpetrators stole my rifle."

"It certainly looks that way."

He handed me back the rifle. "I suppose we're done then."

"Pretty much. I have stones to turn over. And it would be best if I was gone before Phillipa gets back. Don't you think?"

"Yes, you're right. Good Lord. Go, go, go. I hate making up lies, and she never believes me anyway."

We walked out to the driveway and I thought—that house is overheated. It must cost them a fortune. The icy air felt good. I set the big rifle on the backseat of my cruiser, shook the old man's hand, and drove back into town. I knew the first stone I was going to turn over.

She was working as a guidance counselor at the high school.

Chapter Fifteen

The Heiress

My main concern as I pulled into the slant parking in front of the high school was not running into my daughter. Caroline had reached the age where the simple fact of my physical presence mortified her. We had to coordinate show times if there was a movie playing we both wanted to see, so there would be absolutely no chance of running into each other at the theater. Since The Starlight had started running the same movies as the Dreamland, I often solved the problem by going to the smaller venue and getting dinner first at the White Dog. School would be trickier. But the corridors were empty. Class was in session.

I ran into Alana Trikilis carrying a hall pass for the bathroom. She seemed oddly nervous, but perhaps she didn't want to be seen with me either, and for much better reasons than my daughter. "My dad needs to talk to you," she said.

"He already did."

"Oh, good, great. He was freaking out."

"It's fine, now. We spoke. But I wanted to ask you…"

"I have to go. Sorry!"

Then she sprinted down the hall away from me. Something was definitely up with her, but I didn't have time to worry about it. I found Daisy DeHart's office just ahead of the bell, and was safely inside when the corridors filled for the between-class rush.

She stood up behind her desk when I knocked on the half-open door. I paused a moment, off-balance, just looking at her. I'm sure she got that a lot.

She was small, maybe five-foot-two, her body lush and lean, like some dancers I'd known who'd had to give up their ambitions because of their proportions. Her face, framed by short blond hair, had a smudged wounded beauty, like a French film star from the sixties, a Bardot sensuality. Those wide blue eyes shifted something inside you, the way a small tremblor shifts the foundation of house. I could imagine the cracks in the walls. This woman could do damage, and without even meaning to, without even noticing, though I had a feeling she noticed everything. She registered my awkward silence, and the reason for it.

She smiled to set me at ease. "Can I help you?"

"Yes—thank you. I'm Police Chief Henry Kennis."

"Daisy DeHart." She stepped around her desk and shook my hand. "I've seen your picture in the paper. And in *People* Magazine."

"That was unfortunate." Briefly a celebrity after the Preston Lomax affair, I had been included in what my ex-wife called "the nobodies section" of the magazine's Most Beautiful People issue that year. I'd been trying to live it down ever since. We took our positions, facing off on either side of the desk.

"Is this about one of the kids?"

I wasn't sure where to begin. It was a delicate situation. Part of me wanted to say, *"Alana Trikilis told me that you're in charge of procurement for a drugs and pornography ring on the island. How do you square that with your job as a guidance counselor?"* But I had promised Alana I wouldn't do that, and the motive behind that promise was a sound one. If Daisy was involved, the last thing I needed to do was alarm her, without a real case. My grandfather used to say, "If you want to catch the roaches in the kitchen sink at night, don't turn on the lights first." I didn't need these bugs scuttling back down into the drain. If Alana was right, they'd already destroyed most of the evidence by torching their own studio.

Best to skip the innuendoes and preliminaries. "No," I said. "This has nothing to do with the students, unless you know where Jill Phelan got the drugs that put her into a coma."

Her gaze was level, as if she knew all the fabled "tells" for lying. "I wish I did." I let her squirm for a few moments. "I'm not sure what you want to—"

"It's about David Lattimer."

"Oh, God."

"You're his alibi for the Todd Macy killing, but effectively he doesn't have one. Because he'd rather go to jail than have his wife find out about the two of you."

"The two of us?"

"Your affair."

She laughed, more of a short incredulous snicker, as if I'd suggested she'd gotten a nose job, or colored her hair. She was blond to the roots and "rhinoplasty" was the last word you'd ever associate with that face.

"He's in love with you," I persisted.

"He's a million years old! He looks like the Crypt Keeper."

"But you were with him that afternoon, in his truck. You were behind the wheel. You forgot to reset the driver's seat."

"Oh, shit."

"What was going on, Daisy? This could be important. For both of you."

"Is this really necessary?"

"It's crucial."

I sat and waited.

She pulled her hair back with both hands, drawing her fingers over her scalp like a giant comb. She yanked it and then began. "We had a brief…I don't even know what to call it. A flirtation."

"Did you sleep with him?"

"No! Never!"

"Sorry. Go on."

"I kissed him once. That was a mistake. It was the night we met, at a fundraiser for the Maria Mitchell Association. He's on the board. I was there with—a friend."

"Andrew Thayer?"

"How did you know that?"

"Lattimer wrote a letter to you. He never sent it. But he mentioned the idea of killing Todd Macy and burning down Andrew's cottage as a way of...leveling the playing field, I guess you could say. Getting rid of his rivals. It was a crazy fantasy. That's why he never sent it. But he knew Andy was thinking about moving off-island and he figured losing the cottage might be the tipping point."

"This just gets worse and worse."

"So, you were at the fundraiser..."

"Andy left early. Something about short-selling on the Nikkei. And I wound up talking to David. He was charming, I was a little tipsy, he invited me outside to look at the stars. 'Maria Mitchell would approve,' he said. And he kissed me and I let him."

"Despite that Crypt Keeper thing."

"I guess I have father issues."

"More like grandfather."

"Thanks so much. We saw each other from time to time, when his wife was away, but I never let it go any further than that. High school rules, I told him. No getting past second base." She saw the look on my face and crossed her arms over chest, pressed a palm to her mouth. Finally she dropped it to her throat. "He said I made him feel like he really was in high school again. It was very—flattering."

"But you broke it off."

"That day—in the truck. It was getting out of control. He was talking about leaving his wife. So, yes. I had to end it."

"And that's all. You haven't seen him since."

"Just from a distance."

I sat back, listening to the dim thunder of a basketball game in progress in the gym down the hall. "Tell me about your father."

"You're not my shrink."

"Sorry. You're right."

"And he's not my father. He's my stepfather. My father's long gone. I never even knew him."

I stood up. "I think we're done here for now." I pulled a card out of my pocket, and dropped it on the desk blotter. "Call me if you think of anything else."

She sat forward. "I just did."

"Okay."

"That day—the day you're talking about…that's David's alibi for the shooting. It has nothing to do with Andrew's cottage. He still could have done that. He lives right next door. He didn't need the truck to set that fire."

"Are you serious?"

"Yes. Totally. He wrote about it in that letter. You just told me."

"All right. It's a good point. We'll look into it."

"You better—before he burns down someone else's house."

"Thanks, Daisy. We'll be in touch."

I walked out of the school, sat down in my cruiser, but I didn't drive away. I thought about the days just before my divorce, stalking out of the house, jumping in the car and gunning it. It felt good to be on the road, but where was I going to go? Through 'Sconset, around Sankaty and down Polpis Road to town, then back again, or west to Madaket. A U-turn at Millie's Bridge, back into town and then another spin around the Milestone Road-Polpis loop? I might as well have been a lion, pacing circles in his cage.

That was how I felt now—going around and around getting nowhere. I didn't believe David Lattimer had committed any crime more serious than attempted adultery, but I was no closer to finding the real criminals. I had Alana's word about Daisy DeHart, but no hard evidence. I knew she was lying about things but I had no idea which things, no idea what she really felt about Lattimer or where the old man's rifle was hidden, or who might have taken it, or why they killed Todd Macy, or anything else.

No doubt about it: the Nantucket Police Department was batting zero.

But then I searched the LoGran cottage. It wasn't a home run, but as Chuck Obremski always used to tell me, you don't always need a home run.

Sometimes it's enough, just getting a man on base.

Chapter Sixteen

Nancy Drew and Captain Tweedy

The reported break-ins were a good excuse to poke around the place. With Blount connected to Thurman, both of them now tied, however faintly, to Andrew Thayer's cottage, the incidents at the LoGran compound seemed ominously well-timed. I didn't believe in coincidence, and if Sue Ann Pelzer shared my skepticism, she probably suspected I was chasing hunches, following up on leads I didn't want to share. Why else would the police chief himself show up for a minor burglary call? I had my answer ready to that. The NPD was a full-service institution and I was a hands-on leader. But Sue Ann never asked, and if she thought my presence was inappropriate, she never let on.

I followed her out the big French doors, walked across the wide deck, and down beyond the sweep of lawn to the house they all referred to as "the cottage." It was more than enough house for me and the kids—a master bedroom downstairs, two bedrooms upstairs. Big sunny kitchen and living room, two and half baths—all decorated white on white, with beadboard walls, granite counter tops, six-light double-hung sash windows, gleaming heart pine floors—the new-money Nantucket standard.

"We looked around when the policemen left—all three times. We never saw a thing. Some drawers opened, some cabinets messed up. Someone turned on Doug's computer, but of course it's password protected. Whoever it was, they never had much time in here."

"And Mr. Pell said nothing was missing."

"Well…the cut crystal oil and vinegar set was gone, but we assumed the housepainters took it. Turned out one of the cleaning girls had put it in the wrong place! So that was a big non-event."

"Do you mind if I poke around for a few minutes?"

"Be my guest. And you are. Anyone who sets foot on this property is my guest. As long as they're invited! Can I get you some coffee?"

"I'm good, thanks."

"I'll be up at the house—just use the intercom. Dial six and I'll come running."

I went through the place carefully, unmaking and re-making the beds, checking under the mattresses and the rugs, going through the drawers and cabinets, paging through the books on the shelves. I tramped back out to my cruiser, pulled a packet of ninhydrin from the trunk, and dusted for prints. I e-mailed pictures to the station, and ten minutes later Charlie Boyce had run them and come back with the news I expected: Blount and Sue Ann, nobody else. LoGran had their prints on file. Whoever broke in was smart enough to wear gloves.

Finally I did my favorite part of the job—crawling around on my hands and knees. I had crawled over the whole upstairs and was halfway through the kitchen when I found it: a tortoise-shell hair clip, stuck between two floor boards and almost invisible. I pried it out with tweezers and dropped it into a plastic evidence bag.

I stood up, feeling that first rush of excitement, with Obremski's old baseball analogies running in my head. Two outs, maybe—but now I had a man on first. Not bad.

The inning wasn't over yet.

The next hit came when I least expected it, at my daughter's high school chorus concert. As a ninth grader, Carrie was thrilled to be part of the ensemble, and she'd been accepted into the girls' a cappella group ("The Accidentals") as well. Attending these performances—Tim was in the middle school band and they often played a double-bill—had become one of the secret ordeals of parenthood. The band was never in tune, the songs the chorus sang bored me…and then there were the plays, the basketball games and, even more excruciating, the parent-teacher evenings and orientation sessions. Tim's math teacher this year confessed, haltingly, that he had "never actually taught in a school setting" before. I had no answer for that one, but Todd Macy's help had come to the rescue.

One step inside the school building, and I got the creeps. I had always hated school, myself. But of course there was no getting out of these affairs. I had tried reading during one of Carrie's concerts, once—but even though I was sitting way in the back of our new shiny auditorium, my eagle-eyed daughter busted me.

I usually sat with Miranda and we caught up on police gossip and real estate while the audience gathered. We never got much chance to talk, since everyone took the opportunity to accost me about zoning violations, beach permits, noise violations, dog-leash scofflaws, and other complaints.

On this evening, Alana Trikilis' mother, Susan, was at the front of the line. Some rogue trash hauler was poaching her husband's Madaket route, and when he confronted the guy, it turned out he spoke no English. Nothing about the letter or David Lattimer, so it looked like Sam was keeping his word. If he had said anything to his wife, the urge to spread the gossip and double-check the story with me would have been irresistible.

"This other driver was from Eastern Europe somewhere," she said. "Sam was scared."

"Well, the next time it happens, tell him to say nothing and get the guy's license plate. We'll take it from there."

"Thank you. Thank you so much. We've just been so—"

I interrupted her. "Susie…what's that in your hair? That clip?"

"It's a Goody—that's the manufacturer. They went out of business or something. You can still find the short ones, but these long ones…you have to pay twenty dollars for them on eBay. And then my daughter steals them! Once you have daughters, you can't call a single thing your own."

"Especially when they wear your shoe size," Miranda chimed in. Susie laughed and they compared gripes until the concert began.

I stopped listening. I had two men on base now. And I could feel the charge in my blood.

◇◇◇

I pulled up next to Alana as she was walking home from school the next day.

"Get in."

She could obviously hear the iron in my voice. She climbed into the front seat beside me and we drove to the surfside parking lot in silence. The wide field of macadam was deserted at this time of year. I pulled up to the gate beside the concession stand and we sat looking down across the dunes at the milling gray ocean.

"Chief…?

"I found something of yours."

I reached into my pocket and tossed her the evidence bag with her mother's Goody hair clip inside.

"I'm not—it's…where did you find this?"

"In the kitchen at the LoGran cottage on Eel Point Road. What were you doing there, and how did you get in and…what the hell were you thinking? Breaking-and-entering is a felony, Alana."

"I didn't break. I just entered. I had the key."

"You stole the key."

"I borrowed it."

"Without permission."

"And then I put it back in the fake rock. That's not exactly stealing is it?"

"Let's not split hairs. You didn't have the alarm code, so you didn't have time to steal anything."

"I wasn't trying to steal anything! I was looking for evidence, just like you. Except you weren't. Until I got there."

"So it's Nancy Drew and Captain Tweedy."

She smiled. "I was thinking more…Maddy Clark and Police Chief Blote."

"'You keep your nose out of police business, young lady!'" Then I did my best Blote *sotto-voce* double-take: "What did you find?"

Her brief laugh sounded more like a sigh. "Nothing. That's why I kept going back. Finally, I gave up."

I turned off the engine, cracked a window, let the low grumble of the ocean and the sharp salty wind into the car. "How did it start?"

"I followed Doug Blount after he threatened me, and I saw where he lived and where he hid the key. That's all. For all the good it did me."

"Jesus, Alana."

"Chief—"

"You have to stop this. I understand your intentions, but—"

She twisted around to face me. "He's not the only one I followed."

"Oh, God."

"Jared and I have been tracking that McAllister guy and the Land Bank guy, Forrest. Last Saturday they were together. They had a big argument outside the Rose & Crown. I heard them say 'blue heroin.'"

"Blue heroin?"

"I think it may be the street name for the opiate they're getting kids hooked on. Have you ever heard of it?"

I shook my head. "No. But I'll ask around."

We sat in silence for a minute or two. The wind pushed at the car. "Are you going to arrest me?"

"No. I handed you the evidence, and no one else noticed it. But you have to stop this. It's dangerous. I don't want you getting hurt."

She looked down. "Okay."

"Promise?"

"Promise."

"On your *Calvin and Hobbes* collection?"

"How did you know…? Okay." Of course she loved *Calvin and Hobbes*. She was a cartoonist. "On My *Calvin and Hobbes* collection."

"Okay."

"Okay."

But she was lying, and both of us knew it.

She could no more quit than I could.

Chapter Seventeen

Onward and Upward with the Arts

I mentioned the hair clip incident to Jane when I drove out to Polpis for our private reading, dismissing it as a minor footnote to the other cases I was working on.

"What if all the cases are really just one case?" she said. "That's how it would happen in my books."

I laughed. "Yeah, well, unfortunately, things don't work out that neatly in real life."

"But this is small-town real life, Henry, where everyone knows everyone else and everyone's hooked up in all kinds of odd ways. It's not like a city."

"I guess."

She smiled. "You'll see. It's all connected."

Driving out to Jane's cottage in Polpis that evening, I wondered if she might help me with some of these cases. I was at an impasse; she had lived on the island most of her life. She was smart and intuitive. If nothing else, writing mysteries honed her ability to imagine scenarios and poke holes in them. Every crime is a story and I could tell from her reading at Emily Grimshaw's that she had a gem-quality story sense. Maybe I had told myself that this evening was going to be more of a professional consultation than a romance, because of Brad Thurman. I didn't even know if they were still together and I wasn't sure how to ask. I thought of my mother watching TV with me when I was a kid, badgering her about plot points. She would always smile and say, "Let it unfold."

That sounded like good advice for tonight also. Even if Jane had ended things with Brad, the hangover from a toxic love affair could linger, and I wasn't as finished with Franny Tate as I should have been. It felt like a potential mess waiting to happen, "a regular monkey's tea party," as my grandfather liked to say. Edna St. Vincent Millay started an affair with one of her readers after a particularly well-written fan letter. That was the way to do it: translate the love of words into a more urgent carnality without ambivalence or complications.

The drive from town settled my nerves. After the last sprawl of commerce—a lumber yard tucked into the trees on the right, our local Ford dealership on the left—vanished around a curve in the road, and the last ostentatious real-estate boondoggle fell behind me, Polpis Road turned into one of the most beautiful drives in New England. With the moors on one side and the grand old clapboard mansions allowing glimpses of the harbor between walls and hedges on the other, I could feel myself escaping the gravitational pull of the busy town and the crowded "mid-island," with its convenience stores and gas stations. Much of the island had been spoiled—even despoiled—but the farther out you cruised along Polpis Road, the less it seemed to matter.

These old houses weren't going anywhere, though the cars in the driveway had changed (more MINIs and smart cars; fewer Hummers and Expeditions). The moors and the bogs were protected by the Land Bank and the Conservation Commission. This was Old Money country, shabby with a haughty indifference to the granite counter top and the Sub-Zero refrigerator: no one was selling, or moving, or installing a climate-controlled wine cellar or a state-of-the art digital screening room. Instead, they would keep on fishing in Coskata Pond, drinking Bloody Marys on the deck, and complaining about the food at the Yacht Club.

It was fitting that Jane found a place for herself out here, surrounded by the wealthy, but living hand-to-mouth, tucked away in a four-hundred-dollar-a-month cottage among the wild blackberries and the poison ivy. She discovered a few years ago that she was actually related to the owner, going back five generations of landed gentry. The thought clearly terrified his family when she mentioned it over cocktails one evening, as if she were going to rise up with a cold-eyed gang of Boston lawyers and demand her share of the old man's property. Nothing could have been further from the truth. She had been living out there for ten summers and it pleased her to find an ancestral connection to her cantankerous but affectionate landlord. Two years ago he installed a wood stove and now she took the place year-round, ending the "Nantucket shuffle" of seasonal housing that had plagued her since she graduated from college.

I pulled into the bluestone driveway, rolled past the main house, and down to the cottage. The lights were on in the dusk and when I climbed out of the car, the silence of the place closed over me like water. I breathed it like a fish, a new creature in a new world.

"This place is gorgeous," I said when she came to the door. "I could feel my blood pressure dropping about ten points a mile as I drove out here."

She smiled, stepping back to let me inside. "I know. The problem is, you never want to leave."

Her hair was down, a frizzy blond cloud that softened her sharp features, as the gray cashmere cardigan buttoned over a flimsy tee-shirt and loose jeans accented the girlish allure of her body.

She pushed at her hair nervously, pressing the wild mane to her scalp. "I'm sorry. I look awful. My hair gets crazy when it's humid like this."

"I think it looks great."

"It looks horrible. It's okay. You can say so. It looks like I stuck my fingers in a wall socket. The Mad Scientist look"

"I like it."

"You're out of your mind."

"Lucky for you."

She squinted at me. "We'll see about that." Then she noticed the bag in my hand. "What did you bring? I'm starving. I was fine until five minutes ago, then my blood sugar dropped. I was about to start eating shredded wheat out of the box."

"Ugh. That would definitely have spoiled your appetite for the shelled lobster, homemade red cabbage coleslaw, and potato salad I have here. Plus the baguette and the Ecuadoran raspberries. Oh, and a bottle of Pinot Grigio. No, wait a minute. Two bottles."

"Sounds like a wild night you've got in mind. Good thing Sam's with his dad."

I lifted out one of the bottles. "Onward and upward with the arts."

The cottage was a simple rectangle maybe fifteen feet by forty. I stepped into a high raftered, open-stud living room, with yachting pennants, old quarter boards and fishing rods decorating the beams, 1920s Nantucket movie theater one-sheets (Rose Tremaine in *Private Lives* at the 'Sconset Casino), family photographs, and equestrian prints tacked to the wooden walls. The cracked cement floor was softened by sisal rugs, set about with an old velour couch and white wicker chairs. A camp bed with stuffed animals took up the front corner of the room, with a hinged screen folded and leaning against the wall for privacy. "That's where Sam sleeps," Jane said. I had a similar ad hoc arrangement, sleeping on my couch so my kids wouldn't have to be roommates.

I set the food down and pulled off my coat. The wood stove fire glowed red behind the isinglass and took the chill off the night. A dusty television sat on an antique desk between two windows, but it looked as though it hadn't been used in years. Beyond the dining room table, a raised step led to the kitchen, with doors into the bedroom and the bath. Jane had lit candles and hurricane lamps. The place was cozy, lost in time.

I stood looking around, taking it all in.

"It's like some relic of another era," I said.

She smiled. "Just like me."

We walked into the kitchen and I unpacked the bags.

"And what era would that be?" I asked her. "When would you like to be living? The eighties?"

She gave a little puckered wince, as if she had just stepped into a cloud of gnats. "God, no."

"The seventies?"

"Maybe. The seventies had great clothes and movies."

"The sixties?"

"Closer." She handed me a corkscrew and while I was working it she said, "I guess…the fifties. No—the late forties. Just after World War Two. Men wore hats and kids didn't wear bike helmets. Cars had fins. People drank scotch out of little flasks at football games. The Giants played the Polo Grounds. Everybody smoked and nobody cared. John O'Hara world. That's my era."

"I have a fondness for Hollywood in the eighties. David Lattimer would say I miss being a kid."

"You must have had a cool childhood."

"It was weird—bicoastal. I spent vacations in L.A.—enough time to get hooked on my dad's world, but not enough to really be part of it. I was always on the outside. Which was actually okay, because my dad's new family was seriously fucked up. My half-sister was overdosing on LSD, my stepbrother tried to drown me in the swimming pool, and my stepmother was right out of Grimm's fairy tales—the uncut German version. None of this smiley-face American shit. I think she secretly wanted to chop me up and stick me in a batch of cookies. But she wouldn't be caught dead baking, and it's not the kind of thing you can ask the Filipino chef to do unless you're planning to give him a really big bonus, which was not her style."

She laughed. "It can't possibly have been that bad."

"That's why I can't write about that stuff. No one believes it. No one believed the Mary Tyler Moore character in *Ordinary People* and I was like…'that bitch is Mary Poppins next to my stepmother.' I'm not saying it was totally crazy and corrupt. But there's a reason why my real brother and I both went into law enforcement."

"Well, my parents stayed married and I sometimes wish they hadn't. My mom deserves a better life. She—I don't know. She chose it, I guess. She chose him. But I don't think she really knew what her choices were. She could have walked away. She almost did a few times."

"But she came back."

"My dad writes a mean love-letter."

I poured two glasses of wine, handed her one and made a toast.

"To our crazy families, who made us the writers we are today."

I cut the lobster into the bunch of mescal greens Jane had in the fridge, and made an olive oil and vinegar dressing while she put the baguette in the oven and set the table.

We sat down to eat and Jane said, "What made you the policeman that you are today? That's the real question."

"I actually solved a murder when I was fifteen years old. But that's a long story for another time. The real beginning was a few years before that."

She took a bite of bread, chewing expectantly.

"Our apartment got robbed when I was twelve. The place was trashed. This was like…July, 1984. It happened over the weekend—we'd been staying in this little house in Rockland County that my mom rented in the summers. We got back Monday morning and the front door lock was broken. My mom called the police and these two cops showed up, a middle-aged guy and a younger woman, who was some kind of trainee. The guy, his name was Officer O'Donnell, Alan O'Donnell I found out later, he was just—cool."

Jane sat forward. "How so?"

"Very polite but very observant. Like my mom opened the fridge to make some coffee for them before she remembered that the burglars had smashed her coffee machine. Mr. Coffee. So O'Donnell took the other cop aside and sent her for takeout. When she got back, he took the black one, the woman got regular and he gave me an Orangina, my favorite soda. It was still called Orelia then. I was surprised, and so was my mom—hers was half-and-half, no sugar. He noticed the half pint of light cream and the Orelia when she opened the fridge…for all of five seconds. So my mom said, 'No sugar?' and he said, 'Just a guess. Most people who keep half-and-half use it for their coffee and I didn't see a sugar bowl.' She smiled for the first time that day and said, 'Well, you guessed right, Officer O'Donnell.' By that time I was hoping she'd marry him. My mom had lots of bad boyfriends in those days, and I noticed this cop wasn't wearing a wedding ring."

"Did she wind up dating him?"

"No, no. A more observant kid would probably have caught the dent on his ring finger. O'Donnell never wore his wedding ring to work, but he was married, all right. Twenty years, five kids, and three grandchildren—at age forty-seven."

"They were busy."

I shrugged. "Catholics. There's more. He showed up two weeks later with my mom's Betamax. He had noticed one of the tapes in the mess on the living room floor. When they caught some burglar and went through his stash he found the tape-player. Not too many people still had Betamax stuff in 1985. He said, 'You're a diehard, Ms. Kennis. I like that.'"

"So whatever became of Officer O'Donnell?"

"He was killed in a shootout two years later."

"Oh, sorry."

"We went to the funeral. There were like five thousand people there. Not just cops. Lots of people, regular people, people he'd helped."

Jane finished her wine. "So you wanted to be Officer O'Donnell?"

I stared down her smile. "I could do a lot worse."

"My father always said police work draws the best people and the worst people and not much in between."

"Most of us are just muddling through. You should use that line in one of your books, though."

"Actually I did, this morning."

She read me a little of the new book after we did the dishes and I offered a poem or two.

The book was called *Poverty Point*—all her novels used Nantucket landmarks and geographical points of interest as titles. This one referred to the spit of land next door to the Island Home, a gorgeous piece of property with a million-dollar view of the harbor and Coatue. The book involved a classic Nantucket land-grab with greedy developers trying to buy the Island Home property and turn it into a water-view subdivision that would net them millions. But a wily old resident starts to figure it out. Soon he and his spunky granddaughter—the girl who left her husband in the first chapter Jane had presented at Emily Grimshaw's salon—die under suspicious circumstances. At least the circumstances are suspicious to Maddy Clark. The Nantucket police can't be bothered, as usual.

I wasn't in much of a position to protest, with my own desultory investigations fizzling around me right and left. And so we came to her suggestion that all my cases might be tied together somehow. We were standing at her door, me buttoning my coat against the sharp December night outside.

"This was fun," I said. "The one bright spot in a bad week."

She slipped her arm around my waist. "You could have a breakthrough any time. Just stay alert!"

She went up on her tiptoes and our lips brushed in an awkward kiss. I turned my face away, thought better of it, and then she did the same. Then I slipped on a wet paving stone and she grabbed me to keep me from falling.

"Well—good night," she said as I started away from the house.

"Good night. Hey, listen—"

A last smile before the door closed. "Don't worry," she said. "We'll do better next time."

And we did, though neither of us wanted to rush things.

The impasse with my cases continued through that dismal winter and Jane's notion of some sinister criminal conspiracy looked more farfetched and confabulated every day: a novelist's daydream, worlds away from the stubborn random mundane truth

But the murders kept coming.

Part Two: Shoulder Season

Chapter Eighteen

Spring Swell

"Learn from the ocean," Billy Delavane said. "It has a lot to teach you."

He stood next to Oscar Graham, the sand wet and cold under their bare feet. The wind blew steady out of the northeast. Oscar shivered, staring into the booming cauldron of crosscurrents.

Billy worked for Pat Folger, but Pat wasn't expecting him to show up this morning, with the first pulse of waves from a deep Atlantic storm pounding the south shore. For Oscar, it was different. He had a plum job, with guys no better or worse than him lined up to step into his shoes, as his boss loved to point out. Phil Holdgate, the most hated man at Island Resorts. When he said "Clock in by nine," he meant be in uniform and ready to jump by eight forty-five. Oscar glanced at his watch: eight o'clock. He closed his eyes against a lash of sand carried on the wind. He shouldn't even be here. But a chance to surf with Billy Delavane was too good to miss.

He turned to face the older man. "Okay, what exactly can you learn from the ocean?"

"You surf. You tell me."

Oscar shrugged. "Weak swimmers drown? Saltwater makes you puke? I knew that stuff already."

Billy put a hand to his stubble, rubbed his chin. He had a long bony face and deep-set brown eyes. He used them as a weapon. Oscar had seen him close down bar fights at the Chicken Box with nothing but that steady "it-would-be-messy-and-inconvenient-for-everyone-if-I-had-to-kill-you" stare.

"Come on, Oscar. Dig a little deeper."

Oscar shrugged. "Physically fit people have more willpower? Panic is dangerous? Things always look scarier when you're in the middle of them?"

Billy smiled. "Not bad. But you learn that last one the first time you work on a roof. They never seem that high from the ground."

"And the surf always comes up when you paddle into it."

"Yeah, ain't that weird? But there's more."

"So tell me."

A big set rolled through and they paused to watch it. You could barely see the last waves through the screen of wind-whipped spray.

"Sounds like a thunderstorm," Billy said. "God repeats himself. But I like that about him. Makes him more approachable."

"So what are the other lessons?" Oscar prompted.

"Okay. You got to move toward what scares you. You got to duck under the bad stuff and let it go by. You got to lean forward into the thing you flinch back from. You can do any stupid shit you want, but usually just once—like breathing under water. You got to enjoy life even when it's beating you up. Then there's the most important one: You got to watch the horizon and wait."

Oscar nodded. The wind gusted hard. "You going out?"

"You betcha."

Oscar stared out into the silt-gouged water, the dense brown swells reaching up and curling over as the wind streamed giant fans of spray from their crests. It was daunting, but he was eighteen years old and he wasn't going to stand on the beach watching the old man paddle out. You have to pick your humiliations. Maybe that's another lesson from the ocean, he thought sourly. It now offered a full curriculum in the weaknesses and limitations of the body and spirit.

Billy was strapping his leash around his ankle. "Let's go."

Before Oscar could answer, Billy charged across the beach and into the water up to his knees, flung himself onto his board and started paddling. Oscar knew if he didn't move fast he'd be hopelessly far behind, caught inside by big waves as Billy paddled over them. He picked up his board and followed. It was mid-May, a balmy morning, air in the mid sixties, water frigid as winter when it sluiced into Oscar's five-mil wetsuit.

He dug into the surging foam, crested a few small waves and then hit his first wall of white water. He tried duck-diving under it but these were storm waves. They were much too strong for that technique. His board was yanked away and by the time he had pulled it back by the leash, two more waves had tumbled over him, forcing him back toward shore while the cross-rip pulled him toward Madaket. The water felt dense and heavy and stubborn, charged with a malign new energy.

Billy was almost out of sight on his nine-foot longboard. Oscar paddled again, though he could see a steep choppy gray wall massing in the distance, beyond the foamy shore break-swell he was cresting. The big one broke and the horizontal avalanche tossed him off his board again, under the dark violent water. Cold scalded the tiny oval of his face not covered by his hood. It plucked the air out of his lungs. When he struggled to the surface after a few breathless seconds, an even bigger wave was breaking.

He gulped air and dove for the bottom.

He could feel the battering surge above him and the sharp tug of the leash against his ankle. For a second he thought either it would snap or his ankle would. Then he was sputtering to the surface again, wallowing onto the board and paddling. Miraculously, the water was clear and in a few minutes he was bobbing beside Billy, dizzy and panting.

"You made it," Billy said.

"Barely."

"Barely's good enough. That's another thing you can learn from the ocean, kid. Barely's just fine."

Before Oscar could answer, the old man was paddling for another wave. Oscar didn't mind. The rudeness was built into the sport. Conversations in the surf were fragmentary. If the waves were consistent enough, conversations never got started at all. Oscar tracked the top half of Billy, appearing and disappearing above the lip of the wave as he rode almost all the way into shore.

He paddled back out a few minutes later, wild-eyed and grinning. Oscar understood why the surfers used the word "stoked": someone had thrown a few logs on Billy's fire—or maybe doused it with gasoline. He was burning up. "That was great," he called out. "Did you see that?" A wave wasn't half as good if no one saw you ride it—even a jaded waterman like Billy was a little kid that way.

"It's all about decisions," Billy said when he'd caught his breath. A few more guys were paddling out into the lull. "Decision is action, that's the point. You grab a wave and stand up, you don't have time to think about it. Just like real life. Like now: your girl is in trouble. So you want to help her. But you're scared."

"What does the ocean say?"

"The ocean says, make up your mind."

They straddled their boards, floating on the low swells. The sky was clearing to the west. It was going to be a perfect late spring day: bright pristine sunlight, mild and dry.

Oscar knew he had to do something, with the argument he had overheard still playing in his head. But what? The problem wasn't new—it had been poisoning his life for more than six months. He couldn't help Jill—she was still in a coma and might never emerge from it. He had jumped her new boyfriend—and drug connection—Sam Wallace, screaming and kicking and punching him after a Whalers' game, but the other team members had dragged him off and Sam had broken his nose with one punch. No one had pressed charges and Oscar refused to explain the attack—the truth would only get Jill in more trouble, if she ever came back to the world. He let everyone think he was a hot-headed jealous ex-boyfriend. It was easier. The police never got involved, but Bissell wanted to expel him—and would have, if not for Ms. DeHart, who got his punishment knocked down to a three-week suspension.

Jared Bromley and Alana Trikilis had spoken to him during one of those long days at home. They were doing the detective work. They would find out what was really going on.

But they hadn't. And nothing had changed.

Until last night.

Again and again the question spiraled back at him: What was he supposed to do? Confront one of the most powerful men on Nantucket? And say what? Threaten him? But Oscar had nothing to back up a threat and you could tell that, just looking at him. Shame the guy? Trick him, somehow? Manipulate him into making a confession? But Oscar wasn't tricky. He had thought Ms. DeHart would help him, but he didn't know what to think of Ms. DeHart anymore.

He was stumped.

"Heads up," Billy said.

A big set was rolling in, steep walls of water. They were raw and aggressive, they wanted to drown you. That was Oscar's ocean: not a benign guru, but a pig-eyed bully who wanted to dunk you at the public pool.

He scratched over the first couple of waves. His arms were tiring and the ocean ahead was scooped into deep valleys and rising cliffs of brine. The water itself felt heavy, surly, unwilling to let him pass. The final wave was the biggest and he couldn't crest it. He abandoned his board and dove as deep as he could. Again, rolled and twisted underwater, clamped in the iron chill, he felt the tug on his ankle. The pain stopped suddenly. He felt a moment of stupid animal relief, then he realized his leash had broken.

He came up to the surface, trying to gauge his distance from the shore. Billy was paddling out, pushing Oscar's board along beside him.

"Lose something?" He slid it over across the gray water.

"You're nuts."

"And you're taking off on the next wave. Or what's the point?"

Before Oscar could answer, Bill shouted, "Here comes one! Start paddling."

"Billy—"

"Now!"

Oscar pulled himself onto the board and started paddling as hard as he could. The wave loomed behind him. When the moment came, the water felt utterly still. He was paddling but not moving, caught in an elemental trance of balanced forces, sucked back as he thrust forward. He windmilled his arms through the water—these last strokes were the most important. The wave picked him up and he felt the jolt. When you plugged into that live current, that band of pure energy moving through the water, when you were jabbed outward into the swirling roar of the abyss and started skimming across it, the thrill was an explosion of colliding opposites that made your heart burst: death and immortality, flight and free-fall, terror and joy.

Oscar jumped to his feet, leaning back away from the vertigo of the gray gulf in front of him: just what Billy had warned him against. He could feel himself falling backward, the board shooting ahead of him. Then the wave jacked up vertical and he plummeted down the face.

It took him half an hour to swim and body surf back to land. His board was waiting for him, forlorn as a beached porpoise. He picked it up and started the long walk back to the bluff where he had parked. He felt thrashed and humiliated. He should have felt miserable and frustrated. He'd felt that way often enough, crawling out of the surf. But not this morning. He actually felt good, despite the humiliation. He was on dry land; he had tried for the biggest wave of his life and caught it. He had wiped out, but he hadn't drowned.

It gave him perspective and clarity. When things are clear, decisions are easy. You know what's going to happen next because it's up to you, not someone else. At some point, struggling back to shore, it all became clear to him.

He would go to the police. Chief Kennis was a good man. He would know what to do. And now he would have the power to do it.

Oscar started jogging through the soft sand. Right now the most important thing was getting to work. They would fire him if he got there late, and he couldn't afford to lose this job.

◇◇◇

Oscar took the day to think about the situation, alighting on it from time to time throughout his hectic day, like a bird on a statue. But nothing changed, no new options occurred to him, and by the time he clocked out at five o'clock, he had settled the matter. All he needed was a little time to organize what he had to say, and a good night's sleep to fortify him. He'd make his notes, go to bed early, and show up at the police station first thing in the morning.

After work, he was out on the water again. The surf had subsided a little and the wind had dropped to a faint breeze. The ocean was tame and docile. He caught a couple of easy waves and then the swell seemed to die out completely. He blew out a long breath, kicking his rubber-clad feet through the icy water. Tomorrow, this would all be done.

He turned his back to the shore and applied himself to the ocean's most valuable lesson: face the horizon and wait.

Chapter Nineteen

A Probable Homicide

Oscar Graham's body was found floating in the saltwater marsh that edges Nantucket harbor in the early evening of May 24th, 2015.

I was attending a fundraiser at a mansion overlooking Polpis Harbor when I got the news. Normally, Kyle Donnelly would have handled the situation and filled me in on Monday morning—or Tuesday, in this case. But I knew Oscar Graham. I knew his family. We had become friends over the previous winter. Kyle knew how I felt about them. So I was the first call he made that evening, before the State crime-scene techs, before the ME, or the ambulance crew, before anyone. I respected him for that.

I made my apologies and slipped out of the house. In ten minutes I was at the creeks. Oscar Graham's body had been hauled up onto the pier that fronted the harbormaster's shack. Dave Fronzuto nodded to me; he had called in the discovery. I stood on the dock, breathing the low tide aroma. The marsh cordgrass and sea lavender shivered in the gentle breeze. I stared down at the young Jamaican boy. He had been so proud to take the citizenship test, when was it? Four months ago. He had just turned eighteen.

I remembered him grinning at me when he got his papers, saying "I bet I know more about America than you do now, Chief! I know who wrote the federalist papers! Do you?"

I did, but I didn't want to spoil the moment. "Tell me."

"Alexander Hamilton and James Madison! And John Jay."

Most people forgot about John Jay. I smiled, shook Oscar's hand. "I'll take your word for it, kid."

That huge, face-splitting grin was what I remembered now, looking down at the vacant features. Those wide excited eyes. They were open this evening, but Oscar was gone. Elvis has left the building. I felt tears coming on like a chill. I crossed my arms against my chest, and ground my teeth together. The spasm passed.

"Looks like a drug OD, Chief," Kyle said. He was standing just behind me.

I shook my head. "I don't think so."

"The ME's flying in from Sandwich tomorrow. We'll know then."

"Barry Tupper?"

Kyle nodded. "He needs to test the hair follicles. They show the history of drug use. If he was clean until today…"

"Then he got a bad load on his first try."

I stared down at Oscar's body, thinking of the easygoing kid who had insisted on driving me around town the day he got his license, finishing with a parallel parking display on India Street. That had been a little nerve-wracking. I felt the burn of tears rise and subside again.

"Maybe," I said. "Or maybe someone killed him."

I walked away from the others and stood at the edge of the dock, watching sunset gild the harbor, the clutter of boats, almost every mooring taken already. Two stand-up paddleboarders negotiated the still water between the fingers of swamp grass.

It seemed like an immense distance from that lavish Polpis mansion to the gray planking of the town pier, from those animated pink-and-white faces nibbling blue fish pâté and sampling Spanky's Raw Bar to the body of the Jamaican boy behind me, pulled from the harbor. But maybe Jane Stiles was right. This was small-town America and every person and event seemed to touch every other one somehow. Everything that was going to happen that summer, and so much of what had occurred the winter before, had been manifest at the ProACKtive party that evening, like the landmarks in an unfamiliar city.

I remembered returning to Los Angeles as an adult, finally getting to know that immense urban sprawl. So many places I loved—the Nuart Theatre, Griffith Park Observatory, Will Rogers State Park, the Fat Burger stand in West Hollywood, Santa Monica pier, Book Soup, *The Burghers of Calais* at the Norton Simon Museum, El Cholo and La Barca, all seemed to exist as separate islands, disconnected from each other and the rest of the city. Much later, when I could follow Santa Monica Boulevard from the pier to the 405 freeway entrance a block away from the Nuart, drive south to the 5, get off at Vermont Avenue and roll south to La Barca, or north over the pass into the Valley and then east on the 134 to the Norton Simon, when everything fitted neatly into the grid I had learned from my Thomas Brothers maps, after I'd sat stakeouts on those streets, chased criminals through them, canvassed them door-to-door looking for eyewitnesses to a hundred crimes, I could still close my eyes and feel the city as an unknowable swamp, with the places I had loved since childhood floating unmoored, spot-lit in the mist.

That's how it happened on Nantucket that summer, as the case that dominated my life began to unfold. I was lost in an alien world, but everything I needed to see was right there in front of me, like the dome of Griffith Park observatory or the Santa Monica Pier Ferris wheel. Los Angeles was just a scatter of small towns lashed together with freeways; that's what someone from Nantucket could never understand. Cities, finally, aren't all that different from small towns, and neither are people in them. It's just easier to hide in the city.

Or so I thought. I'll lay these new landmarks out for you. Maybe you'll find your way between them better than I did. Or at least more quickly. Quick would have been good that summer.

It would have saved some lives.

Chapter Twenty

The Lay of the Land

The 'Sconset mandarins at the ProACKtive fundraiser wouldn't have particularly cared about saving lives. They were more interested in saving their property.

"I can't believe the way this town has turned against us," Howard McAllister was saying as I arrived. I imagined him waving a hypodermic syringe in front of a young girl's desperate face, explaining in explicit detail what would be required for the next scene. I couldn't put that together with the image of the man in front of me, who seemed like a very different and much more boring sort of villain.

He and a group of his pals crowded around Spanky's Raw Bar, hoovering up the oysters and littlenecks as fast as Spanky could get them open. Spanky was always my first stop at these shindigs, and often he was the only good reason to attend at all.

"Chief," he said.

"Hey, Spanky."

"Prince Edward Island oysters today. Flew 'em in this afternoon." He handed me one.

"Thanks." I took it in one swallow.

"Good?"

"Like eating the ocean."

He grinned as he worked. "Good one. You should write that down."

"You keep it." I took another oyster. "It could be your new slogan."

"Naaa. I don't think too many people would get it, Chief. They'd be like, 'The ocean? I'll be picking kelp out of my teeth. And that garbage island in the Pacific. No one wants to think about that."

"Good point."

I took another oyster and settled in, listening to Howard McAllister. He attended all these functions, holding court, overbidding at the silent auctions, drinking too many dark-and-stormys. I had pulled him over for a DUI just two weeks before.

"What will it cost to make this go away?" he had demanded, the words melting together like curls of grated cheese under the broiler.

"Wrong answer," I said. "You just attempted to bribe a police officer. That's a bigger crime than drunk driving. I can arrest you, impound your car, and search it without a warrant. But I'm in a good mood tonight, so I'll forget you said that and lock you up just for speeding, illegal lane changes, driving under the influence, and an expired inspection sticker."

"My caretaker was supposed to deal with that!"

"Well, he didn't."

He glared at me. "Do you know who I am?"

"Is that a real question? Because if so, you may be more disoriented than I thought." I glanced down at his license. "Your name is Howard McAllister. Does that help?"

We left his car by the side of the road and I took him to jail. He was out in an hour but the judge suspended his license and fined him a thousand dollars. The fine didn't matter, but losing his driving privileges had to hurt.

He glanced over at me now. "Well, if it isn't Chief Kennis! I've been meaning to thank you, Chief. I hired a car and driver after our little incident, and let me tell you—once you've had a chauffeur, you never go back! My father used to say 'everyone wants a car and driver.' I laughed at him, but he never touched a steering wheel after the age of thirty. Smart man."

"I'm sure the roads are much safer now," I answered mildly, taking another oyster.

"It's simply harassment!" Harry Nolan said. Alana had IDed him as an accomplice. Tall and hawkish where McAllister was shaped like a summer squash, they would have made a great comedy team, if either of them had a sense of humor.

"Excuse me?" I said.

"Cops pulling over innocent people, the town trying to stop the beach preservation project. After all we've done for this place!"

My old pal Pat Folger had sidled over, dressed in his usual formal getup of blue blazer and brown turtleneck sweater. The short, scrappy contractor had a big drink in his fist and it obviously wasn't the first one of the evening.

"Like what?" he said.

"Are you joking? We're the job creators! My addition alone employed dozens of people who—"

"Who you shipped in from off-island! So you could get the work done cheap! Oh, yeah—I see them getting off the boat every day, coming in at the airport. You brought your own paint crew from New Jersey!"

"I trust them."

"And they're living in your house for three months, pissing on your toilet seats and breaking your stemless wineglasses, and good luck flying them in from Newark or wherever the fuck, every time you need a touch-up. You've done jack shit for this island, pal. You buy from catalogs. You eat out and stiff the waiters. And now you're trashing beaches with your bullshit geotubes."

"Those geotubes are saving the bluff!"

"You're dreaming. That bluff's been eroding for a million years. Benjamin Franklin made them move Sankaty Light back a couple of miles because he knew what was happening, and that was two hundred years ago. The beach you're trying to save is crap now, the beaches around it are trashed, all because you spent too much on a house you never should have bought to begin with. Well, tough titty."

"How dare you talk to me that way! That is the most outrageous, disrespectful, arrogant—"

"You can push me around all you want, Nolan. That's what you're good at. That's where you got where you are today. Fucking with people. But you're fucking with the ocean this time, pal, and guess what? The ocean don't give a shit. The ocean's going to take your house, geotubes and all, and I'll be standing on Baxter Road cheering the day it happens."

"Don't get carried away, Pat."

Our host for the evening, Jonathan Hastings Pell III, had ambled over, nibbling at a cracker spread with caviar. I was sure he'd have something dismissive to say about the local constabulary—nothing had ever come from our house break-in investigation. But he was leaving me out of this conversation.

"I don't know about Harry here," he said, "but my friends on Baxter Road hired only local contractors for their homes. Scott O'Connor built Ray Davenport's house. Ron Winters just submitted blueprints for Sandy Farrell's new place in Shimmo. And that isn't just knee-jerk localism. These men are the best in the business. Look at the paneling in this house, the mantel, the banisters, the coffered ceilings. All made by Carter Mitchell in that extraordinary workshop of his out by the airport. Remarkable man. A true artist. But without people like us, he'd be hanging sheetrock in some Hyannis housing development. You won't see a man like Carter Mitchell slandering my friends and me. We're his bread and butter! He may be Botticelli or Michelangelo, but we're the Medicis! And he knows it."

A woman's voice piped up. "And the Medicis used slave labor, just like you do."

It was Jane Stiles. We had agreed to meet at the party, but she seemed to have arrived with her on-again-off-again boyfriend, Brad Thurman. For the moment she was ignoring both of us and I glimpsed something old-fashioned in her outrage: Eleanor Roosevelt confronting a robber baron.

Pell was amused. "So you think these lovely homes were built with slave labor?"

"Janey—" That was Brad. He was famous for his caustic temper, especially during the last third of a job with furniture and decorators arriving, big checks in the balance and the pressure of finishing on time jacked into the red zone, but today he was curiously mild-mannered. There was something beseeching in his tone. I could see this was one confrontation he very much wanted to avoid.

"It's okay, Brad," Jane said as she advanced on Pell. "Slave-owners provided room and board. People live here and make exactly enough to make the rent, pay for their truck, and buy groceries. What do you call that?"

"How about—the American Dream?"

Pell smiled, a glamorous high wattage affirmation full of white teeth that deepened his dimples and sparked his eyes. I thought of those three-way light bulbs, clicking brighter and brighter as you turned the switch. It captivated Jane, silenced her, and I realized—this guy has charisma. The real thing was rare. I could only think of one other specimen: Chief Bratton, the man who fired me from the LAPD in his last days on the job, and then caught up to me in the bright lobby of the new PAB to shake my hand and tell me, "That's a helluva a book, kid. Write another one." I told him I'd be sticking to poetry for the foreseeable future and he laughed that big-throated inclusive laugh, threw an arm over my shoulder and said, "You and the Le Eme pastry chef! That pair beats a full house."

I couldn't take offense. I could tell the idea really did amuse him. And I wanted to please him. Despite his financial shenanigans, his racist stop-and-frisk policies, and his possible complicity in the compromised investigation my book described; after he had ended my career, and knowing I would probably never see him again, I still wanted to please the guy.

That's charisma.

Jane Stiles clearly felt the same force of personality radiating from Pell. "I guess…" she said. "I just—I never really thought of it that way. But, well, yeah…I mean it's…"

"Let's get a drink." Brad took her arm and eased her away from the group. When Jane was a step or two ahead of him he turned back to his host. "Sorry," he mouthed silently.

Pell lifted his hands to his chest and parted them like a magician, about to make some small animal reappear out of a top hat. But Pell restored something else with that gesture, something more remarkable, if intangible—the atmosphere of cordiality. We were all at a party again. His self-effacing charm reduced the brief argument to the status of a hastily silenced cell phone or a spilled drink.

Brad smiled gratefully and disappeared into the crowd.

Then Pell turned to me. "This house is a perfect example." He waved a hand expansively, drawing the great room with its thirty-foot ceiling around us like a shawl. "When Preston Lomax died, the place was a shambles—people suing the estate, attaching liens to the property, going unpaid for months. It was a tragedy and a scandal. Someone had to take responsibility for that mess. By the time Preston's estate was settled, everyone clamoring for their proper remuneration would have gone bankrupt. So the company stepped in. More to the point, as CFO of LoGran Corporation, I stepped in, one of those oligarchs the young lady so stridently detests. Well, Chief, sometimes you need an oligarch. To paraphrase my friends at the NRA, sometimes the only answer to a bad plutocrat with a checkbook is a good plutocrat with a checkbook."

The other plutocrats chuckled at this and even I had to smile. The fact was, Pell had pulled a lot of people from the brink the previous winter, and some of them were my friends. I had been picking up my mail at the post office when Mike Henderson got his long-awaited twenty-three-thousand-dollar check. His bark of stunned elation made old Mrs. Tyroler drop her mail. We bent to help gather the scatter of envelopes, and as she walked away Mike showed me the check.

"People say money can't solve problems. They must have the kind of problems money can't solve. Like, incurable diseases or existential despair, or—whatever. I feel bad for them. But I'm lucky, Chief. My kind of problems, money solves just fine. Goddamn!"

He had practically danced out of the post office, and there was a lightness of spirit all over town that week, like a change in the weather, a second Indian summer in the middle of December. At the annual Christmas Eve red-ticket drawing, newly appointed Town Crier Sam Trikilis declared 2014 the island's most lucrative shopping season ever.

"That's the real trickle-down economics, Chief," Pell was saying now, between oysters. "Put money in people's hands and they spend it. Everybody wins."

I nodded. "The house looks good."

"We made some changes. More work for everyone. All time and materials, cost-plus. That's what the tradesmen like. No reason they shouldn't see a little profit after everything they went through."

"I'm glad it worked out."

"But it's just the beginning Chief. ProACKtive isn't just about rescuing one building project. We're going to rescue this whole island. Bring it back to life! Supercharge the downtown, turn it into a year-round destination resort. New people, new money, new spirit. That's our slogan, by the way." He winked. "You heard it here first."

"I don't know, Mr. Pell," I said. "I'm not sure Nantucket really needs to be rescued. You know, we have as many people living here now in the winter as we used to have in the summer. A lot of people actually wish the winters were quieter. They miss the old days. I think they're hoping all the people determined to save Nantucket will just give up and go away. Save another island. Save Haiti. That place could really use the help."

He studied me as he set down an oyster shell. "That's what 'some people' think. What do you think, Chief?"

"Well, for me, your new improved Nantucket just means crowds. Crowded parking lots, a crowded school, a crowded emergency room. A lot of houses, a lot of cars. And a lot of crime."

He patted my shoulder. "That's why we have a brand new police station—and an off-island big city police chief to keep everyone in line. I just wish you were willing to use the available tools."

Pell wanted Nantucket to buy surplus Army equipment—stinger missiles, automatic machine guns, even Bradley Fighting Vehicles, or BFVs as he called them, with a casual intimacy I found alarming. Lonnie Fraker agreed with him. We had fought about it, genteelly, at Town Meeting. I wasn't going to turn Nantucket into a police state, however much the State Police wanted me to. I preferred community policing, a comfortable relationship between my officers and the public. Call me crazy, but I have this idea that it might be a tad difficult to feel at ease with a policeman who's aiming a bazooka at you from the hatch of a tank. Still, Lonnie loved his toys and I knew Sheriff Bob Bulmer longed to deliver eviction notices and subpoenas with a SWAT team for backup.

I won that skirmish—the town voted against Pell's warrant article. He was cheerful about it outside the high school after Town Meeting. He shook my hand. "Democracy in action. You have to love it."

Talk around the raw bar, turned to who had discovered which new vintages at the recently concluded wine festival, and I eased my way out of the group.

"Book festival, film festival, wine festival," someone said, closing in on me from the side. It was David Trezize, the editor of our local alternative newspaper. "Dance festival, comedy festival, cranberry festival. You know what this island really needs, Chief? More festivals. We should have a festival festival, celebrating all the other festivals."

I nodded. "Sounds festive."

He took my arm and walked me over to the big fireplace, beside one of the white plaster mermaids that held up the mantel at either end. I noticed the matching smaller ones supporting the kitchen counter. They were a Grady Malone inspiration. David made a sour face, as if the creatures smelled bad, out of the ocean too long, unrefrigerated.

"What a genius. I asked Patty what makes Grady so wonderful and she said, 'He's deep.' Deep. About as deep as a Disney movie. All he needs is a Jamaican lobster on the hearth, singing 'Under the Sea.'"

"That would be a selling point, like those ten-thousand-dollar animated birthday cakes."

Before David could answer, my phone went off.

It was the harbormaster, calling me to the scene of the crime.

Chapter Twenty-one

The Reid Technique

The next morning, I was interviewing Oscar Graham's family when I got the call from the State Police. They had a suspect in custody and a confession in hand, less than twenty-four hours after finding the body. Fifteen hours, to be precise, as Lonnie Fraker informed me, with a smirk in his voice I could hear through the bad cell phone connection.

"It looks like this one is all wrapped up," he said, drawing out each of the last three words a little too long, with a little too much space between them, hitting the consonants with a guillotine precision.

"Who are we talking about?" I asked.

"Mason Taylor."

I had talked Mason down from a suicide attempt a couple of years before. I hadn't been convinced he could kill anyone, even himself. But a couple of years can make a huge difference, when you're growing from fifteen to seventeen. I thought of the poem we wrote together that afternoon, him comparing Alana Trikilis to a Nantucket rose—not the odorless industrial blooms you could buy in the Stop&Shop, but the real thing, fresh and fragrant, twined into a 'Sconset trellis on an July afternoon. Call me prejudiced, but I couldn't imagine what private tragedies and upheavals could have accomplished such a grim transformation.

From aspiring poet and love-smitten teenager to cold-blooded killer, between sophomore year and graduation?

His parents were still married, happily or not; his two older sisters remained in college. The sweet pit bull the family adopted continued to roam the island, chasing deer spoor and rabbits, but she was always found and returned. No one wanted to take a Selectman's dog to the pound.

Mason's romance with Alana had apparently cooled, but he was still willing to help her with her causes and crusades. Her testimony and Jared's concurred—Mason cared enough about Jill Phelan to confront the men who hurt her. He was willing to take brave, principled action to help Jill—I didn't see him turning around seven months later and killing her boyfriend. That was just crazy.

They were holding Mason at the State Police headquarters on North Liberty Street. "I'll be right over," I said. "Don't do anything until I get there."

"It's already done, Chief."

"Good, then rest on your laurels for twenty minutes. Do not transfer him to Barnstable. Not until I sign off on this."

"Wouldn't dream of it."

I disconnected, and I could see Lonnie canceling the Barnstable flight ten seconds later. But maybe I misjudged him. Lonnie brought out the cynic in me.

"What's going on?" Sylvester Graham asked me.

I slipped the phone into my pocket. "There's been an arrest."

Sylvester pulled Millie tighter on the old plaid couch. "They know who killed Oscar?" she said.

I pushed a breath out through my teeth. "They think they do. I don't know."

"But they must have evidence."

"They have a confession, Mrs. Graham."

"Then it's over."

"I hope so."

"It had to do with his job," Sylvester said. "I know it."

I sat down. Fraker could wait. "His job?"

"On the docks. They had him working as a security guard. For the yachts. Walking the piers. Making sure no one trespassed into the private areas where the big boats were tied up."

"Did he say anything to you?"

"He didn't talk much. Not to us. But he wasn't happy."

Millie sat forward. "Two days ago he told me, 'something's wrong and I have to fix it.' He wouldn't tell me what. Just that it was bad. I told him what his grandmother used to say—don't test the depth of a river with both feet. But Oscar never listened to his grandmother. Or me."

She pressed her lips together. It pulled her whole face tight and I could see tears glistening in her eyes. But she obviously didn't want to cry in front of the police. She was a large sturdy woman, the perfect bookend to her muscular, potbellied husband, still in his plaster-specked work clothes. He levered himself off the couch. "I'll walk you out."

At the front door he said, "We left Jamaica because it was dangerous. My brother's store in Kingston was robbed at gunpoint. Two weeks ago. And that scar on Millie's neck? Someone put a knife to her throat. Lucky she didn't know those men. If she had recognized them they would have killed her for sure. Cut her throat and left her in the road. So we came here. We wanted Oscar to grow up in a safe place."

"I'm sorry," I said. There was nothing else to say. I had no empty promises for him. Most murders go unsolved. "I'm so sorry."

"Just find who did this, mon. Find them and leave them to me."

I couldn't do that of course, but there was no point in telling Sylvester that. I could get him into the sentencing hearing, that was about the best he could hope for. I thought of Liam Phelan on his own private hunt for the people who had overdosed his daughter. A lot of angry fathers on Nantucket this summer. A lot of lost children. I didn't judge Liam or Sylvester. If someone had come after my kids I could easily join them, one more vigilante too full of rage and hate to wait for the sluggish workings of the law. That made my job pretty clear—speed things up. Get to work and do my job properly, before one of those wounded, grief stricken men went out and did it for me.

◇◇◇

"What can I say? Where there's smoke, there's fire."

I studied Lonnie Fraker's wide happy face, spread out in a toothy grin.

"Most of the time," I said. "Sometimes, there's just a guy smoking, who should have quit years ago."

"Speak for yourself, Mr. Nicorette. I never started. I don't drink, either. I try to lead by example. No vices."

"Except pride."

"Are you kidding?" he laughed. "I'm the most modest guy in the world. Nobody's more modest than me, Chief. Check out the cover of *Self-Effacement* magazine this month. I'm Man of the Year."

I sometimes thought Lonnie had no sense of humor. I enjoyed the surprise, and made a note of it. Underestimating people could be dangerous as well as dumb.

"So do you wear that big crown they gave you?"

"Tough one, Chief. Tough line to walk. I wear it but I try to look undeserving. You know…'What, this old thing? I hate it, but the magazine insists.'"

We both laughed. Then it was time to get down to business. "Okay, Lonnie. What have you got?"

"So much, Chief. So much more than I need. I have a confession on video and we printed the texts off the victim's phone for corroboration."

"Let me see the video."

"I have it all cued up. No popcorn or big candy bars, but nobody in the seat behind you talking on their cell phone, either. So it evens out. Come on back."

He had a screen set up in one of the back rooms. The folding metal chairs ranked as marginally more comfortable than the 'director's chairs' upstairs at the new Dreamland theater. I sat down while Lonnie killed the lights and slipped the DVD into the projector.

The screen brightened with the image of a rumpled Mason Taylor sitting alone at a folding table, hooked up to a lie-detector.

"Freeze it," I said. "Where's his lawyer?"

"He waived, Chief. Nothing to hide. Asking for a lawyer just makes you look guilty."

"And who gave him that idea?"

"Just a suggestion. We read him his rights and he signed off."

"The kid is seventeen years old."

"Actually, he turned eighteen on May tenth."

"So he's on his own."

"And he's your special protégé, Cyrano. Yeah, I know that story. Nobody cares. Mao wrote poems when he wasn't slaughtering anyone who looked at him sideways. And don't bother asking—the kid agreed to the polygraph. This is strictly by the book."

I sighed. "Roll it."

Off-screen, Lonnie says, "Your name is Mason Taylor."

"Yes."

"You live on Nantucket?"

"Yes."

"Were you born here?"

"Yes."

"Your father is a Selectman?"

"As you know."

"We're just trying to set the parameters here, Mason, asking basic questions to get a level for the machine."

"Okay."

"So you attend Nantucket High School?"

"Yes."

"And you knew Oscar Graham?"

"Everyone knows everyone at NHS."

"Were you friends?"

"We were friendly. I wouldn't say friends."

"He was Jamaican."

"He came here when he was five years old."

"He was black. Was that a problem for you?

"No."

"Not even when he started chasing your friend Jill?"

"She chased him. And she caught him. I moved on."

"No hard feelings?"

"It was mutual."

"I see."

"We were fine."

"If you say so. Was Oscar a heavy drug user, to your knowledge?"

"No. He never used drugs at all. To my knowledge."

"No Zohydro?"

"What's that?"

Lonnie laughs. "You've never heard of it?"

"Should I have?"

"Do you know the problem with Vicodin and oxycodone? Why people die when they OD?"

"No. Why should I?"

"They mix hydrocodone with acetaminophen or ibuprofen—Tylenol or Advil to you. So people die of liver failure. But Zohydrol is pure."

"That sounds good."

"Yeah, you think so? Well, twelve out of fourteen people on the FDA board didn't agree. But they cleared it anyway. Painkillers make big money and that's all anyone cares about these days. Except the cops on the street who have to deal with the roadkill."

"So this Zo—this other stuff. It's bad?"

"It's like that new wine that doesn't give you a hangover. No rules, no limits. No consequences. So people take more, and the high is sweeter. And then they die from the hydrocodone itself. Like Oscar Graham. And your gal pal. Who remains in a coma. She's still alive, anyway—no thanks to you."

"Me? What are you talking about? I didn't—"

"Where did you get the drugs? Which doctor was involved? You need a prescription for this shit."

"I didn't. I never even—"

"The doctor told you the overdose amount. I blame him as much as you. More than you. You're just a kid. You were angry. You were confused. He manipulated you. He used you."

"I don't know what you're talking about."

"Oscar got Jill into the drugs—he might even wind up killing her if she doesn't come out of that coma soon. Giving him the Zohydrol was just poetic justice."

"No, wait! I didn't—"

"But, see, it was the doctor's job, his civic duty, his moral imperative, to talk you out of that crazy plan. Not goad you on. Was he jealous too? Some kind of perv? Jill was a cute girl. Or was it just an experiment to him?"

"I don't know what you're—this is crazy."

"Why did you put Oscar's body in the harbor?"

"What?"

"Did you think it would sink?"

"I never—"

"Because they don't. Even when you weigh them down, they bob up eventually."

"Look, Mr. Fraker—"

"Captain Fraker."

"Captain Fraker—"

"Where were you on the night of May twenty-fourth?"

"What?"

"Saturday, May twenty-fourth. Between midnight and five a.m. Where were you?"

"I—"

"Just tell the truth!"

"I was home, in bed. I was asleep."

"That's your alibi."

"Yes."

"Your parents will back that up?"

"They were off-island for the weekend."

"So they left you alone?"

"Sure, why not? They—"

"I would call that an error in judgment."

"I didn't do anything."

"When the cat's away."

"Wait, stop. This doesn't make any sense."

"We're done for the moment. Take him off the machine, Carol. We're going to analyze the results. You sit tight."

Lonnie hit freeze frame and touched my shoulder. "We left him in there for three hours. Let him stew."

He started the DVD again. The timecode at the bottom right of the screen indicated that nearly four hours had gone by. Mason was pacing the narrow room when Lonnie walked back in.

Lonnie: "Sit down."

Mason slumps into the wooden chair.

"Want to hear the results?"

"Not especially."

"You were lying, Mason. Every word after the test questions."

"There must be something wrong with the machine."

"It's state-of-the-art. Besides, we know you were dragging Oscar Graham's body along the town pier at two-fifteen in the morning. We have an eyewitness."

"Who?"

"I'm asking the questions."

"Why didn't they try to stop me if they saw me doing something like that?"

"So, you did do it."

"I didn't say that! I just meant…if someone saw a guy dragging a person, a body…in the middle of the night—"

"They were frightened, Mason. They did the right thing. They went to the police."

"They? You use 'they' so you won't have to say if it was a man or a woman."

"That's right. Witnesses need to be protected. They came down here today and identified you through the one-way mirror—on the wall over there. Not one second's hesitation."

"But it was night. How could they—?"

"That pier is lit up bright as day. As you well know. You might as well have been on stage, kid. Time to take a bow."

Lonnie throws a thick file folder onto the table. "It's all right there. All the evidence. Open and shut. So here's what happened. Oscar was moving in on your girlfriend, and it was making you crazy. I don't want to overplay the race angle but it was there. Your dad sponsored that warrant at Town Meeting three years ago mandating INS sweeps on the island. It got voted down and he's still bitter about it. The fruit doesn't fall far from the tree."

"But Oscar was a citizen."

"For less than a year. And not to you, anyway. You don't buy those magic tricks, am I right? Pass a test, wave the wand, abracadabra you're a citizen. So you went to the doctor, got the drugs, lured him out to the town dock to talk about Jill, then knocked him down, hit him with the syringe and dumped him. Looks like he's just some crazy kid on a toot. He falls into the water and boom, it's over. Fifteen minutes later you're back in the sack, sleeping like a baby."

"Look, wait, I never—"

"I get it, kid. You cared about this girl. She was more than a prom date. You've known her all your life. You saw her being lured into some kind of crazy chemical nightmare. You tried talking. You tried to reason with this punk. But you were getting nowhere."

Lonnie's voice turned soft and chummy. "I'll tell you something, kid. That little thug deserved to die. You were doing us all a favor. Kind of like a vigilante in the movies. Like Batman. And we need a Batman right now, because this island is turning into Gotham City, right under our noses. We have a drug problem. Problem? It's a crisis. It's a catastrophe. And this Oscar Graham was throwing gas on the fire, trying to burn this island down for a profit. So no one's blaming you. Hell, I'm proud of you. The way these mooks fuck around with drugs, he was probably going to kill himself anyway. This kid was not long for this world. So what were you supposed to do? Let him take out more innocent kids like Jill? Just stand by and watch? That's not your style, Mason."

He leaned forward. "Look. We have your DNA on the body, we have your texts on Oscar's cell phone, we have an eyewitness. You had motive and opportunity. You have no alibi. And you have justification! If this was the Wild West, no one would blink an eye. You confess, I can get you a good deal, I can make it easy for you. Give up the doctor and you might walk. You might even get a good citizenship award!"

"So...I wouldn't go to jail?"

"Cooperate and we're talking probation, tops."

"But, I just, I...it's..."

"Keep lying and I guarantee you will be doing hard time at Cedar Junction. 'See Walpole and get turned into an Aryan Brotherhood bitch.' That's the slogan. They'll trade you for cigarettes, kid. By the time you get out, there won't be anything left of you. That would be a tragedy. I would hate to see that happen. You do not deserve that."

"Freeze it," I said. "Let me guess. He signed a confession."

"Signed and sealed. Did you see the way he was looking down and sideways? Touching his face with his fingers? Those are classic 'tells' the kid was lying from the get-go. We knew it and he knew we knew it."

"Did you use the multiple choice questions when you walked him through the confession? You know the ones—where all the choices are bad?"

"Hey, I'm not sure what you're trying to—"

"Why did you decide to dump him in the harbor? Was it because you thought the tides would carry the body out into the Sound? Or was it just a place you'd met before? Maybe it was his idea. Pick one. Pretty soon you've coached the whole thing out him."

"Hey, watch it, Chief."

"There was no eyewitness, was there?"

"It doesn't matter. He signed the confession."

"I'm not sure if you're aware of this, Lonnie, but the Reid Technique has been pretty much totally discredited. It's against department policy in like thirty-eight states."

"But not Massachusetts."

"I knew something was up when you started off with the polygraph. Then the folder full of 'evidence.' I couldn't see you, but let me guess. You were standing the whole time. Got to impose the authority. You tell him you know he was lying. But he wasn't, Lonnie. And the prosecution will fight tooth and claw to keep those lie detector charts away from the defense. Maybe that's what you meant by 'sealed.' What next? Right, the 'minimization,' that's the term. It's not so bad, anyone would have done it in your position. Blame other people and make it easy on yourself. Scare the crap out of him, then offer a way out. It's a textbook Reid interrogation."

"So what?"

"So it's the most effective system ever devised for extracting false confessions. People have studied it for years. They did tests at some university."

"Who gives a shit?"

"No, this is interesting. They put two kids in front of computers and had them IM each other. The only rules were no talking and do not under any circumstances hit the 'alt' key. That would automatically shut down both computers. So after about ten minutes, the researchers shut off the computers from the control room and then went into the testing cubicle and said, 'Who hit the alt key?' They both denied it until the researchers told them that they were monitoring the keystrokes. Then the kids started building their own scenarios—maybe they brushed the key with the side of their hand, they were typing too fast, it was an accident, whatever. Sound familiar?"

"Not really."

"Funny, because that's exactly the same trick you pulled with the polygraph and the fake eyewitness."

"I never admitted the eyewitness was fake."

"Admitted? That's an odd word to use. If you really had an eyewitness."

"I have a confession and I have a case and that pisses you off because we beat you to the punch. Plus we have the texts. They're on the phone but I made a transcript of the best ones. Mason Taylor's Greatest Hits."

"Let me see it."

"My pleasure."

He had the sheet of paper folded like a letter in his pocket. He handed it over and I opened it up.

Oscar:	I know everything now
Mason:	SEP
OSCAR:	AYCOOYM??!!
Mason:	DFI
Oscar:	I'm going to the police
Mason:	YBS
Oscar:	GOOMF
Mason:	YHBW
Oscar:	YRW
Mason:	YD
Oscar:	You don't get it. This isn't just drugs or porno. That's just a smoke screen.
Mason:	For what?
Oscar:	I'm not telling anyone but Chief Kennis. Read it in the papers.
Mason:	It's all just OPM
Oscar:	That's ACK! TMSHTF
Mason:	YOYO
Oscar:	EOD
Mason:	AMF

"What the hell are they talking about?"

"You tell me, Chief. They write in code."

I scanned the paper again. "Oscar found something, or overheard something. And it got him killed."

"But what?"

"First we have to figure out what all these acronyms mean. And I know the perfect person to ask."

I took the paper back to the interview room and handed it to Mason.

He glanced at it. "You pulled this off Oscar's phone."

"It was in a waterproof case, fortunately."

"He was always afraid he was going to fall off the docks. Some kid slipped last summer. Lost his whole contact list."

"I need you to translate it for me, Mason."

"Uh, okay. Hold on. He says he knows everything, and I say SEP—someone else's problem. He comes back with AYCOOYM—Are you completely out of your mind? And I say DFI—dumb fucking idea. He says he's going to the police and I say YBS—you'll be sorry."

"Why? Why say that?"

"Because the police don't help."

"A lot of kids seem to feel that way."

"Yeah. Because of cops not helping. Anyway…Oscar texts GOOMF—get out of my face. And I say YHBW—you have been warned."

"Warned? Warned about what?"

"These are dangerous people, Chief. I mean—obviously."

I nodded. "Go on."

"He says YRW—Yeah, right, whatever. Like he doesn't believe me. Like he trusts the cops. And I say YD—you're dead." He caught my frown. "It wasn't a threat! It sounds like a threat but it wasn't! I was just—I was afraid something bad would happen to him and it did. I asked him what was going on, and he wouldn't tell me. It's right there. He wanted to talk to you, Chief."

"So what's OPM?"

"Other people's money. And ACK's Nantucket, obviously. That's what this whole island is about, that's what he was saying—other people's money. Then he says TMSHTF—too much shit hit the fan, and I tell him—you're on your own—YOYO. He says EOD—end of discussion and I say Adios…well, sometimes people mean 'my friend' but mostly, it's…adios, motherfucker."

"And that's not a threat?" Lonnie broke in.

"It was a warning, like I said. But he wouldn't listen. That's it."

"More," I said. "That's the one word that jumps out for me. He said it was more than the drugs and the pornography. What was he talking about?"

"He wouldn't tell me! He says it right there. He's not telling anyone but you. So, like—there's stuff we don't know about, okay. But the stuff we do know about is bad enough."

I thought of Chick Crosby and his cameras. "You're right. Thanks, Mason. You've been a big help."

We left him alone again.

"What a load of crap," Lonnie said. "That kid's a killer."

"He says he was home in bed when the killing was going down."

"So what?"

"I don't know. I'd like to take a look at his room. Maybe there's something there you missed."

"We never checked out the kid's bedroom. Why would we? I'm sure it has a bed. That doesn't mean he was sleeping in it on the night of the murder."

I shrugged. "I'd still like to take a look." I pulled out my cell, called Charlie Boyce and told him to meet me at the Taylor house.

Lonnie was shaking his head. "Dan will never let you in without a warrant, Chief. He already thinks we're out to get his kid. Turns out he's a conspiracy nut."

"We'll see."

We got to see even sooner than I thought. Dan was at the front desk berating Lily Holdgate, the State Police dispatch officer. Lily had known Dan all his life and had learned to let the bluster jostle past her like a joggers on the bike path.

"I'm sure there's a perfectly reasonable explanation, Daniel," she was saying as we walked up to them. Dan spun on Lonnie, cutting off Lily and ignoring me.

"What the hell is going on, Fraker? Mason's letter about police violence must have really hit a nerve!"

"His—what? I don't read the newspaper, Dan. Neither does anyone else. They buy the *Inky* for the classifieds, that's it. And that man on the street feature. That's fun."

"Then what is this about?"

"Try murder. Your son just confessed."

"You useless retarded piece of—"

He grabbed at Lonnie, but the tall Statie danced backward a few steps and Dan stumbled. I took his arm.

"We have to talk."

"Stay out of this."

"I want to help Mason, Dan. I'm on your side and it looks like I'm the only one."

"This miserable little prick is trying to frame my son!" He wrenched himself around, face-to-face with Lonnie again. "Is Mason back there? I demand to see my son."

"No way. Not until the bail hearing."

"Come on, Dan," I said, tugging him back toward the door. "There's nothing you can do here."

"No, goddamn it! I'm not going to let—"

"It's not up to you. Keep fighting with Lonnie and you'll wind up in jail yourself. Your best move is—calm down and think. Come on, let's go. Now."

He let me lead him out of the station, still blustering. I told him my plan, such as it was, on the short walk to his car, parked on the grassy verge of North Liberty Street.

"How will seeing Mason's room help anything?" he demanded.

"I have no idea. That's why I want to look."

"I don't get it. I need to call a lawyer."

"Yes, you do. Meanwhile, Mason was at home in bed when the murder happened. It would be nice if we could prove that."

He shook his head. "With a dated diary entry?"

"How about a time-stamped e-mail?"

"Did he say he was online?"

"He said he was sleeping."

"So he was e-mailing in his sleep?"

"He might have the time wrong. It's worth a look."

"We can't even get into his computer. It's password-protected."

Dan climbed into his car. I slapped the roof. "Go home. Charlie Boyce will be there. Leave him alone and let him snoop. I'll meet you at the house in a few minutes."

"Chief…"

I leaned into the open window, and pressed his shoulder. "I know Mason didn't do this."

He spoke to the steering wheel. "Thank you."

I walked back to the State Police HQ, brushed past Lonnie and stepped into the interview room. I told Mason what I wanted. He swore me to secrecy. I told him I might have to share his password with other law enforcement personnel as well as the prosecution if the case ever came to trial. That didn't matter to him.

"Anyone but my dad," he said.

"You got it."

◇◇◇

Charlie and Dan Taylor were both standing in Mason's bedroom when I got there five minutes later. Dan's wife, Marian, hovered in the doorway. She looked like she was afraid to step inside, as if she might ruin some saving scrap of evidence with a false step. Or maybe she just wanted to keep her distance from Dan.

Charlie gave me a hapless shrug.

"Nothing?" I asked him.

"I don't even know what I'm supposed to be looking for. I thought maybe…a midnight snack? And some forensics hotshot could tell when the kid ate it by testing the bread crusts. You know…bread goes stale at a certain rate, so…"

"Nice thought."

"We don't allow eating after eight o'clock at night," Marian said from the doorway "I always tell him, the eating box is closed.'"

"Yeah, so…I don't know,' Charlie said.

I went into Mason's twenty-seven-inch display iMac. I also noticed a thirteen-inch MacBook air on the bed. The room had its own little flat screen, hooked up to an X-Box. No one could say Mason suffered a deprived childhood. He had a whole little digital world set up here.

I checked his e-mail—Gmail and Hotmail, his Twitter feed, Snapchat, Instagram, Facebook, but it was just like he had told me at the State Police HQ. There was no activity of any kind recorded for the night in question. I checked the desk drawers, on the off-chance that there might be a diary, as Dan's bitter little joke had suggested. But of course there wasn't.

"Give up?" Dan asked.

"Pretty much," Charlie answered.

I stepped back to view the whole room.

And then I figured it out. It wasn't what was on the computer that mattered. It was which way the computer screen faced. I turned to Dan. "I think I have an idea."

"Thank God someone does," said Marian.

◇◇◇

Back at the station, I put in a call to Washington, DC. I had kept the number on speed dial (number four), though I never thought I'd call it again, the same way I still hadn't deleted my father's address from my e-mail contacts. It gave me a strange fleeting comfort to see it there, in alphabetical order with all the living people, as if in some cat-tangled string theory world he were still alive and still threatening to throw his phone into the swimming pool. Or maybe he had already made good on the threat and that's why I couldn't reach him anymore. It was farfetched, but it beat the truth.

I sat down at my desk, enclosed in the luxurious cocoon of my grand new office and touched the four on the screen of my hand-me-down iPhone. I waited while it rang, emptying my mind, focusing on the soft burr in my ear. I got her voicemail, which redirected me to her office number. That same sharp, sexy authoritative contralto. I let it work through me like the first draw on a cigarette (four years and counting since the last time I smoked one), then punched in her work number.

"Office of Homeland Security."

I cleared my throat. "Frances Tate, please."

"One moment."

Mozart played while I waited.

"Frances Tate's office."

"Is she there?"

"She's in a meeting. May I say who's calling?"

"It's Police Chief Henry Kennis from Nantucket." I don't know why I added my title. Maybe to prove I was part of the law enforcement community, marginally more deserving of

Franny's time than some random citizen. "This won't take long, but it's important."

"One moment."

More Mozart—the Sinfonia Concertante. I listened to the sparkling conversation of the violin and the viola, remembering that my mom had won a canned ham for identifying this piece—some little contest on the NPR station in Connecticut where she lived when I was at college. She recognized it from the first few notes, like greeting an old friend. The ham was just the fortune cookie after the meal. But it turned out to be delicious.

"Hank?"

The sound of her voice, living and alert at the other end of the line, snapped me out of my reverie. No one else ever called me Hank. I smiled. "The Mayor of Whoville, at your service."

She laughed. "You'll never let me live that one down."

"Nope."

"So…are you calling to tell me you've had it with the rustics and you're moving to DC? We could use a few cops who think before they shoot."

"No, sorry."

"Then…you're begging me to move to Nantucket and hunt down the bake shop cookie thieves with you."

"That would be hopeless."

"So you need a favor."

"Yeah."

"Spit it out, Hank. I have a homeland to secure down here. Speaking of which…are you in the loop on the big INS sweep of the island?"

"Uh—no. In fact—"

"It's just a rumor, so maybe it's nothing, But I've heard they're going to be running the crackdown of all time out there. Every business, every private employer—arrests, deportations. It sounds like the Japanese internment program. You should check it out."

"I will. Meanwhile…do you know anyone at the NSA?"

"Uh, yeah, I guess so."

"You guess so?"

"I—it's a little—"

"You're dating someone from the NSA."

She made breathed out a soft laugh. "Match wits with Inspector Kennis."

"It's okay. I'm sort of dating someone, too."

"That's great, Henry."

"Another writer." I wondered what Jane would think of my classifying our sporadic private literary salon as a form of dating. It might be worthwhile to find out.

"Oh, my God, I can see it now, both of you banging away at opposite sides of the dining room table. Dueling laptops."

"We're not quite there yet."

"Good."

"Can you ask the NSA dude for a favor?"

"We're not quite there yet, either."

"It's important."

I could hear her pull in a breath. "What's going on, Hank?"

I told her about Mason and Oscar Graham, the arrest and the false confession. "But here's the thing. Mason has gotten politically conscious this year, writing articles for the school paper and letters to the *Inky Mirror* and blog posts about drone strikes and surveillance and putting Cat Stevens on the no-fly list. Anyway, the point is…he's got to have been flagged by the NSA. He wrote one piece asking how Obama would feel if ISIS started bombing farms and kindergarten playgrounds and weddings in America. Just putting the word Obama and bomb together in one paragraph would start the alarms ringing. Am I right?"

"Probably."

"And we both know that the NSA can conduct surveillance through the camera function on your computer."

"Thanks to Edward Snowden."

"Yeah. Thanks to Edward Snowden." She let that one pass, but I knew she took the party line on the exiled leaker. "Mason's computer faces his bed. If the NSA is monitoring him, they have footage that proves he was home and asleep at the time of the murder."

"And you think they'll just hand it over to you?"

"I was hoping they might hand it over to...to—"

"Mark. Mark Hennesey."

"Right—to him. Then he'd hand it over to you, and you'd hand it over to me. Something like that."

"This is your craziest idea yet, Horton."

"A person's a person, no matter how small. Look—Mason needs help. He's in trouble. He matters."

"Not to the NSA."

"But he should."

"This is classified information."

"So, why not use it to help someone, for once?"

"I don't know, I don't know, Henry. This is too weird."

"Will you at least ask him?"

"Okay, but no promises."

◇◇◇

We hung up and I turned to other business: a rash of burglaries, just discovered by returning homeowners, someone suing the NPD because they slipped on the ice in the parking lot during the winter. And the forensics report on the Thayer house fire, long delayed in Boston, had finally landed on my desk. It indicated that the house contained a lot of high-end filmmaking equipment—cameras, editing bays, microphones, lighting gear. That didn't prove Alana's theory—they could have been making totally innocuous movies out there, or even just storing the stuff—but it raised a red flag for me.

The report identified the camera as a high Definition XF305 Canon camcorder, list price around seven thousand dollars. Not a hobbyist's item. You could pick up a serviceable digital camera at Staples for under a hundred bucks; or just use your phone. The State Police arson forensics unit had managed to pull a partial serial number off the unit and they attached a list of seven hundred and eighty-two people in New England who had purchased this particular model, and filed the warranty papers. People came to Nantucket from all over the country, and most people didn't bother with warranty applications anyway. But it was a start. The list of names gave me something useful to do.

On a hunch, I saved the list as a Microsoft Word file and ran a search for the name Chick Crosby.

Bingo.

So it was his equipment. I told Barnaby Toll to set up an appointment and started scrolling through the rest of my inbox. The local film director Mark Toland had sent me the photographs he took on the day Andrew Thayer's cottage burned down. I printed them out and studied them. The attached note apologized for the poor quality of shots. He was moving fast, clicking impulsively, not really sure what he was looking for beyond a sense of the moors as a possible location for his next movie. Alana featured in one shot, posing awkwardly; I could see the tailgate of the F-150 in another. Otherwise, it was just bushes and trees and blue sky. I saved one particularly blurry picture out for Haden Krakauer—it showed red specks on the turf. Cardinals probably, feeding on whatever they could find there. The cardinal was a common bird on Nantucket, but you rarely saw them in groups like that.

I was about to leave the office when the phone rang again.

I picked up. "Chief Kennis."

"Can't do it, Hank."

"Come on."

"Mark could go to jail."

"For helping someone."

"For releasing classified information."

I blew out a breath. Around and around we go. "For God's sake, Franny! It's the video feed of a sleeping teenager."

"And if that teenager shoots up his high school next week? Or joins ISIS?"

"What if he does? How does me having three hours of sleep footage change anything?"

"It's sloppy. It's a mistake. It's a protocol infraction. Senate oversight committees start asking—what other infractions did this guy commit? What other top-secret information did he share with his girlfriend? And who else did she share it with?"

"He can't just borrow the footage and lie about it?"

"I can't believe you'd even ask that. Or ask me to."

"It's three hours of meaningless video. No one will care."

"You'd be surprised at the things the NSA cares about. When they start asking questions, you better have the right answers."

"So, he's just covering his ass."

"Technically, no. Technically, he's choosing not to risk his ass in the first place to help some small-town cop prove his harebrained theory and get a gold star from the Selectmen. The kid's father is a Selectman, right?"

"How did you remember that?"

"I'm sitting in front of a computer, Hank."

"Right, of course." I felt a quick stab of irritation, picturing her clicking away at the keyboard, while we talked. "Splitting the difference," as she called it. I wondered briefly if I'd ever gotten her undivided attention, if anyone ever did, if there even was such a thing anymore.

"So what are you going to do?" she asked me.

"I'm going to be persistent and annoying, like always."

"Oh, boy. Here it comes."

"The night of May twenty-third. Ten o'clock to two in the morning. Just ask Mark to pull the footage and review it. He doesn't have to send it to me, or give it to you. It never has to leave his encrypted computer database. Then if he sees the kid coming in after midnight dripping wet, he can help us convict this kid and take a potential terrorist off the street before he plants a bomb somewhere. It's a win-win."

"But you're absolutely certain he's innocent."

"Maybe they'll catch him talking about ISIS in his sleep."

"If he talks about ISIS in his sleep, they already caught him. That's why the surveillance was set up in the first place."

"Okay, Mark won't help you. But you can still help me."

"Hank—"

"Just back me up on this, if Lonnie calls you. Which he won't."

"How can you know that?"

"I don't—I mean, I'm ninety-nine percent sure. But I worry about that one percent."

"Me, too. In fact that's my job description."

"Look, if he calls, just say something cryptic. Tell him everything's classified, that's not even a lie."

"What kind of scheme are you cooking up in that overheated little brain of yours?"

I told her about Lonnie's use of the Reid Technique. "I'm going to do to Lonnie exactly what he did to Mason with the polygraph and that imaginary 'eyewitness.' I'm going to run my own 'alt key' experiment."

She laughed. "I like it. Poetic justice."

"My favorite kind."

◇◇◇

The next day I met Lonnie Fraker at the Green for lunch. He always said the wheat grass smoothies there were one of the few consolations for being posted on Nantucket. He ordered one. I took a slice of vegan gluten-free pizza and an iced tea. I would have preferred a burger at the LolaBurger but Lonnie was on a health food kick and I wanted to humor him. We sat down on the uncomfortable couch at the low table by the back door, surrounded by yoga moms and ex-hippie cabinetmakers.

"You don't have an eyewitness for the Mason Taylor case," I said. "In fact, you don't have a case at all."

"Dream on, Chief, I know you like the kid, but—"

"I called Frannie Tate. She has connections at the NSA. We have surveillance footage from his computer camera. It shows him home and in bed the whole time."

He stared at me, looking for the "tells" he'd learned at his Reid training course, no doubt. "I want to see the footage."

"Impossible."

"This is bullshit."

"I haven't seen it myself, Lonnie. But Frannie has the report. The footage will be used by the defense and shown to the judge, in chambers, during discovery. But by then it will be too late. You'll have railroaded an innocent kid into a murder trial with trumped up evidence, and a false confession from a discredited interrogation technique. They'll come down on you like a rotten roof in a blizzard. Kiss this job goodbye. You'll be directing traffic on Lyman Street in Springfield. If they let you stay on the force at all. No one wants this kind of publicity."

Lonnie gulped his wheatgrass. "So the kid's just lying there, doing nothing?"

"Well, he snores a little."

"Shit."

"Sorry."

"So now what do we do?"

"You release Mason and apologize to his father. You might think about sweetening that with a case of Duckhorn cabernet. Then we both get back to finding out who murdered Oscar Graham—and why."

Lonnie nodded. "Sounds like a plan."

"Protect and serve."

"Huh?"

"It's the LAPD motto. Kind of says it all."

"Yeah."

Lonnie set out to trace the drugs that killed Oscar. I decided to snoop around Straight Wharf, where the boy had been working. But neither of us got very far with our inquiries because Andrew Thayer's body was found the next morning in the foyer of the LoGran corporate retreat on Eel Point, facedown on a thirty-thousand-dollar carpet with his throat cut.

Chapter Twenty-two

Wrong Place, Wrong Time

At seven-thirty in the morning on the day when he was arrested for murder, Mike Henderson was looking down at his sleeping baby, thinking, "I've been demoted."

It was all right, though, because everyone else had been demoted, too. A baby changed all the family rankings, and there was nothing you could do about it. He was no longer the primary love of Cindy's life, and he no longer had any priority access to her body. Someone else was pawing her and sucking on her nipples. The sheer amount of physical contact with the baby both satisfied and exhausted her. She had the opposite of skin hunger now; skin saturation, perhaps. Offering to touch her was like offering dessert to the winner of a pie-eating contest. For the most part, Mike didn't even care. He was exhausted, himself. And the baby had shifted Cindy in his mind, somehow. She had become the mother of his child, the other half of a team with a daunting project to accomplish. The fact that she was his wife, the love between them, was just fuel, the gasoline in this extraordinary car with its unknowable destination. It was a vital fluid but you never really noticed it until the needle was on empty.

His parents and his in-laws had been demoted, too. They were no longer the center of a nuclear family, however scattered and distracted their grown children might be. Now there was another nuclear family, and they were peripheral to it. They were grandparents, to be used for babysitting when they were nearby, granted holiday visitation rights otherwise. Cindy was closer to her mother now, they shared some vital secret knowledge. But it also isolated them. Cindy's mother had done a lot of things wrong, made a lot of unnecessary mistakes. Cindy's childhood had changed. It was no longer a melodrama full of regrets. It was a cautionary tale.

But it wasn't just their marriage and their families or even their personal histories that had tilted into the unrecognizable. Their friends had been transformed, too. The ones without children seemed to fade away; the ones with children were allies, soldiers in the same platoon, swept into the same incomprehensible battle, talking about bottles and diapers, rashes and fevers, competing for the first smile or the first squeeze of a finger. Ordinary conversation had been demoted. The old topics like films, books, town gossip, politics, national news—in fact anything but the all-consuming pulse of this new life they had brought into the world—had been relegated to the status of background noise, like the hiss of tires on a rainy street.

Mike leaned down into the crib and stroked the baby's head, thinking, so much upset you caused, so much disruption, everyone and everything downgraded.

"Wait till the next baby comes, kid" he whispered to her. "Then it's gonna be your turn."

He leaned down, kissed her forehead, and went downstairs for a cup of coffee. He left it half-finished. He was in a hurry this morning.

He sighed as he started his truck. This was the kind of day that made him question all his life choices. Somehow, at age thirty-four, he had gotten himself into a profession that put him at the mercy of an endless series of exigent women. The husbands never cared about the painting projects. Sometimes he thought they bought the houses (often a second, third, or even a fourth dwelling) for the sole purpose of giving their wives a way to manage the suffocating burden of their endless free time. The women treated the matter of fabric choice and paint color, window treatments and bathroom fixtures with a gravity and teeth-gritting attention to detail more appropriate to nuclear arms treaties or mainframe computer repair. Mike generally found the combination of blithe self-importance and needling perfectionism exhausting, but he had never come up against anyone quite like Sue Ann Pelzer.

Sue Ann controlled all the maintenance work at Pell's LoGran corporate estate and unlike most of the "Miss Ladies" (as Cindy called them) Mike had to deal with, she really knew what she was looking at. He had been refinishing one of the bedroom floors the year before when he looked up and saw Sue Ann perched on the threshold.

"Is that hundred and twenty-grit sandpaper on that machine?" she had asked, squinting into the dust, subtle as a woodpecker. "Because I wouldn't want you to stop at hundred-grit and this floor doesn't look smooth enough for one-twenty yet."

Of course he'd been planning to stop at hundred-grit, firmly convinced that no one could tell the difference. But Sue Ann Pelzer could tell the difference. And she always did.

This morning was going to be particularly awful because Mike had marred the brown copper downspouts with latex paint when he was finish-coating the corner boards. Naturally, Sue Ann had noticed, but he assured her he could clean them off easily.

"Like it never happened" he had chirped.

She stared him down. "Let's hope so."

Of course, he couldn't clean them. Sanding the paint off would ruin the patina of the copper, water had no effect, even with a little soft scrub and a kitchen scrubbie. He had nursed high hopes for the scrubbie. Sometimes fingernails were sharp enough to scrape uncured paint, but soft enough to spare the surface you were scraping.

Not this time.

He bought a variety of latex paint-removing products with names like "Goo-be-Gone" and "Oops." How about one called "You really fucked it up this time, dumb ass"? He'd have bought that one in a hot second but it probably wouldn't have worked. None of the other ones did. Had the latex bonded with the copper? He had no idea. He wasn't a chemical engineer. If he were smart he'd have found a real job by now.

This morning he was making his final attempt. If he couldn't remove the white paint, he might be able to cover it up. He had bought pints of brown and black metal enamel, a plastic bucket, thinner, and a stir-stick. All he had to do was mix up a color match for the copper and then paint out the white latex.

He parked on Eel Point Road and walked up the driveway. This was a stealth mission, but he couldn't help pausing as the imposing front of the mansion loomed into view. He had history with this house. He had been briefly accused of killing the former owner; he had caught the man's wife in flagrante with a kid on his paint crew, and committed adultery himself in one of the big upstairs bedrooms.

It was an oversized, ugly, ill-omened pile, bristling with every ostentatious architectural flourish Grady Malone could scavenge from the Nantucket new money catalog: the giant fan windows, the extra dormers, the absurd cupola and ornate widow's walk, overlooking the endless trimmed hedges and the massive Tora Bora-like stone walls that snaked around the steeply pitched property, cutting it into stepped terraces.

The place felt fake and faintly sinister, like a gangster in the witness protection program, duly acting the part of volunteer fireman and church deacon, eating his tomato sauce out of a jar. Mike wasn't fooled. Bad things happened on this tainted patch of ground and they always would. Maybe it was a Wampanoag burial site. Tanya Kriel had told him the place had "bad vibes" and he could feel them now, literal vibrations, like an alarm going off, beyond the human wavelength. Dogs would flee this place, tails between their legs.

And yet he had taken the offer to stay on as the property's house painter. Cindy couldn't believe he was willing to work here, but he had to work and painters rarely got to pick and choose their customers. He was happy for the extra money, or at least he had been until his first run-in with Sue Ann Pelzer.

He sighed and continued trudging up the hill, his shoes crunching on the crushed-shell driveway. He saw no one as he rounded the corner of the house and started for the back deck. Landscapers would normally have taken over the grounds by this time of day, at this time of year, but the grass looked recently mowed, shaved tight into straight lines of darker and lighter green like a baseball field.

Mike retrieved his stepladder from behind the guest cottage, set out his pots of paint in the mild summery air, and got to work.

Half an hour later he was done.

He allowed himself a moment of giddy laughter as he packed up and put the ladder away. The job was perfect. He had always been good at matching colors, but this was his masterpiece. Even if Sue Ann figured out what he'd done, she would have to bow down at the perfection of his work. He even thought for one leaping second of selling his little mixture to other paint-ers—another million-dollar idea, like the heated screwdriver tip for melting paint in screwheads and the miniature windshield wipers to clear the fog off goggles. Of course, you almost never saw slotted screws anymore, and goggles misted up from the inside. This idea was equally foolish—merely a way to advertise his own ineptitude. Better to keep it as a proprietary cleanup technique. "No trick, no trade," as his first boss had loved to say.

Even better: don't make the mess in the first place.

Still, walking back to the car he was feeling happy and accomplished, the hero of his own mundane action movie—*Indiana Jones and the Temple of Drips*, *Raiders of the Lost House Keys*. Losing house keys—the painter's worst nightmare, the inexcusable negligence that made owners and contractors and real estate people look at you like some demented organ grinder's monkey who needed a choke collar and a short leash. Well, he hadn't lost a set of keys in years, and he'd never made a painting mistake he couldn't fix.

Today was a perfect example of that.

His only actual mistake was not heeding the initial sense of foreboding the LoGran mansion had given him. But there was no way he could have known the truth: he was walking away from a house with a dead body sprawled in the front hallway in full view of any passing eyewitness, his hands covered and his tee-shirt stained with a brown liquid that looked alarmingly like dried blood.

Chapter Twenty-three

The Arrest

The 911 call from the LoGran corporate retreat came at ten forty-five in the morning. Kyle Donnelly and two uniforms answered it. I trailed them by five minutes. I had been heading out to Wauwinet on the Polpis Road when I picked up the call. Sylvester Graham was working on a new trophy house out there and I had some follow-up questions for him. They'd have to wait. I skidded into a U-turn, hit the flashers, and gunned it back to town.

Live-in caretaker Douglas Blount made the call. Apparently ship's engineer Liam Phelan had the guest cottage on the property under siege. The dispatcher could hear him trying to break down the door. He was shouting too. She couldn't make out what he was saying over the phone, but Phelan had clearly worked himself up into a murderous rage, and given the quality of new construction on the island these days Blount's front door wasn't likely to hold up for the six minutes Kyle needed to get there.

Blount and Phelan—two big men with anger management problems. I wouldn't have put my money on either one of them to win the fight, but they'd each be sure to collect their share of bodily damage and felony assault charges before they called it a draw. The problem was that the law would come down squarely on Blount's side. Liam was caught on tape for criminal trespass, breaking-and-entering, and the "assault" side of assault-and-battery. That charge may sound redundant, but verbal threats constitute assault in the state of Massachusetts. Battery comes when you follow through, and Liam was about to cross that line also.

I hit the steering wheel, swerving around a pair of tourists on mopeds. I knew what had driven Liam to this idiotic attack. It confirmed what I already suspected: Blount had given Liam's daughter the drugs she ODed on. I didn't know what evidence he'd managed to dig up, but by withholding it from the police all he'd managed to do was make Blount into the victim and get himself thrown in jail.

Vigilantes—a hundred years of books and movies and TV shows had turned them into romantic heroes. In fact they were misguided and emotion-driven, reckless and inept. They invariably did damage—and when they were as crazed with rage and grief as Liam Phelan, they didn't care. Liam just wanted to hit someone. That he'd probably made the right choice of who to hit this time wasn't going to do any of us much good.

Passing Sanford Farm on Madaket Road, I saw the LoGran F-150 and hit my flashers. We stopped side by side, taking up both lanes as we talked—a long-standing Nantucket tradition. Sue Ann Pelzer was behind the wheel, wearing jeans, a suede jacket, and a beret. She had a pair of binoculars on the seat beside her.

"What's going on?" I said.

"I just saw my first prothonotary warbler! Got my lucky jacket on. It sure worked for me today!"

It was a beautiful brown suede. "Just don't wear it in the rain."

"I've never been caught yet! And it never fails—the prothonotary warblers have usually migrated by now. Long gone! But this one was just strutting around Madaket Harbor under Millie's Bridge. The top feathers are the sweetest cornflower blue. I was thinking—that would be perfect camouflage when you're flying! No one could see you against the sky"

"So, wait—you've been in Madaket?"

"I saw your assistant chief out there. It's a great day for birding."

"Doug Blount just made a 911 call from the cottage."

"What? Why?"

"Liam Phelan is breaking the door down."

"Oh my God. Is Doug all right?"

"Just follow me."

I stamped on the gas, checked the rearview mirror, and saw her making a three-point turn behind me. A line of cars waited patiently for her to finish. In August they'd be honking like a New Jersey tailgate party in a Brooklyn traffic jam. But June was still mellow.

At the LoGran house, Kyle Donnelly had the situation under control. Two officers, Ned Hollis and Jerry Cone, stood at either side of the cottage front door; Kyle was inside with Doug Blount. I told Ned to keep Sue Ann outside and took a quick walk around the perimeter. I heard Sue Ann's car pull up, heard the door slam and her shoes crunching on the crushed-shell driveway—the swift decisive stride of a woman taking charge. For now she was Kyle's problem. I kept moving, checking the windows, the shingles, the lawn, the hedge, and the mulch behind it. I couldn't have told you what I was looking for, but that left me open to whatever I might happen to notice.

Like for instance: the hilt of a hunting knife.

The blade was buried in the mulch against the foundation. I stood still, staring at it. It looked carelessly out of place—like finding my ex-wife's Maui Jim sunglasses in the salad crisper.

It was confusing. This had nothing to do with Liam Phelan. If he had brought a knife, and I doubted he would—he was more the bare-knuckled brawler type—the blade would be lodged somewhere inside Doug Blount by now.

I pulled on a pair of latex gloves, eased through the hedge, and pulled the knife out of the ground. Dirt caked the blood on the curved steel. Someone had used this weapon recently. I hefted it. It was surprisingly heavy, superbly balanced, designed for gutting and skinning big animals—a deer-hunter's tool. But the blood on it was human—I'd seen enough of it, and smelled enough of it to know the difference.

I set the blade on top of the hedge and walked back to the front of the cottage.

Sue Ann had cornered Kyle Donnelly. "If there's a problem here I have to deal with it! Every single thing that happens on the property is my responsibility. If someone is hurt in there, if anything's broken, or—"

"Sue Ann." She turned. "I need you to let me into the main house."

"Is there a problem?"

"I don't know. But, yeah, probably."

We walked across the lawn and along the side of the mansion, skirting the low stone walls, following the path of granite flags to the big front door. Cars passed along Eel Point Road.

The birds chirping in the trees sounded random and purposeful at once, like an orchestra tuning up. It was a gorgeous late spring day, but it felt wrong to me, more like dusk in November. I took a deep lungful of the mild air while Sue Ann worked the key. I had a feeling I was going to need it.

The smell hit us as soon as we stepped inside, that coppery, rotten meat stink of death. There's nothing worse, and you never get used to it. The physical recoil burst in my stomach and bulged up my throat. I gagged back the vomit and glanced at over at Sue Ann. She seemed perfectly composed, calmly studying the splayed body, the head floating in a pool of coagulating blood.

"Well, this carpet is ruined," she said.

I understood the need to banter, to shrug it off, to distance yourself. I've heard the worst dirtiest jokes of my life, standing over dead bodies at crime scenes.

"And forget the floorboards under it," I said. "You can't get rid of blood." We stared at the corpse. "Do you know him?"

She shook her head. "I think I've seen him around. He was a friend of Doug's."

It was Andrew Thayer. I had spoken to him only a few days before, patted his dog, checked out the computer screens he used to plan his investments. Death was always so abrupt, so implausible. We carry our futures around with us, as much a part of us as the sound of our voices or the smell of our sweat. Every living moment implies the next, like mapping one vector in the trajectory of a bullet. Life is movement in space and time. No bullet drops out of the air midflight, but that would seem no less bizarre and dissonant than Andrew Thayer's future collapsing like this, into the black hole of his extinguished mind and spirit. There was nothing left of him now, nothing left of all his decisions and appointments, his plans and his dreams, but this generic human shell, bleeding out from the carotid artery.

It made me sick, it made me frightened, and most of all it made me mad. Someone had done this. Someone had drawn a knife across another man's neck, watched the lifeblood gushing and left him to die. It made me want to kill in turn, to hunt this monster down and let him feel the rough justice of a blade against his own throat. But I couldn't give into that rage. I was no vigilante. Two wrongs never made a right. They made a catastrophe, they made a holocaust, they made a war.

My job was to find this creature. That's all—just find him.

The law would take care of the rest. I unclenched my fists, took a shallow breath through my mouth, and led Sue Ann back outside. The fresh air felt like splash of cool water on my face. A plane droned by overhead. A family of deer bounded across the lawn and crashed into the brush. Life continued. Andrew's departure scarcely registered. When the rug was replaced and the new floorboards installed, the only residue of him would be fading photographs and the flickers of memory along the fragile synapses of his family and friends. It wasn't enough. It seemed pale, pointless, and paltry, an illegible scrawl, a collection of junk in a hoarder's garage.

I turned away from the house. "No one goes inside until the crime scene unit gets here."

Sue Ann nodded. "Okay."

"What was Andrew doing here?"

"I have no idea."

"Had he been arguing with Blount?"

"Doug argues with everyone. So yeah, probably."

"Stick around. I'll need to talk to you later."

I called Lonnie Fraker to fill him in on the situation.

"It's turning into some kind of fucking Fallujah over here," he said. "What the hell's going on?"

"Something bad."

I put the phone in my pocket and sprinted back to the cottage.

◇◇◇

Inside, the place was a shambles. Two cheap chairs lay splintered on the floor among drifts of broken glass, and wood shards from the battered front door. The boys had been brawling, all right. Blount had an angry-looking black eye starting to bloom; Phelan's jaw was puffy and blood seeped from a cut on his forehead. Kyle had both of them handcuffed.

I spoke to Kyle, tipping my head toward Blount. "Take him to the station, read him his rights and stick him in a holding cell. I'll take care of Phelan."

They hustled Blount from the house and Sue Ann followed them. The morning's carnage seemed to register for her only in terms of work hours and money spent. There'd be a lot more of both after this new fracas.

When we were alone, Phelan stepped toward me. "Chief—"

I put a hand up, palm out. "Don't say a word until I read you your rights."

"What are you talking about! My rights? You can't arrest me! I did nothing wrong. I'm the one who—"

"You broke down that door and you landed at least one good punch, Liam. That's criminal trespass, destruction of property, breaking-and-entering, and at least one count of felony assault. If I don't arrest you, I become your accomplice and we both go to jail. You have the right to remain silent—"

"I have the right to a lawyer and you'll appoint one for me if I can't afford it. Probably that strutting useless boozer Timmy Congdon. Am I right?"

"If you choose not to seek counsel, anything you say—"

"Can be used against me. Of course it can. And how about Douglas Blount? Can what I say be used against him, Mr. Police Chief?"

"Eventually. Possibly. But first—"

"He sold my daughter drugs! He tried to force her to shame herself on film. Maybe he succeeded. I don't even know. But I do know this. When she tried to get away from him he gave her the bad load that almost killed her. Might still kill her. Now my Jilly is lying in the ICU ward at Mass General because of that miserable piece of shite and you tell me I'm going to jail? I'll fucking kill the whole lot of you before I let him get away with that."

"No one's killing anyone, Liam." Except for whoever slashed Andrew Thayer's throat with that hunting knife. But Liam didn't know about Andrew's murder yet, and I needed to compartmentalize. "I need to know why you're so certain it was Doug Blount."

"I investigated. I talked to people. Like *you're* supposed to do."

I let that one pass. "Who, in particular?"

"There's a girl, Alana Trikilis—"

"I talked to her, Liam."

"Then why didn't you do anything?"

"Police need evidence. There's no point in arresting a suspect if I can't make it stick."

"But you arrested him just now! I broke into his house and you arrested him."

"That's a different matter. It's—unrelated." I thought of Jane Stiles, and her literary theory of the connections between cases. Or was it a small-town theory? Either way, it occurred to me that she might be right. But that was none of Liam's business. I had other questions for him. "Alana and Jill were pretty good friends," I said. "I'm surprised it took you so long to track her down."

"I've been in Bermuda, with the *Nantucket Grand*."

"That's Pell's boat?"

"It's his ship, Chief. A boat is something you put on a ship."

"His ship, then."

"She needed a lot of work this winter. A new starboard engine, new water coolant filters. We overhauled the electronics and the GPS system. Dry docked her for a paint job. It never ends."

"And you had to oversee it all?"

"I'm chief engineer."

"It must have been hard, though. Being down there with Jill up here in the hospital."

"I had a lot of time to think."

"And brood."

"If you like. I had to fly back to Hamilton Harbor after I brought the *Grand* back here. Arrangements for the winter mooring. And they're building a teak-paneled screening room for the lower deck which had to be inspected before it was taken apart for transport. Good thing I showed up. The carpets were the wrong color, there were no dimmers for the recessed lighting, the finish was supposed to be satin not gloss. Worst of all, the seats were all an inch too narrow, with no lumbar support. Total cock-up. So it's back to the drawing board. And no one gets another penny until Jonathan Pell is satisfied."

"How long have you been back on-island? Let me guess. Twenty-four hours?"

"I took the last flight out of Boston yesterday."

"That was fast."

"The gate opens, the horse breaks."

"Alana was frightened."

"Of course she was. That little wisp of a girl."

"She didn't want Blount coming after her?"

"He won't be."

"Because we showed up. By chance."

"A cell or a box, either way he won't be preying on little girls." I stared at him. "You're saying you came here to kill him?"

"Oh no, Chief! You thought I meant a coffin? I'm talking about a box at Fenway Park! Nothing like a Red Sox game to distract a sociopathic sexual predator. Calms them right down. By the seventh inning stretch they're tame as toddlers."

"Good. We wouldn't want to have any misunderstandings about that."

"Heavens, no."

We watched each other for a few seconds. "You're still under arrest, even if Blount chooses not to press charges. Sue Ann Pelzer's going to want you booked for the B and E anyway. Come on. I'm going to have the boys take you back to the station, see about finding you a lawyer."

"How long will I have to stay there?"

"That depends on Blount. If he chooses to press charges…"

"Of course he will! He hates me. He knows I can take him down. And I will."

I pressed a hand to his shoulder. "Then I suggest you share the evidence you've found with us. We can take it from here."

"That sounds lovely. I know what the bastard did. But knowledge isn't proof, Chief Kennis. As you just explained. My hope was to beat a confession out him, and I don't think that's really your style, if you'll permit me the liberty."

"My way works better, Liam. It might not be as fast or dramatic—"

"The wheels of Kennis grind slowly, yet they grind exceeding small."

I finished the couplet for him: "Though with patience He stands waiting, with exactness grinds He all."

"You know your Longfellow."

I shrugged. "Poets read poetry."

"Of course he was writing about God, not some small town constable. Big shoes to fill."

"I don't play God, Liam. But I don't miss much, either."

Jerry Cone was still waiting outside. I led Liam out to the car and stood watching while they drove away. Sue Ann Pelzer had followed me down from the main house. She sat on one of the low stone walls, texting. I walked over.

"Do you mind if I take a look around?"

She glanced up. "The sooner you all are done, the sooner I can start cleaning up the mess."

"Thanks."

◇◇◇

The guest cottage reminded me of a recently renovated show-house, pristine and uninhabited, as elegantly blank as the last time I'd been there. Blount had left no personal mark on the place—no pictures on the wall, no family photographs, no clothes on the floor, no dishes in the sink. His bedroom held a queen-size bed with two pillows and a cotton blanket, no bed-spread, a dresser next to the window. The drawers held clothes, a wristwatch, some chargers, some condoms, a passport.

He hadn't bothered with reading lights by the bed, but there was a Kindle Paperwhite on the bedside table, so he didn't need them. I opened the Kindle, slid a fingertip across the bottom of the screen to open it, and checked the library: Tom Clancy, W.E.B. Griffin, some survivalist tracts with titles like *Be Ready When the Shit Goes Down* and *When All Hell Breaks Loose*. The book he was currently reading surprised me: Robert Stone's *A Flag for Sunrise*.

Stone had a lot to say about being a man. Maybe Blount wanted to hear it.

The kitchen had no information to offer, except to tell me that Blount ate most of his meals out. Canned soup and tuna-fish in the cupboards, a carton of grapefruit juice, half a dozen eggs, and various condiments in the fridge. A lemon and a wilted head of lettuce in the vegetable drawer, a bottle of Stoli in the freezer. The drawers held the generic rental inventory: silverware, utensils, placemats and napkins, rudimentary pots and pans, an empty trash bin under the sink.

The austerity made it difficult to hide anything, but the place made me suspicious anyway—maybe for that reason. It dared you to find something. It was like a magician ostentatiously showing you his empty hands before the trick began.

I strolled back into the living room and looked around again. The only ornamentation had been built in: nicely worked base-boards, casings with wooden medallions at the top corners, and two wide beams crossing the ceiling.

The beams drew my attention. They were too big to be solid wood—no new construction specs would call for hugely expensive old-growth timber in a guest cottage. I dragged the battered-up chair from beneath the folding table, climbed up and tapped on the shiny white painted wood.

Hollow.

I saw a hairline rectangle in the paint, barely visible even from my perch. You'd never see it from the floor. I pushed up at it, felt a catch and heard a click as a spring released. The panel opened, oiled and silent, until it was pointing down at the floor. The workmanship impressed me. Blount was quite a carpenter, along with everything else.

I paused for a second. I knew exactly what I was going to find up there. I reached up and proved myself right: a Barrett M107 sniper's rifle, the weapon that had killed Todd Macy, along with a box of ammunition. David Lattimer's rifle, still waiting to be switched back. Time had run out for that trick, but it would never have worked for long, anyway. The rifle I found in David's closet felt new and unused. This one was worn and battered, with a patina of age on the wooden stock. This weapon had seen history, and made it. That one was just a replica. The ballistics were an afterthought.

Blount was finished.

Fraker's forensics team had arrived. They were working the crime scene at the main house. I started over. I wanted to check out the mansion and give them the heads-up about the rifle.

Sue Ann fell into step beside me. "Did you find something in there?"

"That's police business, Sue Ann. Sorry."

I was thinking, why would someone who went to such lengths to hide one murder weapon ditch another one only half-hidden in the mulch beside his house? Panic? Phelan was on his way and Blount had to move fast. The rifle's cubbyhole was the product of a lot of thought and craftsmanship, virtually a hobbyist's project. Maybe Blount wasn't as good when he had to improvise. He called 911, knowing that anyone who cared to look would see the butt of his knife sticking up like the mumblety-peg prize winner. He must have been terrified. But I didn't buy that, either. He and Liam made an even match and Blount struck me as the kind of guy who enjoyed a good tussle.

Maybe he thought Liam was armed, and Blount's only weapon was a blood-smeared blade he didn't dare to use. Still, it was crazy to call the cops when you'd just left a dead body next door. Or else that was the strategy. Do the crazy thing precisely because you wouldn't. It made you look innocent—or diabolical.

I couldn't figure it out. But Blount might have some answers for me when I talked to him at the station.

The Crime Scene Unit boss consisted of a fat fifty-year-old with granny glasses and a ponytail named Rick Rogers.

He waddled over to me. "Jesus. This fucking house, am I right? They keep killing people here. Make a good ghost story if they all came back to haunt the place."

"And then they all left because the Nantucket summer people scared them too much."

"They're scary, all right. One of Lonnie's boys was canvassing the neighborhood just now. Some old turd in a bathrobe told him, 'I'll sue you and your department for harassment and ruin your career. Now get off my property.'"

I nodded. "Oh, yeah. That's one of their favorites. As if standing on their sod square insta-lawn smelling the fertilizer stink was a divine privilege and they could ruin your life by revoking it."

"Yeah. Fuck them."

I told him about the rifle, eased past the chalk outline on the stained carpet and started up the stairs to the second floor. I was trying to visualize exactly what had happened. Blount had known that Phelan was coming but the road was invisible from the cottage, and the 911 call came from there. If someone had been in the big house they could have seen Phelan's car; from the second floor they could have seen all the way to Madaket Road and the Eel Point road turn-off. But the house had been deserted: no cleaning staff scheduled for the day, Pell on his boat, Sue Ann birding at the west end of the island. I went inside and checked the rooms with a view of the road anyway: the master bedroom, with the heavy curtains drawn and the shades and louvers closed behind them; and the study, with its dark stained wood paneling and brown venetian blinds, closed against the daylight. The place felt abandoned, the air stale and chilly. The mild weather hadn't penetrated this mausoleum. It felt at least ten degrees colder than the day outside.

I pulled out my iPhone, turned on the lights, and took some pictures of the two rooms. Something struck me as askew—there was some wrong note I couldn't identify. The pictures might help.

I lingered for a few more minutes, but I didn't notice anything unusual—no clues. Finally I left the CSI boys to do their work and drove back to the station.

Chapter Twenty-four

Confessions

I wanted to interview Doug Blount, but when I walked into the cop shop Barnaby Toll had news that sent me off in a different direction completely. It reminded me of getting trapped in the right lane on the highway then forced off onto an unwanted exit. Suddenly you're cruising some woodsy two-lane road in the middle of nowhere, looking for the on-ramp.

Mike Henderson had been arrested for the murder of Andrew Thayer. Haden Krakauer had picked the housepainter up himself. Mike refused a lawyer and wouldn't talk to anyone but me. This had to be a ludicrous mistake.

I told Barnaby to bring Mike up to my office.

"Do you want him cuffed, Chief?"

"No, Barney. No handcuffs. Just escort him upstairs and then get us some coffee."

When Mike was seated across the desk from me, I said, "What the hell is going on?"

"I can explain it."

"I'm sure you can. In fact, I can't wait."

"Okay…but this has to stay here. It's kind of embarrassing, and unprofessional, so…"

"My lips are sealed. As long as you actually didn't kill anyone."

"Jesus, Chief! Of course I didn't kill anyone! I can't even discipline my dog. I say 'sit' and he just stares at me like, 'you have got to be kidding.'"

"So what happened?"

"First of all, I had no idea there was a dead guy in the house. I was touching up the downspouts, I couldn't clean the paint off them and I mean—you're not supposed to get paint on the copper downspouts, you know? That looks bad. I couldn't clean it, so I painted over it. I mixed the paint and I made a mess—it was on my hands, and someone was driving by when I was walking to the car, and it must have looked like blood…but wouldn't it have been really red if I'd just killed someone? Anyway, they called it in and when Krakauer arrived at the house I was cleaning myself up. I guess I looked like Lady Macbeth or something—'Out, out damned spot!' But I mean…come on. Why would I kill Andy Thayer? He was one of my best customers. I bid super low on his interior one winter—the house on Union Street—and when he came back to the island he looked around and said 'No way you could do this job for ten grand.' He gave me an extra thousand in cash and took me out to dinner at the Ship's Inn. That's a guy I'd want to kill? Clone, is more like it."

Barney came in with two cups of coffee. I waited until he was gone. "Just milk okay?"

"Great, thanks."

"So, did you notice anything at the house when you were there?"

"Like what?"

"People, vehicles, screams, crashes, doors slamming? Anything at all."

"A clue?"

"Exactly."

"Why do I want to say Professor Plum in the billiards room with a candlestick?"

"Don't worry about it. Death makes people silly. Until it sinks in. Until you really feel that hole in the world. And the longer you can put that off, the better."

"Yeah."

We sipped our coffee. It had been sitting on the burner too long. "So…anything?"

"I heard a car pull out. But it must have been parked in the garage. I didn't see anything when I got there."

"So someone was at the house."

"I guess."

"Did they seem to be in a hurry? Did you hear the engine revving, or shells getting churned up?"

"No, nothing like that. Just a car heading out."

"Okay, thanks, Mike. You're a good witness."

"Painters notice things. They call each other out. Painter's favorite comment? You missed a spot."

I nodded. "That's the thing. I think I missed a spot here but I can't figure out where."

"Walk away and look at it again. That's what I do. My old boss used to say 'step back and admire your work' because he knew if you did that you'd see all your fuck-ups."

We stood. I came around the desk and shook his hand. "I may give that a try."

When he was gone I drained the last swallow of my tepid coffee and went downstairs to brace Douglas Blount.

◇◇◇

Lonnie Fraker was coming out of the interrogation room when I arrived. He grinned at me. "Ho, ho, ho—Merry Christmas."

"It's June."

"Yeah? Well Jesus was born in June supposedly. You'll believe it when you get in there with that bum."

"You broke him with your up-to-the-minute interrogation techniques?"

"Very funny. I didn't have to do shit. He was ready to confess. All he needed was a shoulder to cry on. But just for the record…I told him my theory. And I nailed it."

"Your theory?"

"It's a classic love triangle, Chief. Crime of passion."

I wasn't sure how Blount would fit into the Macy-Thayer-Lattimer intrigue. Then it occurred to me: Blount was the third party, and he set Lattimer up for the crime. Hence the rifle switch. That was where all the evidence pointed, and it looked like Lonnie had gotten there faster than me.

I gave him a neutral nod. "Sounds interesting. Anything on paper yet?"

"We were waiting for you."

"Thanks."

"Interdepartmental communication. That's my watchword."

I couldn't resist. "But that sounds like two words, Lonnie."

"Fine, whatever. My watch-phrase, then."

"Your motto."

"Right."

"You need to make it catchier, though. Like...working together because togetherness works."

"Nah—that sounds like we're teaching Kindergarten or something."

"How about...'A Safe Nantucket. The State Police and the NPD: Keeping it. Period. Together. Period.' You get a nice double meaning there."

He gave me a grudging nod. "Not bad, Kennis. Now go inside and open your presents."

In the box, as we called it in L.A., Blount was sitting at the table, uncuffed, nursing a paper cup of takeout coffee. He looked deflated, unthreatening, like a man who'd been waiting all night in the hospital for the surgeons to finish. Or maybe just after he'd gotten the bad news—that strange combination of sorrow and relief. At least the ordeal was over.

I sat down across from him. "So Captain Fraker tells me you want to confess."

"Why not?"

"Do you want a lawyer present? You have the right to legal representation."

"If I can't afford a lawyer, one will be appointed for me by the court."

"That's right."

"Probably Jim Folger. Or Timmy Congdon. Am I right?"

I nodded. "It's Wednesday so probably it'll be Tim."

"Either way, I'm better off on my own."

No one had much respect for our beleaguered PDs. "Just so you know, anything you say—"

"Yeah, yeah, I know. They Mirandized me, Chief. Just like on the TV cop shows."

"But this is real."

"And here I thought I was dreaming."

We studied each other across the table. "You killed Andrew Thayer."

"That's right. In cold blood. Except it's hot."

"I think they're talking about your blood there, Doug. Not the victim's."

"Then they know what they're talking about."

"You cut his throat and never got a drop on you. Nice trick."

"You do it from behind, Chief. The blood shoots forward. You step back. Like a little dance. You learn that in Ranger training."

"I missed out on that."

"Lucky for you."

"So…You got Andrew Thayer out to the LoGran house. How did you swing that?"

"He knew we needed to talk. I offered to settle things. That was how I put it. He was happy to come."

"What things?"

"It's a long story."

"That's how people describe a story when they don't want to tell it."

"I'll tell it. I'm glad to tell it."

"Good. I like long stories. The short ones are usually bullshit."

"Like your buddy's love triangle killing spree."

"My colleague."

"Right."

"According to him it was all because of a woman."

"Guys who haven't had a woman in long time always think that. Like poor guys always think it's about money."

"So he was wrong?"

"He saw what I wanted him to see. If he was the top of the food chain the cops would have written the whole thing off as Nantucket winter cabin fever craziness. Shut it down and avoid the bad publicity. But there's too much going on, and there's smarter people than Fraker out there. Not all of them are cops either, due respect. Some of them are high school kids. That was my mistake. I underestimated some shit. I didn't know how fucked up everything was going to get. Actions have consequences, and consequences have consequences, and victims have families, and families have friends and pretty soon it just gets—I don't know, Chief. I'm okay at chess, but three-dimensional chess—forget about it."

I tipped my chair back, let him run down. "So what was really going on?"

"Well, Fraker got one part right. Cherche la femme, brother. In this case it's one Daisy Pell."

"You mean Daisy DeHart."

"I mean Daisy Pell. He adopted her when he married the mom. She kept her real father's name—DeHart. She's been working at NHS for a year or two."

"Right. She's a guidance counselor, a school psychologist."

"Which is fucking hilarious. But I guess all shrinks are a little crazy, right? Why else do a job like that?"

"By that logic all cops are crooks."

"You said it, Chief. Not me. Anyway, she pulled a little disappearing act last week. She was trying to get away from Papa Bear. Smart move. She went to high school here. It feels like home. Pell comes out for a month or two in the summer and he lives on the boat—easy to avoid. Rich people's Nantucket is a tiny little place. If you don't eat at the Pearl, play tennis at the Yacht Club, or golf at Sankaty Head…you're pretty much in the clear. Just make sure you avoid cocktail parties and fundraisers. That was no hardship for Daisy. She hates those assholes anyway."

"So you were in love with her?"

"Love is for suckers, Chief. We had a thing from time to time."

"And the others?"

"Oh yeah—Macy and Thayer, sure. And I know for a fact that Lattimer had a creepy geriatric crush on her."

"That's why you planted the rifle."

"I seized the opportunity. I'm an opportunist. Fraker's version makes sense on that level—Daisy driving everyone crazy. You ever meet her?"

"Just once."

"Then you know what I'm talking about."

"Really? Why is that?"

"Because you're a mammal, Chief. I'd say because you're straight, but fags fall in love with her too. Dogs follow her around. Her mom bought a cat for herself when Daisy was a kid. It drove Mom crazy because it would only sleep on Daisy's bed. They tried locking the cat out of Daisy's room. Nice try. It dug a tunnel under the door. Shredded the floorboards. What can I say? She has animal magnetism. I mean that literally, Chief. Put the palm of your hand an inch from her bare shoulder and try not to touch her. Just try it. I'd like to see that one."

"So let me guess," I said, pulling him back from his swoon. "You used Daisy to get them involved with this dirty movie scheme—"

"They jumped in, Chief. That's like you telling me I used the pastry cart from the Wauwinet to break up the Weight Watchers club. Nice work if you can get it. They've still got the jam and the crumbs all over their faces. Pigs."

"You supplied the drugs, got the girls hooked, Chick Crosby handled the technical side."

"And Daisy recruited from her office at school."

"Why?"

"Why what?"

"Why would she do that? Why would any woman do that? Those girls trusted her."

He shrugged. "People are fucked up. What can I say?"

"That's not good enough."

"Then ask her."

"Where is she?"

"You're the detective. You figure it out."

"Doug, if you know where she is and you withhold that information, it's going to add obstruction of justice to the counts against you. That means another five years in jail."

"That's like saying, they're going to drill another tooth while you're at the dentist's office. I'm in the chair anyway. My jaw's numb and my calendar's clear, so I say, bring it."

This was getting me nowhere. And we had other things to talk about.

"We found Lattimer's rifle in the guest cottage," I said.

"We?"

"I found it."

"You got your nose twitching after you found the knife."

"Something like that." I remembered what Mike Henderson had told me once: a visible mistake at eye-level, like paint on a doorknob or a big miss on a window casing, made the customer inspect the whole job more critically.

"You don't want them to start looking," he said. "Because once they start looking they're going to find more. And when that critical eye starts squinting, they'll never be happy. You don't want to knock down that first domino."

Blount had done that with his hunting knife and he knew it. And he knew what it meant. He sighed. "So now you want to know about Todd Macy and the old man."

"I have a pretty good idea, Doug. Todd wanted to get out of your little movie studio, maybe rat you all out for immunity. You can only drink so much bad water before you get sick."

Blunt grinned. "He was thirsty."

"So he makes noises about getting away and then he has a hunting accident."

"Tough luck."

"You took the shell casings, but you left the actual bullet in the ground. That was your mistake. You switched your rifle for Lattimer's. I was supposed to find it, and when the ballistics report came back I was supposed to figure out the old man was in love with Daisy and lost control when he found out about her little thing with Macy. He was a trained killer. Any doubts about that got burned off in Vietnam. Plus, he wrote a letter that basically makes your case for you. He threw it away but we found it in his trash. So it would have been the perfect plan, except you never managed to switch the rifles back. The ballistics are going to match up with the gun in your cottage."

"It's like Vince Lombardi liked to say—we didn't lose the game, we just ran out of time."

"But he did lose. And so did you."

"And the police chief wonders why I'm confessing. Hey, I was screwed when you found the knife, anyway. They can't put me away for two life sentences. I did what I did. Maybe I want to take the credit. That's the problem with setting someone up. No one ever knows about it. Like putting a word into the language—like 'nonogamy.' That's your dad's word, right? From *The Virgins of West Fourth Street*. Great movie. The horny married dude who bangs his wife's sister? He's the one who came up with it, right? Your dad was funny as hell. And he was right. We needed a word for that. For…" He closed his eyes, setting the words in place, getting them right: "Being sexually faithful to a woman who's not fucking you." He laughed "Perfect. And yet—twenty years later, no one thinks of David Kennis! Or even the movie. They just use the word. Nonogamy. Your dad's anonymous. See? That's the price you pay."

I found the analogy insulting. Bizarrely accurate but insulting. What the hell—my dad would have been amused. And the ability to construct meaningful analogies was a sign of high intelligence, just as much as the one he chose was a sign of severe social pathology. Smart and crazy. I preferred Blount as a dumb bully. But that was his mask. The cunning predator in front of me was the real foe I had to deal with.

"So, Macy wanted out. But I don't believe Andy Thayer was involved with your little games."

"He was involved with Daisy."

"Like everyone else."

"No, no, no. Lattimer had a crush on her, yeah. I used that. And Macy was in love, for sure. But he was nothing to her. Something bad she stepped in. She scraped him off the bottom of her shoe and moved on. I fucked her from time to time but that was it. Thayer was the real deal. He got her to quit—the movie racket, the drugs, everything. He was going to the cops. We burned his house to scare him off, but it didn't work. So boom. Dead men tell no tales. Unless you go to one of those mediums—John Edward, guys like that. Then you find out why dead men tell no tales. They're fucking boring. What's new, dead guy? Nothing, you fucking moron. I'm dead."

"You killed him and you joke about it."

"Yeah, Chief. Nothing's sacred."

"Two men are dead. A third was looking at spending the last years of his life in jail for a crime he didn't commit."

"You're forgetting the kid."

Of course. "Oscar Graham figured everything out. He knew what you did to Jill."

"So I did the same thing to him. It kept those other kids in line."

"And now you get to take the credit."

"Along with everything else."

I felt a quick rush of fear. We should have handcuffed Blount. What did he have to lose by killing me right here and now? This was sloppy police work. I couldn't leave. I didn't want to put my back to him. Maybe I was getting paranoid.

Best to keep him talking. "You must be a very persuasive guy, Doug. Toby Keller, right. You got him to fake the invoices for your truck. He's in a lot of trouble now."

"Well, that's what you get for fixing cars while you're high on oxycodone. He was one of my best customers, Chief. But I always told him—save it for after work."

"He thought you were his pal."

"Big mistake."

"He's not too bright. But you are. You're a pretty smart guy, Doug."

"Sure. Like with Macy—leaving that iPod mini at the scene, loaded with Lattimer's music. That was a shrewd move."

"But it wasn't his music. African pop? Johnny Clegg and Savuka? Mahotella Queens?"

"You found the records in his library."

"Because you planted them there!"

He grinned. "Now it can be told."

"That poor old guy. Just because he let some young girl flirt with him."

"That's the price of nonogamy, Chief."

"At his age."

"At any age. Just wait."

Time to move on. I still had problems with his story. "You're quite the tough guy."

"So?"

"Does anything scare you, Doug?"

"I don't think about it."

"Anyone?"

"Like who?"

"Like Liam Phelan."

He just stared at me.

"You called 911. Why bring the cops to that house at that moment unless you were afraid for your life?"

"I panicked."

"I don't think so."

"Then why?"

"How did you even know he was coming? You can't see the road from the cottage."

"I heard his car."

"Over the air conditioning?"

"I have excellent hearing. Doctors call it 20-20 audition."

"There was a call on your phone from an anonymous number less than a minute before you called the cops. I think you were following orders. You were set up to go down for these killings, and you accepted that. You've been in jail before. From what I can tell, you carved out quite the little nice life for yourself there. But someone must have something big on you, Doug. Something huge. Something that ensures your loyalty and your gratitude and your fear. You're like a serf or a samurai, ready to take the knife for your master. But who's your master? That's what I need to know."

"You're reaching, Chief. I flipped out when I heard Phelan's car. That's all. No one was going to check out the big house and the chances of anyone noticing a knife hilt behind a bush were just about zero. This was pretty much a domestic disturbance call. Two friends duking it out. I wasn't sure I could take him and no one likes a beat down. Especially a bully, and I'm a bully, right? All us bullies are gutless assholes when the chips are down. Everyone knows that. So I panicked, like I said. Guess I'm just a big pussy, Chief."

"That's your story?"

"That's the truth. Sad to say."

"It's also exactly what you'd say if I was right."

He grinned. "So it is. For all the good it does you."

"So when I get a warrant and confiscate Chick Crosby's computer I'll find all the films and e-mails I need to convict everyone."

"Including a little Oscar-bait short subject we were using to blackmail Andy Thayer."

"Or lure him out here so you could kill him."

A shrug. "That, too. He said he was willing to negotiate but I didn't believe him. That boy was on a mission from God. Or Cupid, if Roman gods count."

I stood up and walked to the door. The moment of danger had passed. Blount had pulled into himself like a turtle.

I turned back to him. "I'm surprised you didn't try to make a deal before you told me all this."

"Right—you get me off on multiple homicides because I rat out drug dealers and amateur porn artists? They never even tried to sell those movies. They never posted them online. It was for their private fun. Nah—they're the small fish, Chief. It's just the opposite—you let one of them off the hook for turning State's evidence against me. That's how it really works."

"And which one of them would do that? Who actually knew what you were up to?"

"You mean—who's giving me my orders?"

"Exactly. Someone knew."

"Nobody wanted to know. Would you?"

"Was it McAllister? Chick Crosby? Charlie Forrest?"

"Pick a card, any card. It's your trick, Chief."

"Yes it is. We're done here. I'm asking for an expedited trial. I want you in jail by Labor Day. And don't bother asking for a change of venue. You won't get it."

◇◇◇

It went quickly after that. The State Police got a warrant and raided Chick Crosby's house. It turned out he had cultivated a side business selling the videos. There were buyers in California and Utah, Alabama, and Texas. That made it an FBI matter with charges ranging, in order of severity, from interstate transportation, shipment, selling, or possession with intent to sell visual depictions of a minor engaging in sexually explicit conduct (first offense, five years) to possession of visual depictions of a minor engaging in sexually explicit conduct (first offense, five years), possession of visual depictions of a minor engaging in sexually explicit conduct (no mandatory minimum) to simple possession of the material (no mandatory minimum) to the best one of all: child exploitation enterprise. That once carries a twenty-year mandatory sentence, and the whole sleazy group was going down for it, whether they knew anything about the sales or not.

McAllister and Nolan were arrested together, playing tennis at the Yacht Club, Forrest was dragged out of a Land Bank executive conference and stuffed into a police car on Broad Street, in full view of all the tourists waiting for lunch at The Brotherhood of Thieves. And Toby Keller, the garage mechanic who had faked the invoices that gave Blount's truck its alibi, was grabbed out from under a Range Rover in his own repair shop. We found Daisy hiding out in Andrew Thayer's house on Union Street.

It was huge. The arrests turned into a national story. Lonnie was interviewed on all the cable outlets. There was even a segment on *48 Hours.*

I got some calls from the media but I turned them down. I also got an angry call from Dan Taylor, speaking for the Selectmen, accusing me of wrecking the summer season.

My favorite line from him: "Couldn't this wait until Labor Day?"

I thought of the British Petroleum CEO after the Deepwater Horizon spill in the Gulf of Mexico, pouting: "I want my life back." Dan wasn't in that league but he was playing the same ball game—a Little League brat, running the small-town bases.

Dave Carmichael called me, too, the day after his big press conference on the case, still pushing for me to take the chief investigator job with his office in Boston.

"The offer is still open," he said.

"Dave—"

"And I'm saying that despite all your crazy crackpot liberal bullshit."

"I appreciate that."

"Lonnie's taking the credit for this case, but I know who really broke it."

"We got lucky."

"Take a collar once in a while, Henry. I have a nickname for you around here—crew neck. Get it? Because you *never take the collar.*"

"Nice one."

"What I'm saying—if you're going to give the credit to someone else, it oughtta be me, not that ass hat Lonnie Fraker. No offense. He's a nice guy, but come on."

"I'd love to do it, Dave. But I can't."

"I'll bump the pay twenty percent. That just about doubles what they're paying you on the sandbar."

"That's very generous, but—"

"Plus—Boston."

"You're killing me here."

"A staff of six."

"Jesus."

"Corner office on Ashford Street. Expense account. Never pay for lunch again."

I took a breath. "You and Marsha never had kids."

"Thank God."

"Well, if you ever get married again—"

"Never gonna happen. They say gays are going to destroy marriage. I wish they would. Put the institution out of its misery."

"I'm just saying…if you had kids, you'd understand."

"No, that's the difference between us. If I had kids *they'd* understand! They'd get it that their dad had a career and they'd be on the sidelines cheering."

"Spoken like a bitter childless middle-aged divorced workaholic."

"Which I am, and proud of it! Think about this job a little more, Henry, okay? I have a position to fill and I have to fill it soon."

It was a tempting offer. My kids needed their father in their lives and half an hour later, I had the perfect case in point for the attorney general—but no time to present it.

Chapter Twenty-five

Special Effects

I was sitting with Alana Trikilis when Lonnie Fraker called. She had taken down Ms. DeHart's license plate number and traced it. The car was owned by the LoGran corporation.

"Her real name is Daisy Pell!" Alana blurted. She's Jonathan Pell's daughter!"

"His stepdaughter, actually."

She slumped down in her chair. "You knew this already."

"Sorry."

"I'm going to keep working this,"

"I know. But Alana…I have to ask—who ran the license plate for you?"

"I shouldn't say."

"Then just nod. Bob Coffin. Alana?"

She nodded.

"I have to punish him, you know."

She nodded again. "He knew that. He knew you'd find out."

"True love. You know my dad said something about true love I've always remembered. He said, 'They say all the world loves a lover, but I dispute that. My son is in love, my daughter is in love, my cook is in love, my secretary is in love, two of my friends just fell in love, and they all stand under my window at night baying about it. So I can tell with great assurance that all the world does not love a lover. All the world is bored to tears by a lover.' He was a cynical old prick but he knew what he was talking about."

"Are you going to fire Bob?"

"No. I'll put him on janitor duty for a few months. And revoke his computer privileges."

That was when the phone rang.

"I have something you need to see." Lonnie Fraker, with no preamble. "It's the video of Andrew Thayer—the one they were using to blackmail him. There's something hinky about it."

I loved it that Lonnie still used the word hinky. "How do you mean?"

"I'm not sure. The FBI thinks it may have been doctored, but Thayer's dead and they have bigger fish to fry. They don't care about Andy's reputation. But we do. I made a copy. I'm sending it over. Check your e-mail."

Lonnie could always surprise me. Sure, he was a smug, careless, marginally competent glory-hound; but he was a decent guy, too—and not a spineless one. It couldn't have been easy to get that video away from the FBI. They hoard evidence like Billy Delavane's father hoarded fifty-year-old checkbooks and rusty fishhooks.

"Thanks, man," I said. "I'll take a look at it."

But I didn't get a chance to, not that day. I ushered Alana out and opened up my e-mail. First up—a message from the filmmaker Mark Toland, telling me he was on-island if I wanted to talk about the photographs he sent me, or just pick his brains about the crime scene, and I was about to call him—who better to look at the Andrew Thayer video?—when I got an hysterical call from my ex-wife.

"Tim has run away!" she moaned.

"Wait—what? Slow down. What happened?"

"He's gone! He took his bike and he's gone."

"So…he's riding his bike on a summer day unsupervised. You wanted to live in a place where that was okay. I'm not sure what you—"

"We had a fight. He said he hated me!"

"He's twelve, what do you expect?"

"He wanted to talk about your father—how he died, and my grandparents…and Todd Macy, he's still upset about that…and the poor kid who fell through the roof last winter, and Oscar Graham and Andy Thayer and Jill Phelan…and I don't know. He had a dream where all the dead people were hanging around the Boys and Girls Club. He asked if I was dying, like he thought I was sick or something, and he wanted to know about police fatalities as if you were going to be shot on the job, and…and I—it was morbid and creepy and—and sick, Henry! I told him it was sick and he screamed at me and took off, and he could be anywhere right now."

"It's a small island, Miranda."

"He could be killed the way he was riding! He wasn't looking where he was going. He wasn't even on the bike path!"

"Now you're sounding morbid."

"We have to find him!"

"Does he have his phone with him?"

"You think he's talking on the phone while he's riding? Or texting? Oh, my God, I've told him a million times—"

"No, no—but I installed a GPS app so we could find the kids' phones if they ever lost them. I can use it to find Tim just as easily, if he has the phone with him."

"He always has the phone with him. He's surgically attached to that stupid phone!"

She was the one who had insisted they have top-of-the-line smartphones. I preferred landlines. But this wasn't the best moment to bring up that disagreement.

"I'll find him," I said.

"Good because this is on you."

"What?"

"We came here so we could raise our children away from fear and violence but you carry it with you everywhere you go. It's like body odor."

"That's bullshit."

"Just look at the last few years—Tim's formative years! You were beaten up by that horrible thug in the sandpit, the one who killed Preston Lomax!"

"I remember. Ed Delavane is in prison now, Miranda. He's no threat to anyone."

"But he put you in the hospital, Henry! Then the fireworks last year—"

"I stopped that lunatic from bombing the pops concert!"

"And he practically killed you in the process! And you dragged Tim into the next fight. Goading him on to fight with that horrible bully. I begged you to stay out of it. But no, you had to prove something to Timmy, you had to prove you were a man! And when the horrible bully's horrible father attacked you, your own son had to come to the rescue! Your own son! You needed a ten-year-old boy to save you."

"He and a few other people."

"How do you think that made him feel?"

"He was proud of himself. He was proud of me. We were proud of each other."

"And now he's brooding about death! No twelve-year-old boy should be brooding about death."

"I did."

"Great, so it's in the genes. You've got him both ways, nature and nurture. This is so fucked up. He could be dead himself now while we sit around talking about it."

"I'll find him, I told you that."

"You better," she said, and disconnected. She would have preferred to hang up on me, I'm sure, like in the good old days of primitive technology, when you could slam an actual phone down on its cradle for dramatic effect. Miranda had always been fond of dramatic effect.

But maybe she was right. I tried to shield the kids from the darker aspects of my job but I hadn't been doing so well lately. It wasn't a problem for Caroline—she sailed through life's complications and difficulties like a yacht through kelp. Tim was the swimmer thrashing in the wake behind her, tangled up in the seaweed.

◇◇◇

The GPS app located Tim at the site of the Thayer cottage arson. He had spent time there with Debbie Gibson before Caroline swept in and appropriated her. Tim was a year younger than the girls. Which had proved socially calamitous during the school year. Girls their age liked older boys. Carrie and Debbie were in high school now, which made the gap even wider. A lot of Tim's happiest memories had gone up in smoke two weeks ago. No wonder the world seemed unstable to him now.

I pulled into the dirt driveway. Tim turned around at the engine note of my cruiser, then resumed his study of the ruins. A scorched chimney stood out of the ashes and rubble amid the lingering stink of burned carpet and plastic.

I walked up and stood beside him. "Hey."

"Hey."

"You okay? Your mom was worried."

"She always worries. She's a 'watch out-sayer,' like Granma says. I bet Granma wasn't like that."

"No, she'd let us do pretty much anything. Climb rocks in Central Park, ride our bikes to school on the city streets…even ride the subway!"

"Granma's sick, isn't she?"

I tried to catch his eye, but he was looking down studying the incinerated skeleton of a sleeper couch. "Granma has Parkinson's Disease, but she was diagnosed when she was seventy, so it moves more slowly. She's got a lot of good years left."

"But she could die tomorrow."

"We could all die tomorrow."

"Like the dinosaurs, when that meteor hit."

"Or we could do it to ourselves. We have plenty of bombs."

"Plus global warming."

"Right. Who needs a stupid meteor?"

He gave me a quick look and a wan smile; no laugh.

"I don't want to die."

"Me neither."

"I don't want you to die or Mom to die or Carrie, or…anyone. Except maybe Jake Sauter. Just kidding."

"Immortality would be weird, though. Think about it. Whole clusters of friends and family would keep dying while you stayed young. You'd start to think of other people the way we think about pets. You know—they're a tragedy waiting to happen, don't get too attached. Plus it would be hard remembering everything, once you'd lived for three or four hundred years. I have trouble with what I did on my birthday fifteen years ago. Where was I on June fifth, 1735? Forget about it."

He brightened a little. "Like they say on police shows." He put on a gruff interrogator's voice—"Where were you on the night of June fifth?"

I liked his tough-guy-interrogator voice. "I have no alibi for any time during the Austrian Succession."

"But what if everybody lived forever?"

"I don't know…It would be pretty crowded by now."

"Yeah." He kicked at the ashes. Something that had been the leg of a table crumbled. "Why would someone burn this place down?"

"I don't know."

"It was so nice."

"Yeah, I know you guys liked it."

"Debbie really liked it a lot."

"I know."

"Maybe people are just bad."

"Some of them."

"Most of them, I think. Like whoever killed Mr. Macy."

"Your grandfather used to say ninety percent of everything is bad. Finding the other ten percent—that's the secret of life."

"I guess."

"Look, there's plenty of good people. It's just…the bad people make more noise. They get in the newspaper. They burn stuff down. You don't get in the newspaper for building this cottage, or spending time here and enjoying it. That's not news. Can you see the headline? LOCAL COTTAGE REMAINS

INTACT WHILE CHILDREN INSIDE ENJOY ANOTHER
UNEVENTFUL SUMMER AFTERNOON."

He laughed. "Details at eleven!"

"I'm sure everyone would tune in for that one."

He looked up at me, serious again. "You're going to catch
whoever did this. Aren't you?"

"It doesn't bother you that I have to deal with this awful stuff
all the time?"

"I think it's cool."

"Well, thank you."

His next question took me by surprise. "Do we go somewhere
when we die?"

"I don't know. I hope so."

"Debbie says we do. She's Catholic."

"She may be right. Most people in the world agree with her."

"But you don't."

"We'll all find out, eventually."

"Are you sick too?"

"No! I just meant—it's…who else is sick?"

"Granma Flo and Granny Mary. And Carl at school has MS.
And, I don't know. Lots of people. They were all fine until they
got sick and then bang. You could get sick, too."

"I'll try not to."

"You better."

I could hear the echo of his mother's voice in that mock
threat. Nature and nurture. I tipped my head and touched two
fingers to my forehead. "Okay, boss."

Another silence slipped between us: birds, distant cars, wind
shuffling the leaves. Finally: "If everyone just dies and there's
no Heaven or anything, what's the point? Why bother doing
anything?"

I felt like we'd arrived at the heart of the matter. And I felt
a quick flush of relief. This had nothing to do with my profession. This was just the basic material of being human. "Well,"
I said, "you have to figure that one out for yourself. For me it's
just…I feel like it's a privilege to be here on this gorgeous planet

for a while. Breathe that air. It's so soft and pure, you can taste the ocean on it. Look around, it's beautiful out here. You get to enjoy it."

"I guess."

"Would you skip a ride at Disney World, just because it ended?"

"No."

"So take the ride. It beats standing on the line. It's like Warren Zevon said—"

"Who's Warren Zevon?"

"Okay, my bad. You need hear some Warren Zevon. He was a singer-songwriter. He died of cancer and instead of getting all these awful treatments and losing his hair and being miserable, he decided to walk away from the doctors and do what he loved doing. In his case that meant…recording an album. So he made one last record, and then he died. It's a pretty good record, too."

"So what did he say?"

"'Enjoy every sandwich.' That was his deathbed advice. Speaking of which, I'm hungry and Provisions is open. Want to get one of those sandwiches Warren was talking about? We'll throw the bike in the car."

"Okay, but that doesn't change anything. We're still going to die and Debbie still dumped me and Mom's still mad."

"And you haven't even started your summer reading yet! And one of the books is *The Pearl*. You're going to have to get through that book, somehow. Assuming you survive to the ninth grade."

"You're supposed to be cheering me up."

"Sorry."

"I hate everything."

"Yeah, it's a crappy deal. So…I'm having the Sicilian tuna, what about you?"

"Turkey Terrific. And that iced tea they make with the mint."

I ruffled his hair. "Kid, you're turning into a regular existentialist—Camus style."

"Who was that?"

"A philosopher who thought a lot about this stuff. But he had fun, and he noticed things. He loved life, despite the crappy deal. In his notebooks one day he wrote, hold on let me get this right, because I really love this quote…"In the evening, the gentleness of the world on the bay. There are days when the world lies and days when it tells the truth. It is telling the truth this evening—with what sad and insistent beauty."

"Is he still alive?"

"He died in a car crash at age forty-seven. He was just four years older than I am now. The worst part was he was walking to the train station, and he had his ticket in his pocket. Some friends drove by and offered him a lift. Half an hour later they were all dead."

"Ugh."

"Yeah…and all kinds of mean stupid people live into their nineties, making everyone miserable."

"That's so…not fair."

"Yeah."

I picked up his bike and we started back to my cruiser, rolling it beside us. When we got to the car, Tim said "I'm not hungry anymore."

"You will be. Trust me."

"Just be careful driving."

"If I speed I'll write myself a ticket." He laughed. "What?"

"Granma always says 'don't beat yourself up.' But if you beat yourself up, it would be police brutality!"

"I could get in trouble for that."

We flattened the backseats, jammed the bike inside and drove to town. By the time we got to Provisions, Tim had gotten his appetite back.

We took our sandwiches out onto the wharf—the ice cream shop had wooden benches set up on a deck overlooking the harbor. I could sense Tim's mood darkening again. Had I said something wrong? It was impossible to know. Maybe it had nothing to do with me. There were no rules for parenting, despite the noise of competing experts, who all disagreed with each other anyway.

Our pediatrician had just shrugged. "Make it up as you go along," he said. "That's what everyone else does."

◇◇◇

I dropped Tim back at Miranda's and drove out toward 'Sconset. I felt inept and trapped and frustrated. The feeling had been growing since Dave Carmichael's first phone call, and my knee-jerk refusal of the job at the AG's office. It was impossible, I understood that—Miranda would never had let me move the kids to Boston, and I wasn't walking out on them.

That was my dad's move—ditching his family on Christmas Eve, leaving nothing behind but a present for my mother picked out by his new girlfriend.

There's a photograph of the two of us on one of his movie locations. They were shooting in Brooklyn and I'd been let out of school for the day to watch. I was my son's age in that picture. Dad was the age I am now. I'm looking up at him adoringly; he's smiling down on me. He was the King of Hollywood then—one of the kings, anyway, at the pinnacle of his success. I remember the story in *Time* magazine about the making of that film, and the pull quote from him about the unknown Italian bombshell who played the female lead: "She's a star because I say she's a star."

That's where he was at that moment in his life. Where was I, now? Struggling to make ends meet, giving up on them ever overlapping even for a moment, running the cop shop in what Franny and my brother derided as a tiny backwater, my writing reduced to a hobby, living in an apartment so small I didn't even have separate bedrooms for the kids.

But my son had a father. That's what I told myself: not a super-star who blew into his life the way Elton John arrived in Las Vegas for lavish two week engagements, but a real father. My daughter was going to be one of the only women I'd ever met who didn't have some kind of screwed up relationship with her father—at least that was my goal, and I was working on it every day. I was proud of it. Those kids needed me. And I needed them.

I read a fashionable essay on fatherhood when Miranda was pregnant with Caroline. The man described a day at the playground with his wife and daughter. The little girl fell off the jungle-jim and ran past him screaming "Mommy! Mommy! Mommy!" He might as well have been a fireplug. It broke his heart. I knew even then, before my daughter was born, when she was just a blur on the ultrasound screen that I never wanted that to happen to me.

But here was the alternative: an endless set of self-extinguishing sacrifices for the sake of my children, the two of them presiding over the center of my life while my own ambitions and desires and needs were exiled to the outskirts, junked and forgotten. I could follow my ambitions and wreck their lives or stay put and wreck my own. There was no way out, no ingenious escape plan.

This was the trick where Houdini drowns.

Sacrifice is supposed to be noble. You're supposed to feel good about it, pure and strong and righteous. I felt bad and puny and resentful.

I shook my head hard, as if there was water in my ears. Something bad in there, a tinnitus of unseemly self-pity. Poor me—healthy white American male living on the richest island in the richest country in the world. Snap out of it!

I still had a job to do, an important one with actual rules and metrics and I was good at it, and I'd proved that fact over and over again.

Settle for that, pal, it's pretty good.

I turned the cruiser around and headed back to the station. Mark Toland was waiting for me.

◇◇◇

Barnaby Toll had set him up in front of a video monitor and he was watching the blackmail footage when I arrived. Toland hit pause and stood to shake my hand. He was six-foot-two, exactly my height, but he had the lean, loose-jointed look of a long-distance runner. His clothes hung off him in a casual spill—UCLA tee-shirt under what looked like a thousand dollars' worth of gray Italian silk suit jacket, designer jeans, and black leather dress loafers with no socks. The tan and the pair of sunglasses stuck into the crew neck of his tee-shirt completed the *GQ* photo layout image of a young movie director.

His grip was uncomfortably firm, but his blue eyes shifted nervously over my shoulder to the open door. "Hey, is Haden Krakauer around today?"

"You want to see him?"

His laugh was caught somewhere between a cough and a sigh. "No, Chief. In fact he's the last person I want to see. This is a little nerve-wracking."

"Is there a problem?"

"No, no—I don't know. Yeah, probably. It all happened a long time ago, but, I mean…time kind of folds up on itself when it comes to…"

"What are you talking about? What happened?"

"I'd rather not discuss it. If that's okay? And I'd really appreciate it if you didn't say anything to Haden."

"Of course. Don't worry. And he's off-duty today, so…"

"Thanks, I appreciate it." The tension went out of his shoulders and he glanced around the room. "Quite a place you've got here."

"The locals call it Valhalla."

"That makes you Odin then."

I shrugged. "I don't really get the Norse gods. They didn't create the world. They just kibbitz."

"Well Odin created writing—that makes him a good fit for you. He taught us puny humans to make runes."

"You know about my writing?"

"The magic of Google, Chief. You're all over the Net. Mostly your silly couplets—'I never thought I could love a herbivore/ but I never met a girl who was quite like her before.' Or what was that other one? Right—'Young people think old age is/ a disease that's contagious.'"

"That's actually something my mother said to me a few years ago, rhyme and all. It irritated me at the time. She's always most annoying when she's most right."

"Well, you were right today. This video's a fake." He sat down and started the tape again. I pulled up a chair and sat beside him. "It's obviously an amateur job, too. Some local yokel, no offense."

"How can you tell?"

"I'm no image forensics expert, but whoever did this left some big footprints. See her profile here? The blurred edge?" he paused the tape. "You can use video software to create that look, but it's all about mathematical formulas and algorithms. Any single frame looks off a little, not quite real. Because it isn't." He started the film up again. "Look at the way she's moving on top of him. I know there's a lot of distraction in there, but study her shoulders and her hair. They tried to match the real motion and it didn't quite work. See that little jerk, it's like she got an electric shock, but nothing registers on her face. That's a dead giveaway. The girl in this video was fucking somebody else. Check it out—the shadows don't match up. A professional editor could have fixed that in post. The question is—who was she actually fucking? And who was really on top of this guy?"

I reached over to turn off the video, the way you'd turn away from a dislocated bone or a disfigured face.

"I know the girl they used for this," I said.

It was Jill Phelan.

And I had a pretty good idea who the mystery woman was, also. I had a lot of questions for her to answer. But I had to find her first.

I walked Toland out to his car.

"So you're thinking of shooting a movie here?" I asked him.

"Not anymore."

"Too expensive hauling all that equipment over?"

"Well, yeah, but that's not the reason. I was mostly just doing it to be near this woman, to try and—well, you know. It was pointless. I drove by her house and I saw her and her husband and their new baby and I thought to myself, 'What the hell is wrong with you? You want to wreck that home? Not that you even could. You've spent one night with this woman in the last ten years. What kind of basis is that for anything?' I make movies, Chief. I make up stories. I live in my head. I have this idea about the woman and for all I know it has nothing to do with reality. Nothing!"

"But it was a good night."

"Yeah. We'll always have Paris."

I knew more about this story than I felt comfortable with. He was talking about Mike and Cindy Henderson. Her night with Mark Toland at the Sherry Netherland had been a bizarre footnote in the Lomax murder investigation, one piece in the jigsaw picture of an undocumented day that left Mike without an alibi for the killing.

Toland was about to drive away when he poked his head out of the car window "Chief?"

"Yeah?"

"Do you know a high school student named Alana Trikilis?"

That stopped me. They had both been at the arson scene, but they had never spoken to each other, at least not at the police station, and I was surprised he knew her name.

"Yeah, actually I do. But I'm not exactly sure why you'd be—"

"I was looking through an old issue of the school paper while I was waiting for you today. I'll read anything. When I was a kid I used to memorize the ingredients lists on cereal boxes. I still don't understand how adding butylated hydroxtalene to the packaging material preserves freshness. Anyway…I saw a cartoon she drew in *Veritas*, right?—the high school newspaper?"

So that was how he knew her. My world was getting smaller by the minute. I nodded.

"It was a drawing of the school baseball team—the Whalers? They're standing in some kind of dinghy, being towed by an actual whale, and one kid's holding a bat like a harpoon. They all look scared shitless and the caption says 'If Team Names Were True.'"

I nodded. "I saw that one. She's talented. She did a very good sketch of me once."

"Yeah, that's what I'm saying. I need a storyboard artist. I wonder if she'd be interested."

"I don't know. Give her a call. They're in the book. Her dad actually has a landline."

He nodded and drove out of the parking lot. I was grateful to him. Andy Thayer's name wouldn't be dragged through the looming scandal, now. His innocence wasn't enough—it took the incompetence of his attackers to rescue his reputation from their scheme.

Taking his life? That was something else. A blade across the throat had always been foolproof, if you had the skills.

Chapter Twenty-six

In Memoriam, Oscar Graham

The day before Oscar Graham's funeral, Jonathan Pell and Louis Berman, his rumpled head-of-security, showed up in my office.

"I wanted to thank you for bringing the tragic events at the LoGran house to a swift conclusion," Pell said. "Terrible business."

"Lots of property damage," I agreed.

"Excuse me?"

"That seems to be the main concern among your staff."

"My staff keep their emotions to themselves."

"Apparently."

"I wouldn't want any of these…events…to taint the next Pro-ACKtive fundraiser, or sully the reputation of the corporation."

"Of course."

"So thanks again for your good work."

"You must be…I can't imagine—furious, baffled, sad, disgusted…by your man, Blount."

"We never really know anyone I suppose, Chief."

"You knew he was a convicted felon. You must have."

"I believe in second chances."

"He's not getting a third one."

"Thank God. Now…there is something else. Another troubling issue. My stepdaughter, Daisy, has…well, she seems to have disappeared again. She was released from custody on one hundred thousand dollars bail after her hearing...apparently the judge decided she wasn't a flight risk. That was foolish. She walked out of the Town Building on broad Street ten minutes later—and disappeared."

"Disappeared? I'm sorry, but—I mean...isn't she an adult?"

"Of course she is. She's thirty-two years old! Adults don't disappear? Is that what you're saying?"

"Well...of course they disappear, but not in the same way a child would. A child disappears, it's probably an abduction, or divorce-related incident. A teenager disappears, most of the time you're looking at a runaway situation. Adults don't have to check in with anyone and they usually don't. Personally, I agree with the judge. I'm sure she's still on-island. If I were you, I'd sit tight. You'll hear from her soon. Meanwhile, you could get in touch with her friends. She might be staying with one of them. Does she have any brothers or sisters? Cousins she might be close to?"

I could see his impatience seething. The air between us felt like heat rising off an open grill.

"I don't have time for this. I don't know Daisy's friends. She has no siblings and neither do I, so there are no cousins to pester. She was supposed to meet me two days ago. She never showed up. Her apartment looks like she meant to come back in a few minutes. There's a half-full coffee mug on the table! All her clothes are in the closet. They better be all her clothes, the closet is jammed with them. Her monogrammed suitcases are in there, too. In short, she didn't clean up, she didn't pack, and she stood up her stepfather. How does that look to you?"

I nodded, taking in the whole diatribe. "It doesn't look good, Mr. Pell."

"No, it doesn't!"

"I'll talk to the State Police. But jumping bail is a serious crime, and Daisy knows that. Still, if you want to talk to one of my detectives, we can get a description to the Steamship Authority and the Hyannis bus station."

"I've already talked to the State Police and they were not helpful. In fact they were useless. Worse than useless. That would be—rude and useless. I'm hoping you're right, that Daisy is level-headed enough to remain in the jurisdiction. But that doesn't leave out the possibility of foul play. I've set Mr. Berman the task of finding her. This is a courtesy call. I want to inform you of his activities. Nothing more."

"It won't take long," Berman smirked. "I'm good at my job."

I ignored him. "Thanks for the heads-up, Mr. Pell. I'll coordinate with the State Police. We'll keep an eye out for her, too."

"Good. Then I suppose we're done. I left my card at the front desk inside, if you need to get in touch with me." He reached out to touch my shoulder. "Let me know if you hear anything, Chief. Anything at all. Daisy means everything to me."

◇◇◇

The Thayer family had scheduled Andrew's funeral for Saturday at the Unitarian Church on Orange Street—two days away. Tomorrow was Oscar Graham's memorial service. Too many deaths, too many questions. Supposedly, I had all the answers I needed: a sordid little criminal conspiracy had turned violent—the most ordinary circumstance imaginable in our sad, damaged world. But it didn't quite ring true to me. It covered all the facts, but just barely, the way a queen-size blanket covers a king-size bed, with nothing extra to tuck in, and no way to feel snug or comfortable.

The one person I hadn't spoken to since Andrew Thayer's death was Daisy DeHart. I had been hoping to conduct a gentle interrogation in the safety of the cop shop—and with a six-figure bail, I assumed I'd have time. But she had found the money somewhere. It obviously wasn't from her stepfather. She was probably hiding out with whoever had put up the cash, but the payment had been anonymous. I hoped that Andrew's funeral might flush her out of hiding, but as it turned out I saw her much sooner than that, and so did Berman.

She delivered a eulogy at Oscar Graham's memorial service.

Various zoning laws and noise regulations had made holding a traditional Jamaican "nine night" impossible on Nantucket—the bands would still be playing at two and three and four in the morning, and no one wants the police breaking up a funeral. Instead they set up a tent near the airport in a vacant lot owned by The New Life Ministries International, the Pentecostal church that Oscar's family belonged to. The ministry owned the land on Monohansett Road, though they held their normal services upstairs at the Methodist church in town.

It was still a wild afternoon, with hymns and a hot reggae band, and people talking in tongues. The minister translated. Everyone stood, when they weren't dancing.

"Thanks for coming," Sylvester said to me, shaking my hand.

Millie hugged me. She was crying. "He was such a good boy. He was the best boy. He was a true spirit. He made everyone happy."

"I know."

"Why did he have to die?"

"I don't know."

"He was too young. He had barely tasted life."

"I'm sorry. He was a great kid."

She pushed me away, held me tight at arm's length, staring at my face. "You loved him, didn't you?"

"I…it…yeah, I guess I did."

"You're a good man, Chief Kennis."

They moved off.

Billy Delavane edged through the crowd beside me. "Thanks for coming, Chief."

I saw Jared Bromley and Alana Trikilis at the other side of the tent. They were the only other white faces in the crowd, no sign of Sam Wallace—until Daisy DeHart stepped out of the crowd and up onto the stage. She looked down into the crowd for a moment before she started to speak. The crowd looked back, gradually silencing itself. I joined them.

Her voice, a breathy contralto, had a little catch in it when she started speaking. "Before his fight with Sam Wallace last fall, Oscar Graham had been in trouble just once in his whole short life." She smiled. "But it was a doozy. I think some of you know what I'm talking about. I was his guidance counselor, so I got to hear the whole story, and this seems like a pretty good time to share it with the rest of you. I saw the list of charges afterward. Let me see…speeding, erratic driving, operating a motor vehicle without a license, grand theft auto, and—to top it off—resisting arrest and felony assault on a police officer.

"Quite a night. It started at a party in Shimmo, when his friend Sam Wallace—that's right, the same Sam Wallace—and Oscar's newly ex-girlfriend Jill Phelan starting arguing. Jill left and Sam started drinking. The parents weren't home and there was a lot of liquor in the house. I guess Sam was planning to drink it all. Long before he could do that, he collapsed. Oscar had taken paramedic courses and unlike everyone else at the party, who were either too drunk themselves to care or else simply didn't understand what was happening, Oscar knew that Sam was not merely sick, he was in the early stages of alcohol toxemia. Another kid might have just called an ambulance, and left it at that, but Oscar knew that a slow response time might mean the difference between life and death for his friend—the friend who had just stolen his girlfriend, or anyway that's how the average sixteen-year-old boy would see it.

"So, Oscar grabbed the Land Rover keys off the pegboard in the front hall, praying the car had an automatic transmission—which it did—and got two other friends to help him haul Sam to the car. They shoveled him into the backseat and Oscar took off with Jared Bromley riding shotgun. Jared is here today. It's good to see him.

"So, that night he was bouncing down Shimmo Pond Road, no doubt ruining the car's suspension, crashing through those potholes, lucky he didn't get a flat. He skidded onto Polpis Road, crossing into the oncoming traffic. Lucky there wasn't any. But there was a police car driving into town. The cops hit the flashers and the chase was on. By the time they got to the rotary there was another cruiser blocking the street and Oscar jumped the Belgian block to get around it. Well, not quite all the way around it. He hit the police car bumper and spun it around as he skidded up Sparks Avenue. The other kids were screaming at him to stop, but Oscar knew that he couldn't even slow down, or his friend would die. He might have died anyway. Oscar didn't know. All he could do was hit the gas and pray.

"When they got to the hospital, the other kids dragged Sam into the emergency room while Oscar held off the police. He pushed several officers and threw one punch before he was shoved down on the parking lot and handcuffed. While they were taking him to jail, Dr. Lepore was pumping Sam's stomach, getting him on an intravenous drip and saving his life."

Daisy took a breath and let the story settle on her audience like the blossoms from the cherry trees that paved the streets with pink petals in late May. "I don't have to tell you, no one pressed charges. Not the police—isn't that right, Chief Kennis? And certainly not Sam's family. In fact when Oscar got his license, the Wallaces bought him his first car. But he never got to drive it. That's because someone killed him. No one wants to say it? I'll say it! Oscar didn't just die. It was murder! And no one in this community should be able to sleep or eat or even think straight until whoever did it is arrested and tried and sent to jail for life. They said he drowned. He was a great swimmer—a surfer, isn't that right, Billy?"

Billy nodded as the crowd turned toward us.

Daisy kept going. "They say he overdosed on drugs but we all knew Oscar Graham never took drugs! Not even aspirin! Someone forced those drugs on him and dumped him the harbor and left him there to drown. You have to find out who that was, Chief Kennis. Or Oscar's ghost will haunt you forever."

Every eye in the place was on me. I could feel the pressure of all that rage and grief. I could feel the hot surge of blood in my cheeks. But the case was solved. Blount had confessed. Of course, the news hadn't hit the papers yet—the new edition of *The Inquirer and Mirror* wouldn't come out until Thursday, and as to the mainland papers and the networks—Dave Carmichael had imposed a gag order on all law enforcement personnel. I decided to make an exception for Daisy. She deserved to know the truth as soon as possible. If Blount's ever-expanding confession hadn't implicated her in the porn ring, she wouldn't have been in jail in the first place.

◇◇◇

I caught up to Daisy as she was leaving the tent, two hours and a dozen more eulogies later. Like all good eulogies they took the form of anecdotes. Sylvester told the story of how Oscar had negotiated a small fee for every household chore he completed and then used the money to buy his father the fancy airless paint sprayer he had been coveting for years. Billy described Oscar teaching a kid to surf using his unique trick: plaster a big smile on your face while you're paddling for the wave. It seemed crazy but it worked—it relaxed you somehow, gave you a goofy feeling that canceled your nerves. Billy had started using it himself in big waves, on the heavy days that intimidated him.

"I learned a lot from that kid," he said. "I still have a lot to learn from him. But now I never will."

"Now I never will." The words were ricocheting around in my head like a fly under a lampshade when I caught up to Daisy at the far end of the field, heading for her car.

"Hey—hello, excuse me—Daisy?"

She stopped and turned. The movement smacked the words out of my head and I thought again—that kind of beauty must be a bizarre kind of hardship, a social handicap as extreme as acne or a harelip. "It will be in the paper next week," I said, "but I thought I should tell you now. Blount confessed to Oscar's murder. Along with everything else."

"And you believed him?"

"He was...convincingly unrepentant."

"So you're done."

"We still have the trials to prepare for, but the AG feels confident that we can—"

"Jesus Christ. It's all happening exactly the way he said it would. He could have written it himself. Like one of those

horrible PowerPoint presentations. Thing, thing, thing, each
with its own little graph and pie chart."

"Who could have? What are you talking about?"

She laughed, a strangled little bleat caught somewhere
between a sneeze and a sob. "You have no idea what's going on!
You're all so clueless. Strutting and preening, organizing victory
parades with ticker tape, you should definitely get some ticker
tape, you can buy it on eBay. And all the while he's laughing
because he played you all so perfectly and everybody is taking
the fall but him and he wins again like always. It makes me sick.
I mean—actually sick. I think I'm going to puke."

I stepped back, but she grabbed the side mirror of her dark
green MINI Cooper and steadied herself.

"Daisy, listen—"

"I shouldn't even be talking to you. Not without my lawyer
present. Besides…if they see me—you shouldn't have come here.
Just stay away. Stick your little gold star on the front of your
notebook and get away from me."

She yanked open the door and folded herself into the driver's
seat.

"Daisy, listen to me…if you have information about this
case, you have to share it with the police. That's the law. And
it could help you. You could testify later—make some kind of
deal. But it's also—it's your duty. It's your moral obligation. You
just talked about Oscar's ghost haunting me. How about you?"

"I'm out of it, Chief. I'm done." She keyed the engine. "As
for Oscar's ghost—if he wants to haunt me, he's going to have
to take a number and get on line."

She revved the engine to an angry shriek and the rear wheels
dug up a spray of dirt as she took off.

Alana Trikilis walked up to me as I stared after the vanished
car.

"I'm worried about Ms. DeHart," she said. "I think she's real
near the edge."

"Yeah," I nodded sympathetically. And I was thinking, Daisy's on the edge, all right—and what I need most right now is to push her over it.

Who was she talking about? Her stepfather? Or one of his cronies? And what were they really doing, and why were they trying to manipulate the legal system? If any of that was even happening, if Daisy wasn't busy spinning conspiracy theories. People as superficially smart and sane as Daisy had been convinced over the years that the moon walk was a hoax, AIDS was invented by the CIA, and the Sandy Hook shooting was a government plot to promote more gun control laws. You didn't have to scratch too far below the surface to find the crazy. Maybe Daisy was just one more example. That was the most likely explanation. She had a lot of anger and resentment to work through, and I had a tough, complex criminal case tied up neatly, with a bow. I was happy to leave it at that.

But I was still mulling it over when I drove out to Polpis that evening, for one of my literary nights with Jane Stiles.

Chapter Twenty-seven

On Polpis Harbor Beach

"There's a lot more going on than meets the eye," Jane said. "There always is. There has to be."

I shook my head, exhaling a quiet laugh. "In your books, you mean."

She gave me a stern look. "Life imitates art."

"Not in police work."

"I told you all the different crimes this year were connected and you didn't believe me then, either. But it was true."

"Fair enough. But now you're saying they're connected two ways, which frankly gives me a headache tonight. I have no idea what the second one could be."

"But you have to find out because that's the really important connection. That's the one someone's hiding. And Daisy's the key to it."

We were eating ice cream cones. I had driven out to Polpis with sandwiches in hand, but all either of us wanted was a treat. It was a perfect early summer night and we drove to the 'Sconset Market for a couple of overpriced scoops. The ice cream was good and the market hadn't changed at all in decades. It was a pleasant excursion, driving along the eastern edge of the island, skirting Sesachacha Pond, cutting through the old Sankaty Head golf course and then running parallel to the bluffs of Baxter Road into the little village.

We strolled out into the center of 'Sconset, which consisted of a small rotary, two restaurants, a liquor store, the post office, and the market, with the little rectangle of park beside it. Kids were cruising by on bicycles and you could see that the rich people had already started to arrive for the season, tall and handsome and blond, with perfectly dressed kids and great hair, talking about tennis dates and tee times and Muffy's divorce.

Jane pointed at two big blondes in tennis clothes, climbing out of a Lexus SUV.

"Look at that hair," she whispered to me. "If I had that hair, I'd be driving that Lexus."

"But you don't want a Lexus."

"That's not the point. I could have whatever I wanted, with hair like that. I mean what else do they have going for them?"

"They're pretty."

"They're okay looking. Really check them out."

I did. She was right—regular, ordinary features. The bodies weren't much better. "They have some cellulite happening."

"And they're not that bright, either," she said. "I wouldn't exactly call that a high water mark in political discourse." She nodded toward one of the kids scampering by in a "John Kerry For President—of France" tee-shirt.

I nodded. "Someone bought him that item."

"Someone bought it for his big brother. And kept it for the next kid."

"Dumb and sentimental. Great combination."

"Doesn't matter. She's got the hair."

We strolled back to the car and waited on line and drove down under the pedestrian bridge to look at the water. An old Volkswagen beetle drove by—a powder blue convertible, nineteen seventies vintage.

"That's the car I want," Jane said.

"Nice."

"It just reminds me of—I used to drive one of those. I loved it."

"I'm not sure you need world-class hair to get an old bug."

"Maybe not. But my ex-husband was the mechanic in the family. His idea of a fun Sunday afternoon was climbing under the car to replace the solenoid. Whatever that is."

"I don't think cars even have them anymore."

We drove back to Polpis and took turns eating our sandwiches (Turkey Terrifics from Provisions) and reading aloud.

Before Jane started her story she said. "I have a poem for you! I was thinking of it all day, looking at all the self-important Somebodies strutting around town. It's Emily Dickinson…

> *I'm Nobody! Who are you?*
> *Are you—Nobody—too?*
> *Then there's a pair of us!*
> *Don't tell! they'd advertise—you know!*
>
> *How dreary—to be—Somebody!*
> *How public—like a Frog–*
> *To tell one's name—the livelong June–*
> *To an admiring Bog!"*

I laughed. "That's perfect. I love that. I can't believe I never saw that poem before."

"Apparently she was at some party and all the men were bloviating about their writing and politics and whatever and she was just like—get me out of here."

"Wow."

"She's my favorite hermit."

"And I'm supposed to follow that poem?"

She smiled. "You're supposed to try."

"Well, there's one I wrote about you—actually something you told me this winter—about going back to the town where you lived when you were a little kid, before your family moved here? Checking out your old house, looking up at your bedroom window. I did that, too. My dad owned so many houses over the years I could make it a tour: maps to the drunken screenwriter's homes. So anyway I finally wrote something about it."

She set her sandwich down and took a sip of wine.

"Shoot."

"That might not be the best thing to say to a trigger-happy local cop."

"Fine. Proceed with some thoughtful community policing, Officer."

"Yes, ma'am. It's called 'Homecoming.'" I pulled the folded sheet of paper out of my back pocket.

This happiness is small and fragile
Hope and irony crowded together
Like a Baptist and an abortion doctor
Carpooling
This happiness is like returning home
And seeing how your hometown has changed
The new school
The mall where the movie theatre
Used to be;
The hardware store is gone
Victim of the modern world—
It sells software now
You saw the end of the sign and thought
"Something is still the same"
Too soon.
Still, some things remain
The big sycamores
Still sprinkle the sidewalk with shade
Your house is still there.
It's someone else's house now;
They've added a garage
Someone is sleeping behind your window
Probably someone like you:
A little girl who can't imagine ever leaving
Ever coming back, looking for a homecoming
Among the busy strangers
On the new streets

> *And finding it*
> *In the dry, yeasty smell from the bakery*
> *(It's still there)*
> *Carried through the dark air*
> *On the morning wind;*
> *Finding it*
> *In a smooth piece of glass*
> *Stained amber by sunrise*
> *In the vacant lot*
> *Where your mother warned you*
> *Not to run barefoot.*

She lifted her glass in a toast. "Nice. Especially the end. I never really felt at home there, though. After we moved here it didn't even seem real anymore. It was just—I can't describe it."

"You always say that and then you describe things beautifully."

"Okay. It was like someone had described it to me, and I had this super clear idea of the place from what they said but it wasn't like the real place at all. That was the shock going back. The town in my head was so much nicer. And the hardware store turning into a software store. You remembered that."

"That image summed things up perfectly."

"I was going to use it somewhere. But I donate it to you. For your birthday."

"Best present ever."

We sat eating quietly for a while. The crickets orchestrated the night outside, their own amateur Phillip Glass symphony. Planes heading for Boston and New York droned by overhead.

Jane assembled her papers. In the recent installments of her new Madeline Clark novel, *Poverty Point,* Maddy had searched the house where the murder took place, after the police—under the inept leadership of Police Chief Bill Blote—turned the place upside down and found nothing. Maddy, with her tireless ant-like industry and the patience of a fly-fisherman, had dug out a broken bracelet from the crack between two wide floorboards.

"I stole that from you," Jane confessed. "The hair clip. Tit for tat."

Anyway, Maddy instantly recognized the double pyramid slashed vertically by a cursive capital "S" because Maddy's ex-husband—like Jane's—had been a Scientologist for many years. Jane's ex had left the church in disgust when he finally found out the details of its wacky theology, but Maddy's remained stalwart.

Chief Blote showed zero interest in this new evidence, of course. The man "wouldn't recognize an elephant if it was stepping on his foot." Blote's view: the bracelet could have been there for years, could have belonged to anyone, could even have been placed there to throw the police off the scent.

"But he would have had to assume you'd find it," Maddy said sweetly.

As always happened in Jane's books, the blundering pompous clowns who made up the NPD arrested the wrong person. The evidence was circumstantial and the eyewitness was a drunk. But there was nothing Maddy could do about it. She had no suspect of her own.

Until she did some last-minute marketing.

Here's the end of the chapter she read me:

> After weeks of false leads and dead ends, "red herrings and rotten bluefish," as Maddy called them, she finally solved the puzzle of Raymond Scully's murder in a single moment, driving into the Stop&Shop parking lot.
>
> As usual she was cruising the crowded tarmac trying to find the spot closest to the store. She could walk for hours when she was in the mood, but she hated any unnecessary exercise and dreaded seeing people she knew among the cars and shopping carts. There were all the people she didn't like, and the acquaintances who would invariably want to "catch up." But the worst were the old friends who insisted on having actual conversations in the canned goods aisle. You could lose an hour or two in the soul-sapping fluorescent light, listening to someone's

divorce update or the tribulations of the Whalers' last road trip.

Maddy was on her third circuit when she saw Bradley Morrell wheeling a cart full of grocery bags to his car. An artist who specialized in sea gulls, sailboats at anchor, and cobblestone street scenes, Bradley was always talking about moving to New York where his "real" work (messy abstractions in mud brown and exhaust purple) would be taken seriously. Of course he never left. Nantucket was the capital city of procrastination. It ate away at peoples' ambitions like powderpost beetles chewing away at an old house. Everyone was going to write that book, use all the sound equipment in their basement to finally cut a demo record, get a portfolio of their photographs together—after the summer season, next year, on the first of never.

It didn't matter to Bradley Morrell; he was a trust fund baby who could afford to indulge his airs and affectations. He was normally quite useless, but he was going to come in handy today—Maddy could take his parking space!

She idled the car, watching him.

He lifted the hatchback of his SUV and started loading in the paper bags. His cell phone rang and, distracted for a second, he banged his head on the sharp edge of the raised panel. He grunted in pain, closed his eyes and moved his forehead up to touch the exact spot where he had clouted himself.

Maddy gasped, the real thing, inhaling so hard the breath scraped her throat. She knew that gesture very well. Derrick had done it all the time. It was called Contact Assist, a technique for dealing with injuries developed by L. Ron Hubbard in the 1960s.

Brady Morrell was a Scientologist. She had his clear bracelet in her pocket. She stared at him as he finished loading the car.

She knew Brady was the killer now. All she had to do was *prove* it.

Jane set the papers aside. "Well?"

"Excellent. I especially liked the word 'scrape'—people gasp all the time in fiction but writers don't usually bother to describe what it actually feels like."

She grinned. "I gasped a lot to test it out. That hurts!"

I finished my wine. "I just wish things could work out so neatly in an actual investigation."

"You found the bullet that killed Todd Macy—and the rifle it came from."

"True. But, ultimately, Blount confessed and that's how about ninety percent of all real cases get solved. Not by finding some bracelet and the amateur sleuth making the connection because she happens to be familiar with the killer's weirdo religious sect. And by the way—the real police chief of Nantucket would have found that bracelet. Or at least acknowledged that it was important. I mean—I found the hair clip!"

"But you have to have dumbo cops in a cozy mystery. That doesn't hurt your feelings, does it?"

"No, no. It's funny. Blote without the 'a'—so fat he can't even spell his own name."

She nodded. "That was a little on the nose."

"Loose ends," I said, "that's what you're missing."

"But that's why people read mysteries! It's the one place in life where all the loose ends get tied up."

"We need Madeline Clark to do some digging. Maybe at the Atheneum. She always finds some vital clue in an old library book."

"That only happened twice!"

"Or the Hall of Records."

"Okay, okay. But Maddy is an expert researcher. You have to give her that."

"Unlike the Blote and his Keystone Kops, who let her do all the work and then take the credit."

"That happens in real life. It's the number one thing that happens. I worked for two years as an executive secretary at American Express in New York. I did all the work and my boss took all the credit."

"Which is why you quit."

"I never said I liked it. But that's the way the world works."

The conversation had drifted. I knew the necessary course correction, but it was a topic I'd been avoiding. Jane wouldn't like the questions and I wasn't sure I wanted to hear the answers. Still, I had to address, not the elephant, maybe the pile of drug paraphernalia in the room, the litter of pornographic thumb drives.

"I was hoping Brad might have some answers," I said finally.

She stood up and started clearing off the table. "I don't want to talk about Brad."

"Me neither."

"That's over. For real now. For good."

"I know."

"I pick horrible men. Present company excluded. I hope."

"Thanks."

"Brad seemed great at first, too. Smart, successful, good-looking. He ran in the Boston Marathon. He read my big mother-daughter novel and said, 'You don't read stuff like this. Why don't you try writing what you like to read?' That's how I started the Maddy Clark books. Brad was right. I sold *The View from Altar Rock* to the first publisher who read it. I didn't even have an agent at that point. I hired a lawyer instead. Much better." She held out her glass. "More wine, please."

I took another bottle out of the fridge, opened it and poured us each a glass.

I took a swallow—ice cold, tart and dry. "We've been questioning Brad, but he doesn't seem to know anything beyond the basics."

"A foot soldier in the army of porn."

"Something like that."

"He can be ambitious, though."

"Really?"

"In his own field. He was bragging about some huge deal he had going with Grady Malone, the last time I saw him. Lots of high-end houses, ten years' worth of work, time, and materials, cost plus. He really hit the jackpot, supposedly. But I haven't heard anything about it since. He could have been making the whole thing up. You know—one more Nantucket delusionoid. Sometimes I think this place is actually a government-sanctioned bird sanctuary for weirdos and losers. People who can't make it anywhere else."

"Like me?"

"And me. And everyone else I know. Do you think Brad Thurman could be a building contractor anywhere but here? Some customer yelled at him years ago, "My house leaks!" And he said, "All my houses leak," as if that made perfect sense. Mike Henderson gets forty dollars an hour for spreading paint on flat surfaces. You could literally train a chimpanzee to do that and then you could pay them in bananas. But Mike gets forty dollars an hour!"

"I hear he's thinking of raising it to fifty."

She shook her head. "Only on Nantucket."

I took another sip of wine and made a note to myself—time to have a little chat with Grady Malone.

At the sink, Jane said, "So what did you think of Jonathan Pell's stepdaughter?"

I had to laugh. "How did you know that?"

"It's a small island, Mr. Washashore. Seriously, though—what did you think of her? She always struck me as the kind of woman the hero in a crime novel would fall for. You know…gorgeous, sultry, damaged, mysterious?"

"Nantucket noir?"

She nodded. "The classic femme fatale."

"Not to me. She's too…extreme. She's lived her whole life in this crazy spotlight, everyone focused on her, and so she's focused on them, focusing on her. It turns into this toxic narcissistic feedback loop unless you're really strong. She struck me as flimsy at best. I went to school with this fat girl who lost like sixty pounds in the summer between junior and senior years. She came back to school looking fantastic—she had always been pretty. You know, the kind of girl where you say, if she just lost some weight…Well, she did, and every boy in the school was hitting on her, teachers were hitting on her, random strangers in the street were hitting on her."

"So what did she do?"

"She went out and ordered the first in a long series of chocolate ice cream sundaes."

"That's one solution."

I stood up to dry the dishes and set them on the shelves above the sink. "I prefer a different kind of good looks."

"Really."

"Yeah. Looks that might not be so glaringly obvious, but they're connected to the mind, to the spirit behind the face. Daisy smiles and it's a blow. You dodge the punch or it hits you. It's calculated. It has nothing to do with what she's thinking. You smile, and I want to know what struck you as funny. I want to be in on the joke."

"So you like my looks."

"Is that so incredible?"

"It's odd. But if you weren't a little eccentric you wouldn't be living here."

"Hey—"

"I used to be pretty. You should see some of the pictures from plays I was in ten years ago."

"And ten years from now you'll be saying the same thing. 'I looked pretty good ten years ago.' Why not just accept the fact that you look good right now?"

"Because I don't. I have wrinkles and frizzy hair."

"You're forty years old. You have laugh lines and curls."

"You're demented." But she was smiling a little.

I put the last wineglass away and turned to face her. "Here's my theory. You're beautiful but you don't feel that way because you're on the wrong side—the inside, looking out. No wait, listen to this. It's like…you're in this one tiny room with bad wallpaper, peering out of the threadbare curtains, and you don't realize…you live in a fabulous mansion!"

"In the maid's quarters."

"Exactly! You see your crummy room and the view of the estate. I see the mansion with the girl peering out from behind the curtains."

"So what am I supposed to do about that?"

I pulled her into a hug. "You should get out more."

"Astral projection?"

"Or a stroll in the garden."

She pushed away and took my hand. "Come on, let's go."

She grabbed a flashlight on the way out the door, but the moon was full and we didn't need it. We picked our way through the narrow path behind the cottage, ducking under low-hanging branches and sidestepping the poison ivy. The path opened into rolling fields mowed by the Land Bank, ashen and spectral in the moonlight. We could see the harbor beyond the far trees. A faint wind lifted out of the south west.

We found our way to a dirt parking lot and then down to the public landing, a little beach lined with overturned Boston Whalers and kayaks. We chose a boat and sat down.

"It's beautiful out here," I said.

She nodded. "It's the only place that still feels like home to me."

We studied the sailboats moored on the dark water, listened to the halyards knocking against the masts, the lap of small waves on the packed sand.

"Look at the moon," she said after a while.

I had to twist around to see it, caught and almost hidden in the branches and leaves of a big elm tree behind us.

"It's huge," I said.

"Chekhov wrote somewhere that one moment can change everything."

I turned back to face her and she kissed me.

It was utterly unexpected, though it shouldn't have been. It was bold and crazy and I kissed her back and let the jagged current pass through me. I slipped my hand under her shirt, touched her back and the moment leapt from romance to frenzy. We were really kissing now. We tried to lie down on the damp curved wood of the boat's hull. We almost slipped off and we both started laughing.

"Let's get back inside," I said

Her eyes flashed. She nodded, and grabbed the back of my neck and kissed me again, and then we were running along the moon-bright paths of grass, back to the cottage, and the small cozy bedroom, and the bed.

Part Three: Tourist Season

Chapter Twenty-eight

In Memoriam, Andrew Thayer

Andrew Thayer's funeral was held on June 28th, 2015, at the Unitarian Universalist Church on Orange Street. A rough head count by *The Inquirer and Mirror* estimated that more than three thousand people came to pay their respects that morning. Only a fraction of them actually made it into the church. The line, which started at dawn, stretched down Orange Street, across Main Street and along Center Street all the way to the Jared Coffin House.

Chosen mourners, including Jane, who sat up front with the other friends and the family, stood at the lectern to eulogize and reminisce. I couldn't help thinking that every one of those three thousand people standing outside must have a few stories of their own—thousands of amusing and heartfelt anecdotes jostling each other in the misting summer rain.

How many people would attend the average person's funeral? Wife and kids, close friends, coworkers, cousins from out-of-state, a stray niece or nephew—enough people to fill a living room.

Andy Thayer's mourners filled a town.

Many people spoke during the service, talking about bringing his killer to justice, describing Andy's charitable works (he donated a hundred Vermont farm-raised turkeys to the food pantry every Thanksgiving and routinely gave hundred-dollar tips "to turn the day around" for waiters in his favorite restaurants), his lifelong slow-motion catastrophe as a sailor (he had sunk three different boats over the years—one right outside the jetties during a stormy Opera Cup race in the mid-nineties), and his Pied Piperish appeal to other peoples' children. He could imitate various insects and perform all the parts on Sesame Street with perfect accuracy. "I should open a comedy club for five-year-olds," he once remarked.

But David Trezize's comments touched me the most. I hadn't realized they were such good friends.

"Andy was uniquely…meticulous about other people, and their feelings," David said, as he settled himself at the podium. "When Andy was in love, on the woman's birthday he sent flowers to *her mother*. As a thank you. And he always remembered them—birthdays and anniversaries. If you noticed a David Lazarus watercolor at the X-Gallery months before, you'd find it under the tree at Christmas. He paid attention. If I lost two pounds he was like 'Working out? It shows.'

"Back when I was just out of college, living on Ramen noodles and popcorn, he'd tell me to get dinner at the Boarding House and put it on his tab. And he'd say 'Ignore the right side of the menu.' And there'd be a good bottle of Chardonnay on ice at the table waiting for me. He knew I wouldn't order wine if someone else was paying. So he took care of it in advance. That was classy. But you all know this stuff.

"If Andy stayed in your house for a few days, the place was immaculate when he left, with fresh flowers on the kitchen table. He was the perfect houseguest. He always did the dishes. He was never late. He was always early, in fact—'pathologically early,' that was the way he put it. Maybe so, but he never kept you waiting. He opened doors for people. It sounds petty but it adds up. He'd travel halfway around the world to attend a graduation. If he borrowed your car, it didn't just come back with a full tank of gas. He detailed it. He sent 'thank you' notes. He sent newspaper clippings—anything he thought you'd be interested in, and he was always right. Clippings.

"He wrote by hand and he had the most perfect copperplate handwriting I've ever seen. I won't be seeing it again, and I guess that's the hardest thing to believe. He really is gone and we all have to get used that."

Daisy spoke next. I noticed Pell's private detective, Louis Berman, standing in the back staring at her. So, he just solved that missing-persons case—and picked up the easiest fee ever. No sign of Pell, himself, though.

"Andy was a true friend," Daisy was saying. "And he was the living proof that it's possible for a man to be friends with a woman. We sort of established in tenth grade that he'd always be in love with me, and I'd never be in love with him and we never talked about it again. He cooked me a million dinners, and let me live in his house when I had nowhere else to go. I remember one time he ironed my best pleated skirt before I went out on a date with some boy. How many men can iron a pleated skirt?

"But he was brave, too. Let me tell you this one story. I was at the Chicken Box a couple of years ago and this man was being really obnoxious, hitting on me and really scaring me, frankly. Andy came in and saw what was happening and told the man to stop. Andy was tall but this guy was huge. The guy said, 'Let's take it outside,' and Andy said, 'No I'd rather do it in front of your friends.' Then he reached across the bar—the bartender was cutting limes—and took the knife. He held it out to the guy, who said something like 'What's this about?' And Andy said, "I want you to be armed. I want there to be no question for any of these witnesses when I kick your ass, that I did it in self-defense. I'm not going to jail for this, and you're not pressing charges. Go on, big boy. Take the knife.'"

Daisy paused, glanced over the packed pews. "The guy backed down, and the whole bar started breathing again. Afterward I said, 'Oh, my God, do you know karate or something and you never told anyone?' He said, 'No, that guy would have kicked the crap out of me and cut me up like a pumpkin.' That's brave. And cool. Andy was a great poker player, too. But I guess you figured that one out by now."

When she stepped down, there were prayers and hymns and the Naturals and the Accidentals preformed a creditable version of Andy's favorite song, "Diamonds on the Soles of Her Shoes."

It was a good service—it served its primary function, which was to inhabit the big old building with Andy's spirit for an hour or two. Everyone felt a little closer to him as they filed out into the drizzling street, and a little closer to each other, also.

I caught up to Daisy on Orange Street as she was walking to her car. "I need to talk to you about Andy's death."

She studied me coolly. "I already said everything I have to say about Andrew."

I took a couple of seconds. "I'm talking about the criminal investigation of his murder."

"I know nothing about that. I wasn't arrested for that. And I won't talk to you. I don't want to be seen talking to you."

"We can talk in private. Come to the station. We can—"

"I have to go."

"Ms. DeHart—" I reached out to grasp her arm.

She snatched it away convulsively. "Let me go!"

The shout drew a dozen startled looks and she used the confusion and my embarrassment to break free from the crowd and flee up the street.

Luckily, I had parked my big blue-and-white NPD Ford Explorer a block behind her, and I followed her easily as she drove away. I thought she'd take a left and head down to Union Street, assuming she was still staying at Andrew's house. But she kept on going, taking a right on York Street, across Pleasant and past the old mill, crossing the top of Madaket Road at the monument and curving along New Lane, accelerating into the long curve around the top of Woodbury Lane.

We both raced into that curve too fast, but her low-slung compact hugged the turn and powered into the straightaway. My big SUV rocked on its axle and almost tipped over. I cursed, braked hard, and eased back into my own lane as a line of cars coming the other way rushed past me. Then a Range Rover pulled out of a hedge-screened driveway and forced me to a full stop.

By the time I was rolling again, Daisy's MINI was gone.

◇◇◇

I was going to have to find her the hard way…or wait for her pre-trial deposition, which could be weeks away. I could feel it—Jane was right. Daisy knew the whole story I was trying to piece together, and I needed to hear it *now*. People had died to keep these secrets and anyone might be next, including Daisy herself. Something big was happening, something bad, building to a sinister climax, and I was stumbling around in the dark, helpless and blind, unable to see it or stop it.

Daisy could turn on the lights.

I pulled onto the grassy verge beside New Town Cemetery to think. Daisy had been pulled into the judicial system, and that meant she left a trail. There was paperwork on her now. The first thing I had to find out was who posted her bond.

I pulled out and drove back to town.

At the courthouse, I pulled the records and saw that the paperwork on the cash surety had been signed by "John Smith." That was original. Why not "John Doe"?

I checked the surveillance footage and the clerk identified a tall blond kid with a starter mustache and a Patriots cap as the delivery boy. They printed out a screen grab and I passed it around the station. Barnaby Toll recognized the picture—it was a Jordan Toombs. They had gone through NHS together. Jordan co-edited the student newspaper *Veritas* in his senior year with a girl named Andrea Pellegrini. She had stayed on the island, working for her father's alarm company. I got her on the phone. All she could tell me was that Jordan had worked for *The Inquirer and Mirror*, but quit a few months before. She had no idea what he was doing now. They had dated briefly, broken up badly, and now saw each other only by accident, the punitive chance encounters of small-town life, from the cereal aisle at Stop&Shop to the next table at Kitty Murtagh's, on five-dollar burger night.

I hung up with a thought nagging at me. Jordan had edited *Veritas*, started at the *Inky Mirror,* and moved on. It was something David Trezize had said to me after the Thayer house arson.

He had bragged about poaching writers from the *Inky*, right and left.

I picked up a copy of the *Shoals*, leafed through it and saw Jordan's byline on a story about relocating the Cottage Hospital to Mill Hill Park.

Of course.

The trail was as clear as the bright orange blaze marks on the trees in the state forest. From Jordan Toombs to David Trezize to Kathleen Lomax, who coincidentally happened to have the financial resources to deliver a hundred thousand dollars in cash on two days' notice. And if you were driving to her house on Sherburne Turnpike from the Unitarian Church in town, you could have taken exactly the route that Daisy did.

They were friends. Daisy was living with Kathleen.

I pulled into the driveway ten minutes later. The green MINI Cooper was parked between David's Ford Escape and Kathleen's Lexus.

Bingo.

The front door was open, but the screen door was closed. I knocked, got no response, then let myself in. Past the dark front hallway, Daisy, Kathleen, and David were standing in the big living room, looking out the wide plate-glass window at Nantucket Sound stretching out below the cliff to the haze of the mainland thirty miles away.

"Hello?" I said to get their attention. "I knocked but…"

David turned. "Hey, Chief."

"I don't mean to intrude…"

Daisy spun around. "How did you find me?"

I shrugged. "It's hard to stay hidden on Nantucket."

"That's why I left."

"But you came back."

"Yes, well…I guess I was starting to enjoy not hiding anymore. Silly me."

"You said you wanted to talk privately. I thought we could—"

"You said that! I never said that."

"Listen, you can trust me. I would never—"

"Trust you? Trust you, really? That's the best you can do? Too bad, because that's what liars always say. Trustworthy people don't have to say that shit because *you already trust them*."

"Wait a second, that's not—"

"I'm going upstairs. Unless you're planning to arrest me again."

"No, of course not, I just—"

"Good."

She stalked out of the room, leaving a baffled silence behind her like a dropped platter of food.

Kathleen stepped in to clean up the mess. "I'm sorry, Chief Kennis. Daisy's quite upset right now. It's been a horrible week. And Andrew meant a lot to her."

"That's why I thought she might want to help me solve his murder."

David squinted at me. "My contacts at the NPD say you've done that already."

"Good. Feel free to print the story. But I still have a crime to solve."

Kathleen stepped closer to David, took his arm. "I'm not sure Daisy could help you, anyway."

"Maybe not. But I'd like to find out."

She pulled in a quick breath through gritted teeth, "I understand. This might not be the best day. The Thayers are having a reception at the 'Sconset house and Daisy refuses to go. I don't think she wants to talk to anyone right now. We should be leaving ourselves, actually. It's getting late."

"You go on ahead, Kathy," David said. "I want to talk to the chief for a few minutes." He obviously sensed her reluctance. "I'll be right behind you."

"That means taking two cars. I hate driving in a caravan."

"This is important."

"All right. But don't linger. I hate going to these things alone." She turned to me with a wry smile. "David's my bodyguard."

"I'll be right behind you," he said.

She kissed him, waved to me, and left the room. We heard the screen door squeak and slam, and the sharp engine note of her car.

"I was going to call you today," David said. "I've found out some things."

"What things?"

"Sit down, Chief. This may take a while."

Chapter Twenty-nine

Blue Heron Estates

We settled ourselves on the big wicker couch, and he began. "Remember I told you about the Thayer land parcel, how the family was fighting about selling it, and your ex-wife was in a twirl about the real estate commissions?"

"Yeah, but—nothing happened with that."

"Not yet. Because the family couldn't agree. Edna's will stipulates that the decision has to be unanimous among the beneficiaries."

"Andrew was the holdout."

David nodded. "Most of the family doesn't even live on-island. Joyce and Debbie moved back last year, but the other two brothers live in…Chicago and L.A., I think. The property is just a lottery ticket to them. But here's the thing. None of it added up, Chief. Like—the plan on the table was selling the whole property to the Land Bank."

"What's wrong with that?"

"Nothing, it's the right thing to do. That chunk of land is the heart of Nantucket. But that's what I didn't get—the greedy twins off-island shouldn't have wanted that sale—you never get full market value from the Land Bank."

"So Andy should have been in favor of the sale."

"Exactly. Something more was going on, and that's even more interesting to me than snooping on my ex-wife."

I smiled. "Journalist first, stalker second."

"It's like I told you, Chief, I'm over it. Anyway...I talked to Todd Macy. He practically ran the Land Bank, and he was dead-set against the sale also. He wouldn't say why, though. He didn't want to talk, even off the record. 'You'll know everything soon enough,' that was what he said. Something like that. But then he got killed."

I nodded. "He tried to call me the day before he died."

"So he thought it was a police matter."

"I guess. I don't know. He sounded agitated in the voicemail."

"I tried a couple of other leads—Dan Taylor, he knows everything that's going on; a couple of other Selectmen; Charlie Forrest, who worked with Todd at the Land Bank. But I came up with nothing. There was a potential sale, one of many, negotiations were ongoing, blah blah blah. Then Chris Macy shows up at the *Beacon* office. He just got a poem published in *Ploughshares*, how does that make you feel?"

I let a bitter little laugh swivel my head. "It pisses me off. What do you think?"

"Spoken like a true writer. Chris showed some of your stuff to the editor there. The guy said he thought it was charming—a police chief writing bad poetry."

"Now you're baiting me."

"Sorry, I thought it was funny. My opinion? The kid's stuff sucks. I hate my daddy, in villanelle form with some foreign words and fancy references. Big deal. But it turns out he didn't totally hate his dad after all. He respected Todd. At least—he respected Todd's work at the Land Bank. Chris is one of those turn-the-island-into-a-national-park types. Anyway, he had some documents to show me, stuff he'd taken out of his father's home office."

"What kind of documents?"

"The main one was the plan for a giant subdivision in the moors. Come on, I'll show you."

I followed him into his office where he pulled a folded square of paper off his desk. He carried it into the dining room and laid it out on the table.

"Check it out."

I looked over the blue-inked plot markings. Most of it seemed to be three- and five-acre zoning but there were smaller footprint lots at the eastern edge of the property. The big sheet covered most of the table. The development was huge, spreading over more than a two square miles.

"That's about thirteen hundred acres, Chief. Three hundred homes, counting the affordable housing units."

"Holy crap." I stared at the giant sheet of paper. It represented the death of Nantucket as I knew it. The new roads, the new sewage lines, the cars, and the moors themselves, the pristine heart of the island…gutted like an old house, and turned into some hideous gated community out of Summit, New Jersey. It didn't seem possible. "Have these plans been filed?"

"Nope. I couldn't even find the official surveyor's report. This was all done under the radar. This sheet of paper is the only evidence that anything's even happening."

The thought struck me like a panic attack—the moment when you realize you left the oven on or the skylight open to the rain. "What an idiot I am."

David looked like baffled owl behind his glasses. "Excuse me."

"The surveyor's report."

I pulled out my phone and scrolled through my pictures, into the set that Mark Toland had sent me, the area around Andrew's cottage, particularly the one with the birds on the ground, which I'd never gotten around to showing Haden Krakauer.

Red birds—cardinals.

Well, they were out of focus—and more importantly, out of context. But it was no excuse. I handed the phone to David. "Recognize those?"

He gaped at the screen. "Jesus Christ. Surveyor's flags. When was this taken?"

"The day before the fire."

"So it's real."

I bent to study the western section of the subdivision plan. "This is the area designated for the Moorlands Mall. But the Thayer property…"

"Look again. It's both. The parcel covers both properties."

Nathan Parrish, a local real estate lawyer now serving five to seven at Cedar Junction, had finessed the property from the down-at-heel owners of an Indian quitclaim land deed and gotten a ruling from the Land Court allowing the mall to be built. When his partnership with Preston Lomax went south and the thieves fell out and Parrish had Lomax killed, everyone assumed the deal was dead. Well, that deal was dead.

But this deal was much bigger, and far worse.

"The Lomax property reverted to LoGran Corporation," David said. "But they seem to be out of it, now." He pointed to the logo: the top loop of the capital 'B' turning into a graceful bird's head. "This is the owner. Blue Heron Estates."

Blue Heron. Blue Heroin.

That was what Alana had heard Howard McAllister and Charles Forrest arguing about. It had nothing to do with drugs and everything to do with real estate. But then, real estate was the drug of choice for people like Charles Forrest. I told David what Alana told me.

"Todd was against this," he said.

"So Forrest and McAllister had him killed."

"Or someone did." David blew out a tired breath. "Someone who'd commit murder over a piece of land."

"This is quite a piece of land. It's probably the most significant parcel to come up for sale on the Eastern seaboard in the last fifty years."

"Still."

"Hey, in L.A. I saw kids who'd commit murder over a pair of sneakers."

"I guess I've lived a pretty sheltered life."

"Here's what I don't understand. The Thayers were fighting about selling to the Land Bank. Where does the Blue Heron bunch come in? Can the Land Bank flip a property like that?"

"That's what I wanted to know. So I started digging. Turns out there's this obscure Land Bank charter provision that allows the bank to re-sell the property for commercial or residential use. They also utilize rule 40-B that allows them to build as much and as densely as they want with as much clustering as they require, so long as they provide some percentage of affordable housing...which in fact, they never plan to build. All it takes is bribes to people on the Planning Commission. It's not about zoning, which would require a full vote from Town Meeting. It can all be done behind closed doors. Their lawyer writes the covenant papers so he can slip in even more loopholes regarding sewers, gutters, paving, tree cover, lighting, et cetera. These concessions will net Blue Heron millions of dollars, cumulatively. It's quite a racket."

I nodded. "There have to be kickbacks. The Thayers must get some equivalent of market value after the sale to Blue Heron goes through. That's the only explanation for the greedy ones wanting to do it."

"And Andrew being dead-set against it."

"So they burned his house. And when that didn't work, they killed him."

"But who are 'they'? That's the real question."

"Who runs Blue Heron Estates?"

"That's what I wanted to know. Turns out, it's a dummy corporation owned by another dummy corporation owned by a shell corporation out of Delaware. Which is owned by some other company, which itself is some subsidiary of a holding company in the Seychelles Islands. It just goes on and on. It would take years to unravel it and track these people down."

"But you have a theory and so do I."

"LoGran."

I lifted both hands in a flicking little twist, with a mean half-smile and a cock of the head—universal sign language for 'it's obvious.'

"And Pell."

I nodded. Daisy's "he" and "they."

David stood up and walked over to the bookshelf that covered the whole wall facing the windows. "LoGran's a big company, Chief. Twelve people on the board of directors. A COO, a CFO."

"But only one of them docks his boat at Straight Wharf."

He took down one of his two volumes of Sherlock Holmes stories. "Elementary, my dear Watson?"

"Once you eliminate the impossible, whatever remains, no matter how improbable, must be the truth, as Holmes liked to say."

"But not even Holmes could prove this one. Believe me, I tried. There's no paper trail, no documentation, nothing. I left a trail, though. I got a cease-and-desist letter from Blue Heron. No more document requests without a court order."

"And that scared you off?"

"If they really are owned by LoGran, I was right to be scared off. Lomax practically ruined me and all I did was report on him bullying a waiter at Topper's."

"You were going public about the Moorlands Mall."

He shrugged. "That, too. Listen, I'll get in the ring with them, but I have to have to be ready for the fight. This would be a first-round knockout. I can afford a lawsuit these days, thanks to Kathleen. But neither of us can afford to lose one. Plus—I could be wrong. You don't have to love Nantucket to cash in on it. Larry Thayer, the one in L.A.—he doesn't give a shit about this place. It's just the opposite, actually. Pell cares about the island. Why would he want to trash it? And that's assuming LoGran even owns Blue Heron. It could be anyone, Chief. Take away my grudges and my prejudices, take away your guesswork and intuition…we have nothing. It could be an Arabian sheik, or a Russian oligarch—they love real estate. It's the best trick in the world for laundering money. Or a dot com billionaire. Mark Zuckerberg, why not? Or that guy who owns PayPal. Or fifty other guys we haven't even heard of yet. I get exhausted just thinking about it."

I felt myself coming down from the investigative high, hitting the hard ground with a thump. "You're right."

"Besides, anyone who reads the *Wall Street Journal* knows that LoGran is having some trouble lately. I'm not sure they have the capital to pull this off. They need leverage and they need liquidity and they don't have much of either. There's a bad stretch between buying the property and selling it. Ask Bruce Poor—he lost his shirt developing Woodbury Lane. I remember that development back when he had sold, like, two lots. It was bad timing. Look at the place now. Take a left at the Lily Pond and stroll up to New Lane. It's a gold mine—but not for Bruce. Other people made the money. That could happen to whoever makes this supposed Land Bank deal, too. People get greedy and they overextend themselves and they go down."

"But LoGran is a corporation."

He did his best breathy Mitt Romney impression. "Corporations are people, friend. Greedy people who can overextend themselves, just like anyone else."

◇◇◇

I left the house in a funk, and my subsequent meetings with Charles Forrest—also out on bail—and Grady Malone at his architectural office on lower Main Street, didn't improve matters much. Forrest was outraged and impervious: he knew nothing about the plans I described and knew of no deals pending with any corporate entity, Blue Heron, Red Herring, or anyone else. And even if he did, such agreements were perfectly legal and in fact an essential part of the Land Bank's structure. They sold some properties in order to have cash on hand to buy other, more significant ones. Every prospective purchase was judged on the long-term merits of the property itself and its significance to the creation of a sustainable Nantucket, with as much area kept undeveloped and forever wild as possible. That was the charter and the goal and the moral responsibility of the Land Bank, and to suggest anything else was insulting and very possibly slanderous.

Et cetera.

I thought of my Shakespeare—*Hamlet*, in particular: "The Lady doth protest too much, methinks." Perhaps I should have staged a play myself—not *The Murder of Gonzago* but *The Selling of Pout Ponds*, and see how Charles Forrest reacted to his character's self-righteous screed. But I didn't have time for that and I wanted to avoid an ending like *Hamlet's*, the stage "littered with corpses" as my mother once put it. I was trying to dial down the melodrama.

◇◇◇

Grady Malone made that easy. I could tell he really didn't know anything except the basics: there was a potential development going in, where all the houses would be designed by him.

"I never really expected it to happen," he said, over coffee at The Bean. "Those giant projects usually fall through for some reason. And I wasn't even sure I wanted the job, quite frankly. That's five years of work at least, and I hate to commit that far ahead. You wind up having to turn down something much more cool. You're asked to submit plans for the Frick renovation, and you can't do it because you have another Nantucket McMansion to build. Just an example. The Frick rejected my design two years ago. Not grandiose enough. I hear they've abandoned the whole project now, for the moment at least. Just as well."

I did no better with Pell himself. That same afternoon I drove down to the docks and walked out to the private pier where the *Nantucket Grand* was anchored.

The ship loomed fifty feet high, a hundred and fifty feet long, shifting nets of light from the water reflecting on its massive hull. The giant radar array, looking like a city on the moon, soared over my head, and the vessel itself looked like a low-slung modern office building in Singapore or Dubai—the great slabs of squint-inducing glossy white metal and fiberglass, the giant walls of tinted windows, the layered canopied decks rising into the glare of the sun.

What did such a sea monster cost?

I looked it up: somewhere in the neighborhood of seventy million dollars. How much good could you do with that amount of money? The question wasn't worth asking. It would just make me angry and I wanted to stay calm. Pell was a modern day Pharaoh, and this grotesque, ostentatious cruise ship was the monument to his position—the prize and the proof of it. The boat radiated power, you couldn't deny that, and it was overwhelming. It made you feel small and puny, and anonymous, one of the inconsequential rabble. I might have made a serious tactical mistake.

On board this ship, Pell would have serious home-field advantage.

I started aboard and the uniformed bo'sun stopped me. "Shoes off, please."

"Excuse me?"

"No shoes on board, sir."

"I'm here on police business."

"I understand. I'll inform Mr. Pell of your arrival. But we don't allow shoes on board the ship."

"You have to be kidding."

"It's a universal rule, sir."

"Like Japanese houses? Shoes off at the door."

He smiled, nervous but relieved. "Exactly! That's exactly right. It's a custom everyone respects."

"Fine."

I cocked my leg at the knee, unlaced my shoe and toed it off, did the same with other one.

"We have slippers you can wear on board."

"Thank you."

"Your shoe size?"

"Ten and a half."

"Perfect."

He scurried aboard and I followed him into a high-ceilinged nautical living room, dotted with silk-upholstered couches and Indian sandstone coffee tables, hung with subdued abstract paintings chosen to pick up the taupe and pale green colors of the Berber rugs, setting off the polished mahogany furniture. The cabin felt expensive but cheap and tacky at the same time, a sterile concept of a rich man's world, sleek and soulless. I thought of my mother, saying "All the money in the world can't buy you taste."

That made me feel a little better.

The steward handed me a pair of beige boat slippers with a pale green stripe. "Size ten and a half."

"Just tell your boss I'm here."

"Yes, sir."

He disappeared aft, and I strolled around the big room, noting the hammered silver lamps and the cut crystal vases bulging with white roses. The boat rocked gently on the water and the air conditioning whispered in the background.

"Chief Kennis!"

Pell strode into the room, wearing the full Nantucket summer uniform of blue blazer, polo shirt, and Nantucket "reds" from Murray's, the pink pants that bled down to a dusty rose after repeated washings. As usual I felt the force of his charisma—that potent mixture of charm, willpower, and a restless intelligence that chose to settle its flattering undivided attention on you. It was the size of him too, you tended to forget that when you hadn't seen him for a while. He was tall and broad and fit, with masses of thick gray hair, huge hands, and a crushing grip. I squeezed back as we shook hands but there was no way I could win that contest. He gave the impression that it would be easy and mildly amusing to crush every bone in my fingers, but that he chose to show mercy instead. His blue eyes glinted with combative satisfaction as he registered my wince of pain.

"What can I do for you, Chief?"

"I have a few questions. It won't take long."

"I've got all the time in the world, Chief. It's summer and I'm already on Nantucket! Don't you love that bumper sticker? Says it all. Stop and smell the rosea rugosa, that would be my bumper sticker." He took my arm. "Let me give you the nickel tour."

I looked around. "More like the Krugerrand tour."

He barked out a short laugh. "Quite right. That would be close to twelve hundred dollars, according to today's spot price on the London market. And worth every penny, as I'm sure you'll agree."

I had to admit he was right—the gorgeously furnished open-air decks, the lavish staterooms with king-sized beds and wide windows overlooking the harbor, the interconnected living areas opening into more canopied decks were all dauntingly impressive. There was a fully appointed gym on the lower level, along with quarters for the crew, a huge galley and a pilot house that looked like a NASA control room, with banks of touch-screen computers faced by leather swivel chairs on the gleaming wood floor. One broad cabin on the lower deck was closed off for renovation, soon to be reborn as the screening room Phelan had mentioned.

"We have two Caterpillar engines that run on aviation fuel," Pell informed me. "A fifteen knot cruising speed, and a range of six thousand nautical miles. The *Grand* can cross the Atlantic easily, and we've done it on several occasions. Fabulous trip, if you've got the weather. The *Grand* has two tenders—a twenty-seven-foot Dariel Limo and and 24-foot Rive Iseo. Plus a twelve-foot sky boat and very fast stable rescue boat. We even have a helicopter pad." He recited all this with the barely controlled pride and pleasure of a parent talking about his child's Dean's List grades and equestrian event ribbons. There's a lovely Yiddish word for it: kvelling.

But the ship scarcely seemed real to me. The surfaces were too smooth, the colors too muted, the lighting too indirect. It manifested as a hologram of itself, a CGI trick in a movie. I missed the barnacles and bright work of a real boat, the gorgeous canvas-rigged sailing ships that glided into Nantucket harbor every year for race week. They were connected to the wind. Where did this floating palace connect?

"You spend enough time on board this yacht, and you'd forget the outside world even exists." I remarked.

Pell grinned. "That's the whole idea, Chief. It's a world unto itself. '*In Xandau did Kubla Khan a stately pleasure dome decree. Where Alph the sacred river ran down to a sunless sea.*'"

I was impressed by his knowledge of nineteenth-century poetry, but I couldn't ignore the opportunity he had given me with the quotation. I chose a spot a little farther along in the poem for my response: "*And 'mid this tumult Kubla heard from far, ancestral voices prophesying war.*'"

"I see you know your Coleridge," Pell said.

"Every school child knows that poem."

"Maybe when we were in school. Now they study rap lyrics—to maintain relevance and diversity. Two of my least favorite words in the English language, by the way."

We were standing on the upper deck, our backs to the town, looking out over Coatue and the head of the harbor. A pale breeze ruffled the water, carrying the smells of brine and boat fuel and the fragrant smoke from a barbecue fire.

Enough chit-chat. "So your detective found Daisy."

"Yes, at that man's funeral. And then he lost her again. Last seen haring down the road with the local police chief in hot pursuit."

"I lost her, too. But I tracked her down, no problem."

"And how did you accomplish that feat, if I may ask?"

I smiled. "Detective work."

If my little slap at his employee bothered him, he didn't show it. "So where is she?"

"I think we should let her tell you that herself. She's safe and healthy. She's a functional adult—"

"I often wonder about that."

"If she wants to get in touch, she knows where to find you. This boat is hard to miss."

He smiled thinly. "It's a ship, Chief Kennis."

"Right. So here's what we've got. Daisy was living with Andrew Thayer. Douglas Blount was in love with her. That's why Blount killed him."

"Don't you mean allegedly killed?"

"Blount confessed."

"Tragic. I should never have hired a convicted felon, but at the time I believed that our prison system really does rehabilitate criminals. Doug seemed a perfect example. In fact penitentiaries are more like graduate schools for the aspiring thief or murderer. They come out good for nothing but a life of crime and uniquely fitted for it, well-trained and hardened. That was our Mr. Blount. He talked a good game, at least. He certainly fooled me."

"Some officers at the station believe it was a crime of passion."

"You know he killed Todd Macy. Was that another crime of passion?"

"He seemed like a very passionate man."

Pell laughed out loud. "Did he really?"

"No."

"He was covering up his criminal activities, nothing more. That sickening sex-for-drugs racket he was involved with."

"So you knew he killed Macy?"

This knocked Pell off balance for a second, but he recovered smoothly. "You found the murder weapon in his house! So there's not much doubt."

"How do you know we found the murder weapon?"

"I get around, Chief Kennis. People still talk to me and I still listen."

"Who in particular?"

"I'm not sure I'm under any obligation to tell you that."

"You are if it was a cop."

He lifted his hand and his shoulders, tipping his head in a sort of peacemaking shrug. "Then let's assume it was not."

"I think your daughter may have been involved with that racket, as you call it."

"She's my stepdaughter. I adopted her after her father died."

"Yet she kept his name."

"We didn't always get along."

"Clearly. So you knew about her part in this pornography scheme?"

"I didn't say that."

"But it doesn't surprise you."

"Daisy was always a troubled girl, Chief Kennis. From an early age her looks were…disruptive. And she very much enjoyed creating those disruptions. They say power corrupts. She was very powerful. I tried to impose discipline, to provide her with some sort of moral compass. I only succeeded in alienating her. Still it seemed like we had reached some rapprochement in recent years. She enjoyed being back on the island. She found herself a good job. Her troubled past allowed her to connect with the kids at the school here. She understood their problems. She was able to help. Or so she said."

"That sounds good. But she was recruiting for this criminal enterprise. Suborning under-age sex and drug use, actively working to ruin those kids' lives. Kids who trusted her. One of them is in a coma right now, and it's partly Daisy's fault. She's going to be tried as an accessory, Mr. Pell. Before and after the fact—aiding and abetting the crime and helping to cover it up."

"If any of this is true."

"Is it?"

"I have no idea. I certainly hope not."

I'd taken this path about as far as it would go. Time to switch things up. I put my back to the rail, looking into the connected state rooms of the giant vessel through the open glass door. "What do you know about Blue Heron Estates?"

"You mean the White Heron theater company? I'm a big supporter."

"No, Blue Heron Estates. They're planning a major development in the moors."

"Never heard of them."

"Half the land they're building on belongs to the LoGran Corporation."

"No, sorry. You're wrong about that. We divested ourselves of that property more than eighteen months ago. LoGran is not a real estate company and, frankly, we wouldn't know what to do with a parcel that size."

"Who did you sell it to?"

He leaned his elbows on the polished steel of the railing, staring out at the Great Point lighthouse, a tiny white filament stapled between the blue of the harbor and the sky.

"I'm not sure. Some Canadian group, I think. They certainly weren't developers. I don't recall any 'estates' in their business name. More of a holding company, I think. If they had any plans, they were long-range ones. Tapping the aquifer for a bottled-water concern? Harvesting deer ticks for medical research? I'm just guessing. The kind of work I started ProACKtive to support."

I took a breath. "Okay. Now you know what my detectives think is going on. Want to hear my theory?"

"Of course."

"I'm thinking Blount killed Andrew Thayer because Andy refused to sell his section of the Thayer property. Their land abuts the LoGran parcel."

"I don't see why. That parcel has nothing to do with LoGran or me, or Douglas for that matter." Pell pushed himself upright and took what looked like an invigorating gulp of the humid sea air. "Besides, that's not much of a business model, Chief. Killing people you can't convince. I imagine the corpses would start to pile up quickly—as would the evidence against you. And I can't imagine any business transaction that would be worth taking a human life."

"Well, someone can."

"I suggest you talk to these Blue Heron people, then. They're the obvious suspects, if your theory is correct. But I would look to Doug's other...activities, if I were you. Drug dealers often kill in the course of their business, so I've heard." He smiled. "Realtors? Not so much."

I smiled back. "And where were you on the day of the murder?"

"Excuse me?"

"Do you have an alibi for that morning?"

"I—it's...of course I do. I was on board the *Grand* all day, with a terrible headache. I get migraines, you know. Absolutely unbearable. The crew can vouch for me. Feel free to check with them."

"I will."

"And I must say, I find this line of inquiry rather insulting."

"That's not really my problem, Mr. Pell."

"It is if I complain to the Board of Selectmen."

"Feel free."

"I will. And the State Attorney General's office. They frown on police harassment."

"Good luck making that case."

We stared each other down for about twenty seconds. Finally he said "I think you should leave now. If you plan to arrest me, then do so. You'll make a prime ass out of yourself and I'd enjoy watching that little circus. If not, then disembark immediately, and never board this ship again unless you have either a fully authorized search warrant or suitably humble apology. You'll never procure the first—or perform the second. Because you're too incompetent for the one and you're too proud for the other. Not a good combination, Chief Kennis. Not a good combination at all. Now, if you'll excuse me, I have calls to make."

The bo'sun led me out and handed me back my shoes with a small apologetic grimace of shared distaste that signaled, "I deal with this shit every day."

I crossed the metal gangway and stood on the dock tying my shoelaces, a rudimentary set of skilled gestures most people never even think about past the age of four or five. I had been one of the last kids in Pre-K to master the art, though, and perhaps for that reason, I occasionally noticed the effortless double bow as I pulled it tight. It was nice to feel competent in some small way after having been so comprehensively outplayed and misdirected and dismissed by the tycoon captain of the *Nantucket Grand*.

I had badgered him, baited him, flattered him, threatened him, ambushed him, and tried to catch him in a series of lies, all to no avail. As I walked back along the wide public pier toward the Hy-Line docks and the shops and restaurants of Straight Wharf, it occurred to me that Pell might in fact be innocent. I wasn't missing the target with my little jabs—there was no target to hit. The fact was I wanted him to be guilty. In my own crazy way I was as culpable of profiling as any cop in Ferguson, Missouri, or Staten Island.

Sure, Pell was obscenely rich—that didn't make him a killer, or even a real estate speculator. He was an overbearing asshole but that had never been a crime. Objectively, in this case, I was the overbearing asshole, not Pell—railroading him the way Lonnie Fraker had tried to railroad Mason Taylor in the State Police interrogation room, and with as little proper cause or justification.

The man was right, I did owe him an apology. I had basically decided to go back and deliver it, take another tongue-lashing, slink home, and start re-thinking the whole mess from scratch.

But then I did the dishes.

Chapter Thirty

Circumstantial Evidence

The connection I made was visual, so I have to describe the setup at my kitchen sink.

I have a row of cups on hooks under the open shelving where I keep my plates and bowls. As I was soaping off the breakfast dishes I noticed that one of the cups had been hung up backward. The image rhymed, like a couplet in a poem, with some other jarring detail. But what was it? I stood there with the hot water running over my wrists and hands for more than a minute. Then I remembered.

I dried my hands, pulled out my iPhone and started scrolling through the pictures. When I got to the one I took in the upstairs study of the LoGran house on Eel Point Road, I spread it larger with two fingertips.

There it was: the venetian blinds were all closed, slats down. But one of them was closed with the slats up. They'd been opened and then shut in haste. Someone had been up there, standing lookout on the driveway, alerting Blount of Liam Phelan's arrival, after luring Andy Thayer into the big foyer and cutting his throat.

But who?

The only person beside Pell himself who had access to the big house was Sue Ann Pelzer, and she had been birding in Madaket when the murder went down.

Then, something Pell said on the boat exploded in my brain like one of those illegal cherry bomb fireworks we used to flush down the toilet—the same muted thud, the same ominous shudder in the pipes. The *Nantucket Grand* used aviation fuel, he said on the tour, boasting about the ship's speed and range and power.

Aviation fuel—the propellant for the arson fire at Andy's house! We had investigated the airport—what did we know? We thought jet fuel was for jets.

Yeah—jets and mega yachts.

David Trezize was right. It was Pell, it had to be Pell, all of it—the murders, the island-trashing land deal, maybe even the porn racket. That little conspiracy made the perfect cover, the perfect excuse for all the killings—a routine falling-out among thieves. No one would look farther than that, or dig any deeper. Scumbags kill scumbags—case closed.

But it was Pell's knife in the bushes, his fuel in the dirt around Andy Thayer's house, his name hidden behind the shell companies that controlled Blue Heron Estates. I thought of Jane's heroine Madeline Clark—I was in her situation now: I knew everything.

And I could prove nothing.

I needed help. I needed hard evidence and eyewitness testimony, tearful confessions, and smoking guns. I inventoried the players: Blount would never talk, assuming he was even aware of his boss' plans—Pell must have some unimaginable hold over him. Sue Ann Pelzer knew nothing, and the porn conspirators were ignorant of anything beyond their own sordid affairs. McAllister was a potential weak link, but a short jail term in a country club prison was a small price to pay for his piece of the Blue Heron deal. Besides, he was out of jail on a half-million-dollar bond and bracing him now without some compelling evidence would be pointless—a replay of my fiasco on the *Nantucket Grand*.

No, there was only one person who could help me now, one person who could tell me everything, if I could only persuade her to talk.

So that's how I wound up stalking Daisy Pell, staking out Kathleen Lomax's house on Sherburne Turnpike in my unmarked cruiser, lying in wait like a spurned boyfriend, like David Trezize reading his ex-wife's diary. Lucky for me he'd done that. It set him on his own investigative trail and he had proved far more helpful unraveling the case than Lonnie Fraker and his State Police army, or even my own detectives. But stalkers had it easy—snooping and skulking and keeping out of sight. My task was different.

I had to pounce.

Predators spend most of their time waiting and I waited below the driveway of "Sea Breeze," as the house was called, for almost three hours. I started to suspect that Daisy had left the car and gone for a walk into town, or a bike ride to the beach…or, more ominously, that she had left the MINI Cooper there as a decoy, to keep me stuck in place while she fled to the steamship terminal or the airport. A neat trick if she wanted to escape the island and my questions and her part, whatever it was, in the events of the last eight months. But she wasn't crazy enough to jump bail; I knew that.

My speculations were nothing but the product of boredom and an overactive imagination. A bad combination, the personal version of mixing a secluded town and a choice item of mendacious gossip. Still, gossip had a way of doubling back on itself, slipping up behind you with one sly push that made the silliest trumped-up lie turn true. That same thing could be happening to me right now. If I did a good enough job of treating Daisy like a panicky fugitive, I could easily turn her into one.

Down, boy. Sit tight and wait.

Good advice. Daisy skipped out of the house ten minutes later, calm and unconcerned. She didn't notice me and I almost missed her, checking e-mails on my phone. That's why I'd made a firm rule forbidding social media on stakeouts. Leave the smartphones at home. They make you stupid. Being somewhere else instead of where you were supposed to be—the central purpose of today's interconnected communications web—was the exact opposite of what you needed for a surveillance detail…as I had just proved.

That would give the boys a laugh back the cop shop.

Fuck that, I had no time to think about it. I threw myself out of the car and sprinted up the steep driveway. Daisy and I reached the MINI Cooper at the same moment.

"Daisy—"

"Chief, get in, take a drive with me. I need to talk."

This was progress. I folded myself into the passenger side of the little car, which I have to say was startlingly roomy once I got inside. She drove down to Sherburne Turnpike and onto Cliff Road toward town. I rolled down my window and tasted the mild breeze. Most of the time, the best interrogation technique is to say nothing. Not that this was technically an interrogation. I wasn't sure what it was. I let Daisy take the lead.

"I wanted to apologize," she said on Easton Street when we stopped at the corner of South Water Street for a pair of jogging super-moms pushing strollers. "I've been rude to you. I treated you badly and it really had nothing to do with you and I'm sorry."

"No problem. I was only frustrated because I had some questions I wanted to ask."

"I know."

"And it didn't seem like you were ever going to answer them."

She made a small apologetic grimace. "I'm not."

"So, I'm not really—"

"I just hated that you thought I was a bitch."

"Well, bitchy. On occasion. Like everyone else."

"Thank you. That's a lovely distinction."

We had skirted the bottom of town and started up Washington Street with the harbor on our left. It was crowded with boats, every mooring taken now. High summer.

"Here's the thing," I said. "I have witnesses who place you at Howard McAllister's house in 'Sconset at a meeting of the group who—"

"I know what they were doing. Obviously."

"I'm interested in what you were doing."

"I was recruiting. Obviously. That's why you arrested me."

We passed Marine Home Center as traffic slowed down moving toward the rotary. I took a breath and let it out slowly. "There's more to the story than that. Guidance counselor fast-tracking troubled kids into sex traffic and drug addiction? For money? For kicks? I don't buy it."

"Thank you for that."

"So?"

"So what?"

"So tell me the rest."

"You tell me, Chief. I think you know it."

"All right. It's about your stepfather. He and McAllister are friends."

"Friends, I don't know. That's a term mostly used in human society."

"But they're animals?"

"Animals have packs. They're loyal to the pack."

"Then what?"

"I don't know, Chief. Call them partners. Business associates. People like my stepfather don't have friends, but they do have known associates."

"Right."

She drove on. We had rounded the rotary, and turned off onto Polpis Road.

"So when did you figure it out?" Daisy asked as we took the curves uphill past Moor's End farm. "I'm guessing…today."

"This morning, actually."

"So now you need me to talk."

"You had a falling-out with your stepfather. But you still have unfinished business there. That's my theory."

"And the origin of this theory?"

"I have a stepparent, too. A stepmother in my case."

"Not all stepparents are horrible, Chief."

"Absolutely. I'm thinking about a potential stepparent for my own kids right now. And she's delightful."

"But yours?"

"She could go head to head with Pell any time."

"Bad idea. She'd lose."

"Tell me."

"I can't. I don't want to. I wouldn't know where to start."

And that was the moment I realized we were being followed.

She turned to glance at me. "What?"

"Check your rearview mirror. You see that gray SUV behind us?"

"The Escalade?"

"Right."

"What about it?"

"It's been tailing us since…well, since we left your house obviously. I first noticed it on Washington Street. But I mean—a gray SUV. It's like noticing a shingled house. But they followed us around the rotary, and they're still back there."

"Who is it?"

"I was going to ask you. Recognize the car?"

She shook her head, studying the mirror. "No. My people drive Beemers—and the occasional Lexus."

I checked behind us. They were closing the distance.

"Who are they chasing?" Daisy said. "Me or you?"

"Maybe they were waiting until they got us both together. They saw us talking at Andy's funeral. The detective was there. Louis Berman."

"Shit. This is exactly what I was talking about."

"I must have led them right to Kathleen's house today."

"Shit shit shit. They're going to kill us."

"Daisy—"

"I know Jonathan Pell. This is how he operates."

"Okay, he's got my stepmother beat."

She snorted. "You have no idea."

"Maybe they're just trying to scare you. Get you back in line."

"Maybe. Let's hope."

With a rising growl from its big V-8 engine the Escalade rammed the back of our car. The jolt banged me back against my seat and then forward. The seat belt snapped tight across my shoulders. Daisy yelped, but managed to steer the little car out of its skid.

Another impact. Daisy screamed but kept us on the road. The Escalade pulled up next to us. I couldn't see anything through the tinted windows.

"Oh, my God," she squealed. "They're going to run us off the road!"

We came around a turn where a landscaper's truck forced the Escalade back into its own lane behind us with an angry bleat of its horn. They were going slowly, dragging a trailer of mowers. A line of cars straggled behind them.

The reprieve didn't last long, and I quickly realized the new danger: every car going the other way on Polpis Road had piled up behind that truck. Once the last of the traffic passed us, the Escalade would get a shot at clear road.

They sensed it, too, and roared up beside us, twisting the wheel sideways. A sickening smack of metal on metal and Daisy was off the asphalt, wheels chattering on the sandy grass of the shoulder, swerving toward the start of a split-rail fence. She wrestled the car back on the road as the fence blurred past us, then hit the brakes. The big SUV surged ahead of us—another respite. We flew past the Quidnet turnoff.

She was chanting, "What do we do, what do we do what do we do?"

They braked to come beside us again.

"Floor it," I shouted. We pulled ahead and I remembered almost flipping my NPD Ford Explorer on New Lane the day before. We were about to hit one of the only other sections of road on the entire island where a small, low-slung car like Daisy's could have a chance against a top-heavy SUV. I had almost toppled that same NPD Explorer on this upcoming set of "S" curves when I first arrived on the island, siren-screaming on my way to Hoick's Hollow to make sure my first drug bust didn't turn into a firefight.

"Hit these next turns as fast as you can," I said.

They bumped the back of the car again. "I can't! I'll flip it!"

"No, you won't. You'll flip them. Stamp on it! Accelerate into this turn. Hit it hard."

She did it and the inertia slapped me back against my seat like a big hand.

"Brake a little, then go! Go go go!"

She took the next turn fast, too fast I thought for a second as the little car rocked and righted itself. I turned back to see the Escalade tilt on its wheels, teeter out of control for a heart-stopping second, and then keel over sideways. It hit the pavement with a tearing screech and slid off the road onto the grass.

Daisy let out a shout of glee. "We did it!"

The accident vanished behind us around the next turn.

"Go back," I said.

"What? Are you kidding? We have to get out of here!"

"Go back. I'm not leaving the scene of an accident." I dug my cellphone out of my pocket And called the station. I got Barnaby Toll on the line. "We have a one-car crash just beyond Quidnet on the Polpis Road. Send two cruisers and an ambulance. Proceed with caution. Victims possibly armed and dangerous."

"Okay, yes sir, right away, I'm on it."

I disconnected and turned back to Daisy. "I mean it. Go back."

"You just said they could be armed and dangerous!"

"They're probably unconscious. They might need CPR. They could be bleeding. They might need a tourniquet. I have to find out. It's my job. If you're afraid, I understand. Just get me close and let me out."

"You're out of uniform. You're unarmed! What about 'proceed with caution'?"

My gun was safely locked up at home. Much to my assistant chief's annoyance, I never carried it without some compelling reason, and a chat with Daisy hadn't qualified. Haden always wore his, off-duty or on, because, as he put it, "things can go sideways anytime."

This moment would justify his paranoia. But if you had a gun, you tended to use it, even when you shouldn't. It was the quick, easy solution, but it caused more problems than it fixed. We had argued about the topic for years.

All I said to Daisy was, "I always proceed with caution."

"Jesus Christ. At least we won't be outnumbered."

She spun the car around. We drove back, not talking, catching our breaths, getting ready.

The big SUV lay sideways across the bike path like a wounded animal. We pulled over and I climbed out of the car. Daisy moved to join me. I leaned back in the window. "Wait here."

"But—"

I jabbed the flat of my palm at her. "Stay."

She pouted at me, fully recovered from the incident, or so it seemed. "Woof, woof."

I crab-walked to the Escalade, looked down through the side window. They were out, all right. They had banged against each other and the windows like shoes in a dryer. The glass was starred, cracked, and bloody, with more blood on their clothes and the leather seats. A Glock 9mm autoloader and an iPhone rested on the glass of the driver's side window.

Daisy appeared behind me. Bad dog.

"They should have worn seat belts," she said.

I nodded. "It's a good lesson in basic automobile safety. Always strap in when you're planning to commit vehicular homicide on a crowded road."

"Are they okay?"

"They're breathing."

"Should we try to get them out?"

"I don't want to move them unless the engine starts smoking. We'll leave that to the EMTs."

She shook her head, registering the lightning events of the last few minutes with distant thunder of a sigh. "Wow."

"Yeah."

"That was unbelievable."

"Do you recognize them?"

She went up on tiptoe for a good look down. "It's hard to tell with all the blood. But no."

"Hired hitters out of Boston, probably. But who sent them?"

"I think we both know the answer to that."

I heard sirens in the distance. "We're almost done here."

She put a hand on my arm. "You were amazing. Talking me through it. I guess that's what they mean when they say riding shotgun."

"Except I didn't have a gun."

"You didn't need a gun, Chief. That was the coolest part."

I gently removed her hand and stepped back. Her sensuality was a physical force, like the acceleration that had pressed me against my seat when she floored the gas pedal. We were both giddy, nervous, coming down from the adrenaline rush. We could easily have another type of accident. A head-on crash.

I badly needed that not to happen. "Here they are," I said. The cavalry arriving in the nick of time.

The EMTs checked us out. One of them was John Macy, Todd's younger brother. I hadn't seen him since a bomb went off at the Steamship Authority the summer before. Bob Coffin and I helped him and his assistant pull the victims out of the car. The men were half-conscious, groaning and bleating in pain as we angled them out of the side door and eased them onto the grass.

John did a quick catalogue: concussions, broken noses and cheekbones, a broken collar bone, assorted cracked ribs. Severe lacerations, a fractured wrist, possible internal injuries. Five minutes later he and his partner had strapped the men onto stretchers, slid them into the ambulance, and driven away.

I gave Bob Coffin a bowdlerized version of what had happened: a speeding car glimpsed in the rearview as it took a turn too fast and flipped. Daisy slipped me a raised eyebrow as I told the story, but information regarding this case was now on a need-to-know basis and Bob Coffin didn't need to know anything. Neither did the rest of the station, and anything I told Bob would spread like jam on toast. Mmmm, delicious. Another slice of law enforcement gossip, please.

Not today. Finally the boys drove off and left us alone, with a Nantucket Auto Body tow truck on the way for the SUV.

Lonnie's forensics team would check the Escalade when it reached the station garage. I was happy to leave it to them. My day was done.

We stood on the grass and watched as traffic slowed briefly to check out the overturned behemoth and then sped on. Two deer bounded across the road, nearly causing another accident.

"They were trying to kill me," Daisy said.

"We don't know that. Look on the bright side. They may have just been trying to kill me."

"No, no. They wanted to kill me. It was my car. They'll do it, next time."

"There won't be a next time for those guys."

"There'll be other guys. There's no shortage of…guys. If you have the money to pay them."

I nodded "You should think about what you want to do next." It was just a prod, I knew she'd already decided.

"I want to help you. I want to burn my stepfather to the ground. But first I have to tell you my story. I need you to understand it."

"You told me you didn't know where to begin."

"That was a lie. I know exactly where to begin. At the beginning, like every good story. And it is a good story, at least. I could tell it at The Moth, if they were X-rated. Do we have to go to the station? Will there be tape recordings and papers to sign and lawyers and…all that?"

"Not yet." I still wanted to keep this under wraps for the moment. There might be a spy a the cop shop and even if there wasn't, I didn't trust anyone except Haden Krakauer to keep this information secure. Pell knew too much about police business already. We drove to a secluded stretch of beach she knew about in Squam and we settled in on the warm sand and stared into the calm blue-green ocean, and I listened and Daisy told me everything.

Chapter Thirty-one

Daisy's Story

"I did the first job for my stepfather six years to the day after he touched me for the first time. I was sixteen. The incest had been going on since my tenth birthday—January 24th, 1991. I was nine when my mom married him. So he didn't waste much time. It was a whirlwind courtship. My father had died two years before. We were broke. My mother met Pell working for the company that catered some big party in Montauk. One minute she was bussing dishes, the next minute she was fucking this millionaire on the beach. I remember when she came home, I was on the couch, I'd been trying to wait up for her but I fell asleep with the TV on. I woke up when I heard her come in. She looked so happy and I said, 'What happened, Mom?' And she twirled around the little living room and laughed and said, 'I got fired.'

"They were married a month later and it was like…winning the lottery, or—or like that fantasy where you find out you're really a princess. Suddenly we were living on Beekman Place and my room was bigger than our old apartment and I was going to Brearly and all the girls liked me and I had an allowance and I could buy all the clothes I wanted. We went to concerts— I'd never been to a concert before! My first one was…we saw Madonna in New Jersey, at the Brendan Byrne Arena. It's called the Izod Center now. The Blonde Ambition tour. I couldn't talk for two weeks, I screamed so much. I adored Pell, he'd saved our lives, he'd given us this whole new secret world of limousines and country houses on the beach and people who did your laundry and playing tennis on the roof at the CityView racquet club and lunches at Lord & Taylor and—and—Italian spring water and sweet butter and having to learn which fork to use for which course at dinner.

"I guess I was sort of in love with Pell right from the start and I'd always been jealous of my mother so I liked it when he flirted with me, and told me I was pretty. But he could be cold. He was moody. He could be demanding and tough and mean. He'd critique my homework and make me do it over and over again until he was satisfied. He wouldn't tell me what was wrong. I had to guess. Once it was the indentations. I wasn't indenting far enough. I went to bed crying that night but he explained everything in the morning and helped me fix it. When he slipped his hand under my skirt after my birthday party, it felt good. I was happy. He liked me. He was sweet and gentle when he touched me. And it gave me power. I figured that out right away. I could use his feelings to get what I wanted. And it wasn't just him."

She shifted herself on the sand and her skirt slid up her thighs. I looked away, out to sea.

"Jesus Christ," she said. "I'm doing it to you now. I can't help myself. It's pathetic."

I was about to say, pathetic? Most women would kill for legs like that, but I thought better of it. She didn't need a compliment and even the appearance of flirtation would be toxic. I said nothing. She seemed to be forming sentences and discarding them.

"Most people would enjoy being seduced," I said finally. "I don't really see what—"

"But I do it with everyone, Henry. Can I call you Henry?"

"Sure, yes. Absolutely."

"Thanks. What I'm saying is…I seduce the lady at the drug store counter, the paper boy, the old man next door. Everybody. I even know why. I've had the million hours of therapy. I know all my syndromes and issues and pathologies. I learned them by heart. It all comes from Pell—you never could have guessed that one. It's such a cliché. But cliché is like a rank, it's earned, you know what I mean? Some idea gets promoted by being repeated over and over and by being true every time, until it's so true for so long we're just sick of it. But it's still true. Seduction was the only way to please Pell, and it worked really well, so I never bothered to learn any other techniques. But knowing that stuff doesn't help me. That's the real problem. It doesn't get me anywhere. It doesn't change anything. I'm still flashing the police chief when I should be helping him with this case and explaining why we both almost got killed today."

I held up a hand to slow her down. "Let's go back. Pell started touching you when you were ten."

"I got older and it didn't stop. It got worse. I hardly ate for a year. I started flunking at school. I was scared of him. He warned me not to tell mom, but I finally did. And this wasn't some hokey 'recovered memory'—this was stuff that happened yesterday. But she didn't get it, she didn't believe me. She was furious. She didn't talk to me for weeks. About a month later she caught us. I was wearing nothing but one of his t-shirts and he had his hand between my legs. She still didn't believe it. She said we were 'rough-housing.'

She rubbed her cheekbones, dug her fingertips under her eyes, breathing in and out. I didn't speak. I just waited. Two seals surfaced and dove again twenty yards out to sea. They were adorable but they drew the sharks.

"The worst part," Daisy said at last, "was afterward. He'd be colder than ever, as if I was some stray his wife had adopted against his will. Any little thing I did that was particular to me, any thought I expressed, any enthusiasm I showed, any opinion—he'd go into a rage. So I had to sort of not be there. That was the trick—to disappear, to become this sort of—this generic person. The fact that I'd be grown up in about a million years wasn't much comfort."

"Why didn't you run away from home?"

"I did. Why didn't she? That's what I don't understand."

"Fear of being alone? Fear of the unknown, fear of rejection? And real physical fear. Did he hit her?" Daisy nodded. I pushed on. "She probably didn't think she could make it on her own. She was angry and couldn't express it. That's tiring. She was busy pretending this stuff wasn't happening. That has to be exhausting. A couple of years doing that and you can barely get up in the morning. Being a hero is out of the question."

"So she's the victim? I don't think so. She was a criminal. There's a legal term for it—accessory after the fact. It's a felony. You go to jail for it. Your partner can commit the crimes. All you have to do is not try to stop him."

"I'm sorry."

"You have children. Would you let that happen to your children?"

"No." But you did the same thing to Jill and the others, I said to myself. Just to myself, for now. I needed to let her talk.

"Don't apologize for my mother. She should have killed him."

"Daisy—"

"But he killed her instead."

"What do you mean?"

"He finally told her the truth. He didn't just tell it, he…he weaponized it. That's a favorite word of his, weaponize. He told her every little detail, he knew she couldn't handle it and he was done with her. Divorce was out of the question for a man in his position. But it wasn't necessary. She killed herself. She took all her antidepressants at once with most of a bottle of Grey Goose. No cheap vodka in our house. Only the best for Johnathan Pell."

"Then it was just the two of you."

"I was like his child bride. Of course it was all secret. I hated him but I wanted him, too. I was like an addict. Maybe it was Stockholm Syndrome. Boys my own age seemed dull and stupid. I was an orphan. I had no extended family, I'd never made any real friends, except for a few people here, but by then we were only here in the summer and the one school year, tenth grade… and I—it was hard. I didn't know where to start. No one wants to hear this stuff. So there was no one I could talk to. Pell was all I had. And I told myself…he wasn't really my dad, it wasn't incest, he was just this wildly attractive older man who adored me."

"Legally it was incest, though. You know that now. It goes with the statutory rape and corruption of a minor."

"The whole thing was sick and fucked up. I know that. But he said he loved me. And then he weaponized me. I was sixteen, like I said."

"He weaponized you."

"Someone else in the company was trying to block the purchase of this biotech company, GoRX. They had a bunch of cancer treatments and an MS drug about to be approved by the FDA, but this other executive found out that Pell had a huge stake in the company and would cash in big time if the sale went through. It was rush deal and this guy…well, let's just say it. The executive was Preston Lomax, and he thought the trials had been rigged and the drugs were phony and Pell was trying to get out before the whole thing collapsed. He said he was going to the LoGran Board with conflict of interest charges.

"Then he met this girl in a bar, that would be me, and I took him home to my studio apartment in Tribeca and more or less fucked him stupid. Seriously—I think he lost about twelve IQ points that night. There were only two problems. I was sixteen and the whole night was recorded on high definition video. Pell had bought the apartment and set it up as a state of the art sound stage. I hated the sex with Lomax, but I loved the look on his face when he got the news."

"Power."

"Right. That night was very empowering. I was turning into quite the little feminist. For a brainwashed sex slave."

"So he started using you that way all the time."

"I was a good weapon. Sometimes I didn't even have to blackmail them. Sometimes, all I had to do was ask."

"And you never had a real boyfriend?"

"I just laughed at them. They were all so obvious and clumsy and weak. I could make them do anything, but why bother? I was a professional by then. I didn't work for free."

"Until Andrew."

She pressed her face into her hands. "We'd been friends for twenty years before I fell in love with him."

"And you finally told him the truth."

She nodded.

"And he was okay with it?"

"Andrew didn't judge people."

We studied the ocean for a few minutes, saying nothing. I watched sea gulls diving for their lunch, a speed boat drawing a thin white line across the blue water, its engine silenced by distance and the rustle and sluice of small waves on the beach. Two black labs bounded up the hard-packed sand near the water, followed by a couple who nodded to us as they walked by. Down the beach, a little boy was flying a kite, its translucent yellow wings caught in a high breeze we couldn't feel. He played out the string, let it go taut. That was it—the kite motionless a hundred feet up, the kid holding the line. Nothing more was going to happen; there wasn't even a tree for it to get stuck in, but the translucent plastic was pretty against the blue sky, a carnation pinned to the summer afternoon's lapel. I dug my elbows into the sand and waited. Daisy would tell me the next part when she was ready.

A few minutes later she pushed a breath out from between pursed lips and launched. "When Preston Lomax died and Pell took over the LoGran Corporation, he went through all the files and ledgers and spreadsheets, all the tax records going back twenty years. He identified the Moorland Mall property and a title search of the area led him to the Thayer family. Edna had died, and the land was potentially for sale. With the LoGran holdings, it would be the biggest parcel of privately owned land ever developed on the island. Edna's will was very clear: the land could only be sold to the Land Bank, and all the beneficiaries had to agree. So Pell worked out a deal with the Land Bank using Charlie Forrest as his point man.

"But there were problems. Todd Macy was against the deal and Andy refused to sell his four-acre lot on the Thayer estate.

The courts could make him go along, but they wanted to keep things quiet, and Andy could make a lot of noise. Plus, Charlie had gotten involved with Howard McAllister's home-movie business. Pell got him out of it, Charlie had to be clean, but Pell has a way of turning calamities into tactical advantages. He always says, 'Never let a crisis go to waste.'

"This movie thing was a perfect way to control McAllister, and a perfect cover for any drastic actions he might need to take. So, naturally, I had to get involved, to supervise and recruit and make sure the whole scandalous mess could be…"

"Weaponized?"

She etched a cold little smile onto her face. "You're getting to know Pell pretty well."

"And he knew you."

"I was bad and he made me that way. Or I don't know, maybe I was born that way, and he recognized it. I had started a new life here, I was working at the high school, I was trying to move forward, using my real father's name, like living underground. But I was kidding myself. I couldn't say no when Pell needed me. So when the call came, I—it was fate."

"You got involved with the porn business."

She swiveled around, brushed the hair off her face. "Yes."

"I don't get it. Those kids trusted you. This wasn't messing with some middle-aged businessman. Those girls were innocent."

"I know that."

"You must have seen yourself in them."

"Yes."

"But you couldn't refuse Pell."

"It was—not just that."

"Tell me."

She turned back to the ocean. Twenty yards out, a couple poled past on standing surfboards. Honeymooners. "I loved the kids but I kind of hated them also. Like that happy couple out there. It's the way poor people think about rich people, it's the way crippled people think about people with healthy bodies. You don't even have to be crippled. Did you ever sprain your ankle and look at people running around, taking everything for granted?"

"I think I know what you mean. But it just made me appreciate being able to walk again, when I could."

"But I couldn't! Don't you get that? I could never be happy like them or normal like them. I could never have their sunny little lives, their smiley emoticon casual who's-taking-who-to-the-prom dream world. It was a clean brick wall and I wanted to spray paint my graffiti on it. I wanted to mess them up. I wanted them to hurt like I did."

"And you got your wish."

"Yes."

"You showed them."

"I showed them."

I let a silence go by. A fresh breeze lofted a scouring of sand at us. We both looked down.

"But you pulled out," I said. "Eventually, you had to stop."

"Everyone has a limit."

"What happened?"

"It was a lot of things at once. Pell wanted me to seduce David Lattimer—he was the only abutter who might make trouble about the deal. The old man was smitten, but it just seemed too horrible. I'd gotten involved with Andrew by then and he saw what was happening. He wanted me to make a clean break. I never could have done it without him. I started to see a whole other life, a normal life. The job at the school had felt like a sham, like playacting, just kind of going through the motions on faith—pretend it's real to make it real. But I felt bad about the kids, the ones I'd recruited and the other ones. I could see some of them were hurting as bad as I was, and I could tell they needed me. And Andrew was like, 'This is who you are now, you can be good, you are good, it's easy.' And it felt easy when I was with him. I know that sounds corny."

"Not at all."

"So I told Pell I was done. We wound up having a terrible fight about it onboard the ship, and Oscar Graham overheard us. He was working security on the docks, that's why he was there, and Pell caught him listening. Oscar knew Pell had seen him and Pell could see I knew the kid. The next thing I knew, Oscar was dead. And then—and then Andrew. I know Pell had Andrew killed, and Oscar and Todd Macy."

I scooped a handful of warm sand, let it sift through my fingers. "I believe he had Andrew's house torched as well. And there was something else. A blackmail film. We have reason to believe that Pell installed surveillance cameras in Andrew's house. He filmed you and Andrew together and then doctored the film to look like it was someone else with him. A girl, one of the girls you recruited."

"Well, that's Pell's M.O. I should have known he'd turn it against someone I cared about. Eventually. If they got in his way."

"This girl in the film was—"

"Jill Phelan. Andrew told me. He knew I'd believe it was fake."

I nodded. "The house fire didn't work and the blackmail didn't work, so they took the next logical step."

"They're all in it together and I'm in it with them. There's no way out."

"There may be."

"No. Edna's will just came out of probate, everything's official now. They're signing the deals soon. Maybe tomorrow. Maybe today. Maybe they already signed."

"But what about Andrew's will?"

"It doesn't matter. Edna's estate was *per stirpes*—all the legatees are treated collectively, as a single person. Andrew's share is automatically distributed among the remaining beneficiaries. Pell knew that. He does his homework. He wouldn't have killed Andy just to get himself into another probate limbo."

I sat up, dusted the sand off me. "You can help me take Pell down."

"It's too late."

"You don't know that. This is your way out."

"There's no way out. I don't deserve a way out."

"Yes, you do."

"I'm bad. I'm poison. Everything's done. I can't fix it."

I took a breath, "You can't fix it. That's true. But you can end it. You can make sure it never happens again. You can't change the past but you can change the future. At least you can try. It's the best chance you're going to get. I can stop Pell, but I can't do it without you."

She looked at me and I saw hope soften her features. She said, "What can I do?"

I had worked out the plan while she spoke, putting it together on the fly as she made her confession. I told her, and she agreed.

She said, "I'll be your weapon now."

I helped her up and we jogged through the soft sand, and ran back along the dirt road, and flung ourselves into the little car. She keyed the ignition and pulled out with a spray of gravel. We got to the police station in seven minutes, and before we reached the rotary I was on the phone with Dave Carmichael in the State AG's office, setting up the wire.

Chapter Thirty-two

Strategy and Tactics

I left Daisy with Lonnie Fraker at the State Police headquarters. He could coordinate with the various law enforcement agencies, get the necessary authorizations, set up the microphone and the live feed. He knew the drill—the mike had to be waterproof and invisible, or close to it. Daisy could wind up in a bikini, or wearing nothing but a towel in the ship's sauna.

I explained my conditions: "No break from routine, no hesitation, no uncomfortable moments."

Lonnie grinned. "No problem."

"You're sure—"

"Don't worry, Chief. We have the technology."

But Daisy needed more than electronic gimmicks. She needed backup. I couldn't send an officer on board with her. Andrew Thayer would have volunteered in a heartbeat but he had proved unable even to defend himself with these people. I thought of David Trezize and almost laughed. The hapless reporter would be a liability, despite his good intentions, and Pell would never talk freely in front of him anyway.

No, it had to be someone Pell knew, someone Daisy liked, someone I trusted. There wasn't much overlap there. In fact, it came down to one person. I had to convince her to help us, and I had to do it fast.

"That's crazy talk!" said Sue Ann Pelzer.

We were standing in the foyer of the Eel Point house, five minutes after I left the State Police headquarters.

"It's the truth."

"Jonathan Pell is a good man."

"He's not."

"Bad things happen around him. I admit that. A man was killed in his house here. That doesn't make him a killer."

"I never said he did his own dirty work, Sue Ann. He gives the orders. That's how people like Pell operate."

"You can't know that."

"I know it. I just need to prove it."

"Have you seen the new Boys and Girls Club building?"

"It's hard to miss."

"Well, it wouldn't be there if not for Jonathan Pell."

"He's generous to strangers. He wrote a tax-deductible check. I don't see how that—"

"One time we were walking in the moors—he loves the moors, Chief Kennis. And we saw this adorable little King Charles spaniel puppy being attacked by these two awful bull-mastiffs. They were off the leash and the owner was just kind of dancing around saying "Keats! Byron! Stop! Stop that now!" while those vicious dogs just laid into this poor little puppy. Mr. Pell stepped in and pulled them off him. Two bullmastiffs! He got bitten, he needed stitches later, but he stood them down and he saved that pup. That's Jonathan Pell. Then he pushed the leash law warrant through at Town Meeting the next year. That's Jonathan Pell, too. He cares and he has follow-through. Not many people have follow-through. They talk a good game and forget about it. Not Mr. Pell."

I allowed myself a bitter little smile. "I can agree with you there, at least."

"I don't like your tone, Chief Kennis."

This was taking too long. "I talked to Daisy. She told me everything."

"I don't know, but I bet the statute of limitations is up on all that shoplifting. And the rest of what she's done isn't illegal. Except in Alabama."

"We didn't talk about her. We talked about Pell."

"I can't believe she would slander her stepfather."

"She didn't. Slander is making false statements with malicious intent. I believe Daisy was telling me the truth, and trying to help."

She squinted at me and I met her interrogating stare. Finally she glanced sideways and crossed her arms over her chest, submitting. She squeezed her eyes shut and then opened them wide. She pointed into the living room. "Sit down and tell me what she said."

I ran through it for her and then said, "I need you on that ship with her. I want to make sure she gets what we need on tape and make sure she gets back on dry land in one piece. This plan could go wrong in an instant and Daisy has to be protected. I wouldn't use her if I had any other choice."

"I could do it."

She wasn't thinking clearly. "No, you couldn't. He's kept everything secret from you. He's not going to start confiding in you now. Sorry, but that's just—"

"I know, I know. You're right."

"Anyway, there's more to it. I need you to vouch for Daisy. Pell's going to be wary, Sue Ann. They argued, she walked away. His detective saw her talking to me, his goons tried to run us off the road. You have to spin all that. The chase scared her, made her realize the rift she'd created. She's remorseful, she's afraid, she needs him to know she'd never betray him, that she told me nothing, that she can't make it alone out there with Andrew gone. She needs Pell. She loves him. She wants to help. She wants to make things right. She wants to prove herself. She told you all that. In tears. You have to sell it."

"I'm not sure I can."

"He trusts you. And you trust her. It's that simple."

I glanced at my watch. Time felt like a big dog chasing me.

"I want you with her all the way," I said.

"Don't worry, Chief. I make a good wingman."

"Good. Thank you. I'm glad to hear that."

I left the mansion feeling a wary sense of confidence. All Daisy had to do was spend an hour making up with her step-father, coax out a casual confession, and get away clean. The plan was simple, the backup was solid. I'd been forced to confide in Lonnie Fraker, but he loved being in the loop and his new superior knowledge energized him.

He clapped me on the back as Daisy—wired-up, on edge but determined—walked out of the State Police building. "It's in the bag," he said, watching her drive away. "What could go wrong?"

The short answer was "everything"—as we were about to find out.

Chapter Thirty-three

The Visionary

It started when Haden Krakauer gave me the files. He brought them over to the hastily organized command center at the State Police headquarters, partly to check the boxes of a routine inquiry and partly to give me papers to read for distraction while I sat like a general behind the front lines, waiting for news of the battle. Some delay was inevitable. Daisy had to go to the LoGran house on Eel Point Road and call Pell from there to set up the meeting. He insisted on a landline call from a known location before anyone was allowed on board the *Grand*. No drop-ins, no surprises. If he was paranoid, his paranoia had served him well so far.

Meanwhile, I was glad to have Haden's files. He had done thorough, meticulous work, even if it didn't add up to much beyond deep background. He knew and I knew that deep background could break a case, if you knew how to look at it, or maybe I should say, if you knew what you were looking for. Some facts lingered in people's histories like viruses with long incubation periods, flaring up with a shocking new relevance years later in a new context.

Haden had worked up dossiers on the crew of the Nantucket Grand, including all the stewards, the chef, the bo'sun, the first mate, and the chief engineer—Liam Phelan.

There were write-ups on the Eel Point house personnel, too—Blount and Sue Ann Pelzer, of course, along with the groundskeepers, cleaning crews, and kitchen staff. There were also two secretaries and a party-planner who organized large events at the estate.

I started with Sue Ann. Born in Charleston, South Carolina, attended McBee Elementary School, and Provost Academy in Columbia. Sophomore year as an exchange student with a Catholic school in Johannesburg, South Africa. There was an Interpol notation there: she was briefly arrested at an interracial concert in Cape Town when the police broke it up. The rest of the year was uneventful. She finished up high school in South Carolina and then moved north and west, attending college at Montana State University because of an interest in winter sports developed over numerous ski vacations at Sugar Mountain in North Carolina. She took up competing in biathlons and was named junior biathlete of the year in 1993 and picked up a bronze medal at the world championships that year in Borovets, Bulgaria. She competed in the winter Olympics the next year in Lillehammer, but never got close to the winner's circle.

I had read a little further—a masters degree in business administration from the University of Chicago Booth school, a stint with McKinsey, doing consulting work, various low-level corporate jobs in public relations, the LoGran hire in 2004—and then I stopped.

I set the file down. This had to be wrong. I was standing on the beach in California watching the sun rise over the ocean—it was that disorienting. I was on the wrong coast, turned around a hundred and eighty degrees. I felt nauseous, dizzy, as if I had been physically spun around until the vertigo hit. I scrabbled for the file again, found the Interpol report. The band playing at that interracial concert back in 1986 was Juluka. Of course no one caught it; you'd have to be a fan to know the name of this particular artist's first group.

Johnny Clegg: the featured performer on the planted iPod.

And the biathlon: the event where you skied around and shot at targets with a hunting rifle.

I had to be wrong. This couldn't be happening.

She had an alibi, an airtight alibi.

At that moment Lonnie shouted from the next room, "Get in here! Daisy's talking to Pell! And she's got him on speakerphone."

We lurched through the door in time to hear this exchange:

"What's going on, Daisy? What's this about?"

"I need to see you, Jono."

"Really."

"Come on, don't be like this. Please. We need to talk."

"Apparently you need to talk. I need to be somewhere else— anywhere else—when that happens."

"No, no, listen to me. The police are pressuring me. I'm scared."

"Louis saw you talking to Kennis. You seemed to be getting along fine."

"I was terrified! What was I supposed to do, slap him? I had to find out what he knew."

"So you were spying for me."

"Is that so hard to believe?"

"Almost impossible. And it doesn't matter anyway. The police know nothing."

"Oh, God. That's not true. If those…those men were trying to kill me today to stop me from talking, it's too late. And it's—it's pointless, Jono, they already know so much and not from me. I didn't say anything. I never would say anything, ever. You have to believe that."

"Even after Andrew, Daisy? Even after what happened to Andrew?"

A long silence. Was he going to confess to the murder right here and now? But it was Daisy who spoke next.

"With Andrew gone I have no one in the world but you."

I thought, what an actress! Or was she acting? That was the real question. What if that was the truth?

"Nonsense," said Pell. "What about your friends?"

"They don't know me. I can't talk to them. They'd never understand. They'd hate me. I have to fake it, I have to lie all the time, to everyone. Except you."

"And you're telling the truth now."

"Do you remember that beautiful little Grimm's fairy tales book you gave me? With the David Hockney illustrations?"

"What has that got to do with anything? Why bring that up? You lost that book years ago."

"I was seventeen! I had no idea who David Hockney was and I was too old for fairy tales. I was stupid. He's my favorite artist now. But it's too late. The book is gone."

"Actions have consequences, Daisy."

"I don't want to lose you, too."

"Daisy—"

"Let me prove myself to you. I know what the police know. Kennis told me everything. I worked him, Jono. Just like you taught me."

"So you're the prodigal daughter now? The prodigal step-daughter."

"Whatever you want me to be."

Another silence. This was where the plan came together—or fell apart.

Finally Pell spoke. "What did Kennis say?"

"We can't talk about it on the phone."

"This line is secure."

"It's 2015, Jono. No line is secure."

"Then come. Come now. I'll be waiting."

Lonnie turned to me. "This is it."

Then…silence.

"I'm getting nothing," the tech guy shouted. "The connection's dead. They must have found the wire. We're dark."

"Maybe it's a technical glitch," Lonnie said. "I'm not blowing this operation because someone got a wire crossed."

"So what do we do, sir?"

"We hold tight and wait. They may be on their own but they know what they're doing. And we trust them—right, Kennis?"

Trust! Jesus Christ.

"Haden!" I turned on him so fast I spilled his coffee onto the front of his shirt.

"What? What the f—? What is it? I'm soaking wet!"

"Tell me about that day."

"What day? What are you talking about? What's going on?"

"Sorry." I took a breath. "The day Andrew Thayer was murdered. You were birding in Madaket."

"Right."

"You saw some bird you'd been hoping to catch sight of."

"The prothonotary warbler."

"Did you tell anyone about it?"

"I tweeted it. I have like—I don't know…five or six hundred Twitter followers—@birdman. And a lot of them re-tweet."

"So anyone who checked your Twitter account…"

"What is this? What's going on?"

"Tell me about the day. Who you saw, what you did, where you were, how the weather was, everything."

"You're not going to tell me what this is about?"

"Haden, please. Just think."

"Okay, okay, give me a second." He was holding a cup of takeout coffee, obviously gone cold. He swallowed the last of it and set the paper cup down on a desk. "I remember I was amazed we saw anything in that rain. You've gotta be dedicated to stick it out in a downpour like that. We were miserable."

"Wait, stop. It was raining?"

"Are you kidding?"

"It was raining in Madaket."

"Yeah, so what?"

"Didn't you notice? It wasn't raining anywhere else on the island that day."

"Well, yeah, but that happens all the time, Chief. Those storm systems push up the coast and just brush the west end of the island. Ask anyone."

I wasn't spinning anymore, I was on my knees in the sand. Impossible as it seemed, that was the Atlantic Ocean in front of me, not the Pacific. The sun rose in the east, I was sure of that. Facts were facts. "Jesus Christ. Jesus fucking Christ."

Haden took a step toward me, grabbed my shoulder. "Chief, what is it? What's wrong? What's going on in that crazy head of yours?"

I reached across my chest and squeezed his hand. Then I stood up. "I saw Sue Ann Pelzer that day, just after the murder. I was responding to the 911 call. She said she'd been birding in Madaket. She even told me about the prothonotary warbler."

"Okay, she saw it, too. What difference does that—?"

"She was wearing a suede jacket, Haden. And her jacket was dry. We even talked about it—her lucky jacket."

"Well, that's not possible. It was coming down in buckets out there. She would have been….Oh."

"Yeah."

I told him the rest: the Johnny Clegg connection, her riflery experience in the biathlon. He could see he was as disoriented as I was. "But…but Blount confessed."

"Blount took the fall. God knows why. Pell must have some hold over him."

"Then—if that's true…if he…then it was Sue Ann, all along. She burned down Andy's house."

"Yeah. And then cut his throat when that didn't work. And she shot Todd Macy, Haden. She knows to handle a rifle. Apparently she could have done it while she was skiing. And as of right now she has no alibi for the Andrew Thayer murder."

It only took him a second to figure out the rest of it. "Holy crap," he said, "She's with Daisy! Right now."

We didn't have time to react—Lonnie's phone started buzzing. He picked it up and listened. "What? Wait, back up, what happened? How the hell—? And they just let him? How is that even—? Jesus fucking Christ. Get an APB out on the guy! Full description, armed and dangerous. I don't care if he is or not! He could have stashed a gun somewhere. Just do it. This fucking island. I don't believe this shit."

He ended the call and turned on me. "Jill Phelan died in the ICU ward at Mass General fifteen minutes ago. And your boy Barnaby Toll just walked her father out of the police station. They're both in the wind."

After the first punch of shock it made sense. Barnaby Toll had been Jill's babysitter back in the day, and they had remained close friends. He had access to the holding cells. He and Liam must have been talking, sharing stories, stoking each other's outrage and hate and despair. Jill's death had obviously snapped both of them and Barney was smart enough to use our special relationship to bluff his way through the escape. What would he have called it? Some sort of transfer? A plane ride to the Barnstable facility? Or a quick ride to the State Police HQ? That would explain the routine follow-up phone call that set off the alarms. Except—that all was supposed to happen before you let the prisoner out of the building. The NPD was getting careless. This would never have happened in L.A. Time for a crackdown.

But that could wait. Right now I had Liam Phelan and Sue Ann Pelzer to deal with.

And Pell.

"Phelan's not in the wind," I said. "I know exactly where he's going."

"Tell me! We can chopper in a SWAT team and—"

"No, Lonnie. We're de-escalating this one. It's a one-man job."

"Hold on one minute! That's totally contrary to the SOP! If you fuck this up—"

But I was already halfway out of the room. Haden put a hand on my shoulder and handed me his Glock. His eyes said, "Just in case."

Mine said "Thanks."

And then I was gone. I heard Haden behind me saying, "Alert the Coast Guard."

He knew where I was headed.

I sprinted to my cruiser, backed out of the State Police driveway spitting gravel and skid-turned down North Liberty Street, calculating the route as I drove. I popped the siren to clear the road and stamped on the gas. I'd have to go silent when I got close to Straight Wharf, but the louder the better for now. North Liberty is twisty and narrow, but everyone pulled over as I passed the Lily Pond, skirted Lily and Hussey streets, and tore down India. It was a straight shot to the bottom of town, and the path was clear.

Then a cat stepped off the sidewalk and sidled across the street in front of me. A black cat, of course. He sauntered across the street, and slipped out of sight behind a parked car. I accelerated again, trying to make up for the lost thirty seconds, hitting the siren at the Centre and Federal intersections, keeping it howling for the turn onto South Water and the jolting traverse of the Main Street cobblestones.

I was maybe twenty seconds from Straight Wharf, and starting to feel confident, when I hit the gridlock of the Harbor Stop&Shop parking lot. How could I have forgotten the summer traffic, here of all places? The siren wouldn't help me—there was nowhere for anyone to go, no shoulder where they could pull over. I jammed the cruiser into the first restricted parking slot and took off running.

I brushed past some people, I may have knocked someone down. I heard angry shouts behind me as I hooked a left on New Whale Street, and pounded past the open plaza of Harbor Square and the Hy-Line ticket office. In another few seconds I was on the pier, racing over the slats with the low-tide smell of the harbor in my nose. I glimpsed the spires of the *Nantucket Grand* with a gasp of relief. They were still docked. I might have even beaten Phelan to the ship. People leapt out of my way. I heard a splash—that couldn't be good—and kept on moving, past the forty-foot boats tied at the pier, then a hard right, through the turnstile to the restricted dock. Past two big yachts, *Becky's Promise* and *Harpooner*.

The *Grand* was pulling away, churning whitewater from the big twin engines. There was no one visible on deck, no way to stop the ship. I had to jump for it. I slammed through the gate as I made the decision, clattering across the gangway in my heavy shoes. So much for tiptoeing around the deck in your sock-feet. I had the feeling that by the end of the day, scuff marks were going to be the least of Pell's problems, or mine.

I landed the last step and hurled myself over the gap. A horrible moment of suspension caught over the water, and then my chest hit the chrome guard rail and smacked the breath out of my lungs. I flipped over the metal tubing and landed flat on my back on the deck.

Welcome aboard.

I took a second to catch my breath, then scrambled to my feet and eased myself over beside the big sliding glass doors. The wharf slipped farther and farther behind us. I could feel the big engines vibrating smoothly under my feet, a giant cat purring.

I risked a glance inside the doors.

Sue Ann had a gun at Daisy's head, Pell had a girl I'd never seen before in the same position, using her as a shield against Liam, who was pointing a FNP Tactical autoloader in their direction. The detective, Berman, stood off to the side in front of an upright Steinway piano. Liam's hand was shaking. This situation could explode at any second. No more time for skulking around.

I slid open the doors, pulled Haden's gun out of my pants, and stepped inside.

Maybe I'd seen too many movies, but I had the surreal sensation of stepping into the overheated last reel of a Tarantino film. This crazy Mexican standoff was real, and it was my job to defuse it.

"All right everyone," I said. "Put the guns down."

"I don't think so, Chief," Pell said. The girl squirmed under his arm, the gun jabbed up under her chin. "Or I should say… not everyone. Just you and my chief engineer. Take their guns, Mr. Berman."

"Yeah, sure. What the hell." He stepped toward me, extended his hand.

Pell said, "Let me clarify the situation, Kennis. You two are armed but neither one of you is willing to kill another human being in cold blood. Your weapons are a bluff, and I'm calling it. You know I'll kill this girl. I was planning to fire her anyway. She can't even do proper hospital corners when she makes a bed. Think of the money I'll save in unemployment payments."

I gave Berman my gun. I had to keep the situation fluid. My opportunity would come. When he took Phelan's weapon, I turned to Sue Ann.

"Why?"

"He's my boss. It's my job."

"And you like it."

She grinned. "Are you kidding? I love it."

"Especially when Doug Blount takes the fall for everything you do." I looked back at Pell. "How does that work, anyway?"

Pell shrugged. "Doug owes me everything. I made sure he got the life insurance payout after his wife died. I'm putting his boy through school—Hotchkiss—at the moment. Some Ivy League school later. I'll make sure of it. I'm the boy's new father now. Just as well, Doug was never really happy out of jail. Did you see the way he lived at the LoGran cottage? He managed to turn it into monk's cell…or a lifer's. Doug is my creature, leave it at that."

Daisy looked terrified. Phelan was unreadable. I expected to see fear and despair on his face. I saw nothing but tension and resolve.

"Here's what's going to happen," Pell continued. "Daisy here is going to have an unfortunate accident…a bit too much to drink, bad habits reasserting themselves, and then she's going to fall overboard, the old Natalie Wood trick. Tragic. Even worse, the heroic police chief is going to die trying to save her. On the off-chance that your bodies might turn up we're going to water-board you before we throw you overboard. Well, perhaps that's somewhat inaccurate. Waterboarding only simulates drowning. But you get the idea. And don't worry, we use only good clean Atlantic brine. We wouldn't want a coroner to find fresh water in your lungs! As for Phelan here—alas, he went postal…or should I say 'aquatic'? Too many lonely weeks at sea. He always was unstable. Then his daughter's death pushed him over the edge. Terrible business. Very traumatic. But I'll recover, don't worry. I'm quite resilient. And I have a mission to pursue. I have a dream."

"And what is that?" I said. "What was worth killing Oscar Graham and Andrew Thayer and Todd Macy for?"

"And you two. Don't forget you two! You're as good as dead already."

"So why? It can't only be about scoring some big real estate deal."

"The biggest real estate deal, Kennis. But no, you're right. It's a vision, my vision. It started with this ship. The *Nantucket Grand.* That's where the epiphany struck me. Nantucket is a ship, too. A giant ship, permanently anchored, thirty miles out at sea. Do you understand?"

I stared at him. "No."

"Of course not. You're nothing but a pedestrian little bureaucrat."

"So enlighten me."

"We're taking back this island, Kennis."

"Taking it back? To what?"

"Not to what. From who."

"What are you talking about?"

"Blue Heron is just the beginning. This island is going to become what it was always meant to be—a haven for the leaders, the job creators, the true royalty of the capitalist world."

"The one percent."

"The one-tenth of one percent. The people who make this world function. The drivers, the makers, the masters."

"The Pharaohs."

"But the Pharaohs were parasites."

"Exactly."

"I'm not going to argue political science and macro-economics with a local cop. I suppose you think it's the eight-fifty-an-hour worker bees who make the world go round."

"At least they pay their taxes. Unlike General Electric. And LoGran Corporation."

"America achieved its greatness in the era before income tax. And not just in business. Have you ever taken a trip to the

Isabella Stewart Gardner Museum in Boson? Lovely place. The art in that extraordinary building constitutes *her private collection.* She could never have accumulated such a spectacular array of art in the age of income tax."

I didn't want to get sucked into his laissez-faire philosophy. "None of this matters," I said. "Your plan is impossible. It could never work."

"It's already working! We're well underway. That's the real work we're doing at ProACKtive."

"What about your slogan? 'New People, New Money, New Spirit'?"

"You have quite a memory."

"Well?"

"That's just for the rubes, Chief. 'This way to the egress,' as P.T. Barnum would say."

"There's a sucker born every minute."

"Exactly. They thought they were going to see the eagle and they wound up outside the tent."

"And that's where you want everyone else. Outside the tent."

"Well put. The governor's commission has put together the necessary eminent domain takings, and a majority of your Selectmen are ready to sign off on them. We'll be clearing out every ugly patch of commerce and squalor—the 'mid-island' merchants, the developments at Friendship Lane and Essex Road, the hideous public housing off Miacomet Avenue. In ten years they'll be moorlands again. We're coordinating that with sweeps by the INS—comprehensive raids that will clear every non-documented worker off the island. We'll rake them up and bag them like autumn leaves."

"And who'll do all the work in your Capitalist utopia?"

"Every homeowner will handle his own staffing needs."

So that was what Franny had been talking about. This stuff was coming from the highest levels of government. Pell must have extraordinary connections. But why wouldn't he? They all knew each other. The world of real power was a small one, much smaller than Nantucket. He didn't have to "buy" the politicians.

They were all members of the same tiny community, all dining together at the Yacht Club, dividing up the world over drinks and raw oysters.

"What about the regular homeowners?" I said. "Middle-class people, upper-middle-class people? How are you going to get rid of them?"

"We're buying them out, Kennis. Most of them are dying to cash in on their property here, anyway. They've been fleeing in droves for years, taking their big house sale money and buying land in North Carolina and Vermont. Half the native Vermonters come from Nantucket by now!"

"And the ones who don't want to sell?"

"We can exert pressure on them."

"Like the pressure you exerted on Andrew Thayer?"

"Well, not quite so extreme, I would hope. Most people get the message."

"Then what happens to all those empty houses?"

"That's the best part! We buy them at market value, but once phase one of the Blue Heron project is complete, we resell those homes at an unimaginable profit to the richest individuals in the world. This island will become, over the next decade the most exclusive, elite, desirable community on the planet. Some will buy just to shelter their money. Others will come for the unparalleled privacy and the company of their equals. Price no object."

"And you'll make hundreds of millions of dollars."

"I refuse to audit the value of paradise, Chief Kennis. But, yes, Blue Heron stands to make a substantial sum of money in the next few years. A very substantial sum of money."

I allowed myself a disgusted grunt. "And the hilarious part is—when you build this gigantic gated subdivision—call it what it is, Pell—when you build it and create your perfect Utopian community, you'll be ruining the island! The beauty of this place is your best selling point, those moors are the heart of Nantucket, and you're going to destroy them, like a little kid smashing his favorite toy. Because smashing things is the real fun for people like you."

"Bravo, Chief Kennis. Bravo. But I have no intention of 'destroying' this island, as you put it. The acres in question are nothing but bogs and shrubs and scrub pine."

"They're moorland! They're thistle and heather and high bush blueberries and wild grapes—those moors are unique. They're a bird habitat and—"

"They're a tick habitat, Chief. Another nuisance we will be eliminating. Along with the poison ivy."

"Good luck with that. And what happens when someone blows a fuse or their toilet backs up?"

"We've considered those eventualities. Some of the tradespeople will stay on—the crew, as it were. Every ship needs a crackerjack crew. Isn't that right, Mr. Phelan?"

"Fuck you."

"I'll take that as a yes. The electricians and plumbers will have their own separate little community, Chief—their own quarters. Everyone else we'll fly in, as necessary. The school will become a private academy for those who wish to live here year round and raise their children on-island. The hospital expansion plans will be scrapped, of course. The current facility is sufficient for a small, elite population. We'll upgrade all the equipment, naturally. Only the best, Kennis, only the best. The finest stores and restaurants will remain, we'll make sure the staff housing is luxurious but…inconspicuous. The rest of the business clutter? We'll turn it into…museums, reading rooms. We'll tear some of the uglier buildings down for vest-pocket parks, Bocce courts, croquet lawns. It's a long-term project. But the goal is nothing less than Arcadia."

I thought back to the ProACKtive fundraiser, the night we found Oscar Graham's body in the salt marsh, the innocent boy this creature had killed for convenience. I had been so impressed with Pell's charisma! Well, this was the flip side of it—a raging narcissism that had sucked him to the edge of madness.

"You're insane."

"Am I?"

"You'll never get any of this past Town Meeting."

"Town Meeting? Really? That's your answer? First of all, hardly anyone even bothers to attend Town Meeting anymore. What did Oscar Wilde say about democracy? It will never survive—it takes up too many evenings."

"You'll get a quorum on this one, believe me."

"It doesn't matter. Eminent domain is not adjudicated by Town Meeting. The voters have nothing to say about it. And individual home sales are a private matter. Everything is poised to begin, Kennis. Blue Heron is fully subscribed, and when the last deed is registered, phase two will begin: the next round of sales, the INS action, the eminent domain takings. All we have to do is sign our deal with the Land Bank. And that happens… let me see…twenty hours from now. Set your watch."

I studied him, smug and comfortable with a gun pushing into a young girl's jaw. "You're like some absurd James Bond villain, planning to take over the world. All you need is a Siamese cat in your lap."

"You misunderstand me, Chief. I have no interest in taking over the world. Just my little corner of it."

"But it's not yours."

"Not yet."

"And if someone gets in the way, they die."

"Preston Lomax used to say I was reckless. A liability because of my…impulsive nature. I remember once he yelled at me—'Do you plan an accident? Do you? Do you plan an accident?' I took his words to heart, Kennis. I've been planning my accidents ever since."

"Here's one you missed," Phelan said quietly. Then he shouted, "Now!"

Chapter Thirty-four

Fifteen Fathoms

A torrent of events—the bo'sun who had ushered me onto the boat last time leapt out of the shadows that led to the galley and wrenched Pell's gun hand away from the girl's jaw. The gun went off with a deafening bang and punched a hole in the ceiling. At the same moment, Daisy reared her head back and hammered Sue Ann's nose with her skull. The compact little assassin reeled backward as the bo'sun punched awkwardly at Pell's face, hitting his neck and shoulders. Pell tried a counter punch but the movement opened him up and the bo'sun landed a solid blow to his solar plexus.

Pell went down to his knees, the girl fled into the depths of the ship and Daisy hurled herself at her stepfather.

It all happened in less than five seconds.

I grabbed Daisy before she could pounce, and when I looked up, the situation was upside down. Phelan had his gun digging into Sue Ann's neck, the mirror image of a moment before.

Pell shouted to Berman, "Louis, you've got the cop's gun! And your Beretta! You have the angle on Phelan. Take him out!"

Berman shrugged. "I don't think so. This ain't my fight. And I haven't been paid in three weeks. For the record."

"Typical," I muttered, struggling to keep Daisy under control.

Gasping for breath, Pell still managed to croak out a laugh. "That's profiling on Nantucket," he said. "Rich guys are all cheap bastards."

"You want to buy your loyalty—without paying for it," Phelan said. "That was your first mistake, you worthless slab of shite. You thought your crew was on your side. Wrong. They hate you! They wanted to break out the Perrier Jouet when they heard the plan."

"The plan?" Pell looked nervous for the first time. "What plan?"

Phelan turned to me, shifting Sue Ann as his human shield. "Here's the thing, Chief—step back! I'll kill her and you know I will. Then I'd bring her back to life if I could, just to fucking kill her again! So listen…LoGran isn't doing so well these days. Lots of bad investments, lots of gambles that didn't pay off."

David Trezize was right again, I thought.

Liam kept talking. "The only way they could raise the money for the big Land Bank deal was leveraging this ship. You're standing in the collateral, Chief. Without it, they can't buy the Land Bank property, and without the Land Bank property, Blue Heron can't close with its subscribers. Without that core group to secure the deal going forward, there's no eminent domain action, no INS raids, no ancillary house sales. It's just one deluded sociopath's wet-dream. It's nothing."

"Don't do this, Phelan," Pell croaked. "You do this, your life is over."

He ignored his boss, still talking to me. "My life is over already. I had a dream ten years ago, when Jilly was six—most vivid dream of my life. She was playing near an open elevator door, and I knew she was in danger and I tried to call out but I couldn't make a sound. She was dancing around, closer and closer to the edge. I started running, but it was like wading against a cross rip. I was almost close enough to reach when she fell. Do you know what I did then?"

A chill washed over me. I'd had this same dream, or close enough. Maybe all fathers had. "You jumped in after her."

"That's right, Chief. I figured I could get below her and cushion her fall. I might die but if she died I didn't want to go on living anyway. Of course I woke up before we landed. But then it really happened. Jilly's dead and the dream came true. Only I couldn't even jump."

He faced Pell again. "So don't think for a second I give a shite for the consequences of my actions at this moment, Mr. Jonathan Pell."

We could all feel the engines strike a deeper note.

"Where are we going?" Pell shouted. "Where are you taking us?"

"Just under five nautical miles from shore, off Tom Nevers Head. A little north of Old Man Shoal. A lot of ships have run aground there over the years, but that's not going to happen to the *Nantucket Grand*. You can salvage a boat that's run aground. Now, a little ways north of the shoal it's a whole different story. The water is fifteen fathoms deep there—that's ninety feet, for you landlubbers. This vessel is going all the way to the bottom. And your precious deal is going down with it."

"No!"

Pell lunged up and the bo'sun clobbered him, knocking him flat on his face on the polished ash wood deck.

I stared at Phelan. "You're going to sink this boat? Is that even possible?"

"Don't make me laugh, Chief Kennis. It's easy." He addressed the bo'sun: "Get Daniels to launch the tenders, get the crew aboard. Hand luggage only." He pointed at Pete. "If this rat moves, knock him out. He's going down with the ship."

The bo'sun nodded. "Got it."

Phelan glanced over at me. "Come with me. Bring the girl."

The rage and even the energy had drained out of Daisy. Phelan held her responsible for his daughter's death, and she knew it. She had recruited Jill in the first place. She must have assumed Phelan was going to kill both her and Sue Ann, and the posture of resigned, exhausted dread telegraphed that she thought she deserved it. She was finished, no matter what happened. She didn't have a chance and she'd never had a chance, lost from the moment her mother met Pell and checked out his Tom Ford suit and his Franck Muller wristwatch and started planning a brighter future.

This was where that future ended up.

Phelan led us out to the stern deck, into the sharp salty wind, and down the metal stairs to the engine room doors. The south shore of Nantucket had shrunk to a low green ridge on the horizon, off the starboard side. The big ship moved steadily through calm seas. I saw a couple of sailboats, the speck of a kite surfer, a brief raucous swarm of sea gulls, but no other big ships—no Coast Guard cutter.

"I killed all the electronics, Chief," Phelan said, reading my mind—or noticing my desperate scan of the water around us. "We're dark. No one can track the ship now."

I had to give Phelan credit—he had thought this one through: picked and manipulated a plausible accomplice at the police station, organized his crew, mapped out his destination. He clutched Sue Ann in a brutal half nelson. She grunted in pain with every step, but said nothing. I could see her mind moving, turning over the elements of the situation, recalibrating her options, looking for an opening.

Phelan led us into the heat and buzz of the engine room, past the bank of blacked-out electronics, and between the two giant engines, the pistons of some immense machine lying side by side. Thick white pipes, maybe two feet in diameter, rose from the deck beside each engine, capped with clamped metal lids and smaller pipes connected to the turbines.

Phelan walked Sue Ann to the far end of the cramped little chamber and stood between the engines. "See these, Chief? The engines are cooled with sea water, and these are the filters—there's a lot of particulate junk in the cleanest sea water—algae, plankton, kelp, you name it. We have to shut the engines down to clean the filters. If we opened these seals while the engines were running…all that water would flood the engine room and then the rest of the lower deck compartments at a rate of a hundred gallons a minute. That would be catastrophic."

He released Sue Ann and pushed her at us. She stumbled across the floor, lurching into Daisy. The impact woke Daisy up and Phelan laughed. "You can keep those two wildcats off of each other. I have real work to do."

"Liam—"

"Don't bother, Chief. This is my world. You're just a passenger."

He opened the hatches one-handed, waving the gun at us. There was no way he couldn't get a shot off if any of us moved, and he was right—I had my arms full keeping Daisy off her nemesis. In a few seconds we had more important things to worry about—the sudden geyser and then the churn of water from the two pipes, and sloshing and swirling over the floor, sluicing into our shoes, dense and icy. The shock of cold ocean at our ankles brought every other action to a halt.

"You'd best find your way out of here," Phelan said. "This end of the ship goes down first. And don't even think about closing these hatches. Ten people couldn't do it. There's no going back now."

The water surged around my knees. It was survival time and we all knew it. We started wading back toward the door. Phelan was right behind us. And somewhere above us, Pell lay unconscious on the main cabin. I pulled myself out of the engine room and up the exterior stairs. The ship was tilting to vertical already, poised above that ninety-foot gulf of water beside Old Man Shoal. I could hear things sliding inside—chairs and lamps, a crash as the upright piano hit the cabin wall.

My job now was to save Pell. Whatever Liam's plan, the man was going to stand trial for what he'd done. Whatever his crimes, that was a fundamental right as a citizen of this country. It wasn't Liam's job or my job or Daisy's job to determine his guilt or innocence. That was up to a jury of his peers, after a fair hearing in a court of law. But he would never get there unless I could drag him off this boat. As for Daisy and Sue Ann, I had to hope that the immediate need to get away from the *Nantucket Grand* and the suction field it created as it sank would trump their schemes and grudges. If they didn't drown, the law would determine their futures. Pell was my job now.

I hauled myself into the main cabin, past a coffee table that had shattered the glass door. Pell was groggy but conscious. A couch scraped past me and I heard another impact. In a few seconds I'd be slipping backward, too. I clambered up to Pell on all fours, sat him up and dug my shoulder into his stomach. He groaned but didn't struggle as I wrestled him into modified fireman's carry. Could we exit by the canopied deck on the bow? The glass doors behind us were hopelessly blocked by a jumble of furniture.

The end tables were bolted into the floor. I used them as handholds to reach the far doors as the ship continued to tip. The opening had become a hatch, bombarded by redwood deck chairs that shattered the glass and tumbled through the opening to land with the rest of the furniture at the stern. The attached tables probably saved both our lives. I swung from the support leg of one table to the next.

As I reached up to grab the edge of the table, Pell regained full consciousness. After a second of disorientation and panic he grasped the situation. I could feel my shoulder start to separate as he scrambled over my head and used my shoulders for a foothold to stand upright, teetering on the blade of the table edge, reaching for the metal door frame, pulling himself up and out.

I followed him, managed to stand on the same thin ridge of mahogany and jump for the metal frame. I caught it and dangled for a few seconds thirty feet over the rear wall of the cabin, with its jagged clutter of smashed furniture. I wrestled myself up and onto the intact sheet of glass beside me. Pell had already reached the end of the window wall. He jumped the gap to the railing, spun around it in a grotesque pole dance, and vanished over the side.

I was on my feet as he made the leap, and I could feel the heavy tinted glass of the window wall shivering ominously under my feet. If it broke I was a dead man. But it held my weight and I plunged after Pell, grabbing the slick wet rail and pivoting myself around it to fall beside the massive white hulk of the sinking ship.

The frigid ocean closed around me and paralyzed my lungs for a second; my shirt, pants, and shoes turned into ballast, weighing me down, tangling me up. The thought of pulling my shirt over my head hit me with a vivid stab of physical memory, the claustrophobic panic I had felt during lifesaving practice when my shirt got stuck halfway off, the fabric blocking my nose and mouth, pressing down on my head. Forget it—pull some oxygen into your lungs! I thrashed my way to the surface and took a deep gulp of fresh air.

I looked around. Pell was five feet away, choking and flailing, going under. Was it possible he didn't know how to swim? Maybe he was too disoriented to function properly. I could feel the tug of the subsiding boat, a vertical riptide pulling me under. We had to get clear and we had to do it fast. I stroked over to him, weighed down by my clothes, and got my arm around his chest.

After a brief struggle, Pell gave up and I sidestroked him away from the surreal overwhelming vision of the vertical mega-yacht, still more than a hundred feet of it above water, a blinding white fiberglass slab the height of the Unitarian Church from the side-walk to the steeple, slipping into the roiling maw of frothing water that was swallowing it whole.

The ocean's throat was deep but not deep enough to wholly submerge the *Nantucket Grand*. It shuddered as it struck the bottom, then gradually, majestically, tipped over and fell in slow motion, slapping the surface with a dull thunder, shoving out a bulge of water with the impact.

The slap of the wave tumbled us under for a second or two, but I got us to the surface again in time to see the whole opulent length of the giant ship slowly sinking into the water until there was nothing visible but the radar towers. Finally they were gone, too. There was nothing to show the ship had ever been there but the field of churning foam that marked its descent.

I thought of a telephone pole struck by lightning when I was a kid. It happened on a road in rural Vermont, a flash summer downpour. The pole had tipped over the same way, with the same eerie sense of deliberation, and crashed across the black strip of asphalt, pulling the wires with it in a tangle of sparks and disconnection—severed links and broken conversations, tarred wood across the blacktop, phone lines coiling like snakes in the flood. I remember staring at the new chaos, awestruck even at ten years old by the fragility of the complex modern world I had taken for granted.

The *Nantucket Grand* had pulled down much more than itself. Pell's grand scheme, his distorted, disassociated vision of Nantucket's future, the very survival of his teetering company, had all of it capsized with his grandiose yacht. And floating there in the frigid ocean I felt a pulse of animal ecstasy, a rude angry joy to see this man so utterly defeated. I jacked a fist into the air with a shout of triumph.

The gesture snapped Pell out of his daze.

"You…bastard!" he grunted, and twisted out of my grip. He lurched at me, getting his hands on my head, ducking me under the water.

We punched at each other in ludicrous slow motion as we struggled back to the surface. He clipped the side of my head and jammed me under again before I could get a breath. The guy was actually trying to drown me after I had just saved his life. I had no air in my lungs and I was starting to black out.

A second later he was yanked off me from above—the bo'sun had him by the collar, dragging him up into the first of two tenders.

"Don't kill him," I sputtered, gasping for breath.

The detective, Louis Berman, helped me up into the second boat. "So that's it." He inclined his head toward the field of whitewater where the *Nantucket Grand* had been floating a few minutes before. "We need Celine Dion to sing it down for us."

"I was thinking more about *Gilligan's Island* than *Titanic*."

"Really? *The Minnow?*"

"It shows appropriate disrespect."

I checked out our tender—various crew members, along with Daisy and Sue Ann. But no Phelan. I couldn't see him on the other boat either. I finally caught sight of him in the water, swimming away roughly in the direction of Portugal.

The kid at the outboard saw him too. "It's Mr. Phelan! We're coming, Mr. Phelan!" He gunned the motor, turned the little skiff in a fan of spume and chugged toward the engineer.

Phelan rolled over onto his back as we approached. "Leave me alone," he said. "Go on, get out of here."

"Liam, get in the boat," I said.

"No."

"Come on, don't be crazy, just—"

"I'm not crazy, and you know that very well. Now leave me alone."

I turned to the boy at the motor. "Hand me that rope!" It was coiled up at his feet.

"You mean the bowline?"

"Jesus Christ—whatever you call it! Just give it to me!"

He handed it over and I heaved over the side toward Liam. It spun in slow motion like a giant Frisbee, unwinding. The bulk of it hit with a splash a few feet from him. "Grab it!"

"No thank you, Chief. I'm done."

He started swimming again, and the boy at the motor revved it to follow. I grasped his arm, shook my head. Liam had made his decision. In his position I might very well have made the same one.

I lifted my own hand in a final wave and then turned back to the other passengers.

Daisy had a knife against Sue Ann Pelzer's throat.

Pell, the yacht, Phelan and his swim to oblivion—all gone in an instant, dragged under by the gleam of the blade.

I heaved myself forward. "Don't do it!"

Daisy flinched back. The knife drew blood.

"Get away from me!"

"Daisy—"

"I'll cut her throat, I mean it." Sue Ann squirmed but Daisy had her in a vise. She was stronger than she looked.

I took a breath. "Daisy, don't do this."

She tossed her head toward Phelan, still swimming strongly away. "Why not? My life is over anyway—just like his."

"But it's not. You never wanted any of this. You were coerced, and now you're the main witness against Pell. All you have to do is tell the District Attorney what you told me today. If you agree to testify, they'll cut you a deal. You could get immunity—or a stint of community service."

"Working with kids? I'm sure everyone would love to see me working with kids again."

"No, no—obviously not. I mean—but there's all kinds of things you can do. Park clean-up, working at the food bank—"

"I don't want to do any of that. I just want to kill this bitch and die."

"Think about Andrew—"

"She killed him! Don't you get it?"

"But what would he want you to do? What would Andrew say now? You're no killer. He knew that. I know that. You're better than she is. Let me arrest her. Let the State put her on trial. She'll be convicted—she's confessed! She'll go to jail for the rest of her life, Daisy. She'll have a whole lifetime to think about what she's done. And you'll be free."

"No."

"You kill her and your life will be over. You'll be finished and you'll deserve to be."

Quieter now: "No."

"Let her go and you can start again. You can try to make things right."

"Will I bring Jill back?"

"You didn't kill her."

"I helped. I did my part."

"She was a drug addict before you ever met her, Daisy. You understand that disease. You've lived that life. But you have changed. This nightmare has changed you, Daisy. I can see that. Anyone could see that. You're like…a clay pot. You've been fired in the kiln, and you didn't crack. Don't crack now. You're one flick of your wrist away from losing everything."

"I've got nothing."

"You have friends—David and Kathleen…me. You have a chance to walk away from the past and you have the future. You can make that future into anything you want."

"But first I have to want it."

"Yes. First you have to want it."

"But I don't."

"If that were true you would have let yourself go down with the ship. You'd have killed Sue Ann already. But you haven't done any of those things. Your hand is shaking. You think you want to do it but you can't. Pell is finished. He and his cronies are going to be in jail for the rest of their lives. It's like—the Berlin Wall finally came down."

"People hated it when the Berlin Wall came down. I read about that. They thought they'd be happy but they weren't."

"At first. But then they started living. Start living, Daisy. It beats the alternative."

That tricked a tiny smile out of her. "I want a front seat at this bitch's trial. I want to see her face when the judge reads the sentence."

"Done."

"You promise?"

"It's easy." I thought of Dave Carmichael. "I have friends in high places."

Sue Ann stared down, silent and defeated, no more moves to make, no more angles to play. Daisy dropped the knife and let herself cry. She cried for most of the trip back, deep shuddering sobs, but her eyes were dry when we pulled into the Easy Street public landing.

She was a survivor. She'd be fine.

Chapter Thirty-five

The Phoenix

We drove back to the station, where I took a long hot shower, found some dry clothes, booked Pell and Su Ann, and arranged to set Berman free on his own recognizance. Kathleen Lomax came to the station to pick up Daisy. I headed home for a night with the kids. "Kidding" as Haden Krakauer liked to put it. It was anything but a joke—I was exhausted, wrung out, pounded flat. I almost called Miranda and asked her to take them for the night, but I knew what her answer would be. The last thing I needed was an argument or a guilt trip.

I thought about Dave Carmichael—his office would handle the Pell case from now on. It was out of my hands. Guilt would be tested and justice dispensed elsewhere. My part was done. I was a bystander again—a passenger, as Phelan had so aptly put it. Soon the island would subside into its normal somnolent rhythms…the odd domestic disturbance or DUI, barfight or B&E. While we slowly nodded off again into our small-town nap, Carmichael would be finding the big cases, important cases, and someone would be investigating them. It wouldn't be me.

The old jailhouse sulk had begun again. The kids kept me tethered to this place, to this dead-end career—nothing else.

Then Caroline got sick.

She felt queasy at dinner, and she woke up at two in the morning with the bug raging.

"Daddy," she cried out of sleep. "Daddy!"

I rolled out of bed and ran to the room she shared with Timmy, charged with adrenaline but still thinking somewhere: "She called for me, not her mom." It made sense—she was at my house not her mother's—but she could have called for Miranda anyway. I would have phoned Miranda and awakened her and she would have come over, driving on the nighttime roads in her PJs. But that wasn't going to be necessary.

Because Caroline called for me.

I got her downstairs and into the narrow little bathroom, and she projectile vomited all over the walls before I could guide her to the toilet. I held her hair back, talked her through it, gave her a cool glass of water, helped her navigate her way back upstairs, put a lobster pot near the bed in case there was another emergency, and read her to sleep.

Then I went downstairs and started cleaning up.

And that's where it happened. I was on my knees, scrubbing my daughter's puke off the bathroom walls at three in the morning and I realized—I would much rather be doing this than investigating bank fraud in Boston.

This was where I belonged.

I was in the right place, doing the right thing.

I finished up and went to bed, feeling a satisfied exhaustion, a quiet, resonant bliss and something else, something more— gratitude, perhaps. The resentment was gone, banished in the space of an hour. And I felt pretty sure it was never coming back.

◇◇◇

"I told you so!" said Jane Stiles. "Everything did tie together, two ways! Todd Macy and Oscar Graham and the house fire and the drugs and porn mess, and—and Andy Thayer—all of it! Just like in my books. Sorry."

We were standing in the moors, watching Pat Folger's crew as they pushed the frame of the rebuilt Thayer cottage vertical and banged it into place, the rhythmic clatter of hammers reverberating in the clear summer air. It was a cool, dry day, more like early fall than high summer. Caroline was holding one of my hands and Tim grasped the other. Debbie Garrison stood next to him. That seemed to have worked out nicely. David Trezize and Kathleen Lomax hovered at the edge of the clearing with Daisy. He was taking pictures for the paper. Everyone else just wanted to mark the occasion.

Haden Krakauer strolled up to me. "I was thinking about that prothonotary warbler," he said. "The bird that nailed Sue Ann Pelzer. It got Alger Hiss, too. Did you know that? True story."

"Alger Hiss? The spy?"

"Well…he was accused of selling nuclear secrets to the Russians. During the House Un-American Activities Committee hearings in 1948, Whittacker Chambers claimed that he and Hiss had been friends as members of the Communist party. Hiss denied it, but Chambers told the committee that Hiss was a birder and he'd mentioned sighting a prothonotary warbler—told Chambers all about it. Anyway, that's how the committee knew Hiss was lying. The bird gave him away! He knew Chambers and that proved he committed perjury. And that meant he was a communist and probably a spy, like you say. He went to jail for perjury. They would have tried him on espionage charges, but the statute of limitations ran out. Still, the point is…he was busted by a bird! That was a big moment for ornithologists, let me tell you."

We contemplated the peculiarities of fate for a few moments. A rare bird-sighting, a freak rainstorm, and a new suede jacket had done in Sue Ann Pelzer and revealed her true self. I thought of Chuck Obremski, my old boss in L.A. He used to say, "Nothing is what it seems, everything is different under the surface. Blueberries are green. Peel one, K. See for yourself."

It was easy to guess wrong about people. Pell was so much worse than he seemed. Maybe Daisy was better. I hoped so.

Haden was watching a turkey buzzard circling overhead. "I guess birding helps in police work sometimes, Chief, just like poetry."

I patted him on the shoulder. "Absolutely."

Joyce Garrison and her two brothers had also come to watch, along with various town officials. It was a big moment. The Land Bank was donating the property to the Conservation Commission, creating a massive swath of land that would never be developed. They had agreed to give the Thayer family life rights to the use of the cottage. The good guys won.

Jane leaned against me as Billy Delavane set a ladder against the gable end of the house, climbed to the top of the raw plywood structure and nailed a holly branch to the peak. Pat Folger unpacked champagne and paper cups. He poured out the wine for a toast as Billy climbed back down and scooped Debbie up into a hug.

"The Thayer cottage—rising like a Phoenix from the ashes!" Pat said, lifting his paper cup. "With a little help from the best goddamn carpentry crew on the island."

"Amen," said Billy.

It was getting late in the afternoon, though the sun was still high. I said to the kids, "How about a Pi Pizza?"

"Just a salad for me," Caroline said.

Tim said, "Can Jane come?"

I nodded. "Absolutely." And softly, to Jane: "You're in."

We walked back to the car, through the rosa rugosa and poison ivy and wildgrape vines, and it felt good, being awake after a deep thirsty night's sleep, submitting finally to the simple animal pleasure of the cool air on my skin, the dazzle of the sun in my eyes, the glitter of light on Polpis Harbor through the scrub pines, my weight pressing down smoothly through the linked system of joints, pressing my feet against the ground, gravity like some filmy adhesive, barely attaching me to the world.

I was unshackled and so was the land, forever wild thanks to that tragic beautiful unbowed elemental giant, Liam Phelan, whose body was caught in the gulf stream, heading south into the tropics probably, never to be found.

I thanked him silently one more time, and then we drove away.

Chapter Thirty-six

Pilgrims

After the harbormaster pulled Oscar Graham's body from the Saltmarsh creeks, after the drug overdose and Jill Phelan's death, after the arson and the murders of Todd Macy and Andrew Thayer, after the sinking of the *Nantucket Grand*, and the arrests and the news reports, there was a teenage boy, on a high summer afternoon, sitting in Logan Airport rehearsing what he was going to say to the girl he loved.

Jared Bromley had been watching Alana for half an hour. He considered himself an agnostic when it came to fate, but this encounter shook the foundations of his skepticism. He had lost touch with Alana after their investigation blew up. She hated the publicity and associated him with everything bad that happened—Jill's death, Oscar's murder, Ms. DeHart's dismissal, the sex scandal, her new notoriety, everything. He had approached her just once, at Fast Forward. They were both on line for coffee. But the propinquity hadn't helped. She had been cold.

She said, "I don't think we should hang out, Jared. I'm trying to stay out of trouble for a while," and turned back to her oatmeal cookie.

Rejected for an oatmeal cookie. He left her alone after that. He even stopped writing about her on his blog. He let the blog dwindle; he had other things to write. He was trying to finish as many screenplays as he could before he left for Los Angeles.

Now he had five finished scripts in his suitcase and four thousand dollars that he had managed to save over the last few years zipped into a side pocket of his computer case. It was enough to get started. He knew his scripts were good, but he expected to be rejected for a while. It was the real world, not the psychotic Nantucket dreamscape where girls who couldn't sing or act were given the lead role in school musicals, treated like stars and told they were brilliant. They weren't brilliant and they'd find out the truth if they ever took their stammering, self-conscious, stage non-presence into a Broadway audition room.

Jared had no such illusions. His writing was clumsy in places. His characters talked too much. He had a lot to learn. But he was a quick study and he was persistent. That was the key. If you refused to give up, you were miles ahead of the quitters.

He had left home with little ceremony and hadn't expected to see anyone he knew in the airport. The beauty of airports was the way they extracted you from the familiar. They were the perfect prelude to an adventure, setting you down among fast-moving strangers headed for unknown destinations and making you one of them. He relished the indifferent bustle of Logan. After the unwanted intimacies of a small-town childhood, simply being anonymous gave him a sharp physical pleasure, like climbing out of a car after a long drive.

He watched Alana from the bank of pay telephones.

He remembered the day she had come to work at *Veritas*, two years ago next autumn. They were going to be working together every day, rubbing elbows in the cramped little *Veritas* office. He shouldn't have been looking forward to that; he certainly shouldn't have been happy about it.

But he was. He might as well admit it: he was ecstatic. He was dancing in the snow like an Eskimo Gene Kelly. He twirled and stomped to his truck, a soft shoe seal fisherman in heavy boots and down parka. What an inspired improvisation. What a coup! He was going to be seeing her every day. She would get to know him. His wit and charm and unrivalled paragraphing skills would wear her down, it was only a matter of time.

A car almost hit him: a Buick Riviera from the late nineties. Superintendent Bissell was driving. He slowed down, squinting at Jared's antics. Jared did one more turn and took a bow. He was dizzy, he fell back against his truck. When he caught Bissell's eye, the old man was smiling. He had somehow managed to amuse the school superintendent.

Anything was possible now.

Of course it hadn't quite worked out that way. But now here she was, a pad in her lap, twenty feet away from him, sketching someone, probably the nun in full habit sitting across from her. He loved watching her hand move across the page, the quick confident pen strokes. Her self-assurance gave him the push of confidence he needed. Or maybe it was the half-smile on her face as she worked. Anyway, without making any conscious decision, he walked toward her. The next seat was empty. He sat down. Her eyes flicked to him for a suspicious split second, the stranger who had ignored so many empty seats to crowd her this way. She was probably wishing she'd staked out the seat beside her with her carry-on bag. Then she recognized him.

"Jared!" she said. "What are you doing here?"

"I'm going to Hollywood," It sounded stupid to him. "Los Angeles, I mean. I'm going to be a screenwriter. Like I always said I would."

"Wow," she smiled. She closed her pad and stuffed it into her bag with her pen. "That's incredible, Jared. That's so great. Do you have, like—a job?"

"Nope."

"Do you have an agent?"

"Nope."

"So you're just…going out there."

"That's right. Someone once asked Preston Sturges what he'd do if his movies started to fail and he couldn't get a job and he went bankrupt and wound up on the street. Sturges wasn't worried. He said 'I'd buy a ten-cent pad and a two-cent pencil and start all over again.' That's how I feel…the modern version, with a used laptop and an ink jet printer. It beats sitting at home and thinking about it." He sat back, a little winded, feeling he'd said too much. "What about you?"

"It's really weird. This movie director was visiting Nantucket, the one who helped Chief Kennis with the case. He saw some cartoon of mine in *Veritas,* and he just called out of nowhere to offer me a job working for him, drawing storyboards. Is that bizarre? I Googled him, he was for real. So I said yes."

"So something good came out of all this."

"I hate thinking that way."

"Don't say that. Jill would be happy to know something turned out okay. She always said you should get off the rock."

"Yeah. I guess."

Jared shook his head. "I can't believe you didn't tell me about this."

"I wanted to, but everything got so weird between us, and I wasn't sure how—"

"E-mail is safe."

"I'm sorry."

She touched his knee. He jumped as if she had spilled hot coffee on him and they both laughed.

"So we'll be out there together," she said.

"Yeah."

"I was getting a little nervous. I've never been west of…well, of Hyannis, actually. Which is pathetic."

"Me, neither. No, no, my parents took me to Philadelphia when I was six. But that's it."

"We can cling together for warmth—that's what my dad always says when he and my mom are at a party where they don't know anyone. Like they were in a life raft or something. Not that it's ever actually cold out there. Mark Toland—he's my boss, the director?—Mark says it hit ninety degrees last February."

"It sounds nice to me. I won't miss the snow, I'll tell you that much."

"Me, neither."

"I'm not going to miss Nantucket in February, just in general."

"Or being hassled constantly by those State Police with the jack boots and the buzz cuts. Ugh. We were having a party on the beach last summer and they made us pay a hundred dollars each because you need a permit or something if there's more than ten people. I was like, ever read the Constitution? There's something called freedom of assembly. Well, I didn't actually say that. But I wanted to."

"That's something I won't miss—freedom of assembly for rich people only."

"How about—just two stupid movie theatres all winter long?"

"And going standby on the steamship."

"And having to use air freight if you want a Chinese dinner."

"And ticks and mildew"

"And Lyme's and babesiosis."

"But you know what I want to get away from most? This will sound weird."

She sat forward a little. "Tell me."

"The stars. I mean it. I'm so sick of seeing all those fucking stars every night and the way people from the city ooh and aah over them. You know why we can see the stars on Nantucket? Because there's nothing interesting enough here to block them out."

She laughed out loud. "Oh, my God, I can't believe you actually said that! I feel exactly the same way. I even wrote it in my diary. I have to show you. Almost those exact words."

"Wow."

They stared at each other, suddenly off balance. Before either one of them could say anything else, their flight was called, first-class passengers ahead of everyone else.

"That's me," Alana said, standing. "How are you going?"

"Steerage, I think. In the baggage compartment with the dogs."

She laughed. "Well…see you on the other side."

She lifted a hand. He almost stood. But she started walking away before he could move. She turned back once and smiled at him, though. He took that smile with him onto the plane and into his narrow window seat, and tucked it around him with the thin airline blanket when he fell asleep, with his tiny pillow pressed against the humming Plexiglas.

Maybe anything was possible after all.